WHY WE DIE

MICK HERRON

JOHN MURRAY

First published in Great Britain in 2006 by Constable,
an imprint of Constable & Robinson Ltd

First published in 2016 by John Murray (Publishers)
An Hachette UK company

This paperback edition published in 2020

1

A CIP catalogue record for this title is available from the British Library

Paperback ISBN 978-1-47364-702-2
eBook ISBN 978-1-47364-703-9

Typeset in Bembo Std by Palimpsest Book Production Ltd, Falkirk, Stirlingshire

Printed and bound in Great Britain by Clays Ltd, Elcograf S.p.A.

John Murray policy is to use papers that are natural, renewable and recyclable products and made from wood grown in sustainable forests. The logging and manufacturing processes are expected to conform to the environmental regulations of the country of origin.

John Murray (Publishers)
Carmelite House
50 Victoria Embankment
London EC4Y 0DZ

www.johnmurraypress.co.uk

To Nick
(from word one)

Prologue

IF THERE IS AN answer to the question, it is this: because our bodies are designed to lie in boxes in the dark; arms neatly folded on our chests. Feet together. Eyes tight shut. This is why we die: it's the end we were shaped for.

. . . When she unwrapped her arms, her hands touched the cold sides of the container she'd been planted in, and she understood that everything that passed for normal had slipped out of reach. She was in a world of new instructions – try not to whimper; try not to scream; especially, try not to breathe. She had never been good with instructions. But these bore down with the weight of the earth, and could not be ignored.

And everything that had ever happened carried on happening elsewhere; out of sight or reach, in a time closed off to her. She recognised this, and even as she forgot her instructions and began to scream, felt the intense regret of being out of the loop – of knowing that, whatever came next, she'd play no part in it; nor ever know how it came out.

And this, too, is why we die; because we are only part of the story. And never to know how the story ends.

ONE

THE SMART BOMB

I

I

DEATH WAS ON HIS mind when he first saw the woman. It was her dress caught his eye; a white cotton dress that hung just above her knees, patterned with large blue almost-leaf shapes. *Like a Matisse in motion*, he thought, then wondered where that had come from – Matisse? Leaving the bar, descending the steps into the hotel lounge, she paused and looked round, verifying the obvious; that all of the tables were taken. The sunlight breaking from the window behind her lent shifting life to the dress she wore.

What death wore, he didn't know yet, but the clever money was on black.

He returned to the book he wasn't reading. Words swam into vision, took their usual route to his brain, and evaporated immediately, leaving no discernible impression. Twice in the last twenty minutes he'd turned a page in case anybody was watching, and now did so again, noting as he did the way the same light that played with the pattern of her dress lay flat on the table before him: room key, wine glass, ashtray littered with corpses. If he turned, he'd find the view through the window – the car park, and the ivy trailing down the high wall separating the car park from whatever lay beyond.

Will sir be eating this evening? he'd been asked.

Sir wouldn't be eating this evening.

. . . Last time Tim Whitby had been here, ten years to the

day, he and Emma had been the only couple dining. That was how he remembered it. This evening it was full. Some of the room's occupants were presumably residents like himself; others were here just to eat. There was a futile permanence about the word 'resident', but that was how the bartender had identified him while taking his order. *If the information below is not correct, please amend by crossing out the names of persons no longer resident,* Tim had read lately, on his electoral form, and had had to look for a pen . . . Some moments passed while this crawled across the landscape of his heart. And then the light altered, because the woman had approached and was gesturing at the unused half of his table. His face must have remained blank. She resorted to speech.

'Do you mind?'

He shook his head.

She sat on the far end of the sofa, leaving a good two feet between them; placed her glass and a folded newspaper on the table and leaned back, closing her eyes.

On any list of things Tim did not want right now, company came first, second and third. For a start, it called for a rearrangement of his body. He compromised by pulling the ashtray closer; a gesture that ceded territory. He wasn't eating this evening. He wouldn't be taking up space much longer. He planned to have two, or possibly many more, glasses of wine, then go upstairs. Her being here did not alter his plan . . . This was a comfortable dining room, favouring armchairs and sofas. Guests weren't pressed to hurry. But soon she could have the long table to herself. He tried to convey all this in the way he picked up his glass, but it was impossible to know if she understood.

The wine – which Emma had taught him to enjoy; he'd been a beer man – should have been a treat, but it was simply the next thing happening. He wasn't drunk yet. Just dislocated enough to feel his fingers rubbery as they negotiated glass back on to table; he didn't spill but sloshed a little; she didn't notice because her eyes remained closed. She had long dark wavy hair – almost black – and maybe this made her skin seem paler than it was, or maybe it was pale anyway. And she wore a lot of make-up. This was presumably to cover a bruise on the side of her face nearest him – not a terribly large bruise, nor old enough to have purpled and blacked, but definitely there, for all the careful layers she'd painted on top. He looked away before her eyes could open, and let his gaze sweep the room once more. As if he had enemies who might have sneaked in while his mind roamed elsewhere.

But there was nothing here that did not always happen: people eating, drinking, talking; being happy in a public place. The English were supposed to be repressed – beaten to a pulp by the weather and an ineradicable sense of loss of empire. So why was everyone so bloody cheerful? In the far corner a young couple looked about two minutes off conceiving their first child, while in the opposite, a pair who might have been their grandparents were toasting each other with smiles whose wrinkles matched like bookends. The time it took Tim's gaze to cross from one to the other, a whole lifetime of promises had been kept and twice renewed.

And waiters came and went, of course; and plates were scratched by knives and forks. Whatever the music was changed to something precisely as tasteful. Outside, a car left, and another arrived to take its place . . . All this just scratching Tim's surface, as if life were a TV he wasn't watching, but couldn't ignore. It was impossible, while alive, to divorce yourself from events: even the boring, even the stupid. When the last thing you wanted was conversation, you found yourself discussing the merits of various whiskies. When the last thing you wanted was company, a woman joined you, wearing a noticeable dress . . . Tim looked out of the window again; watched for a while early evening sunlight reflecting off the windscreen of a blue

Toyota; a windscreen whose wipers had cleared a stylised M-shape on a background of reddish dust. He wondered why this detail mattered. He wondered why he bothered noticing.

Time to stop. He returned to his book; the novel he was struggling through. It was a Graham Greene, one of Emma's. Emma had left her books behind. And though he'd made a genuine effort to concentrate, the story's fundamental unreality hummed away beneath the narrative: it was set in 1953, for God's sake. Didn't the characters realise that? Didn't they understand they were interim; that the natural state of things was twenty-first century; that by the time they'd caught up with history they'd be dragging round colostomy bags, or cuffed to Zimmer frames, or just plain dead? That was the problem: these people were dead, but didn't know it. It was the only convincing aspect of the story.

When he looked back, her bruise seemed to have grown darker, and to his horror, she saw him notice.

She said, 'It was a cupboard door.'

. . . If he'd left it baldly alone, if her statement had withered and died in contextless silence, they'd both have remained frozen there forever.

He cleared his throat. 'I'm sorry?'

'You were looking at my eye.'

'I didn't mean to.'

'It's okay.' Her voice was deep for a woman's, and carried a faint accent, though Tim couldn't register from where: never a strength of his.

He picked up his glass again. It was strange, and also expensive, how easily a glass of wine emptied – though expense was hardly a consideration. Otherwise he'd have stayed home, and drunk himself stupid on supermarket offers. Home, though, was not where he wanted to be, and as if he were broadcasting this thought out loud she picked up on it, and spoke again:

'Have you been here before?'

'. . . This hotel?'

'Oxford.'

He lived here. This was his home, where he did not want to be. Explaining that, though, would have involved open-heart surgery. 'Yes.'

'It's our first visit.'

'I see.'

'Our' was an affront; one of those red flags the coupled wave to piss off the newly single. Lately, everywhere Tim went he saw people in pairs, flaunting happy, secure futures. And now it seemed even people turning up on their own had to trumpet their significant others. Tim had shared an 'our' once; now he had simply a 'his'. This unalterable fact made the woman's attempt to hide her bruise laughable.

. . . But this was good, this was fine, this was nothing. It was a sequence of moments time would carry him through the way gravity would see him through a fall: there was little preparation needed; only the ordinary social stitching which held him together anyway – which kept him saying *please* and *thank you* instead of *leave me alone.* He could smile pleasantly for as long as the situation demanded, which would not be terribly long, and all the while his alcoholic buzz would grow until it blotted out even the agonisingly pleasant chatter of the other diners. This woman would eventually run out of conversation and subside into silence. Tim would finish whatever drink he was on, nod politely, and go upstairs to his room. And there he would kill himself, and the whole fucking mess would be over.

Focus . . . She was silent now, but he could feel tension building. At any moment, she might begin talking. Her eyes, he noticed, were brown . . . He looked away. Today had been a day of *lasts* – the last time he'd get dressed, leave home; the last time he'd be caught, last in line, by the lights at the junction near his house. It always felt like last in line, even when others queued behind you . . . The last time he'd think *always*. Her dress left her arms bare, and he thought he could see – it might be a trick of the shifting light – faint yellow marks, the size of thumbprints, above her elbows.

'It was a cupboard. One with double doors, where one's held in place by the other? And I tugged the wrong handle, so the outer door swung and hit me in the face.'

This seemed a long answer to a question he hadn't asked.

'I think some of us are just accident prone,' she said.

There was a second or two's silence into which the conversation fell like a stone dropped down a well. He should say something. It wasn't enough to sit wrapped in his own intentions. This was the social stitching at work. It took a moment to play back where he was: a cupboard door had hit her in the face.

'I'm no lawyer,' he said. His voice came out rusty, and in his head various available sentences incompletely suggested themselves. *You could sue for. Maybe they'll reduce your. Or offer a complimentary.* 'Have you complained?' he managed.

'It didn't happen here.'

'Oh.'

'I'm disturbing you.'

'That's all right.'

Which was the wrong thing to say, the English policeman who patrolled his conversation informed him. It sounded rude; sounded as if she *were* disturbing him. Which she was. Which did not make it okay for him to say so. Fuck it: there was suicide happening here, albeit – so far – in slow motion. Why did life conspire to produce sitcom, when the audition had promised tragedy? Just this morning, at the off-licence . . .

She smiled faintly and picked up her newspaper.

Just this morning, at the off-licence, he'd become involved in a choice of whiskies. What should have been a two-minute exercise – you pointed at a bottle; you produced your wallet; you paid – became a discussion about the merits of various brands, one in which his own part was minimal. Something of an expert, the man behind the counter. Which meant he'd made a fine career choice, but this didn't soothe Tim much. *It's medicinal*, he wanted to say. It would stop the pain, he meant. A smart woman had once remarked that what put you off drugs was the embarrassing slang you had to use. Suicide, too, had its downside. There was a shameful amount of self-dramatising involved.

Upstairs, along with the Macallan he'd been talked into, was an almost full bottle of amitryptilline – no slang necessary. Between the two, the job would get done.

But first, it seemed, he had to make up for his unintentional rudeness to this bruised woman.

'Have you come far?'

A line that creaked as it was delivered.

If she noticed, she didn't let on. 'Totnes,' she said. 'Do you know it?'

He didn't. Then he did. He'd never been there. He knew where it was.

And so she talked for a while: about Totnes; about what brought her and her husband to Oxford. And where her husband was at the moment. Details Tim immediately forgot. Her name, he gathered, was Kay. Or rather (she corrected herself) Katrina. He supposed he told her his. A certain oddness about the situation suggested itself, but there was a certain oddness about everything today – a *last* oddness, that would be. Mostly, their conversation moved as if it required little of his attention. Mostly, his own undercurrent drowned out what was happening on the surface . . .

It wasn't a slow accretion of feelings he was subject to; it was a wave of blackness that hit him at once, and often: who would love him now? Who would be there when he felt lonely, or needed contact? And it would be the same tomorrow, and every day after; the rest of his life dipping like a long slow road underground. They said it got better. It took him a moment to remember who 'they' were: they were the experts, who explained what was happening to you long after it had become obvious. They said it got better in time – call it two years. So what would he be in two years? Two years older. His body would have slackened further into that Babapapa shape men declined into; he'd have become seedier, the way men on their own did. Would be making his shirts last an extra day. And there'd never be anyone else again, because who would love him now? He'd been lucky the first time. Luck wouldn't happen twice. And he really didn't think he could take another unlucky day. The important word here was *really*.

. . . At some point he ordered another glass of wine. Things were speeding up, the way water did as it drained down the plughole. Soon time would have run dry. They seemed to be talking about poetry now. This wasn't something he'd consciously thought about since school, and not even then, to be honest. *Tiger, tiger, burning bright.* It occurred to him that this evening was going on a bill he wouldn't be around to pay. He should have ordered drinks for the house . . . And then came a moment, all too sudden, when he was alone, smoking his last cigarette. She had left. He remembered a hurried goodbye, but couldn't recall the reason for it – maybe her husband had shown up. The cigarette burned his fingers, and when he stubbed it out it came alive in the ashtray. Its burning smell mingled with others – with the wine; with the trace of her perfume hanging in the air; with his own bodily odour – and all of it produced a self-disgust so enormous, he wished he could disappear. Carefully, Tim stood, and managed to leave the bar without incident. Then, a resident, he retired to his room, to set about the tiresome chore of suicide.

*

When he woke, he forgot for a while that he was dead. Everything felt still and muffled. Noise grumbled elsewhere – the rattling of a breakfast trolley; a synchronised murmur of voices – but it felt dubbed; artificially added to satisfy those hungry for detail. All that counted was the body he remained sealed in: limbs like concrete; head broadcasting action from a distant war. The pounding of mortar bombs hitting sand with the dull rhythm of a heartbeat. Slowly, facts percolated while he lay motionless: the first, that the light was on. It burned directly on to his closed eyes, brighter than the average sun. The second, that he was fully dressed; on top of, not under, the covers.

Tim was dead, of course. Except he wasn't. Pieces of yesterday evening came back, and he imagined gluing them together like you might a favourite vase – entering the room, sitting on the bed, opening the Macallan. Fantasies he'd entertained while doing these things returned now with the heft of memory, as if he'd actually been dancing with Emma that recently; as if they'd made love – that recently. As for drinking the whisky, memory shuddered at the notion, and backed away. Like his favourite vase, memory wasn't holding water any more. But Tim didn't need memory to know he'd punished the bottle. Eyes closed, he could feel it poisoning his system. Eyes open – when he dared – he could see it, three-quarters empty, on the bedside table.

Next to the bottle of amitryptilline he'd not even opened.

He groaned, and alarmed himself with the noise . . . As if he'd just disturbed something nesting in its pit. He was the pit. This was the pits. Words that dizzied him, chasing their own tails round his mind: he made it to the bathroom, but just barely.

Tim wasn't keeping count, but it was two hours later he checked out of the hotel, doing so with a heavy sense of shame, as if he'd abused the premises somehow – sneaked in a prostitute, or accessed a pay-per-view that would have the staff sniggering in his wake. He barely glanced at the bill, though it was a lot more serious than it would have been if he were dead. Standing at the desk, watching the woman process his credit card, he almost excused himself – *I was here once before. With my wife. The weekend we married* – but recognised that for what it was: yesterday's alcohol talking. The remains of the Macallan, he'd left on his bedside table. The drugs, he'd flushed away – a corner had been turned, and he wouldn't be trying that exit again. Plans were not to be trusted. A sudden jump in front of a heavy vehicle might work, but anything more considered, he was bound to fuck up.

That afternoon, safely home in the small terraced house Emma wouldn't be returning to, he went to bed again: slept the sleep of the newly suicided between sheets unwashed in a month. When he woke, it was just before 5 a.m. His limbs were heavy and his stomach still churned, but mostly with hunger. He ate a bowl of cereal, then sat in his tiny back garden while autumn flexed its limbs, trying out a variety of small cloud formations before settling for plain blue. He smoked cigarette after cigarette until they were all gone, and their fumes infused his skin as if he were toxic.

The following morning, Monday, Tim called in sick, but got up in the afternoon anyway and washed his bed linen. He showered, and afterwards spent a while staring into the bathroom mirror. Lately he had been avoiding his reflection, the way he might cross a road to avert an encounter with a former friend, one who'd been out of touch too long for conversation to be anything but awkward. Now, though, Tim stared, as if indifference had crossed into hostility. 'You worthless shit,' he said to the familiar face with its few new creases; with the mole just under the jawline which had never bothered him, but did now. 'You pointless jerk.' He wondered what Emma would say if she could see him. But tears were sealed inside him so tightly they might never work their way out. He'd have to crack and fissure like a wrecked kettle for that to happen.

He slept. He woke up. Everything that had already happened for the last time happened again . . . He dressed, ate breakfast, and left for work; was caught once more by the lights at the junction, and then was delayed again near the shopping drag, before the long dip towards Oxford city centre.

An ambulance was parked by the subway, and somebody was being loaded into the back; there were policemen everywhere – Tim counted twelve, though he might have missed a few – blocking pavements; stringing yellow-and-black crime scene tape around the jeweller's. Cars were waved past one at a time. Stuck in line, Tim tuned the radio to the local station and picked up a story about an armed robbery so recent it was barely over. A passer-by had been shot: unconfirmed reports suggested he was dead. And this is how it happens, Tim thought; this is how it *really* happens. Unplanned, unexpected, when you were on your way somewhere else – death is not a rehearsal. Like the T-shirts say about life, only with more of an edge to it. Death is not a rehearsal.

Traffic began to move, and Tim moved with it: slowly down the hill, and into the heart of the city.

II

Some nights, there was a problem with the rats. The problem was, there were no rats. While Arkle stood in the centre of the yard, the only noise came from the road; a passing taxi's heavy-clutched grind, baffled by the high wooden gates which hadn't been opened in a year. And even that was blotted by the underfoot crunch of sand and pebble; the carefully graded piles of which had leaked from their enclosures and drifted to the centre of the yard, where it would have taken an expert to tell them apart, though the old man would have managed all right – on a lightless night would have done that with his feet: just the odd taxi for a soundtrack, and no rats in evidence at all.

Though Arkle could imagine the little bastards cowering in the darkness, waiting till he'd gone.

He'd borrowed Baxter's fancy watch. It withstood pressure fifty metres underwater, explained due north, and, more relevantly right now, lit up when he pressed a button: 10:45. Price was due at eleven, which realistically meant he might turn up within the next three hours. After one last look around – the weapon heavy in his hands: he hated it when he came out shooting, and found nothing to shoot – Arkle trekked back up the metal staircase to the temporary cabin that had perched there twenty-five years, a big tin coffin on a stepladder. Through its grimy window the portable's blue flicker leaked. Arkle's boots on the stairs made that dull thudding sound you got in submarines.

When they'd been smaller, Trent had worried about that, and also about the missing slats – you could see right the way to the ground. Trent was worried he'd fall through the gaps.

'No one in recorded history,' Baxter told him, 'has ever had that happen.'

'You don't know all of recorded history.'

But Baxter was pretty sure he'd have been informed.

At the top Arkle stopped and looked back. He wore a long black coat, and even in the dark his shaved head shone, as if recently charged. The lights of Totnes stretched up the hill, the chains they made broken where buildings or trees interrupted them. Somewhere out of sight, beyond where the street lights dipped into invisibility, Kay's old man still lived: a confused idiot last time Arkle had seen him. Years back you could have laid a garden rake against his backbone, touching all the way. It was one of those lessons life taught: that getting old was just another way of fucking up.

So: he placed his weapon on the flat roof. When he pushed the door it jammed briefly, and when he put weight on it, the office shook. Inside, Baxter and Trent perched on wooden stools that were just this side of firewood, watching the TV buzzing soundlessly in its corner like an electric aquarium. Despite the hour, Baxter looked – as always – splinter sharp: tonight a dark grey suit over a collarless white shirt, no tie. He looked like a poster boy for something expensive but ultimately soulless, like alcohol-free lager, or a New Labour policy initiative. Trent, though, looked like Trent. When you saw those newspaper articles about Britain today, how everybody was getting rounder and pastier, it was quickest just to think about Trent and nod.

But then, Trent had always had a problem. Fifteen years back, Arkle's first impression was Trent was terrified all the time. He'd thought there must be something basic, something all-encompassing, that gave Trent the willies twenty-four seven: hair, shoes, the weather, paving stones. Turned out, he was frightened of Arkle. So at least the little mutt had some brains.

It was Baxter who cleared this up. 'He's worried you'll forget your lunch one day, and bite his head off to keep you going.'

Arkle tried to imagine this. 'Does he think I'll chew clean through, or just scoop the insides out?'

Baxter had never had problems being scared of Arkle; or more likely, Baxter had quickly got used to not showing fear. Probably before he was three. Baxter was light brown, so when it was summer, looked like he had a really good tan. But when it wasn't, you knew there was mixed blood going on.

'Is your dad a brown man?' Arkle had asked him, back then.

'Don't know.'

'Why don't you know?'

'Don't know.'

'That all you fucking say?'

And Baxter had fixed him with huge oval eyes, dark as chocolate. 'Don't know.'

These days, Trent wasn't as scared of Arkle as he used to be, because Arkle had learned how not to put the fear on, which was energy-saving. Also, Trent was hung-over. You could always tell when Trent was hung-over; his hangovers clouded round him like a separate weather system. Trent reckoned he was a champion drinker because he drank so much, but this was like thinking you were a champion boxer because you got punched lots. Right now, he looked recently mugged.

When Arkle slammed the door it rattled the window: reminded everybody they were one small accident away from being bounced like a can of marbles.

'Price showed?'

Arkle barely got halfway through patting his pockets, looking over his shoulder, before Baxter said: 'Christ, enough, okay? Just thought his car might have pulled up.'

As often happened, and for no reason he could put his finger on, Arkle's mood lifted, tension leaking out of him exactly as if there'd been rats to shoot. Everybody had their own way of dealing with the climbdown after a job. Trent got drunk. Baxter – Baxter was wrapped pretty tight; probably had ways of letting off steam Arkle didn't know about. Probably involving Kay. Arkle didn't drink, and rarely touched women, but he had his moments. 'He'll be here. It's early yet.'

Baxter put his hand out.

Arkle tossed him his watch back.

On TV, a guy with a dark suit, bow tie and American teeth was displaying an empty top hat to a studio audience: you could almost taste the rabbit. It was funny how stuff that was naff ten years ago was cool again – Arkle rated TV magicians below radio ventriloquists. That guy who hung himself in a glass box over the Thames? They should have seized the opportunity and microwaved the prick.

But to be friendly, he said: 'Why's it quiet?'

'Sound's buggered. He just made a car disappear, though.'

Arkle was staring at him.

'What?'

'It's fucking TV, Bax.'

'And?'

'You watched *Superman* last week. You think that guy can really fly?'

Trent said, 'That was a film.' It came out 'fillum'. He sounded like his throat needed rodding. 'This is telly.'

'You probably have a point. I wonder what it is.'

'They said it was real. No mirrors or nothing.'

'And if Price offers magic beans, you'll believe him?'

Trent said, 'Films are made up. Telly isn't,' but said it largely to himself, so Arkle didn't let it spoil his new-found well-being.

Baxter said, 'I've never worked out whether I prefer you in a good mood or a bad one. Or what the difference is.'

Arkle rose above this. Baxter had occasions when basically he was just going to grumble, but the office was Arkle's space, and he wouldn't be crowded out. Baxter didn't like it, there were other places he could be.

Most of which were cleaner. Apart from the TV, the room – the crow's nest, the old man had called it – held a metal table, the stools Baxter and Trent were using, a chair which was Arkle's, a filing cabinet stuffed to buggery with invoices, receipts, catalogues, *paperwork* – not a scrap of it less than a year old – and one of those hatstands with horns, had to have fallen off the back of a lorry. And every last inch of everything, Baxter excepted, covered in dust. That was a rule: you couldn't run a gravel merchant's without a lot of airborne particles invading your space. The surprise was how Baxter avoided it; like he actually repelled the stuff.

The TV buzzed on wordlessly. Dust – dust would be doing that; choking its workings, so the words tangled up inside, and never got loose. Not that some dickhead with an undone bow tie had anything Arkle wanted to know.

'He'll be here soon,' he said, just to be saying something.

Baxter grunted.

'Price.'

Baxter grunted.

'I'll be outside.'

Arkle scooped the weapon off the roof on his way down the stairs.

Big clouds shifted overhead; the moon a bright edge behind them – a silver thread knotting in the middle. He could hear his own breath; hear his clothes rustle as he lifted the weapon to his shoulder and waited. Something would happen. His eye and the weapon were ready; a conjunction that demanded a third party: a victim that didn't know it was willing yet. Above him the crow's nest creaked, but Arkle was focused now; was all vision and trigger finger. Any moment now, the last living rat would show its whiskers. And half a second later he'd be on it, in it, through it . . . The rat would never know life was over. The last thing to pass through its mind, Arkle's steel bolt.

III

Death was on her mind when she heard about the money. Death and taxes: the two great constants, the latter somehow guaranteeing the former – nobody could afford to live forever. The interest alone would kill you.

'Four thousand, seven hundred?'

'Four thousand, seven hundred and thirty-one.'

She nodded.

'And twenty-six pence.'

'Where did they get that from?'

'Well, they're rather hoping to get it from you.'

This was what Zoë Boehm needed: a comedian. This was why she'd come through the door marked ACCOUNTANT.

'I fill in the forms. Every year. The self-assessment—?'

'The SA100.'

Thanks.

'I fill it in. I declare everything. So how come I suddenly owe four thousand, seven hundred and thirty-one pounds in unpaid tax?'

'It's a system. Like all of them, it has its flaws. You know what the problem with self-assessment is?'

She was about to find out.

'*Self.* If you'd come to me in the first place, you wouldn't be here now.' He hesitated, as if aware of a paradox lurking in that. 'An expert would have avoided the pitfalls.'

'So you can make it go away?'

He said, 'You realise we're talking after the event.'

Four thousand, seven hundred and thirty-one pounds.

Zoë – forty-something, five foot nine, dark-eyed, curly black hair – had been leading one of those second-chance lives lately: air smelled fresh, coffee tasted great. When she walked down the street, attractive details jostled for attention. But there was a use-by date on second chances, and she'd reached hers. The floral displays hung on lampposts, autumn sunlight stroking sand-coloured stone – they'd revert to visual irritants on her way home. Everything would be back to normal.

'I've never tried to cheat the Revenue.'

This was about eighty per cent true. She'd never tried to cheat the Revenue in a way she could be found out, and this was what was pissing her off now.

'There's a policy about ignorance being no defence? It turns out you're not entitled to some of the set-offs you've claimed.'

'Four grand's worth?'

He looked down at the papers in front of him. 'They're going back a while. It adds up.'

'They can do that?'

Short of walking through walls, his look said, they could do pretty much whatever they wanted. And don't place bets against the walking through walls.

'So what made them decide to look at me?'

'Roughly twenty-eight per cent of all small businesses—'

'What made them decide to look at me?'

'I imagine somebody gave them your name.'

Autumn sunlight slanted through the window. On the ledge birds shuffled and cooed.

'Nice.'

'You're a private detective. I assume you've made enemies.'

This was nice too.

Damien Faraday was mid-thirties, so hadn't had as much practice as Zoë at making enemies. Zoë imagined he'd be a natural, though. She'd picked him out of the phone book, and there was always a sense, doing this, that you were conjuring somebody from yellow paper: an origami miracle. In which case, the product ought to conform more closely to what was needed. This one was a little too smooth, a little too self-satisfied.

She said, 'I haven't worked in a while.'

'Such people have long memories.'

She assumed his experience was born of celluloid.

The desk between them was hi-tech, a polished black surface with chrome edging, on which sat a photo cube, displaying pictures of Damien, and a sleek computer whose screen was angled away from her. She had a sudden vision of the numbers he poured into it: an endless stream the machine would chop and change, delivering them back again as fractions, percentages, roots and dividends. And he'd be shaving points all the time, of course. It wasn't like he sat here for free.

'Have you been away?'

'Why do you ask?'

'You've not been working, you said.'

She wasn't about to give him her medical history. 'Yes. Which has kind of hammered my savings.'

'We can arrange a payment schedule. They won't be expecting a lump sum.'

'This is your advice?'

'Like I said, Miss Boehm.' *Ms*, she didn't bother saying. 'We're a little after the event, here. We can make sure it doesn't happen again. But there's not a lot we can do about what's already done.'

She wondered if this was what talking to a backstreet abortionist was like.

'You no longer have an office.'

'No. I run the business from my flat.'

He made a spreading gesture: what did she expect? The office had been her biggest business expense, a handy hole in the tax demand. Deciding it was also a luxury had been a bit hasty, judging by the man's obvious disappointment in her: he might have been offering Zoë tax windows for years, on which she'd insisted on pulling the blinds. *So pay the bill, woman. Forget about it.* Just one tinsy problem with that, Damien.

'We could throw together a list of legitimate expenses. Expenses you unaccountably forgot to claim. I doubt they'd look at them at this stage, but if you wanted to make the effort . . .'

Did she want to make the effort? For a while, this past year, life had ganged up on Zoë Boehm. She supposed she'd let things slide. It was certain she didn't have a trove of receipts she could wave in the taxman's face . . . Zoë had been flying under the radar so long, she got a nosebleed signing official documents. Waking up to a demand like this might be just what she needed, if you went in for that tough love crap. Mostly, though, she wished the taxman's spotlight had passed over her without registering the bump.

'Are you working at the moment?'

It was on her tongue to tell him to mind his own business, but by entering his office she'd made it his business. 'I had a call on my way here. A job, yes. I'm not sure what yet.'

'It might be an idea to take it. Regardless.'

Regardless . . . That was a good word. It implied that consequences were things that happened to other people – though looking at Damien Faraday, it was possible that that was true. Events might slide off his basted surface. If she were a cruel woman, she'd be wondering what he looked like with a pair of those bird thermometers stuck into him; the kind that pop up when the turkey's done.

'Ms Boehm?'

'I suppose you're right.'

'Filthy lucre, eh? Where would we be without it?'

'I'll keep you informed.'

With it, without it: she was on the street five minutes later. If she charged as much as Faraday did for doing bugger all, she'd not have required his advice in the first place. Another paradox there, but not as big a problem as remembering where she'd parked . . .

Except her memory wasn't that bad. She'd parked exactly where she thought she had, and the space remained exactly as she'd found it: a nice vacant kerbside stretch barely halfway over the No Parking line. It was only the car that was missing, and no matter how many times she turned and stared along the row of vehicles behind her, it didn't reappear when she turned back. Her car was gone.

Some crime scenes looked the part: broken glass and fractured furniture; the sense of something large having passed through, thrashing its tail and not giving a damn about the chaos. Others, eerily still, were often the ones where the most violence had taken place; violence carefully considered in advance, and focused entirely on its victim. Sometimes death was a private creature, and kept itself to itself. Zoë had seen a room once where a murder had taken place, and it simply looked recently vacated. She'd not have been surprised if the unspilled coffee cup on the table had been warm.

The jeweller's shop she stood in now was more akin to the former than the latter, though it had not been laid waste, exactly. Two men had entered, and with threats and visible weaponry had taken what they'd come for. Harold Sweeney had been left shaken but unharmed. Little damage had happened indoors; the violence – the ripped bone and cartilege; the spilt blood – had taken place on the pavement outside, and pavements didn't retain event memory. Harold Sweeney's, though, was working overtime:

'I'm unlocking the door, and first thing I know they're breathing down my neck, closer than my shadow. Looming up out of nowhere.'

The nowhere in question being a white BMW parked round the corner; stolen that same morning, and later found abandoned in the railway station car park.

'And they were armed,' Zoë said, to remind him she was there. He'd slipped into a fugue state; had travelled back in time three days, and was reliving it breath by breath.

'The tall one.'

'How tall's tall?'

'Taller than me.'

This wasn't as helpful as he might have liked to imagine. Harold Sweeney wasn't one of life's giants; nor did he especially make up for this in other departments. Under the shop's dim lighting – the mesh-inlaid windows blocked out the morning – his skin had a sallow sheen, as if he didn't venture above ground often, and his suit smelled like it had been rinsed then hung to dry in a smoke-filled room. Two smallish triangles of hair sprouted at his cheekbones. Presumably he thought this looked good, or that you weren't allowed to shave there. Either way, a second opinion would have helped.

But it was a job, Zoë reminded herself. Whatever he wanted, he'd be paying for it. And money would be useful, any time soon.

Sweeney had called just before her appointment with Faraday. Of course, she hadn't known then that she wouldn't have a car come eleven o'clock. She'd had to wait twenty minutes for a bus up the hill, time she spent reporting the theft on her phone. More officialdom. Was she sure she'd left it where she thought she had? Only she'd be surprised how many wom— how many people reported their cars missing, only to remember later where they'd actually parked.

She said, 'Is it true most policemen are failed traffic wardens?'

'I think you've got that the wrong way round, ma'am.'

'My mistake.'

Traffic wardens were a possibility, of course, but not a major one. In London, lorries with winches removed offending cars, but somebody had to examine the target for pre-existing damage first – she'd watched wardens with clipboards jotting down bumper scratches, to ward off later litigation. But that didn't happen in Oxford yet, and besides, she'd only been with Faraday half an hour. Nowhere near long enough to catalogue her car's damages. The policeman-shaped dent in the offside front panel was a page in itself.

And there was probably some law of modern life operating here: everybody gets a divorce, everybody gets their car stolen. Zoë had never been divorced, though that was largely a matter of timing. Now she'd had her car stolen, and while she couldn't say she enjoyed the feeling, the timing wasn't so bad here either. Like her marriage had been, her car was a wreck. But unlike her marriage, she was going to need to replace it.

Back to the present. 'What about the other one?'

'He was taller than me too.' His vision was sharper suddenly; the eyes had a spark to them. 'I've heard all the short jokes.'

'I'm sure.'

'The second one, he could give me an inch, tops. The first was about six foot.'

'And they were wearing stocking masks.'

'I doubt they walked up the street like that. Must've pulled them over their heads as they came up behind me.'

Zoë glanced through the dismal glass at what could be seen of the street. If their car had been round the corner, they'd had to cover fifty yards to get here: further than anyone would want to travel with a stocking mask on.

'I doubt that too, Mr Sweeney. Did they speak at all?'

'Bare minimum. They knew what they were after, and didn't waste time discussing it.'

'And what did they take?'

They both looked at the main counter display, whose glass was gone, though slivers remained in the crevices of the dusty velvet inlay. This was moulded to hold necklaces and bracelets. The wooden pegs were presumably mountings for rings.

'Everything from there.'

'Do you have—?'

But he was already giving her a typed list: one prepared for police and insurers.

'Thanks.'

He said, 'Do you know much about the jewellery trade, Ms Boehm?'

No: do you know much about the private detective business? But there was no sense antagonising a potential client; besides, *yes* – everybody knew about the private detective business. 'Just what everyone knows.'

He raised an eyebrow.

'You sell expensive stuff. What's on your mind, Mr Sweeney?'

'Much of what passes through my hands is never actually offered for sale to the public.'

'I see,' said Zoë, who didn't.

'It's a nice city to do business in, Oxford. There's a lot of overseas visitors, a lot of tourists. People on holiday like spending money. Main reason they leave home in the first place. You can make a nice piece of change off the holiday trade . . .'

Zoë could see a *but* coming before it cleared the horizon. 'Except this isn't really Oxford, is it?'

'This isn't really Oxford.'

It was Oxford, of course, but it wasn't. Oxford, for the tourist trade, was half a square mile – built largely of Cotswold stone – around which visitors could wander, asking where the university was. It was a stop en route to Stratford, around which they could also wander, asking where the Globe was. But Sweeney's jeweller's was well outside that zone: was up the big hill, past the house where a famous fat crook once lived, and nestled between a chemist's and a charity shop on the road to London. Passing trade was exactly that: passing. Oxford was a nice address, but nicer the less you knew about it.

'I do a lot of selling on. To bigger fish in the trade, you know?' Whose shops, presumably, boasted loftier addresses and kerb flash.

'Selling on of what?'

He shrugged. 'People die. Their relatives sell their jewellery.'

'Where are we heading here, Mr Sweeney?'

'It's what you might call a grey area.'

For a moment, she thought he meant Headington.

A shadow stopped outside the window, examined its contents for a moment, and moved on. Uncommitted interest. Sweeney got a lot of that, no doubt. Zoë had had a certain amount herself, when she ran an office: people dropping in to run hypotheticals past her; hoping she'd indicate an easy way they could find out what they wanted to know, and save them the expense of hiring her. Time-wasters were less of a problem since she'd quit the premises, though the species hadn't been eradicated entirely. Cold calling had brought it to something approaching an art form.

She tapped the paper he'd given her. 'You gave the police this list of the stolen valuables.' She was starting to sound like a box that required ticking.

'I gave the police a list of the stolen valuables that were officially in my possession.'

More shadows passed, this time without stopping. The dark blue rumble of a London-bound bus growled to a halt at the lights. Zoë – who'd been making occasional notes on a pad – put both it and pen in her pocket. Her jacket was dark denim, and hugged a little tighter than she'd like. The black leather one she'd had for years, she'd recently lost. 'There is, shall we say, a slight discrepancy between the actual value of what went missing, and that which I'm able to claim on the insurance.'

'It sounds like we're pushing the envelope here, Mr Sweeney.'

'I don't plan to hire you for moral guidance.'

'What do you plan to hire me for?'

'I want you to find these men.'

'It's a police matter, Mr Sweeney.'

'I'm aware of that.'

'A serious one. They might have stolen your goods, but they also shot a man on their way out.'

'And for that alone, they deserve locking up. But if the police catch them, and I have to say I'm not wholly impressed with the available statistics, it isn't going to help me much, is it?'

'Because you lied about what they took.'

'Because I was unable to furnish them with a full inventory.'

At this point, she supposed, she should be thinking about the ethics of her job . . . Instead, she was thinking about her tax bill, and the shallow grave of her current financial position. She was thinking about a cheque she'd written yesterday – to Vicky, her local teenage Webhead, who'd unscrambled Zoë's software – and wondering if it would bounce. She didn't want to piss Vicky off, who'd no doubt left trapdoors in the system, and would rescramble it without a moment's thought . . . Joe, her former business partner – her former husband – would be approaching high dudgeon about now. Joe had never lacked principles. Common sense, yes, but not principles. But the thing about Joe was, he was dead. Argument from him could be postponed indefinitely.

'So you want me to find them. And then what?'

'Then nothing. All you need do is tell me where they are.'

'And you'll ask them nicely for your jewels back.'

'There are . . . people I can turn to. Who would ask them for my jewels back.'

'Nicely or not.'

He inclined his head slightly.

'These people. They'd be your trade connections, would they?'

'Yes. That's who they'd be.'

'So why don't you use them to trace these guys?'

He said, 'I'd much prefer it if they didn't know the stock was missing.'

'Because then they might think you were unreliable.'

'We're all at the mercy of forces beyond our control,' he said. 'The small businessman more than most. It's sometimes difficult for the bigger fish to see that.'

'Are we talking stolen property here, Mr Sweeney?'

He said, with a passable attempt at dignity, 'We're talking about property without, perhaps, the full complement of paperwork.'

'Provenance and the like.'

'Have you ever filled in a form incorrectly, Ms Boehm? It's easy to make mistakes. It doesn't necessarily make you a criminal.'

Zoë became aware of a clock ticking while she swallowed that one.

'I'd hate to think you were using me to set up another robbery,' she said at last.

'It's not stealing to take back what's yours.'

'It's not the repossession worries me. It's how violent the process might get.'

'The tall one shot a passer-by. You're worried about what happens to him?'

'His conscience is his problem. It's mine I'm worried about.'

He said, 'In your line of business, I'd have thought a conscience a luxury item.'

Yes, well. It had been lost property not so long ago. Now she'd got it back, she didn't want any more blood on it.

Then he said, 'I'm sorry. That was uncalled for.'

'I've heard worse.'

'No excuse.' He looked up as another shadow passed; fooled, perhaps, by some slight hesitation in its step into thinking it was about to enter, take out its chequebook, make his day . . . It moved on. He looked back at Zoë. 'There'll be no vigilantism. Do I look like a soldier to you?'

'Hardly. But your friends sound the part.'

'I might have overstated our relationship. Acquaintances would be nearer the mark.'

This was getting nowhere. 'Mr Sweeney, I'm not sure I can help you.'

'Your involvement wouldn't be great. You find these people, you drop me a line. Anything else, you never know about.'

'Even that far. Finding them? I wouldn't know where to start.'

'Five thousand,' he said.

'. . . I beg your pardon?'

'Five thousand pounds.'

. . . It was, she decided later, the reality of the sum that gave her pause. Twenty thousand and up, even fifteen, she'd be shaking her head, laughing a little, as she made for the door. But five thousand was a plausible amount. It wouldn't make an especially big pile of notes. She could pretty much see it on the counter in front of her. She could pretty much pick it up.

She could pretty much wave goodbye to the tax bastards with it.

'Mr Sweeney—'

'That got your attention, didn't it?'

'Mr Sweeney,' again, 'I wouldn't know where to start. A couple of strangers rob your shop? They could be from anywhere in Britain. Hell, they could have flown in for that matter.'

'Just to rob me?'

'Cheap flights, why not? A day trip from Spain would pay for itself.'

'They weren't Spanish.'

'I didn't mean— Mr Sweeney, the point I'm trying to make is, they could be anywhere.'

'The five thousand,' he said, 'is a cash offer.'

And if he was willing to spend five grand getting it back – on even the chance of getting it back – it was a safe bet it was worth upwards of fifty.

Zoë tried not to sigh. Money was unsubtle stuff, and led to blunt situations. One of those had occurred just outside this shop: somebody walking past at the wrong moment, and ten minutes later he was being packed into an ambulance while traffic backed up as far as the ring road. Though it was interesting to speculate if that had been deliberate: a bit of random chaos thrown in, to make the getaway easier . . . But she was supposed to be counting reasons to stay uninvolved. Organised or not, they'd shown they were prepared to hurt people. And the big fish, Sweeney's 'friends in the trade' . . . Zoë didn't want to meet them either.

'I assume you have police connections.'

This was a big assumption. Some policemen had tried to kill her once, but they didn't exchange Christmas cards.

'I mean, wouldn't you be able to—'

'Mr Sweeney, it's not easy to get details of ongoing police investigations. You'd have to be a lot better connected than I am.'

'Your daily rate. Your daily rate, plus a five thousand bonus.'

Another ghost passed the window, disappearing without the slightest hesitation. Another cash sale, walking by without happening . . . There came a point where you had to be mad to turn opportunities down.

Her notebook was back in hand. 'The bonus happens when I find them. The rate happens whether I do or not.'

He said, 'The first one was about six foot. You'll want to take this down. The other—'

'He could give you an inch, tops,' Zoë remembered.

'Yeah. A real short-arse.'

'And it was the tall one had the gun?'

Sweeney said, 'Gun?'

'They shot somebody. It was on the news.' Sounding stupid even to her own ears: if they'd shot somebody, it had to be on the news, didn't it? Had to mean a gun.

'It wasn't a gun,' Sweeney said. 'It was a crossbow.'

2

I

SHORN OF LANGUAGE, WHAT Price had said was: 'Fuck did you think you were up to, fuckhead? Did I say shooting was *required*?'

Not totally shorn of language, obviously, but cleaner than the original.

Arkle explained it was one of those things could happen to anyone, not clear even in his own mind whether he meant releasing the bolt or being shot in the leg, but figuring same difference. Except Price said, 'Not if you left that fucking thing *home* it couldn't.'

(A couple of things about Price. First, he looked frighteningly like a younger Van Morrison. Unfortunately for him, only about ten minutes younger. Also, he had the habit of stressing random words, which made it tricky to work out his meaning. 'Did I say shooting was *required*?' Which could mean it was optional, right? Which wasn't what he meant.)

All this had been late last night, well after midnight. Trent was asleep, stale beer wafting off him; Baxter, meanwhile, had gone on to the gantry with his mobile, and was murmuring to Kay in a voice so low it might have been threat or promise. Baxter was always controlled, always focused; listened when Kay spoke. Kay too was tightly wrapped, though Trent had called her 'accident prone' lately – Arkle didn't know what that was about.

What Price said next was: 'Can I assume you at *least* took the right fucking goods?'

So Arkle showed him: not the lucky-bag assortment scooped from the counter display, but the stones they'd made Sweeney dig out of his safe. Price sorted through them with greedy fingers, while the TV span silent webs in its corner.

Price went quiet when assessing merchandise. He'd pick up the pieces one after the other and scrutinise them from all angles, in case he came across one that hadn't occurred to him before. Arkle left him to it; crossed to the window, whose wire mesh reinforcement cut the pane into tiny diamond shapes, and looked at Price's car. Price always parked over the road from the gate, or rather Win, his peculiar driver, did.

. . . That time he'd spoken to Win, it had been with genuine friendliness. Arkle had seriously wanted to know why the fuck Win dressed in retro leather like an extra in a Nazi porn film. But maybe his choice of words had been poor. Win, in reply, had invited him not to lean on the car, like he was about to smudge it or something. The car was a shit-brown Audi: a smudge would have lent it character.

'You actually his . . . ?'

'His what?'

Get that voice.

'His minder?'

'Try causing a problem. That way, you'll find out.'

Which had freaked Arkle, all right: *try* causing a problem. Like there'd be difficulty noticing if he decided that's what he'd do.

What with the irritation and all, he hadn't felt inclined to offer his advice; this being that when you were minding somebody, it was an idea to vary your routine. Instead of, for example, always parking over the road from the gate.

Always, though. There was a big word.

Baxter came in, looked at Price, then sat on his stool again, facing the TV.

Always meant seven: seven times they'd done this now, so must be experts. Not that a lot of skill was involved. Price provided names, times; spelt out the merchandise; took it off their hands. From his point of view, it must have been like shopping online with Tesco's, except the right stuff got delivered.

And what Baxter said was, Price was playing both ends against the middle. The targets were guys Price fenced for, which was how he knew what they were holding – small fry, so lacking in comeback. Price, big in his own field, was poaching in others': the way McDonald's sold fish nuggets to choke the local chippies. Baxter knew stuff like this, and could have been an economist if being a thief wasn't quicker. Baxter took charge of the money.

But Price didn't totally squeeze the targets – no: he paid sympathy visits; took some legal junk off their hands, to cheer up their cash flow. That was probably good for another forty per cent under market value, Bax reckoned. You couldn't underestimate the human touch. Once you'd got that faked, you were raking it in. Again: McDonald's – have a nice day! If they wanted you to have a nice day, they wouldn't be selling you that shit.

Price grunted now, as if he'd discovered a flaw. Arkle turned from the window. 'Something wrong?'

Price said, 'You know much about diamonds?'

Baxter said in a bored voice: 'I know a bit.'

'Yeah?'

'Yeah. I know you're not the only guy in the West Country buys them.' Still in the same bored voice, making Arkle proud of him.

'We've got a deal,' Price said, after a moment.

'So don't start chiselling.'

'For fuck's sake, I'm clearing my *throat* here. Where's the problem?'

Baxter just looked at him.

And if he wasn't sitting watching a soundless TV in a tin box, Arkle thought, Baxter could have been, not just an economist, but a banker or TV evangelist: someone making serious money . . . If the old man had had his way, they'd be supplying the basics to construction companies, instead of raking in more in three days than he had in six months. But then, if the old man had had his way, he'd still be alive. Death hadn't been on his wish list. It had just been on his agenda, like everybody else.

Price said, 'Let's try and keep this on a civilised fucking level.'

Arkle said, 'You parked in the usual place?'

'Why?'

'No reason.'

Price said, 'You enjoying this conversation? Or shall we shut *up* while I get on with it?'

Arkle shrugged: get on with it.

'Only it looks like the hobbit's settled in for the night.' Nodding at Trent, who was snoring rhythmically, sounding like his own respirator.

Baxter, without taking his eyes from the screen, said, 'Don't dis the hobbit,' and even Arkle couldn't tell whether he meant Trent or that pixie from the film.

Price went back to the merchandise.

Arkle returned to the window. If it was open, and he had the crossbow, he could put a bolt right through Price's radiator. Or any other part of the car he chose.

And that had been last night, and Price had gone eventually, having said the merchandise would do, which was the word he'd used: *do* – as if there was anything else it could have done. Thirty grand . . . And if he'd paid thirty, it was worth more.

But thirty grand would *do*.

And now they were in the pub down the road from the yard – Arkle, Baxter, Trent – having lunch, which for Arkle was tap water and for Trent lager. Baxter was drinking wine. The pub was done up to look like a library which had become a pub by accident: like, how did *that* happen? Except Baxter made a point of plucking the occasional book from its shelf, sniffing, putting it back. Then explaining they'd been bought by the yard, as if this was news – there were fucking hundreds of them.

Trent said, 'Good couple days' work,' and it was the first sensible thing he'd said all morning, or at any rate, the first thing he'd said all morning.

Baxter looked at him. 'You ever consider detox?'

Trent took a pull on his pint and set it down, dead centre of his beer mat. He looked around the room: at the books on their shelves, at the barman, at the couple of ancient Chinese men drinking Guinness at the far end, then back at Baxter.

Bax said, 'It's something you might want to think about.'

'Know what I've been thinking about?' Arkle asked.

'No,' said Baxter, turning to him. 'But I know where you've been. Just this side of fuck-up central. Price was right. You were looking for an excuse.'

'He was in the way. He had this uniform—'

'He had a pair of overalls.'

'You weren't there.'

'We've each got our part to play. Mine's to drive. Yours is to get the stuff with the minimum fuss.'

'We got away, didn't we?'

'No thanks to you.'

Arkle stared at him a long moment, then looked away. It was an old building, and the windows were cramped uneven openings through which dusty sunlight fell in slanting beams. Every time you raised a glass you caused turbulence: swirls and eddies multiplied in the streams of dancing dust. Consequences. This was what Baxter meant. That actions had reactions. Except there came a point where you had to stop worrying, else you'd never get anything done. So he'd shot a guy on the way out: so? The guy would live. All they had to do now was not get caught, and they'd had to do that anyway.

Trent mumbled something nobody heard.

Arkle said, 'I'm going for a piss.' He didn't need one especially, but those Chinese pensioners were weirding him out. Wasn't there something oriental they should be drinking: gin slings or tiger beer? Instead of Guinness?

When he'd left, Baxter said, 'He's losing it.'

Trent shifted. 'He's always been losing it.'

'This is worse. The crossbow? He's going mental.'

'It was under his coat. I didn't even know he had it until—'

'I don't blame you.'

They both knew Trent couldn't have stopped him if he'd been a traffic light.

'So what you saying?' Which whatever it was he'd better say fast, because Arkle would be back soon. And Trent didn't think Arkle wanted to hear it, which meant nobody in the immediate area wanted to be near Arkle hearing it either.

'I'm saying' – and Baxter leaned forward: 'I'm saying he's going to blow it, Trent. Soon. And that's not something we want to be caught in the middle of.'

'We're okay so far.'

'Skin of the teeth. Think about it, that's all.'

Baxter leaned back and the conversation was over. Trent took a pull on his lager, and felt his body start to relax.

In the corner, a trivia quiz machine went through its endless routine: snippets of games, each of which guaranteed a fifty-quid payout, unless the snippets weren't telling the whole entire truth. Somebody had lit a cigarette, and the sunlight vectoring from window to bar billowed suddenly with blue-grey smoke, the way a river swirls with mud when you drop rocks into it. It took Trent a moment to notice that the cigarette was his.

'Kay coming?' he asked, without knowing he was going to.

'No.'

'She all right?'

Baxter said, 'Why shouldn't she be?'

'No reason,' Trent said.

Arkle appeared through the door from the toilets, and stood surveying the scene for a moment, as if presented with an unexpected vista. It wasn't clear whether he'd lost track of where he was, or was just momentarily appalled by it. On his way back he paused by the Chinese men, or Trent assumed they were Chinese, and said something, pointing to their pints of Guinness. The Chinese men looked at each other. Arkle said something else, or maybe the same thing again, and this time pointed to the bar's top shelf and its row of bottles: the usual suspects, plus a couple of fairly exotic interlopers, notably more dusty than the rest. The barman arrived. Arkle kept pointing, and the Chinese men were served with a couple of glasses of one of the exotics. Then Arkle nodded, satisfied, and came to join Trent and Baxter, wiping his shaved head with his big right hand as he approached; letting it rest there a moment as if he were about to test his skull's strength; see if he could squash it in his own grip. It was the kind of competition, whatever the result, Arkle would figure he'd won. Which was a good reason for not getting involved in serious disagreement with him.

Sitting down, he said, 'So what I've been thinking is, maybe it's time we did things a little differently.'

They looked at him.

'I mean, Price? Seriously? He's taking half of everything we earn.'

'He sets it all up,' Baxter said in a neutral tone.

'So? How hard could it be?'

He began humming, a tune Trent didn't recognise, though

it was a safe bet its composer wouldn't either. Down the bar, the two Chinese men rose and went.

'You know,' Arkle said, 'I've got a good feeling about the way things are going.' Though he wasn't happy about the unfinished glasses they'd left behind them.

II

'They come out of nowhere.'

'What time was this?'

'Must've been . . . half nine?'

Derek Hunter – Derek *Raymond* Hunter: D. R., aka the Deer Hunter (Zoë had had this explained twice already) – had come off shift at 9:00 a.m.; had got off his bus at 9:27; had been walking past Harold Sweeney's at 9:29 – he lived just round the corner – and had been shot in the leg roughly then, as 'two armed men' burst out of the looted jeweller's. Zoë had only heard about one weapon so far, and wondered how divisible that was. If there'd been five men with a single weapon, would they still have been 'armed men'? But being injured with the weapon in question probably altered your perspective.

And the weapon being a crossbow altered Zoë's, truth to tell. Most situations, something not being a gun could only be a good thing. But when it was a crossbow instead, you were beyond dealing with the average muppet and looking at someone less clearly focused. Possibly a moral half-wit for whom other people's pain was a party trick. But possibly somebody worse: who knew the pain was real, and liked it.

Derek worked as a security guard at a supermarket.

'Seventeen years and never a shot fired in anger,' he said proudly. Derek wasn't allowed weaponry, of course. But he was man of the moment, and it wasn't his fault if the only words he could find were hand-me-downs. Seventeen years, and probably nobody had paid much attention before. 'And here's me getting plugged off-duty.'

'What else do you remember? About the men?'

'There were two of them.'

'Yes.'

'And they were armed.'

'Did they say anything?'

Across the ward a nurse pulled a curtain around a bed, and proceeded to act as if she'd thereby constructed a soundproof chamber: *Let's see to the doings then, shall we?* Zoë faded her out; tried to concentrate on the Deer Hunter, who was fiftyish, with teeth like a broken fence. Who wore no ring. Who might harbour crucial information – there was a first time for everything – but who most likely was going to enjoy his fifteen minutes then melt into the background, while his front-page appearance yellowed on his sitting room wall: the one that informed him that, contrary to initial reports, he wasn't, after all, dead. And one day even that wouldn't be true any more.

. . . She had to snap out of this. Morbidity was starting to stain her outlook; starting to taste like the air she breathed. Which this morning had mostly been other people's exhaust fumes.

The hospital was barely ten minutes' walk from Sweeney's, and a bus had arrived after a mere fifteen, so it hadn't taken more than half an hour to get here. Finding Mr Hunter hadn't been difficult, either: he was the only crossbow wound admitted lately. But it hadn't been visiting time, and the staff on duty hadn't been impressed with either of her business cards: not the one which said what she actually was, nor the one claiming she was a journalist.

'It's your lot were saying he was dead the other day.'

'I think you'll find that was TV,' Zoë said. 'Or radio. I'm strictly ink and paper.'

'Nice for you. You can wait along there.'

Waiting was never her strong point, and especially not in a cheerful room; one of those places whose very paintwork screamed *Could be worse.* Paintings by children she had to assume had been patients; whose fortitude should have been a lesson, yes, Zoë knew. But she'd had her car stolen, as accompaniment to a bill she couldn't afford, and this was not her day regardless. Through the window she looked down on distant undramatic roofs. Sounds carried of doors shutting, of everyday shoes on institutional floors. Half a dozen chairs had been stacked against one wall, beneath a notice reading AWAITING REMOVAL.

So she'd flicked through a magazine, and encountered an article about Positive Thought, the cure for everything. The Secret To Health, apparently, was A Happy State Of Mind. Happy? Totalitarian state of mind, more like: no sulks, no anger, no kvetching about the weather. No wondering why things went wrong, even when they obviously fucking did. No swearing. And, of course, no cigarettes, no alcohol, no fatty foods . . . One of those Total Health Diets where you lived to be a hundred, but every last minute felt like death. Capital Punishment – punishment by capitals – had sneaked in through the back door.

And death was the ultimate removal, of course: death was change of address, no forwarding. Your number disconnected for all time. Right that moment, at the end of this corridor, sitting in a plastic bucket seat, it was hard not to figure this an anteroom to death – maybe the entire building was. Like the joke says: you don't want to end up in hospital, they're full of sick people. And sick people died. As, in the end, did healthy people . . . Just one more change of identity, in a lifetime spent being one thing then another. Young/old, happy/sad, alive/dead. The ultimate deed poll alteration. You could change your name, change your habits, but eventually, you got what was coming.

And here was why death had been on her mind: she had had her own scare lately, Zoë Boehm. It had come to nothing, her brush with death, but the best you could say of that was that it was rehearsal only. It had been an act of subtraction: a good doctor had taken away the thing that had frightened her, which had turned out not cancer, but a cyst. So what still frightened her? How come she still had nights where sleep ended before it began, and dawn found her upright in an armchair, sipping tap water in a room with open curtains? Because she wanted to retain her identity was why. She was not yet ready for removal. And she'd come close, if only in imagination, to what that removal would be like. It would not simply be the end of Zoë Boehm. It would be the end of everything – of armchairs, tap water, curtains: everything. The fact that they would continue for other people didn't count. She'd discovered she wasn't going to be around forever any more.

In her good moments, Zoë worried she'd allow a few bad months to turn her into a health zombie. And the rest of the time, she took her pulse and checked the calendar and carried on giving up smoking . . . And besides, and besides, and besides. There were many possible futures, and one of them was hers. The slow decline into senescence, or the rapid burnout of a mattress fire. Positive thinking only took you so far. You could look on the bright side – that it was the knowledge of inevitable closure that made the remainder sweet. That the trite was also the true: all good things come to an end. That this was the natural state of things, and nature must have its way. And that two positives don't make a negative. Yeah, right.

Or you could carry on being yourself, and try to put what lay ahead behind you. Which was her current plan.

In time, she'd been allowed to come and speak to Derek Hunter; in time, she'd reached this point in their conversation:

'Did they say anything?'

'I think they might've . . .' His face scrunched into concentration. Fiftyish faces had earned their lines. Zoë tried to read what these might mean, and guessed at puzzlement, spite, confusion . . . Concentration looked like it might be new. 'I think he might've. The one with the crossbow.'

'You remember what it was?'

He paused. 'I was too busy being shot to notice.'

Fair point.

Over the way, the patient was succumbing to something approaching panic. His words weren't clear, but the tone was unmistakable: querulous, importunate. The voice of someone who'd been giving it a little thought, and wasn't keen on the conclusions. Not when these invoked a curtained bed and a loud-voiced nurse.

'Did he have an accent?'

'Who?'

'The one who spoke. The one who shot you.'

She gave him a moment to think about it. They'd been through most else: height, weight, clothing. He'd had nothing to tell her she hadn't gathered from Sweeney. The masks might have been interesting, if the villains had gone for something post-Tarantino – American presidents, Disney characters, Spice Girls – but stockings were useless. Sometimes it was hard to tell traditionalism from lack of imagination.

'De Niro. He sounded like Robert De Niro.'

'De Niro.'

'You know him?'

'I know of him. Yes.'

'Well, that's who he sounded like. Bobby De Niro.'

'. . . Thanks, Derek. You've been a help.'

She tossed the notes she'd made into a bin on her way out. The Deer Hunter. Robert De Niro. Life was too short, really.

A sign by the door reminded her that her mobile should be turned off. She remembered that hers wasn't just as it started to ring.

*

Smoke that had been a thick black smudge blotting out sunlight was now a greasy ribbon spiralling skywards. On her walk from the city centre – she'd taken the route past the multistorey and through the estate; across the bridge which overlooked the vacant space where the house had exploded a few years previously – it had reminded her of those hot air balloons which took off from the meadow next to the ice rink. Usually with an advertising logo attached, though all this one said was USED CAR.

Zoë was reasonably proud of not smoking any more. It was definitely a retrograde step that her Sunny had taken it up.

She'd walked down the main residential road this side of the river, then taken a right which led her past the local nursery school, and along a lane bisecting an adventure playground and a playing field which had once been dead ground: the former site of a gas works, whose industry had rendered the land dust-grey and hopeless. But it had been reclaimed in recent years; there was a basketball court now, and a five-a-side pitch whose goal mouths were muddy with use. On it, some kids were kicking a ball about. There was no good reason for the scene not lifting the heart. Except for the greasy black ribbon up there: the one that said her car was dead.

A gate blocked the lane halfway, but it was swinging open. The chain that should have secured it glinted in the ditch that ran alongside. The lane itself, heavily rutted, ended in a broad fenced area alongside the railway tracks, which were spanned by a concrete bridge with metal railings. A police car was parked dead centre, and a Dormobile on bricks, which had been in place long enough for bushes to have grown round it, was rusting quietly in a corner, its panels daubed with psychedelic whirls and swooshes. Short of carbon dating, it was impossible to tell which particular sixties revival this had died during.

There was a policeman sitting in the cop car, writing in a notebook, or possibly doing a crossword. Another stood by what had been, earlier this morning, Zoë's car: her red Nissan Sunny, which was now kind of melty grey.

'Ms Boehm?'

The standing cop had removed his jacket. Various bits of equipment rattled against his frame.

'That's right.'

'Well, here it is. I'm sorry.'

He seemed friendly and sympathetic, which meant he'd never heard of Zoë Boehm.

'You were quick. It only went missing a couple of hours ago.'

'It was phoned in. Parked in town, were you?'

'Yes.'

He shook his head. 'Makes you think, doesn't it?'

Zoë supposed she'd missed a fire vehicle. Her wreck of a car was streaked with foam. Its flames hadn't died by themselves.

The policeman said, 'You have to wonder, don't you?' This was his theme: you had to wonder and it made you think. 'Adventure playground to one side, football pitches to the other. And they tell you it's having nothing to do sends kids off the rails.'

Zoë wasn't so sure you could draw such straight lines between events.

'Then there's the fire-starting. Erases the evidence, sure, but it's a kick in itself.'

'Kids?'

'Who else?' He took half a step back, as if the heat had grown too much. 'It's not an especially grown-up thing to do.'

'It wasn't an especially joyride kind of car.'

'We IDed it by the plates. Couldn't tell the make, just by looking.'

Point. Whatever it was now couldn't be called a *make*. An unmade, perhaps.

'It was a Nissan. A Sunny.'

'Red?'

Zoë nodded.

'That'll be it. Honey for the bears, red. It's a go-faster colour.'

And Zoë had seen them before, of course: under motorway bridges; in the corners of fields. Cars reduced to exoskeletons; scorched the colour of rust, as if time had bullied them into their own future selves: relics from a future which didn't enjoy machinery, and whose plastics couldn't stand the heat . . . She'd seen them before, but she hadn't seen this one. This had been *her* car, dammit. Her car, which she'd taken care of. Which Jeff from the garage had monitored regularly. Which Zoë herself had cleaned religiously – i.e. once a year, round about Christmas.

'It usually happens at night, doesn't it?'

'Time was they were all tucked up by eight. Biggest thing happening was the tooth fairy.'

'But I get lucky in broad daylight.'

'There's always someone at the sharp end of the averages,' he said, with a philosophy born of observing something happening to somebody else.

He took her details, explained some stuff about insurance, and confessed he had no idea what would happen to the car. He imagined the council dealt with burnt-out wrecks. He'd put a POLICE AWARE sticker on it; meanwhile, there was nothing to see here. Move along, now. He didn't actually say that last bit. She nodded and walked away, from both him and her car's smoky ruins; took, without considering what she was doing, the steps up to the bridge over the railway line. A little to the south, this side of the gravel mounds bordering the tracks, sat disused rolling stock: canvases for local tag artists. In the opposite direction, across the river, lay the station. The sky above was a blue surprise, embroidered with just the odd scrap of cloud, and on the far side of the bridge, vaguely visible through the trees, were buildings belonging to a college sports ground: squash courts, maybe a cricket pavilion. Immediately below

Zoë, four sets of tracks pointed in both directions at once. You could hear them singing moments before a train arrived, but they were quiet as she fished her mobile from her pocket.

It surprised her that she had his number locked in her memory. Perhaps it was just locked in her thumb, which jabbed it out as if pushing needles through his skin . . .

'Poland.'

'One day, Bob, I'm going to finish the job I started and squash you like the bug you are.'

'Zoë Boehm. Having a good day?'

'Bob Poland. Not at work?'

'Fuck you.'

Needle or not, it wasn't hard to get under his skin . . . She'd cost Bob Poland his job. However he was earning his keep these days, she doubted it gave him the kick being on the force had.

Against the odds, this lifted Zoë's mood. She looked back, and saw a thin comma of smoke curling into the overhead: her car's last punctuation mark. At least she wouldn't be spending the next two years trying to coax another month's life out of it.

'How're the job skills shaping up, Bob? Hot-wired anything more upmarket than a Sunny lately?'

'Taping this?'

'You're watching too much daytime TV.'

'Gosh, Zoë, you sound like you're out in the open. Not calling from your car?'

'You know what gave me the clue it was you, Bob? It was something only a real fuckwit would do.'

'This one's for your dictaphone.' He cleared his throat, and spoke slowly, his faint Scots burr humming through. 'I have no idea what you're talking about.'

'Thanks, but I don't need to hear you deny it to know you're lying. Just opening your mouth does that much.'

'I hear you got your nose caught in a VAT trap. That must sting. Your sort don't like parting with money, do you?'

'Works every time. Scratch a thug, you'll find an anti-Semite.' Vice versa worked too. A train was coming, Oxford-bound, but very very slowly. 'I've a job on at the moment, Bob, but I'll get back to you soon. See how life's been treating you since you last tried messing with me. And then I'll fix your wheels, like you just fixed mine.'

'You've had your go, bitch. You think fate's gunna swing your way again? Your good luck's used up. It's downhill all the way.'

'So I could strive real hard in this life and still have a haircut like yours in the next?'

'Hang on to your sense of humour, Zoë. You're going to need it.'

The phone died, then the train blotted the silence out as it crawled asthmatically towards the station.

Bob Poland . . . Describe Bob Poland. He was a six-foot jawless stringbean who used to be a cop; a man whose nearly spherical head topped a narrow frame like a concrete ball tops a gatepost. It would be the most obvious thing about him, if it weren't for his being a prick . . . For the first few years of their working relationship, he'd been Zoë's police contact; someone she gave money to in return for information. Then he got involved with people who wanted to kill her, which had ultimately cost him his job. Apparently, he remained pissed off about this.

She slipped her mobile into her pocket and leaned on the rail to watch the train come to a halt by the cemetery. Last time she'd caught a train from London, the fifty-minute journey had taken a shade under three hours. It was a wonder ties and shoelaces weren't confiscated on boarding, as a suicide precaution.

Back on ground level, the cops had gone. On the field, there were kids still playing kick about, though not with a ball, she realised, but something ball-shaped: a rolled-up wodge of wet newspaper, or a human head. They had better things to do than watch a car expire. Happened every day. She left them to it, and walked into town.

III

It was office procedure to give one week's notice of time off. Tim Whitby had always set a good example, and hesitated now to say he wouldn't be in tomorrow. A dozen small but cumulatively significant obstacles suggested themselves as he sat tapping a pencil against his thumbnail. His office was small, windowless, would have passed for a cupboard without effort, but it allowed him a certain amount of privacy despite his open-door policy. And there were usually people outside that door, because the office was off the staffroom, which wasn't much larger but had more chairs.

The previous Monday, of course, he had called in sick. This had felt legitimate – he had, after all, planned on being dead – but had not gone unnoticed.

'Feeling better?' Jean had asked, every morning since.

Jean was the shop mother. Jean fussed over everybody; even – especially – those who didn't welcome it. *Fuss* was Jean's default setting. If Tim announced that he was taking tomorrow off, she'd assume he'd had to make an emergency appointment with a specialist. So he needed a plausible explanation for absence; another sick day, and she'd send an ambulance round his house.

. . . And this was what his decision to live had returned him to. He favoured an open-door policy, but was locked back in his old life as severely as if it were a cell; worrying about how much notice he should give for a day off. He'd planned on taking the rest of forever off: how much warning had he given of that? Tim had the feeling he'd passed a fork in the road, and there was no turning back – suicide was a one time only offer, if you were Tim Whitby. Like those rubrics in job adverts: previous applicants need not apply. He'd sometimes wondered how he'd feel if he saw one of those and knew it meant him. Well, this was it. Death had rejected him. It would catch up eventually, of course, but at a time of its own choosing. Not his.

He realised that he was bent forward over his desk, eyes closed, and that anyone could have looked in. In case they had, and were still there now, he tried to adopt an expression of intense concentration, provoking instead a fleeting amalgam of self-disgust, amusement and despair, which convulsed his shoulders in a kind of emotional hiccup. Great. Now his observer would think he was crying. Tim opened his eyes. There was nobody there. On his desk various invoices craved his attention, but not loudly enough to warrant it. He stood and walked through the staffroom to the storage area, and let himself out of the side door.

It was another bright blue day, too windy to be warm. There was something he ought to be doing now; for a moment he couldn't imagine what, and then decided it was smoking – he should be smoking. This was your alibi when you'd walked out of your office and were standing doing nothing much while work piled up behind you. But his occasional nicotine binges left him sick and hungover, and he wasn't in the habit of carrying cigarettes. So he stood doing nothing, while the wind rearranged his hair. He yawned suddenly and largely. He hadn't slept much last night.

His bedroom was at the front of the house, and though it was a quiet neighbourhood, noises from the street carried to him nonetheless, offering a commentary on lives unconnected to his. Last night, he'd heard footsteps – a woman, in heels; their regular click click providing a rhythm for his insomnia.

And as they reached their loudest, directly beneath his window, they stopped, and for half a beat he imagined the next sound he'd hear would be her key in the lock, and that this was Emma come back to him. But Emma wasn't coming back to him. *This is what your life is like now.* But he allowed himself to dwell for a second on what would happen if she did; the readjustments that would ensue; the endless explanations to friends and neighbours. The rot that would result from this attempt to repair the irreparably sundered. It wasn't going to happen. She wasn't coming back. Something rasped on the street below – a match or an inefficient lighter – and the footsteps started again; grew quieter, more distant, disappeared.

He'd somehow dozed off after that, and had the second dream.

The store was part of a complex of large retail outlets – the others sold sporting goods and DIY materials – arranged as an open-ended square around a car park; a probably accidental parody of the quadrangle effect older buildings in the city were famous for. The car park's level expanse was relieved here and there by strips of greenery intended as chicanes, but which also served as fast-food packaging depositories. Red-and-white-striped cardboard cartons nestled under exhaust-stripped shrubberies like a terrible taste of Christmas yet to come. And the whole complex was just one of a series of such lining this busy road leading west out of the city: a consumer paradise, or possibly hell on earth.

He walked a little, to avoid capture. By the DIY store he paused. Its window stickers offered unbeatable bargains with a gusto bordering on the desperate. He peered past them to pyramids of paint cans; to racks of tools designed for home improvements. Everything here came with the promise of a future attached. He left, kept walking; found himself tracing the car park perimeter with no real sense of purpose, but at least it was a ready-made route. At the main road he stopped, and thought about the dreams.

Emma had often described her dreams to him, and they had always been – or had seemed in the telling – coherent narratives, with defined beginnings, middles and endings, even if the endings turned out to be that hoary old staple *And then I woke up* – it was all a dream. But Tim had rarely recounted his, and she'd never, of course, pressed. Dreams are more interesting related than listened to. And Tim's were pointless, shambolic episodes: fragments too scattered to shore up any ruin. But last night, and the night before, he'd dreamed about the woman.

The first time had felt like an act of infidelity. Something very like guilt clouded him that morning; dogged him all day until he burned it off with alcohol, the way Emma used to sear their Christmas pudding – infidelity? It was Emma who'd betrayed him. He was still here. At which the usual bout of hatred and self-pity enveloped him: the usual old snake, swallowing its own tail. It took the second dream to make him think about the dream itself.

Which had been almost eventless. They had not been in the hotel bar where they'd met, but in a cottage somewhere. She had her back to him, and he had been asking a question which had seemed, at the point of asking, to carry the weight of his entire life, but whose import he'd immediately forgotten. And when she turned, any answer she might have made became irrelevant because all that mattered was the bruise, which was no longer a slight discoloration under one eye but a whole continent of purples, blacks and oranges; a bruise which blazoned not only the blow which had made it, but all the other blows suffered by the same body. That there had been others, he had no doubt. Perhaps it was that sense of certainty that woke him: it was an unfamiliar feeling these days. And dreaming the same dream twice was strange, too – but perhaps, in fact, he hadn't. Perhaps the dream had arrived with familiarity hardwired into it: trailer and movie at once. Just another retail con trick; one with the promise of a history attached.

. . . His mind drifted. Concentration was hard to come by these days. His mind, in fact, didn't drift: it took a predetermined route he was helpless to forbid. It began at his feet, stepped into the main road, and instantly hurled away into the traffic like a paper bag in a slipstream; whistled past shops so they blurred into a single endless mall: one huge window, plastered with insincere offers. Then on to the ring road: past estates bridges garden centres; skirting small communities long islanded by traffic. Through green lights red lights amber; over roundabouts; shaving corners. On to the London road, and a sudden shift of gear before rocketing away to what waited: a long sloping curve towards the motorway . . . And here, at this junction, somewhere under the road's ever scribbled on surface, there would be skid marks still. Like the plastic slate he'd drawn on as a child, which could be wiped clean repeatedly but retained every mark on its backing board: an incoherent mess of squiggles, each of which had meant something once . . . The skid marks he was thinking of were Emma's. What they meant was, she had lost control. They meant she was never coming back.

He did not know how many cars used that stretch of road every day: easily thousands, though; tens of thousands. And he did not know how many people died on the roads every year: but hundreds, tens of hundreds. That vaguely appreciated big number was not information consciously acquired; it was simply part of the condition of life. In a motorised society, there will be a certain amount of collateral damage. Tim had always known that, just as he had known that every time he picked up a newspaper, he'd find some version of that same story. But he hadn't expected to find himself in it, and Emma gone.

But death was the smart bomb. Death could unerringly pick an individual from a crowd and obliterate her so particularly, so precisely, it was amazing any memory of her survived. As for those closest, they were left wondering what happened; the smoking crater beside them all that remained of their recent companion. And those approaching sirens heralded emergency counsellors, come to cut the survivors from the wreckage of their emotions.

Tim wished he had a cigarette after all. But the nearest pack would be across this busy road: a rushing metal river he didn't care to step in once, let alone twice.

She had lived for two days. This was not precisely right. The quick, the true, the *ugly* fact was, she had not died for two days. Which was when Tim, who had not slept during that period, gave permission for the machine to be turned off: the machine being all that was keeping Emma breathing, though in his stricken exhausted mind, the machine *was* Emma by then; he was giving them permission to switch Emma off. And afterwards, he slept.

'There is no sense in which you are responsible for her death. None at all.'

'I know.'

'She had the bad luck to be on the same stretch of road as a drunken—'

'I know.'

These were the words of friends, and were meant to help.

'There was no chance of recovery. It wasn't that it was the kindest thing to do, it was the *only* thing to do.'

Consolation, though, wore off. People trod round him on eggshell feet, then gradually normalised, as if his own rate of recovery were somehow equivalent to theirs.

But there was no way of measuring the speed he was moving at. And as for time, it was ever divisible. Even seconds broke down into smaller units, which frequently snagged on events like a loose thread – pauses in conversation seemed to last for days. Responses had once come automatically. Now he had to sift everything twice: what had been said, the available replies, which he should choose . . . Grief was slow motion. This was what was meant by funereal pace.

And because there was so much of it, time was impossible to ignore. Clock-watching became obsession. It was as if he weren't just passing time but accumulating it: one more thing he had to carry through the day. What would he do with all this time he was gathering? He'd find some way of killing it . . . Work became purgatory. He had always enjoyed his job, or more accurately, had enjoyed the knowledge that he was useful; that he could garner a salary for the time spent doing it. Now, it was barely credible they still paid him. What was it he did, exactly? There was a shop, and it sold electrical goods. Part of a nationwide chain, with a turnover in the mid-millions. Twelve staff under him; more at weekends; and God only knew how many above, when you took the national hierarchy into account. Once, he'd seen himself climbing this pyramid – but then once, he'd been good at what he did. Once, he'd been on first-name terms with his staff, even the Saturday part-timers. Lately, he kept forgetting what Jean was called. Once, he'd filled the store: it was his territory, and everybody breathing was a potential customer. Now, he'd become two-dimensional: he took up space, and wasted time.

Time, which passed so slowly.

A horn sounded somewhere behind him, and he came back to the present, looked at his watch. It would be lunchtime within the hour. He'd better return to his desk.

Where he dealt with invoices; returned a phone call; fended off Jean, who had logged his temporary absence: 'Are you sure you're—?'

'I'm fine.'

She looked doubtful.

'I'll be taking a day's leave tomorrow. Wednesday. Could you put that on the roster, please?'

'Doing anything nice?'

'Let's hope so,' he said, 'Will you close the door? I need to make a phone call.'

So that was that.

Tiger, tiger, burning bright . . .

And that was something else that popped into his mind every time he recalled that evening. The line, of course, he remembered from school: *Tyger, tyger,* his textbook had read. There was more to poetry than spelling. Blake had been the poet's name, and still was, because fame was a kind of antidote to death – your name lived on. But only kind of, because you were still dead. He didn't know why it kept ringing in his head, and could only imagine that it was his brain's way of preserving a memory he didn't know he had – her name was Katrina. Her name was Katrina *Blake.*

It was not surprising, perhaps, that his subconscious had had to resort to subterfuge to preserve such shards. Saturday would have been his and Emma's tenth anniversary. The hotel was where they'd spent their wedding weekend.

. . . Katrina Blake, then. What was she doing in his dreams? And where had her bruise come from: oh, right, the cupboard door. Tim tried to retrieve exactly what she'd said about that, but all he could recall was that it had been a long detailed answer to a question he hadn't asked. A prepared story; one he'd failed to respond to adequately.

I think some of us are just accident prone, she'd said.

And had gone on to talk about her husband.

No huge leap in logic was required. It needed a leap in emotional understanding, that was all: a jump back in time to a point where this had been a language he'd been versed in; one he'd spoken at home – the ability to understand what was meant when a subject was talked around, not over. The ability to read between lines, and interpret silences. So say it was true, say it was so – say her husband beat her up. Why, then, would she talk to a strange man in a hotel dining room? Tim wished his recall extended beyond that bruise, that dress; the vague recollection of a voice deeper than expected.

Do you come here often? Had she really said that?

Tim thought he'd remember if she had looked at him with those forgotten-coloured eyes and said, 'Help me. Please. My husband beats me up.'

And what business was it of his anyway?

But that was a question for another time. Meanwhile, there was the other fragment that had pushed its way to the surface of his mind; the one he'd found there when he'd woken – had she come far?

Totnes. Do you know it?

He didn't. He did. He'd never been there. He knew where it was.

Voices from the staffroom told him the shift was changing. It must be the lunch hour. For the first time in a while, Tim Whitby felt the stirrings of appetite; something that reached beyond the body's automatic response to time passing. For the first time in a while, he had a plan which stretched beyond the first drink of the day.

He would go to Totnes. He would find Katrina Blake.

He would do this tomorrow.

Meanwhile, he'd have lunch.

3

I

MEN ARE GOOD AT watching and waiting. Zoës, less so. With men, it was doubtless something primitive; a lonely instinct programmed for the forest, where the ability to remain motionless and alert meant the difference between feast and fast. With Zoë, it was straightforward biology: she wasn't designed for taking a leak in a bottle. So she'd done the next best thing, and lied.

'It's for the council. They're actioning antisocial driving.' 'Actioning' was a good local government word, like 'prioritise' or 'backhander'. 'I'm taking notes of illegal turns, double parking. Horn-blowing.'

'People emptying ashtrays on the kerbs?'

'I'm prioritising that.'

'Filthy business. Well, if you're out there all day, you'll need to use the facilities, won't you?'

This was in the Cancer Relief shop opposite Sweeney's, and the woman was so sweet – all pink wool and white hair; a charming stereotype – Zoë might have felt bad if it hadn't felt so good. She refused a cup of tea for obvious reasons, and returned to the car, reminding herself to jot down number-plates if any of the cited infractions occurred. Pink wool, white hair – the old duck might be Miss Marple, and come checking.

The car in question was from her local garage; lent by Jeff, who'd tended her Sunny through most of its recent illnesses, and who had accepted its demise with equanimity. 'I'd have given it six months, max.'

'Thanks for the sympathy.'

'Yeah, well. You weren't planning on putting it out to stud, were you?'

'No,' she admitted. 'But I hadn't organised a Viking funeral either.'

He'd showed her some used cars, and they talked money without finding common ground. Insurance companies were mentioned, and their famous reluctance to pay out on policies. Zoë had been prepared to whistle this theme, but Jeff explained he had work to do.

'And you'll only be happy,' he said, 'when they give them away with boxes of cornflakes.'

'It'd have to be the supermarket brand,' Zoë said. 'Lend me a car, Jeff?'

'How long for?'

'. . . Couple of years?'

So now she had a Beetle until Wednesday – an orange Beetle. 'Sometimes I have to follow people,' she'd reminded him. 'Have you anything in taupe?'

'I'm straight, Zoë. I've never heard of taupe.'

The orange Beetle worked, though, despite being sticky on hills. And it was somewhere to sit while she watched Sweeney's. Watched and waited . . . She'd brought a bag of apples along. Since giving up smoking she'd been hungry all the time, and rumour had it apples were healthy.

This was Monday morning. In Sweeney's shop, there'd been no activity since nine thirty, when he'd opened. It was now pushing twelve. Divide the business rates by the pre-noon profit, and you could see why Harold might have been tempted off the straight and narrow . . . A lorry passed, chugging exhaust fumes, while on the pavements parents pushed prams and buggies, stopping to compare children every so often; a demographic varied by the odd group of students flexing their youth – talking too loudly; fondly imagining the interest of others. In the doorway of a boarded-up shop, a woman of indeterminate age huddled in a blanket, swearing at an ancient enemy who wasn't there.

A creep in a used-car salesman's coat with a face that belonged on Gollum oozed past.

There was nothing new here. Zoë had seen this before. Life was a series of vanishing circles that sucked you in faster, the smaller they got – life was a whirlpool. Life, in fact, sucked. She couldn't remember the first time she'd sat in a car, watching the same door never open, waiting for the same face never to appear . . . She could hazard a guess, though, that the job had involved something unpopular: another bill to pay; another court appearance. She'd pretty quickly grown used to being unwelcome. It must have wreaked havoc on her character, though nothing like the damage it did to her opinion of other people's . . . It was possible there were trustworthy souls out there, but a glass wall had dropped between her life and theirs. When she'd been those students' age, one million and twenty-five years ago, she'd no doubt had a vision of how life would be – so what happened? It must have had something to do with Joe, her late husband, whom she didn't miss. She rarely thought about him, and even when she did, he was still dead. There was nothing new there, either.

Puffed-up contrails cross-hatched the sky, as if something large and bored were about to play noughts and crosses.

To work. Sweeney, in Zoë's view, was dirty; or perhaps, in the grand scheme of things, merely grubby – the difference being, how rough you played. Either way, she was ninety per cent sure, he was a trafficker in stolen goods. As for his 'trade associates', they'd be his fences, and ugly pals like that weren't in the game to shore up a failing business. She wasn't surprised he didn't want them knowing he'd been ripped off. She wondered, though, that it hadn't occurred to him they'd been the ones doing it.

She plucked another apple from the bag. She was approaching her limit already – would wind up with stomach cramps if she didn't watch it – but she was so damn hungry, or at least, so damn needed to be doing something with her hands . . .

Anyway: the ugly pals were playing rough. Two men (there'd have been a third in the car) had paid an early call on Harold Sweeney, relieving him of loot he kept out of sight of the public. How did they know about the loot? Inside job . . . The ugly pals' version of victimless crime: one that didn't involve police. Who wouldn't have heard about it at all, if D. R. Hunter hadn't copped it as they left . . . Which was where her scenario might collapse if it weren't for the desperately fucking stupid element – in any group of more than two criminals, one would operate best at room temperature. And when you married poor impulse control to a low attention span, then dumped the mix into a lawless enterprise, someone was going to get hurt.

Something else worried her. She was pretty sure there was a fictional private eye who drove a cute VW. Probably in California. Jeff might be taking the piss.

Action happened over the road – a woman paused by Sweeney's window; spent fifteen seconds clocking its contents, then moved on briskly: either putting all thoughts of jewellery behind her or hurrying to tell someone of her plans, who could tell? That was it for half an hour; thirty minutes during which Zoë tested her logic and found it held. There was no way on earth she was going to find Sweeney's robbers by looking for them. Sooner or later they'd do it again and be arrested on the job, but that wouldn't mean Zoë got paid. Meanwhile, she knew something the police didn't, which was that these guys had known exactly what they were after, and where Sweeney had kept it. Getting a line on who else had known that was her only available starting point.

She browsed. In the glovebox she found a tube of Polos, an A to Z of Santa Teresa – wherever that was – and a nice pair of nail scissors she put to use: she'd been meaning to buy a pair for ages. Meanwhile, on the radio, an internationally megaselling author explained that he'd chosen popular rather than higher fiction because he'd never write anything as good as *Ulysses*. Zoë, who'd read one of his books, doubted he'd ever write anything as good as *Where's Spot?* In the window of the Cancer Relief shop she caught an image of white hair/pink wool, and pretended to be taking notes.

Lunch was an apple, followed by a Polo. At one, Sweeney left, to return ten minutes later with a sandwich. Zoë sank into her seat, donning her favourite disguise of trying to look like somebody else, but he didn't glance in her direction. He seemed curiously shorter today. Money worries, she guessed. Her own loomed large behind her. She could almost hear them squabbling in the back seat.

Sweeney had more customers in the afternoon, but none of them excited her. The first, a man in a grey suit whose joints shone, looked more salesman than customer. She could imagine the stand-off that must have made. The others were a young couple, early twenties; the male half eager, the way Zoë read it; the woman going with the flow – outmanoeuvred, perhaps, by her own disinclination to cause hurt. A ring was a ring; a bracelet, a bracelet. Sometimes promises were handcuffs. When they left twenty minutes later, he seemed to be halfway through a list of points that needed making: reasons to be cheerful, perhaps. The woman listened, nodded, half smiled . . . Waited for a break in the traffic through which she could hurl herself, screaming.

That was about it. Cars ebbed and flowed with the clock: school run, office exodus. Sweeney closed at six, though his enterprise had had a needy, unfulfilled air since four thirty at least. Walking away, he stooped like a man on whom gravity had done a number. For a while, she wondered about following him home; then for a while longer wondered what would be the point of that? Instead, she went home herself: ate a bowl of pasta, drank a glass of wine . . .

Doing nothing exhausted her. Her body felt like she'd put it through an uphill, dangerous struggle. It craved exercise, she supposed. Weariness was a con her mind was hoping to pull. In another life she'd have gym membership, or a robust callisthenics routine. In this one she had another glass of wine and went to bed.

Where she slept the fitful, punished sleep such shirking deserved. She dreamed she was cuffed to the steering wheel of an embarrassing German car, while Bob Poland watched through its windscreen . . . Poland was a man best left under his rock. She woke with that thought in mind, and couldn't sleep again.

On bare feet she padded to the kitchen; with a glass of water padded back, but found herself instead in her study: big word, small room. Small cluttered room, stacked with books she no longer needed and would one day shed, along with a filing cabinet full of Joe-related documents she supposed she'd keep forever. Zoë stood by the window, and looked out on the night-time world. A mist had fallen. No house lights shone. If she believed in ghosts, now would be the time to see them: pale spectres over the rooftops, barely distinguishable from the air they occupied. But all that carried to her was the sound of distant traffic. The dead don't drive, Zoë. There are no ghosts. There was, though, a fat cat from next door, scrambling over the fence with a noise like a John Bonham drum solo, only rhythmical. She let the curtain drop.

No ghosts, but haunting remained possible. Bob Poland, a man who by his own reckoning owed her harm, had threatened her life. How frightened should she be about that? It was true that he was not impressive: in the flesh or on the phone. She had cut bigger threats down to size; had once shot a man who could have crippled Poland with an elbow. Bob had the heart and mind of a stalker, and Zoë had encountered a few stalkers – all shared the same drab profile: middle-class under-achievers with hygiene problems. But Poland, an ex-cop, had a vicious streak, and it would be wise not to forget that. Besides, he didn't have to be brave or interesting to cost her money. He'd proved that already.

She went back to bed in the end. She didn't dream again, but on the other hand, she didn't sleep either.

Back on stake-out next morning, she thought through the robbery again. It involved neat moves. The BMW hadn't been discovered in the station car park until Tuesday evening, once the commuters' day was over, and their vehicles had dispersed. It was probable that the robbers had had a second car waiting, but always possible they'd simply boarded a train . . . Westbound they might have been noticed, but there was never a shortage of people heading for London. They might have lost themselves in the crowd. Or it could have been double bluff: they could be local. Either way, they knew their ground; had checked things out in advance. Only that pointless use of the crossbow suggested amateur status, and the more she thought about it, the more they sounded like a professional trio incorporating a loose cannon. Perhaps her time would be better spent scanning the papers, waiting to read about some minor thug being hoisted from a river, medicine ball welded to his ankle. Crooks with ambition didn't carry passengers. Unless something else bound them together, of course, but it was pointless speculating further.

No: her best bet was getting a line on Sweeney's 'trade contacts', and since he wasn't likely to tell her who they were, watching his shop in the hope of a personal appearance was the obvious move. It was a long shot but so was everything else, and she stood to win five grand. The most she had to lose right now was a bag of apples.

She was back in the charity shop before long.

'Are you collecting lots of data?'

'Masses of it.'

'Only you don't seem to be *doing* very much, dear.'

Which just went to show that sooner or later, long observation resulted in a conclusion or two.

The rest of the morning crawled. Lunchtime was a meaningless punctuation mark consisting of a cheese sandwich. If she still smoked, the car would be a death chamber by now: her skin, her fabrics, even the windows, would be suffused with dead tobacco. It had been something Jeff had checked on before he'd agreed to lend her the car.

'I figured you for giving up around when they made you Pope. How long?'

'Couple of months.'

'What, you're not going to break it down to the nearest second?'

'Since the first twenty minutes,' she'd confessed, 'it's all been a bit of a blur.'

A middle-aged woman entered Sweeney's about an hour into the afternoon, and came out again shortly after. It was all Zoë could do not to chase her down the road, asking what she'd wanted . . . Minutes passed. Hours. The day.

Late afternoon, something happened.

II

In a house on a hill in Totnes, a man sat looking at nothing in particular.

Sometimes she would arrive, and it was as if he were frozen the way she'd last seen him – glued to the chair like some patriarchal version of Whistler's mother; the dull cardigan still missing a button; the shirt still frayed at collar and cuff. The once sharp beard straggly and ungroomed. Even the point he was staring at never varied, but remained an invisible dot on a blank wall, causing her to wonder what he saw – whether he was looking back on all the lives whose endings he'd tended, or searching for a clue to his own beginnings; a little light shed on how he'd got here from there.

She stepped into the room, but he didn't look round. In profile, by the light that found its way through the ivy strangling the window, the lines age had carved into his face seemed deeper than natural, like wounds from a battle he'd been lucky to walk away from. And he wasn't that old, she had to remind herself. Early seventies. Life laid waste to some sooner than others.

'Dad,' she said.

He didn't appear to hear.

'Dad? It's me. Katie.'

Two ways of saying the same thing. He'd only ever had one daughter.

He stirred, as if passing weather had ruffled his surface, then blinked and turned to her. 'Katie?' Something missing in his eyes swam back under her regard: not quite a spark of life, but an acknowledgement of involvement – that things went on; that he was part of them. That one of these things was his daughter. The eyes were misty blue; the skin pale. The hair gone grey.

'Are you okay, Dad?'

'Katie. I'd just been doing a bit of clearing up.'

This, too, was how it ever was: he'd always 'just been doing' something moments before her arrival; had sat down the instant her key hit the lock. There'd been a children's programme in which a doll came to life and danced when everyone's back was turned. Her father cleaned up. That was the fable. Except there were always dirty dishes in odd places, and other, more peculiar untidinesses, such as piles of leaves in the bedroom. A neighbourhood girl did odds and ends, but left no evidence she ventured upstairs. The rooms there seemed part of an abandoned museum; one of those life as it was lived exhibits, whose roped-off bedside tables hold hatpins, boxes of Bryant & May, and folded-open green Penguin paperbacks. A bit like that, except not roped off.

She was certain he never went into her old room. Those days were long gone.

Putting down her bag, she crossed the room; bent and kissed his cheek: sandpaper. Talked about ordinary things, like the route she'd taken and the weather she'd encountered, which gave him time to recalibrate his existence to allow for her presence. This was age, but not just age. It was something age was doing to him. But at the same time, it was part of what he'd always been; never entirely present, it seemed to her.

The clock on the mantel had wound down months ago, but even so, she knew when ten minutes had passed. That was how long it took for his light to go out; for her presence to stop being a surprise, and start being just something else in the room, like a broken clock, or the oddly shaped metal figure on the mantelpiece. When that happened, she said, 'I'll go and see if anything needs doing in the kitchen, shall I?'

'It's mostly tidy.'

'Then I'll have a quick dust upstairs.'

So she left him swaddled in unravelling memory, in a chair

placed so perfectly, the sun slanted on to him through a break in the curtains he either hadn't drawn back yet or had pulled across too early – time slipped past so slyly, it might have been a mouse. He often spent whole days here. He couldn't be sure how long this had been happening, but it was somewhere between not very and forever. Once there'd been work, and work had meant death – death was something he'd been good at; something he could do business with. These days death was a mark on the calendar, the difference being, the calendar was now his own.

He could hear Katie overhead, though the sound seemed to be coming from the back of the house. It was easy to grow alone, when you were often confused. Katie aside, company for Kenneth Blake mostly took the shape of young Tamsin, or perhaps her name was Rachel, who lived across the road, and would call in to make sure he'd eaten and that mould spores hadn't evolved to upright status in the kitchen. She'd bustle away through there, occasionally calling out something bright and cheerful, as if they were friends or family, and she were here out of duty and affection. A curly-haired, dark, overweight cherub: very much the saucy minx. Once she had stood in front of his chair and lifted her skirt, leering at him. He can't decide now whether he's remembering imagining this, or imagining remembering it. Whichever, he must be careful not to mention it to Katie.

Some days he has bright passages, and for hours at a stretch can put a name to everything that matters, but at other times he descends into a fog. And more or less in both of these states, he fears that Katie's husband is beating her, though he cannot for the moment recall her husband's name . . . However unravelled he's become, he knows a bruise when he sees it.

This, too, he's always known: that the clocks might stop, but calendars never do. That the days tear off and whip away like a fleeting years montage from a black-and-white movie: the pages autumn leaves blown damp and dying on the wind; their summer green thumped the colour of bruises. And at calendar's end your blind date waits, who arrives in different costumes, but is always only after one thing. He's everybody your parents ever warned you about, though they rarely called him by the right name.

. . . And after a life spent negotiating with it – moulding it; arranging the empty shapes it left behind; superintending the rituals for those devastated by its passage – death should have been a colleague: not liked, necessarily, but certainly respected, understood, bargained for. But life didn't work like that. Death didn't work like that. Long cooperation had produced no uneasy truce, but simply the knowledge that it was always there, always waiting, and might turn at any moment to wonder why he was still alive. Had he really ever thought it *needed* him? Had he really thought, like collaborators down the centuries, that his obeisance would lead it to spare him or those he loved? No, probably not . . . When his daughter was born, when Katie was born, he had thought *Here is another one* – another one to whistle for, in the long run; another who'd eventually vanish behind glazed eyes, skin turned plastic, and the utter silence of worn-out organs. In the normal run of events, this would not be until long after he was dead, but what did that change? – it was a detail of chronology, no more. She would still be dead. And all the while she was growing, he remained starkly aware of this: the knowledge lived under a trapdoor in his mind, and sometimes strained at the hinges, aching for the light. She would die. How could he successfully pretend this wasn't going to happen? She would die. Sometimes, long after midnight, he'd stand in her bedroom doorway to watch her sleeping – *death's counterfeit*, he'd heard that called: some Elizabethan, who ought to have known better. It was nothing like. It was all grunts and shiftings, every last one of them a match lit in the darkness. Death was never like this.

She was still alive . . . Children should reconcile you to your own mortality. All parenthood had done for him had been make him aware of his child's inevitable end.

So, of course, he'd put up barriers. The less you seem to care for something, the more it seems to flourish.

The truth was, there was nothing he wouldn't do to keep her safe.

Though she lived just half a mile distant, Katrina always felt like Alice down the rabbit hole on revisiting her childhood home; was always faintly stunned by the way everything familiar had grown smaller. Smaller and dustier. In her father's bedroom, she tested the environment's resistance to intrusion; moved the scorpion paperweight that lived on the mantelpiece slightly to one side, wondering if it would inch its way back as soon as she turned. But all that happened was, a scorpion paper-weight-shaped patch of dust-free mantelpiece appeared. Perhaps the neighbourhood girl could be persuaded to do a little more . . . But that way guilt lay; an abdication of the role of dutiful daughter.

Which was only one of many roles she played. Katrina to the world; Katie to her father; Kay to her husband – small wonder a subtly different woman answered, depending on which was addressed. It was a vocal version of Find the Lady: you overturned a name to see what it uncovered. Today she was Katie, who had grown up in this house. There was no corner of it her imagination hadn't occupied; not a nook she'd not hidden in, playing one-sided hide and seek, waiting for the calls of *Katie? Katie!* that never came . . . Once, she'd spent an afternoon investigating her father's bookshelf on the landing, and found – among the mishmash of MacLeans, Wheatleys, *Reader's Digest*'s condenseds, and a pamphlet outlining the uses of a pressure cooker, which was probably the large forgotten pan in the cupboard under the sink – a dusty *Names for Girls*, and had sat thumbing from Abigail to Zandra; waiting for the perfect name to jump out, the one that should have been hers. And there, right in the middle – first column, centre page – was a neatly inked tick next to *Katrina*, as if a short list of one had been instantly settled upon . . . When you wanted to know how to use the pressure cooker, you bought the booklet. When you needed a name for a baby girl, you did the same. The pressure cooker eventually went to live under the sink. Katrina . . . Katie was still around. Still haunting the same house, though not on a full-time basis.

On impulse, she visited her old room. Downstairs was quiet. Her father had probably re-entered that near catatonia in which she suspected he spent most of his waking hours. She wondered if it was his past he visited; wondered if somewhere in his remembered corridors a little girl hid, waiting for a cry of *Katie?* that never came . . . Her room smelled of dust, and possibly mould. She ought to rectify this; to make sure the house wasn't about to collapse about her father's ears, but that might draw attention, which wasn't sensible. Other than the smell, everything remained the same as ever: bed, dressing table, bookshelf, wardrobe. The window looked townwards, and had always reminded her of a storybook illustration: the rooftops it viewed so pointy; the street lamps old-fashioned. Smudges on the walls indicated where posters had been Blu-tacked: pop stars (Numan, Spandau, Duran) giving way to art (the Impressionists, and then the medieval masters) giving way to nothing at all – was that a fair summary of her changing taste? Tucked into the dressing table mirror were two photographs, each capturing an attempt at a smile. The first was of her mother, who had died when Katie was eleven. And while the mother Katie recalled had been always distracted, or angry, or perhaps just unhappy, she had been aware that when a camera was pointed at you, you smiled. So what the camera had seen was a pretty woman, who had known how to smile. Her hair was fairer than Katie remembered; her eyes brighter.

The other showed her father as a young man, and his smile might have illustrated a relevant page in a physiology textbook. It reminded Katrina, obscurely, of the *Mona Lisa* . . . Hadn't da Vinci studied the skull beneath the skin, and everything else it hid? – all those bloody strings and lengths of gristle which worked to make things move? Then clothed it in flesh, and painted it in action? And this was her father facing the camera, as if the photographer, coaxing the required reaction, had asked *What makes you smile?* and he had replied *The muscles at the corner of your mouth*. They *make you smile.*

When she returned downstairs, he was standing. 'I thought I might go for a walk later,' he said.

It was the kind of statement he primed himself to make in her presence: one that transmitted loud clear messages of health and independence.

'How are you for groceries?' she asked.

'Oh, Rachel does that.'

'Tamsin.'

Whoever. As if he didn't have better things to do than remember the names of the neighbourhood girls.

They stood for a while looking out of the window. After some moments he shifted, and she thought he was about to lay an arm across her shoulder, but he didn't.

III

Price's driver was called Win, and like everybody else, he had trouble remembering it wasn't short for Winston. Roughly the size and shape of a phone booth, Win had been with him four or five years, so folk assumed she had something on him, video or DNA, because why else would he let a uniformed walrus chauffeur him round? A lot of women, the uniform wouldn't be a problem, but on Win black leather suggested a seventies dining room suite more than sex on wheels. But while it was true he'd rather Win had a body he could happily imagine in or out of a bikini, there were other factors at play. He'd seen her bounce a man off the side of a building once – 'bounce' was usually an expression, but this guy had been airborne. This had been the first time Price had seen Win, not long after he'd had to fire his regular driver for being stabbed. The airborne joker, in pre-flight mode, had been a door supervisor at a club. And what made it funny, when you thought about it, was that the proper name for a door supervisor was—

'Someone's following.'

For all her big-boned frame, her voice was pitched higher than likely. It could take a moment to focus on what she was saying, rather than how she was saying it.

'Boss?'

'You sure?'

She glanced reproachfully into the rear-view.

For some reason the first thing into his head was Arkle – he didn't trust Arkle. Baxter, he could do business with: Arkle, you'd be better off chaining to a kennel and forgetting to feed.

'Recognise the car?' he asked.

But Win was shaking her head: 'Orange VW.'

'A *Beetle*?'

She shrugged.

'What, they couldn't have found a, a, a pink Rolls *Royce*? Something less noticeable?'

But it wasn't Win's job to have ideas about cars for other people, and he couldn't really blame her for not replying.

Besides: what mattered was she'd picked up the tail, and he didn't doubt her ability to lose it. Of course, then he'd have no idea who it was, which would be a complication, and the best thing to do with a complication was stamp on it before it grew up, sprouted little complications of its own . . .

'Do you want me to lose it?'

Like she was reading his mind.

He said, 'Let me think a bit.'

Price wasn't carrying a lot: just odds and ends he'd taken off Sweeney's hands. A relief operation: the man was happy to see commerce happening on his premises, even at twenty per cent under trade prices. Price didn't feel great about ripping somebody off in front of their eyes – he preferred doing it at a safe distance – but even so, it was hard to get worked up about Sweeney's situation. The way Price saw it, either you survived in business or you didn't. Making a fuss was like complaining you were drowning when you'd never learned to swim.

Except Sweeney hadn't been making a fuss.

Price had said what he always said: 'Bastards. It's hard enough making an honest *wage*, without some scumbag coming on the rob.'

'They'll slip up. That sort always do.'

He'd expected the normal rant: the mournful accounting, to the last lost penny.

'Yeah, well. Won't *help* us, will it?'

'You never know.'

Almost as if Sweeney had a plan of some sort.

'Boss?'

He met Win's eyes in the mirror.

'There's a good bit coming up.'

For losing a tail, she meant. They were still on the motorway – heading into London – but there was an exit approaching. Win was good at exits.

'I could dump her.'

'Her?'

Win nodded.

That was kind of interesting.

'Leave it,' he said. 'Wait till we're in town.'

She nodded again, and moments later the exit was behind them.

He had stuff to do, but that was okay. Win would take care of it. She was good at this sort of thing.

This one was good. Zoë had slowly become aware that the Audi driver knew she was there – a matter of opportunities left begging: gaps in traffic unfilled; exits untaken. He could have blown her off half a dozen times, which meant he'd decided not to.

She'd taken off after him more on impulse than evidence. The Audi hadn't been the only car to park near Sweeney's that morning, but it had been the only one with a liveried driver. Of him, Zoë had barely caught a glimpse; her attention was on the man getting out of the back seat, who put her in mind of someone she couldn't put her finger on, and wasn't so much wearing as was hunched inside a brown suede coat, possibly chosen to match the car. When he'd stepped on to the pavement he'd tapped the car's roof, and it had pulled out, heading away from Zoë. Mr Toad, she thought – that's who he reminded her of. Mr Toad. After the past two days, it was like watching a Hollywood spectacular being mounted in front of her eyes.

Mr Toad went into Sweeney's. The car drove up the main road and turned right at the traffic lights; looking for a parking spot was Zoë's guess.

For the past hour, she'd been aware that the old dear in Cancer Relief was checking on her every five minutes: peering between wickerwork stands holding knick-knacks and greetings cards; her eyes hardened into marbles; her pink wool forged to steel. She knew Zoë was up to something. Whatever this was, it definitely didn't involve further use of the facilities. All these things Zoë had weighed in the balance, but the main reason she followed Mr Toad was, he had a driver. Having that kind of money and choosing to spend it in Sweeney's struck Zoë as offbeat enough to warrant attention.

So now she was on the motorway, and if nothing else, at least she was moving. Traffic was medium heavy, with no jams yet: ideal for tailing, but here it came again – the feeling that the Audi's driver had spotted her, and was choosing not to leave her sucking dust. Which, if true, confirmed a couple of things – that an orange Beetle wasn't the best choice for surveillance, and that Mr Toad was one of the Ugly Pals. You had to be really paranoid to be legit and still keep lookout for a tail.

Zoë passed anonymous fields and the usual motorway sculptures: directions to towns she had no interest in, and small brick fortresses marking where bridges once stood. And all the while, the Audi kept even distance two cars ahead, until it became difficult to say whether she was following it, or it was luring her.

And of course she lost it once they'd come off the motorway. She didn't like driving in London, which always felt like joining a game whose rules had never been explained properly, or perhaps just never formulated, and the area she'd reached now – somewhere near Paddington, she thought, though the city's shifting geography had fooled her before – was a whole new landscape: the kind people meant when they said a place had 'character', though this particular character would be one you'd cross the road to avoid. With few other cars for cover Zoë had had to drop back, and lost her quarry in small streets lined first with warehouses, and then with blocks that had started life industrial but now seemed residential. An antique shop on a corner; an off-licence; a hardware store – she slowed to a crawl, feeling useless and annoyed. The last she'd seen of the Audi it had been turning left a hundred yards ahead, and by the time she'd reached that corner, it had vanished. Zoë drove slowly down the road, swearing under her breath. There were too many lanes it could have gone down. There'd be lock-ups too – weren't there always, near railway stations? – and the Audi might be stowed thirty seconds away: she'd never find it. Alternatively, the driver might have simply decided it was time to throw her off, and be back on the motorway now . . . She'd memorised its plate, but damn: this was supposed to be her job. There'd been a time she'd been invisible. That's what she told herself, coming to a halt on half a legal parking space. It wasn't true, but it was a handy stick to beat herself with.

Zoë sat with one hand on the wheel; with the thumb of the other tapped her front teeth thoughtfully. There was nothing to do now bar drive home, and how much fun would that be? She didn't trust her own moods these days, and didn't think she could face an evening at the bottom of their well. All this in the time it took to tap her teeth; she was on the pavement before she'd formulated an exact plan of campaign. Just wander round a bit, was her afterthought. See if there *are* any lock-ups. Failing which, drop into that antique shop: might find something of interest. Zoë hated antique shops; never found anything of interest. But she hated being planless even more.

In the end, she didn't get that far. She walked past some shops and a café, then found herself at a corner, looking down a lane which angled out of vision twenty yards from the main road, but seemed to lead to a row of garages – was she supposed to resist this? Nosiness was a virtue in her profession. Scaffolding callipered the wall to her left, though no builders were in evidence. A bucket hung from a strut. It was odd that you could hang a bucket in a public place here, and expect to find it when you got back. Though of course, nobody was back yet. Anything might happen.

Where the lane crooked she met, to her right, a row of garages; to her left, a continuation of the wall. The garage doors were a uniform blue, and all but one were closed. It would be grand if there were a brown Audi parked inside, but it proved empty save for the usual mess – a hose coiled round a hook on the wall; a shelf lined with paint cans and other stuff she couldn't identify. The floor was patched with oil, and in one corner a tap dripped into a steel sink. This had been a small waste of time, except a leather-clad arm snaked round her waist as she stood looking, and another wrapped itself round her neck and lifted her off the ground – *fuck*, she was dangling mid-air, her breathing cut off. A little late her instincts kicked in and she back-heeled, aiming for the guy's balls, but nothing doing: she hit his thigh, heard something fall softly to the ground a moment later. *His cap* – it was the Audi man's cap: the liveried driver.

Black spots blossomed before Zoë's eyes, and burst into sausage-shaped rainbows.

'I'll hurt you exactly as much as I need to,' a voice said, and for a moment Zoë wondered where it was coming from: it was too high too squeaky too—

'Until you tell me who you are and why you were following me.'

—fuck, too much of a *woman* to be the man suspending her like this. Except that's who it was: the man was a woman. A six-foot barrel-built woman, with arms like branches and a voice like David Beckham on helium.

'Is there any of that you didn't understand?'

Zoë pulled her left arm free and swatted backwards at the woman-thing's head. This had the effect it would have had on a concrete bollard. So she did it again, and found herself squeezed harder: black balloons were bursting all around now, and more words floated into her ears: 'I can keep this up all day. How about you?'

How about her was, she was trying to loosen the woman's grip on her neck: like trying to prise roots from the ground with bare fingers. Zoë's lungs were aching. She might not be smoking any more, but she hadn't planned on giving up breathing . . . And what difference did it make this was a woman? Zoë slapped an elbow: feebly perhaps, like a dangled fish; but the intent, she thought, was clear: *loosen up. I'm ready to talk*.

Maybe a man would have taken two slaps to get the message. Maybe that was the difference.

Zoë's hand dipped into her pocket.

'Okay. I'm going to let you speak now.'

The woman's grip tightened round Zoë's waist and loosened round her throat. Air rushed back into her system and the world flushed red for a second, her vision clearing so swiftly it struck her this woman knew exactly what she was doing – had held her in that chokehold not a moment too long.

'Who are you?' the voice said again. 'And what do you want?'

'I just want to know,' said Zoë – her voice a dull rasp – 'I just want to know if you want to keep your ear?'

Because she'd taken the nail scissors from her pocket, and was holding them to the woman's left lobe: nipping just sharply enough to remind her what *slice* meant.

The silence that followed lasted seven of the longer seconds Zoë remembered . . .

And then she felt the ground beneath her feet again, and the other arm unwrapped her: she took a quick step away, and turned to face her new enemy.

Who was a woman, of course, but it wasn't that surprising Zoë hadn't noticed earlier. From behind, with the cap on, she'd have gone with the odds nine times out of ten, and called this male. But face-to-face told a different story: the woman's skin was pale and baby soft; her lips full roses; her eyes brown and damp. Her uncapped hair, cropped to a buzz, was so blond it was colourless. This wasn't beauty, quite – the effect was startlingly like an inflatable come to life – but it wasn't masculine. In the moment it took Zoë to register those damp brown eyes, the other factors – the broad shoulders, the branchlike arms, the thick columns of legs; all cased in black leather, like an implausible SM fantasy – faded to insignificance, but only for that moment. And then the woman's weight and thickness reasserted itself, reminding Zoë that whatever gender she espoused, she was solid and dangerous.

Though the voice remained a bit of a hoot.

Heavy or not, she moved quietly, and even standing still looked ready as a dancer. Which was exactly what Zoë wanted: to get in a rumble with somebody bigger than her, who'd put some training in. She must have been six foot easy. Her reach – Zoë didn't want to think about her reach. She already knew the important bit: that she wasn't far enough away.

But she looked troubled, as if she were having similar thoughts about Zoë. Or maybe she was just aware that this was a little public: barely twenty yards from a main road. Anybody could be watching from any of a hundred windows.

When things stall, push them. Zoë pushed. 'Are we going to fight?'

The woman thought about it. 'Were you really going to cut my ear off?'

'Yes. Well, probably.'

She was still holding the scissors, and didn't think there was any harm in carrying on doing so.

'You were following me, weren't you?'

'I was following your boss.'

'You're not too good at it.'

'I'm better in a normal car.'

'I was behind you by the time you parked.'

'You're smooth. Light on your feet, too.'

The woman's eyes narrowed, as if Zoë were setting a trap.

'On the other hand, I could have cut your ear off. Where's your boss?'

'Things to do.'

'So it's just us girls. That's nice.' But also fucking ridiculous. 'Look, let's not get too alarmed about this. I've no idea who you are, or him either.' She put the scissors back in her pocket, making it clear she was doing so. 'There's a few questions I have to ask, that's all. It needn't involve trouble.'

A man would assume she was trying to make an idiot out of him. She was hoping a woman would recognise a desire to avoid hurt.

After a beat the woman said: 'So what does it involve?'

'There's a place round the corner,' Zoë said. 'Nice cup of tea?'

'So what's it like? Being a private eye?'

'Compared to what?' Zoë asked. 'It's a long time since I've done anything else. Never had an office job, never worn a uniform. What's it like being a chauffeur?'

'Compared to stacking shelves?'

'If you like.'

Win said, 'Different world. Different *galaxy*. That pink plastic coverall? I could have been anyone.' She looked down at her black leather jacket; her shining trousers. 'Now, I'm somebody.'

'There you go. You've things to measure it against. I've done bar work, but not in twenty years.' She didn't drink tea, nice or not: she'd ordered coffee. She took a sip, and told Win her life story: 'I married a private detective. I've done this ever since.' The end.

Win, still thinking about plastic pink coveralls, said, 'I read they're calling it "ambient stock replenishment" now. You ever come across something, they change its name, there's a significant improvement?'

'They tried it with "date rape". I'm not sure "date" adds much. How did you get to be a driver?'

'Made an impression on my boss.'

'Handbrake turns?'

'I bounced a man, for calling me a name. One thing led to another.'

Zoë bet. Sitting opposite, watching her speak, it was hard to deny Win's gravity, even if most people would label her freak. Certainly, nobody in the café was unaware of her presence. The girl behind the counter couldn't peel her eyes away: probably stuck between thinking her gross, and knowing that wherever she went, people would pay attention. A good half of those people would be men.

Mr Toad, for instance.

'But it was more for your bouncing than your driving.'

'He didn't want a driver who couldn't take care of herself.'

'Have you trained?'

'I passed my test.'

'Fighting, I meant.'

'I know you did. Don't think I'm stupid, just because I'm big.'

Zoe raised her palms: 'Hey. I already surrendered.'

'But you didn't, did you? Not really.' Win raised her teacup. She had a strangely delicate manner, but then, was probably used to finding things fragile. 'I dance. Fighting's just movement.'

An unwanted vision from *Fantasia* swam through Zoë's head.

'But it's not real fighting anyway. Fighting's when there's two of you. Mostly, when I do it, it's just me.'

'I can see how that might happen,' Zoë said.

'You're a fighter.'

'I don't make a habit of it.'

'Yeah, I bet.'

This was getting cosy.

Zoë said, 'So. You drive. You look after yourself. And him too, I presume. Have you been inside yet?'

'No.'

'It's a matter of time. Your boss is a crook, right? What's his name, anyway?'

'Price.'

'Anything in particular Price?'

'Oswald. He doesn't like it much.' Win paused. 'He's a pretty good crook. He's careful.'

'Still comes down to the law of averages. Careful or not, he's involved with a gang who shoot people with crossbows. That makes him a high-risk type.'

'How do you know that?'

'You kind of just told me,' said Zoë. 'By not denying it. And let's face it, Win, once he's been bagged, your long-term career prospects look about as good as a Defence Against the Dark Arts tutor's.'

'I could always go back to ambient stock replenishment.'

'No you couldn't. That's the kind of job they mean when they say it's a small world. You're too big for it now.'

'You planning on shopping him?'

Zoë said, 'You'd not believe how much it's hindered me in the past, but the courts don't usually bang people up on my say-so. They like charges, trials, evidence. Stuff like that.'

'So remind me why I care.'

'Because I can be an unbelievable fucking nuisance when I

try.' Zoë drank more coffee. Her throat hurt, but she didn't let it show. 'I notice you're not in a hurry to contradict.'

'You're already a fucking nuisance. And I can tell you're not trying.'

'But once I start, he's got trouble.'

'I could stop you.'

'Probably. You're bigger than me, and we've both noticed you're stronger.' She wished she still smoked. Now would be a good moment to light up. 'But why bother? This isn't TV, Win. The guy your boss ripped off doesn't want cops involved, or no more than William Tell's involved them already. Here and now, we can make it all go away. All you have to do's give me the names of the guys involved in the robbery.'

'Which robbery's this?'

'You're five minutes late asking, Win. But on the off chance there's been more than one lately, we're discussing last Tuesday's. The one that happened at the jeweller's your boss just visited.'

'Maybe he was looking at rings.'

'And maybe you didn't just try to pull my head off. Back in reality, we both know Price set it up, but the client doesn't, and I'm not about to tell him. All he wants are the guys who took his stock. You give them to me, I give them to him. That way, he gets what he wants, I get paid, and your boss discovers the thugs doing his dirty work aren't just whackos, they're unreliable whackos he'd be safer not using. Everybody's happy.'

'We haven't mentioned me.'

'You? You get to stop worrying about your boss mixing it with guys with crossbows.'

Win thought for a moment; said, 'Any names I give you, your client's going to pass right back to my boss, yes?'

'On the assumption he'll wreak vengeance on them.'

'Whereas all he'll do is give 'em the boot, because what use are they if they're found that easily?'

'Like I said,' Zoë repeated. 'You get to stop worrying.'

'You think you've got me typed, don't you?'

'I think I could study you for a decade, Win, and still find you an original. But all we've got's the next five minutes.'

On the wall above their heads, the clock chipped this away.

TWO

THE DARK OUTSIDE

4

I

IT HAD THE AIR of a prison break: a day Tim Whitby should have been at work, and wasn't. Okay, he'd given notice, but . . . The roads were quiet at first; more happening overhead than in the lanes – seagulls, presumably lost, flapping about in noisy convocation; kestrels hovering, alert for ground life on the hard shoulder. There did not have to be much traffic for things to be deadly.

Enough, though. One day off from grief.

But it was like trying not to probe a sore tooth with a tongue. There were times when it seemed that Emma's death occupied his thoughts more than Emma, alive, had done, with the probable exception of the moments he'd spent inside her. Because what else did he have? While they'd been together, the future had been one blank page after another, waiting for their story to be written. Now, instead of blank, Tim's future was empty; the best he could scribble on it being versions of a life he'd already had, and couldn't now retrieve.

Signs punctuated the motorway: service stations; emergency phones. As if it were that simple. As if you could be given directions, and helped to get there, and rescued when it all went wrong.

'Be reasonable,' he said. Talking to himself was a recent mannerism. 'She's dead. You're not. Get a life.'

There were parallel universes in which all possible realities expressed themselves. In one, Tim had died on a wet night in a lightweight car, and even now, in that one, Emma was tooling off to Totnes on some hare-brained pretext she'd have difficulty articulating even to herself. And if driving very fast into this approaching concrete abutment would lift him from his world into hers . . .

'But I wouldn't, would I?'

The abutment was history by the time he'd reasoned this out.

'I wouldn't. Because I'd know it was just another way of saying I want to die. But I don't, not really. Suicide didn't *let me down*.' He wasn't above sarcastic intonation. '*I* let *it* down. Otherwise I'd be dead now. QED.'

Another set of signs. Tim pulled into a service stop, drank a cup of coffee; by the time he rejoined the traffic there was more of it, as if folk had now cottoned on that you could just say *Hell, I'm not working today*, and hit the road. One among them blared vehicular rage at Tim for some imagined infraction. Tim gave her the finger, then noticed his door wasn't closed properly . . . Slowing, he secured it; wondered for a second what an apology flare would look like, and wished he had one. Then flashed his headlights, hoping she'd catch this in her rear-view, and recognise it for what it was.

'And that is what you do,' he said a little later.

This was what you did, if you were a functioning member of society. You noticed other people; offered them help; apologised when they trod on your toes. All of which Emma had understood, of course; as – equally of course – had Tim, while they were married. And had to learn again, because otherwise he'd be forever the man he was now: a self-hating failed suicide, whose tongue, memory, kept probing his sore tooth, life.

'All I know is her name,' he said. 'And I'm not even sure of that.'

But he knew she'd been asking for help, however she'd chosen to code it.

'A distress signal,' he said, his mind still designing an apology flare. 'She was sending up distress signals, only I didn't realise that's what they were.'

And I am not the Lone Ranger, not Batman, not Simon Templar . . . No, but I've not even been Tim Whitby lately, have I? And if that was the best I could be, that's the highest I can aspire to now.

Whatever happens, he thought, Emma would approve of the impulse that had driven him here today.

And having driven here today, he thought, entering Totnes, what he needed was a car park.

Tim was wearing white chinos, or cream chinos that had faded white, and a dark blue top under a black jacket he couldn't remember when he'd last worn, though he'd found a cinema ticket in the pocket for a film he was pretty sure had been remade since. Not especially smart, but not a hopeless scruff. All of which occurred to him now because he was after all paying a visit on a woman – provided he found her, and, having done that, kept his nerve and knocked on her door, or rang her bell. Whatever.

He'd arrived just after twelve, and found a car park at the foot of the town. He'd never enjoyed negotiating strange traffic systems, and, like everywhere else, Totnes appeared to have one of these. The car park was by the river, and from the branch of an overhanging tree a tyre swung on a thick grey rope. Tim's immediate thought was what a charming, Huck-Finn image this cast, but his second was to wonder where the tyre had come from, and what kind of security they had round here anyway. There were swans on the river, and ducks, and some other birds he couldn't put a name to. He watched for a while, then set off for the town centre.

In a post office, he found a payphone with a local directory next to it. This was chained to a hook in the wall which came loose as he opened the book; it was a moment's work, though, to trace *Blake, K.* At the stationery counter he bought pen and paper, and jotted down the address. He also bought a map of the town, and was careful to fix the hook back into the wall before he left. It was the small touches that counted; that when you put them together, pulled you back into the fold.

A minute's study, and he knew which way he was headed. The route was not hard: straight up the High Street; a left-then-right wiggle at the top. The High Street was on the far side of an open square and displayed the hallmarks of a nice, quirky town. There were the usual landmarks – banks, shoe shops, pubs, church – but a number of second-hand bookshops too; a toyshop with working wooden models on display; and a sweetshop piled high with fudge, details of special offers crayoned in primary colours on its windows.

The road grew narrower near the top. A clock set in an overhead arch rang the half-hour as he passed beneath.

It was busy for a weekday, and the pavements too narrow to allow unimpeded progress. Tim found himself trapped behind a group of teenagers traipsing so parodically slowly, it would have required less effort to jog. But this at least postponed whatever came next. *Katrina Blake. Totnes.* He was reasonably sure about Totnes, but was guessing the Blake. The odds, then, of *Blake, K.* being the woman he was looking for weren't great, and anyway, what was the protocol for these situations?

Hi, I don't know if you remember me but . . .

Hello. We met in Oxford . . .

Stop me if I've got this wrong, but did your husband give you that bruise? Is that what you were trying to tell me?

And even if it had been, did that mean she'd be happy to see him now?

Plus: what if her husband were home?

Tim hadn't been in a fight since school, and not really then. He'd been hit once, and it hadn't hurt, but the shock had forced tears out of him . . . I was *twelve*, he reminded himself. Like most men, he carried a secret hero within; like too few, he recognised his as fantasy, but still had faith he'd no longer burst into tears at the threat of violence. He was strengthened in this by the folk wisdom that only cowards hit women, and that cowards shrivelled like wet triffids when a man – any man – took them to task.

At the top of the hill, the road bore left. Tim passed a scattering of junk shops and health-food cafés, a hairdresser's and a record store, before commerce petered out. He checked the map, then turned right to find the houses taller, and painted Mediterranean colours: faded yellows, pinks and blues, with small, disorganised front gardens. Tim counted numbers down. K. Blake's was on the end, just edging on to, though elevated above, the road skirting the town centre. The garden here surpassed untidy – resembled a wildlife sanctuary – and the front door was tented by a none too robust wooden porch.

Because it was, if he stopped to think about it, a moment of decision, he decided not to stop to think about it, but simply rang the bell and stepped back, looking out across the road below while waiting for an answer. In the distance, over the moors, clouds gathered. He wondered if it were raining, and if the rain were heading this way.

After a while he rang the bell again.

This time he leaned forward as he pressed the button, but heard no answering buzz within. Which meant that the bell didn't work, or that it did work, but was inaudible on the front step. Either the house was empty, then, or it wasn't; and if it wasn't, whoever was inside either wanted him to go away, or didn't know he was there. An analytical mind was a useful thing. At a pinch, it always knew where the exits were.

From the railing a few yards distant, he looked down on the road below. This was why he'd driven this far: to lean on a railing and breathe in fumes. Nice going, he thought, then said it aloud. 'Nice going.' He turned, and studied the house in more detail. Like its neighbours, it was three storeys high; unlike them, it had once been painted milk chocolate, though was peeling badly now. Slates were missing from the roof, and the guttering to the left of the ramshackle wooden porch had rusted and appeared barely functional. The porch itself was painted darker chocolate than the brickwork, as was the length of guttering, though this turned a fresh bright blue where it reached next door, as if someone were making a point. Even with anyone inside, Tim thought, it would still be an empty house. One whose lights had gone out.

By the side abutting the main road, a path ran through to the back. This had a wooden door at the near end, which wasn't locked but would barely open – the hedge behind it had grown so wild it was touching the brickwork. Tim discovered this a few minutes later – there'd come a moment when he was no longer leaning against the railing, but was instead making his way along this passage, with no clear memory of having decided to do so. Squeezing past, he had the impression of a hundred green fingers clutching at him, most of them wet, and when he reached the back garden he felt like he'd walked through a car wash. The ground was thick and spongy, as if coated with sea moss. The first thing he saw, parked under a makeshift carport – a transparent sheet of corrugated plastic held up by wooden struts – was a hearse.

Quite literally, Tim stopped breathing.

Before long, he began again. It was a car, no more; a car used for the transportation of the dead. This, in and of itself, did not make the vehicle more to be feared than any other car not actively bearing down on him. Besides, it was on blocks. Despite, judging by the paintwork, being in better nick than the house – though lacking its hood ornament – the hearse wasn't actually usable. Why this should be a comfort, he didn't immediately analyse.

There was other stuff under this carport-cum-shelter: what looked like an old workbench, on which a few ancient tools quietly rusted; a freezer, presumably decommissioned; a wardrobe with its doors removed. To one side, next to what might have been a pond if its overgrowth were napalmed, sat a two-foot-high stone frog. A crack had formed in its head, running ear to ear, as if it were an oversized money box. None of this was terribly important, but it distracted him from the immediate problem of what, exactly, he thought he was doing.

A door into the house, probably the kitchen, lay immediately to his left. He put a hand to its handle. There was a word for this, wasn't there? – three words: breaking and entering. For half a second he wondered what his colleagues would have made of it: Tim on his day off, miles from home, looking to break into a house in search of a woman he'd met once. They probably thought he was having a lie-in. He took his hand away; made to knock on the glass, then didn't do that either. Instead he walked further round the house until he reached quite a large window, partly obscured by ivy, but not so much he couldn't see through.

In a chair in the centre of a room sat an oldish man in a threadbare cardigan, his attention focused on some out-of-view spot on the wall.

A hand dropped on Tim's shoulder. Something sharp tickled his chin. 'What the fuck's your game, soldier?' Tim felt the morning's dreaminess slip away, and nasty cold reality take its place.

II

Cherchez la femme. This was French for find the lady, which was one of three cards, but not usually the one you thought it was. Hunting the lady was a good way of losing your money.

. . . Last night, he'd been playing cards with Trent, or watching Trent play cards: same thing. Clock patience. Trent always so nearly got this out without cheating, it was painful. Trent was drinking vodka, but Arkle was just prowling: table to window, window to table. This was in Dunstan Senior's house – he could come back to life and die all over again: it would still be his house. Arkle and Trent lived there, was all. They moved in the spaces between furniture he'd bought; lived under the gaze of pictures he'd hung.

'Do you,' Arkle said at last, 'ever get tired of this place?'

Trent looked up, looked round, looked down. 'No.'

'Do you get tired of anything?'

'What's the matter?'

'What were you and Bax talking about?'

'Nothing.'

After a moment Arkle explained, 'You didn't ask when.'

'. . . When?'

'In the bar,' he said. 'The other lunchtime.'

This was Tuesday again. In the seven days since the robbery, Price had paid them for the diamonds and Baxter had stashed it, minus walking-around money. Arkle didn't require much, mostly drinking tap water and mostly eating toast. In a wardrobe upstairs hung a tropical suit, but otherwise he spent little. Like he was going Buddhist, Bax once said, except Buddhists frowned on armed robbery.

'When I was taking a piss,' he added.

And it hadn't mattered until now because everything had been fine: they all had their roles, like Baxter said, and Arkle was happy with that – if asked, he'd have said this was because there was a mountain of money growing in the background, which, when it was big enough, they'd all go and live on. But actually Arkle was happy doing this because he was happy doing it. Only everything didn't seem fine any more, for some reason.

'What were you talking about?'

'This, that. Jesus, I don't know. What we always talk about. Usual stuff.'

But what was the usual stuff they always talked about? Arkle had no clue: the only conversation he could recall right now had happened when he was out of earshot. He reached out with a sigh and began collecting the cards in front of Trent. He did this one-handed, tapping the edge of the pack on the table to square it off. Then he squeezed the top and bottom edges, and squirted the cards into Trent's face.

Who batted them away without speaking. Which was an admission of guilt, you asked Arkle.

When the cards lay in a mess on the floor, on the table, in Trent's lap, Arkle said, as if nothing had happened, 'Did you think about my idea at all?'

'Which idea?'

'The one about Price.' The one where they robbed him. He'd not actually said this out loud, but they'd known what he meant.

Trent said, 'These jewellers' shops, it's in/out. Mess with Price, we're going to war.'

'He's supposed to be some kind of face,' Arkle said, dreamily. 'But he's driven around by a walrus in drag. How difficult would it be?'

'Bax is right. You're just looking for the edge.'

'That's what Bax said, is it? In the pub?'

'He didn't mean anything,' said Trent, and began collecting the cards, as if that would make things tidy again.

But coming back from the gents, Arkle had sensed everything was different. They'd been talking about him. More: they'd come to a decision, something that had been brewing ever since he'd accidentally shot that guy in Oxford.

Accidentally was the word. It wasn't like Arkle had arranged him being there.

'He's pissed off that guy tried to stop us, isn't he?'

'He wasn't,' Trent began, and then quite sensibly stopped.

'He was a security guard. It said so in the paper.'

'At a supermarket. He was on his way home.'

'Those guys are always on duty.'

(When he'd said as much to Baxter, Bax had said: 'What, he thought you were a lost trolley?')

'Price,' Arkle said now. 'One big score. Then we can . . .'

Then they could what, he didn't know, but it was important to have a plan – a plan involving the three of them. When he shut his eyes and imagined their future, it was always the three of them. That was as far as he'd got until recently, when it had become more specific. They'd be somewhere far away and hot, and there'd be animals: sleek things with teeth and tusks. In the evenings he'd stride out with his crossbow, in his tropical suit. It would be more of a challenge than the fucking yard rats.

'Baxter says that's just looking for trouble.'

Arkle rubbed a hand over his hairless head. He'd lost his place in the conversation: then he hadn't. 'Baxter says?'

Trent wouldn't look up. He was laying out another hand of patience, and somehow his glass had refilled – Trent could pour a drink with both hands in his pockets. Arkle watched while he turned over a card. Then said, 'When did Bax get to be the oldest?'

'Arkle—'

'When did Bax get to be the oldest?'

A faint hiss, as if air were escaping Trent. 'You're the oldest, Arkle.'

'Don't forget it.'

And that had been last night, and Arkle hadn't slept since – had left his bed in the tiny hours, and walked to the yard; had perched on the gantry outside the crow's nest, aiming the bow at anything that moved, which wasn't much. Scraps of paper bothered by the wind. One big black crow, unless it was a rook, that flapped down as dawn was breaking to pick at something wet lodged between broken stones where the sand elevator had once stood. Arkle had sighted on it, had been half an ounce of pressure off releasing the bolt, but in the end hadn't – not in case he'd miss, but because he wouldn't. The Oxford man had crumpled when his leg was pierced; had uttered something recognisably human. But the crow would just explode into sticky feathers. It wasn't the same.

While the bird took off, Arkle was thinking about Kay.

Who had long been on the scene. You could be forgiven for thinking there were four of them, not three; that was okay up to a point, but the point had been reached some while ago. The day she and Bax married was the last time Arkle had drunk alcohol, and everybody pretended it was in celebration. They all had their role: fine. What was Kay's role, exactly?

'She's my girl, man,' Bax had told him, when Arkle had brought this up.

'But kind of like a sister, right?'

And Bax had laughed his deep dark laugh which, more and more, seemed to be aimed at Arkle, rather than anything Arkle said.

So things changed. Bax got married and moved out; Dunstan Senior died. First thing Arkle had done was close the yard down. First thing Bax had wanted to know was, what the fuck was he playing at?

'You want us to be wage slaves all our lives?'

'Tell me your better idea.'

Said with that *thing* tone Bax had developed. Superior, something like that. Arkle didn't have a word for it.

He walked down the metal steps, his heels ringing like bells in the early morning. There was a milk float chugging along the road, and a girl in a short black dress making her unsteady way up the hill. Arkle had left his crossbow behind the lowest step. You could get into trouble for carrying one around.

He'd met Price in London, when Dunstan sent him there on a bullshit errand: delivering a bid on a cement deal. Arkle had spent the morning traipsing round a building site, being shown a lot of empty space that would one day be filled with glass and girders, maybe with the old man's cement holding it together. Turned out, he was just making up numbers – there were two serious bidders, and everyone else was scenery. All Arkle needed do was go with the flow, which meant by and by finding himself in a club down some stairs off Brewer Street, the only one among them not drunk. The contractor was happy because the bigtime bidders were looking competitive, and everybody else was happy because they were on exies, and also because there was a girl under their table. Then a friend of the contractor joined them, and this was Price.

'Been inside?' was the first thing he asked Arkle.

Couple of overnighters, Arkle explained: some car crime when he was younger; agg battery too, which had withered and died when witnesses changed their minds. All the stuff Dunstan Senior hadn't been able to cure him of. Something about the club, about it being daylight outside but midnight in, loosed his tongue. 'It's the hair, isn't it?' he'd asked, meaning it wasn't: he had no hair. Pointless denying it made him look dangerous. He wouldn't have shaved it otherwise.

'The eyes, too.' Price wasn't large but acted it, like a cut-rate Joe Pesci. 'You've done institutional. Don't tell me it was boarding school.'

So Arkle had talked, and Price had listened, and then, after a while, they'd done it the other way round. So when, months later, Bax said, 'Tell me your better idea,' Arkle had the details pat. He'd met someone who had this project, and the three of them were perfect for it.

Superior or not, Bax had recognised a plan when he heard one.

Arkle walked home from the yard brooding; lay down in

curtained darkness, but didn't sleep. Bax and Trent had something going on. This was not the proper order of things. Time was, when Arkle had a plan – like that they rob *Price*: which was genius – they'd say yes, great, do it. When had this changed?

When Baxter married Kay.

After a while he got up, made toast, drank water. Trent was sleeping off last night's vodka: that or he had a pig in his bedroom. Arkle sat in the kitchen and thought about Kay, and also about the money.

Baxter handled the money, and that was fine, was common sense. Trent wouldn't have known what to do with it, and Arkle himself – well, *delegation*. And here was the score: when they had enough money, a sum which kept adjusting upwards, they'd take off somewhere cheap and friendly; somewhere Arkle could practise his crossbow unharassed. Anywhere that laid-back would be bound to serve alcohol, so Trent would be okay too. And Baxter could bring Kay. Happy families.

Except Kay didn't fit so snugly into this scenario, did she?

The toast was ready. He ate it dry. Kay was an odd one. Accident-prone, Trent had said lately: Arkle hadn't noticed. 'Why?' It was possible Trent was more observant than he was, just like it was possible we'd be visited by intelligent life, or the Tories would win an election. Bound to happen one day, but no time soon.

'You haven't seen her black eye?'

Arkle hadn't. Would have quite liked to.

'She walked into a cupboard. She said.'

She'd said, and maybe that was a cover-up? Maybe Bax had blacked her eye. Argument? Over money, perhaps? And how much money was there to argue about? Not a lot, if you weren't counting Arkle's.

He supposed it was obvious, when you got down to it, that Kay knew where Baxter kept the money. Man–wife stuff; Arkle didn't pretend to be an expert, but Kay would be. When Arkle thought about women the woman he was thinking about was Kay, and he didn't understand Kay, which meant she was sneaky. And Arkle was older than Baxter, so if Kay confused *him*, what was she doing to Bax? She knew nothing, Bax said – but she'd been with him in Oxford, when he'd been scouting the layout. She'd gone as background colour, and stayed in the hotel, but in the long run which did you believe – a woman or your instincts? Whatever secrets the three of them used to share, four were sharing now, and if things were wobbling, it was Kay wobbling them. Baxter knew that really – once you added up the details, it was scary how obvious it was. Bax had blacked Kay's eye. It was a classic cry for help.

Cherchez la femme. Arkle finished his water, and went out looking for the money.

And he might not know about the man–wife stuff, but he knew this much: if you were looking for something a woman helped hide, you had to think sideways. They were devious creatures.

Bax and Kay rented a downstairs flat near a supermarket junction; not far from where Kay had grown up, but a drive round the houses all the same. Where Arkle and Trent lived was off the other side of the High Street; beyond the concrete square where they'd hung out as kids. It had been a handy place to congregate: there were toilets where you could trap the unwary, and a flat arena for skateboarding. Arkle had never been much cop on a skateboard, but he'd been good at punching people who were better on a skateboard than him. It was where they'd met Kay, way back when.

She had dark hair and was kind of skinny, and wasn't there for the 'boarding. Arkle wouldn't have paid her a second glance if Baxter hadn't noticed her. Bax was seventeen, and all the teenage stuff – spots, smells, greasy hair – had passed him by, though they were happening to Trent twice, to maintain their average. Girls looked at Baxter like they couldn't work out if he was threat or promise, but wouldn't mind trying. And Bax mostly ignored them, which seemed to be the trick of it.

. . . That was the first time Arkle had seen her. He couldn't offhand remember the last: within the fortnight, but before she picked up this black eye Trent had noticed.

He drove past the flat, wondering if she was in. Maybe they were both home, Kay wearing Baxter down – doing the maths. The way things were, she got no share at all and Bax got a third. Her way Bax got everything, and she got half of that.

No wonder Bax had hit her. But how long was he going to put up resistance? Women crawled beneath your defences; used logic when you least expected. The three of them had been solid as cement, but now Bax and Trent were whispering in corners. Arkle needed to re-establish the old order before everything crumbled to bits.

Around the houses it was, then. If you wanted to know Kay's secrets, dig into her past . . . Kenneth Blake's house was last on the row, just before the drop to the road; he remembered leaning over those railings as a kid, spitting on cars. He didn't do that now; just parked, got out, looked at the house. A loose gutter rattled as he watched. Through the open side door, he could see the hedge sprouting like a raggedy monster, planted to stop strangers squeezing past. Except somebody had done that recently; there were bent back branches and green leaves littering the passage . . .

He could move quietly when he wanted, Arkle; he could surprise a cat. The man peering through old man Blake's window wasn't a cat, but made a peculiar meowing noise anyway when Arkle dropped a hand on his shoulder; pushed a sharp fingernail into his chin's soft underside. 'What the fuck's your game, soldier?' he asked. And already he could feel it tightening in his belly: that sense of pleasure yet to come; the knowledge that he'd found somebody to play with, without even knowing he'd been looking.

III

Life was a dangerous business, Zoë reflected, easing past a bottleneck. The accident had happened in the oncoming lane – two cars sat motionless some hundred yards apart; one of them sideways, glassless, its lights punched out; the other concertinaed to what would have been a comedy shape, if it hadn't involved people. The delay in her lane was caused by drivers slowing down to witness the aftermath – police cars, motorbikes; a sense of recently departed ambulances – and like everybody else, Zoë sped up again as soon as she could; partly to put the scene behind her, but mostly to take advantage of the empty road ahead. On motorways, the wisdom went, the dangerous drivers were the ones who drove too slowly. This required shifting definitions of 'slowly', 'dangerous' and 'wisdom', but was too well established to challenge now.

To one side, an angry metal worm of cars sweated out the wait. To the other, shades of green and grey piled into the distance. It was morning, reasonable and fair, though the damage in her wake suggested that for some, the day had come to a shuddering halt. But then, death was always on the case. She remembered a fable about a bird flying through the window of a feasting hall on a winter's night, then flying out the other side: one bright flash between two eternities of darkness, only one of which was destined to end. It wasn't a difficult message. Life was the light and the feasting. Death was the dark outside. It didn't matter how long you lived, the dark was always longer.

So there was little point clinging to the safe side of everything. Survival was a lifetime project, and bound to fail in the long run. Most things had sharp edges, if you used them wrong. Machines were unreliable. People turned nasty, sometimes first chance they got – look at Bob Poland. Even children couldn't be trusted; were basically walking germ factories, primed for use inside forty-five minutes. And even here, even now, some idiot was leaving a service station with his door not properly closed. Zoë tooted him, then put him out of mind.

She was heading for Totnes, because that was where Price's thugs hailed from.

'Tell me about them,' she'd said last night to Win.

'It's not like we're best mates. I generally wait in the car.'

'But you met them?'

'Once or twice. Talked to one of them. If the others are madder than him, I'm happy we're strangers.'

'And he'd be . . . ?'

'Arkle.'

'What's his first name?'

'Arkle,' Win said. 'What you have to understand is, they're not your average family.'

She stopped and bought a sandwich in a lay-by. Of the other customers, the lorry driver was obvious (he had a lorry); salesmen were never difficult to pin down, and the youngish guy, who was tall and acne-splashed, and wore jeans with a blue–white check that had probably looked good in the shop, was definitely a student. That established, she paid them no attention. Zoë was not paranoid, exactly. But she liked to know who was closest at any given moment.

Technically, she reminded herself, she didn't have to be here. All she had to do was give Sweeney the names, and then all he had to do was give her five grand. Already, she was thinking of it as her money . . .

Win had said: 'Their old man ran this gravel merchant's. Been in the family for generations kind of thing. You think there's money in that?'

'Probably.' Unless you were rubbish, of course, though that was pretty much the universal rubric.

'Except old man Dunstan – that was his name – didn't have

children. So his firm was going down the tubes, as far as the family bit was concerned. Do you have kids?'

'Not that I know of,' Zoë said. 'Price told you this, did he?'

'Some nights he likes to talk.' Zoë must have signalled a false understanding, because Win added: 'In the car, coming home from wherever. Business trips. Says he doesn't want me dozing off at the wheel.'

'I can see how that might spoil his evening,' Zoë agreed. 'And he talks about these Dunstans?'

'He likes to think he's an expert on human nature,' said Win. 'Most men think that, don't they?'

There were probably a couple of realists out there as confused as everybody else, but it was kind of rare to hear it admitted.

'So anyway, he adopted three boys. To be the sons in Dunstan & Sons. If you can't beat 'em, fake it, sort of thing.'

'And one was called Arkle?'

'Arkle, Baxter and Trent. What he did was, he kept their actual surnames, only he stuck his own on the end.'

'That's cold.'

Win shrugged. 'What I've seen of Arkle, it could be arctic, he'd not notice. My boss breaks the law, okay. But he does it for the money.'

'Whereas Arkle does it for kicks.'

'Arkle does it because it's what he does. And if it's what he's doing, why should anybody stop him?'

A law unto himself. They were the hardest kind to break.

Zoë said, 'Sounds like old man Dunstan made some unwise choices on his one-stop shop for progeny.'

'They weren't babies when he took them on. They'd been kicked round various foster homes, and God knows what. You hear stories, don't you?' Win finished her tea. The cup looked ridiculously small in her hand. 'The old man died last year. They folded the business about five minutes later. They still use the place, though. There's an office, like on a building site? One of those cabins, up on scaffolding.'

Dunstan & Sons. A gravel merchant's. It didn't sound hard to find.

It had been late when Zoë got home, and the drive from London had left her cross. She ate a half-hearted sandwich, drank a large glass of wine, and went to bed, to be woken half an hour later by a talentless yoyo in the house opposite, murdering an electric guitar. Broken sleep was irreparable in Zoë's world, so she left her bed, poured more wine, fired up the internet. She found no mention of Dunstan & Sons. What she did find was a street map of Totnes, which she printed. It was handy when decisions were reached with no conscious effort needing to be made.

After that she shut everything down and sat in the dark for a while, waiting in vain for her brain to stop churning. Random thoughts were their own special torture; circulating endlessly, arriving nowhere. *Contents under pressure*: we should have that tattooed on our foreheads at puberty. Zoë must have slept at last, curled on the sofa, because that's where she was when she woke.

She drank coffee, showered and dressed, catching herself in the mirror halfway through: black pants, white bra – zebra underwear: something Joe said twenty years before. It was strange how such fragments kept recurring, like shrapnel working its way to the body's surface years after the wound had apparently healed.

In the car, it occurred to her that it was her last day for use of the Beetle – another reason, if she needed one, for heading off to Totnes now.

Other people's accidents and sandwich stops apart, she was there before she knew it.

*

It was a bright day, not long past morning, and the sun caught glass everywhere she looked. To establish her bearings, Zoë headed up the High Street; found herself having one of those near bodiless experiences in which every detail is brilliant and every surface shines. The wheels on a passing pushchair. The multicoloured frames on a teenager's shades. When she crossed the road to examine a bookshop window, and had to wait for a van to pass first, she could have sworn she saw the driver's eyes flash – a shaven-headed man with a smile tight as a shark's.

The books were all hard-backed; their titles embossed and glittering. Even as she read them the sun slipped behind cover, and the words faded to drab, cluttered cliché.

Zoë checked her map, though she was good at holding streets in her head. She knew where she was, and where she needed to go. Heading back down the hill, she passed an alternative grocer's, whose noticeboard she paused to browse: *Bleed beautifully with hand-crafted moon pads.* A surprisingly tasteful illustration went with that. And, *Rediscover the traditional art of ear-coning, under a trained therapist*. What? When she'd finished, she moved on, replaying in her head the rest of her conversation with Win: 'Where did Price find them anyway, if they live in the West Country?'

'He met Arkle in a Soho club.'

Chains and chokers, Zoë thought. Women leashed or leashing.

But Win said, 'Not Arkle's usual stamping ground. He hasn't much use for women, and I don't think he drinks.'

'Obvious place to hang out, then.'

'There was a reason he was there, but I don't remember. Oz – my boss – says he knew straight off he'd found talent.'

'But you think he bit off more than he can chew?'

'I don't think it's him doing the chewing. Arkle's got a look to him, like everybody else is a victim. They just don't know it yet.'

'Your boss is hardly an innocent though, is he?'

'We're not going there.'

And Zoë supposed she knew what Win meant by this; knew, anyway, not to go poking it with a stick. Love took different forms, and one of them obviously dressed in black leather, and looked like a fairground attraction.

'What about the other pair?'

'Trent's the runt of the litter. Drinks. Doesn't look much, but probably vicious when cornered.'

'I know the type.'

'And Baxter's the brains. Part West Indian by the look, and handsome with it.' She glanced away from Zoë, momentarily distracted.

'But looks aren't everything.'

'I've never spoken to him. Watched him on their cabin landing once, making a phone call. What's that stuff, supposed to be really hard? They make statues from it.'

'Obsidian?' Zoë guessed.

'Might be. Anyway, that's him. Hard as . . . whatever. I think he could be cruel if he wanted.'

'His gang robs jewellery stores. They fire crossbows at passers-by,' Zoë reminded her. 'I doubt the RSPCA's planning on canonising him any time soon.'

'I just meant he's not somebody I'd want to know better.' Win picked a paper napkin from the table and carefully began shredding it. 'So what do you do next?'

'Me? I pass this on to my client. All he needs are the names.'

'And he tells my boss, who realises the Dunstans are blown. So he distances himself from them.'

'That's the idea.'

'He – Price – he's not going to like it when your client suggests he retrieve the gear. He can hardly tell him he's already got it.'

'Do I care? They're all crooks, Win, Sweeney included. On the scale of things, he's paddling down the shallow end, but the stuff the Dunstans took from him was stolen in the first place. And the only reason your boss knew Sweeney had it was, he's a fence himself. This way, Price may lose a little capital, but he gets to understand the Dunstans are bad news. If he cuts them loose, he's ahead of the game.'

'He'll probably tell Sweeney it's not his problem.'

'Then Sweeney learns a hard lesson. But I still get paid.'

'And what about the Dunstans?'

'What about them?' Zoë agreed.

'You think, if my boss ditches them, they'll head back to the straight and narrow? Back into the cement business?'

'Stories I've heard, the cement business is anything but.'

'That's not what I'm asking.'

'I know.' Zoë looked around the café. They were the only customers, and the staff were getting edgy: sweeping corners, stacking plates. The evening light had a silvery shade. She looked back at Win. 'Maybe I'll have a word with whoever's investigating the Oxford end. Not that I'm Miss Popularity there.'

Win didn't nod; didn't say anything.

'What?'

'You don't seem the type to let them get away with it, that's all.'

'How would you know what type I am?'

'That thing with the scissors? That was pretty cool.'

'Are you trying to play me, Win?'

Win shrugged. 'It doesn't matter to me. And all you want is to get paid, right?'

'If I'm looking for the moral high ground . . .'

'You'll what?'

I won't look for the space occupied by a thieving fence's gopher, Zoë didn't say. She fished in her pocket for a note to pay the bill. 'If you're that concerned, there's a payphone in the corner. Maybe you could call the cops yourself.' She'd have thrown Win a coin, if that hadn't been a Bob Poland trick.

Win laughed: a high-pitched, strangely airless laugh. It was like listening to Minnie Mouse choke on a fishbone. 'You think that's what I'm after? You have your slow moments, Zoë.'

'Yeah, right. Tell me, Win, does your boss get to hear about this? Or does it stay between us girls?'

'What does?'

'This idea you've got to rip the Dunstans off.'

A sudden gust of wind rattled the window. Win smiled a long slow smile.

Zoë crossed the square at the foot of the hill; double-checked the map in her head, and set off into narrower backstreets. Most towns were the same at heart: rivers and brick; war memorials, clock towers. She almost felt at home here, the way she almost did where she lived, and might have described this next street before turning into it: the row of narrow terraced houses with tiny front yards leading down to basements; the high wall on the opposite side with wooden gates set into it: a wall that hinted at industrial machinery behind. The gates didn't open often. This wasn't intuition so much as the rust on the padlock binding them shut. There was a small door in the left-hand gate. And parked on the kerb opposite was a van she recognised, though it took a moment to work out why – *a shaven-headed man with a smile tight as a shark's*. It had passed her as she walked through town. She'd seen the driver's teeth.

Looking at it more closely, she could make out painted-over writing on the side. DUNSTAN & SONS.

So: that would be Arkle.

From here, she could see the cabin in the sky; a tin box perched on scaffolding, its windows blank squares. Zoë guessed they were meshed over, easier to see out of than into, and if Arkle were up there he might be wondering what she was staring at. She crossed into the lee of the wall, and walked the length of the road and back. There was nobody around, though she could hear voices inside the yard. The sign above the gate also read DUNSTAN & SONS, written as imitation scrollwork, as if in invitation to posterity. Zoë stopped and crouched where the gate hinged to the wall; looked through the gap into the yard, where a man in white jeans and black jacket stood, caught in the act of raising an arm as if to fend off a projectile. When she shifted focus she saw Arkle was there too, and even as she watched he fired the crossbow he held.

IV

What he liked was the sound of the bolt hitting home. Wood was good. Glass, too: a bolt could punch through glass with a noise like somebody opening a Coke can. Metal was noisier, but had less stopping power than you'd think. Arkle had once spent an afternoon taking potshots at an abandoned car, and found few points outside the engine block the bolt couldn't carry straight through. Flesh was a whole other story. It didn't make a noise that compared to any other kind. On the other hand, it didn't offer much resistance either.

He fired and the bolt whipped past Whitby, and buried itself in the wooden upright behind him. The margin was a couple of inches, which it seemed Whitby thought way too narrow because he went white, and looked ready to puke.

'I hardly ever miss what I'm aiming at,' Arkle said.

Whitby didn't say anything.

''Course, I sometimes hit other things too. If they're in the way.'

Back at Kay's dad's, Arkle thought he'd found a prowler: someone nobody was going to get upset about when Arkle bounced him round the garden. But then the guy said he'd come looking for Katrina, and Arkle had back-pedalled, let go of him; had even dusted him down, though he'd barely dusted him up yet. 'Katrina?'

'Yes . . .'

'You a friend of hers?'

'We met just once . . .'

Not often enough to know that everyone called her Kay.

Arkle glanced through the window. Kay's father was still staring into nowhere. He was riding his own mental iceberg these days, ninety per cent of it lost from view. 'She doesn't live here. Didn't you know that?'

'I was passing through town. I looked her up in the phone book.'

'You got her father.'

'Are you . . .'

'I'm her brother-in-law.' Actually, that sounded kind of strange. He said it again: 'I'm her brother-in-law. This's her old man's place.'

'I'm sorry. I didn't mean to trespass.'

He looked relieved, for some reason, that Arkle was the brother-in-law.

'Passing through on your way where?'

'Oh, uh . . . St Ives.'

'From?'

'Oxford.'

Arkle stared hard, waiting for him to embellish that, or perhaps change his mind.

'We met the other week. She was staying at a hotel? With her husband?'

Statements turning into questions, as if he could feel the ground giving way beneath his feet. Oxford was beyond coincidence, but whoever this guy was, he wasn't copper.

'What's your name?'

Which was when Whitby had told Arkle his name was Tim Whitby, looking relieved saying it, as if the social formula offered protection. Maybe, in Oxford, it was only people who didn't know your name you had to worry about.

'You drove here?'

'I'm parked down the hill.'

Arkle said, 'The old man's a fruitcake. Should be living in a tree.' He said, 'I'll give you a lift back. Drop round Kay's on the way, see if she's in.'

'Kay?'

He smiled. 'Katrina.'

Whitby burbled in the car, though he might have been acting; might have been, if not copper, some kind of investigator: private or insurance. But Arkle didn't think so. He was too nervy, too retail – like someone who approached you in shops, asking if you needed help. Besides, he was hardly under cover: he'd already told Arkle about meeting Kay in the Oxford hotel . . . Which had been Baxter's idea, of course. Whoever booked into an upscale hotel to case a jeweller's?

'That's what makes it smart,' Bax had said. 'Kay'll come too. Cover.'

Which was when Arkle asked him straight out: how much did Kay know?

'I told you. Nothing.'

'Right.'

'What's the matter? Don't you believe me?'

Did he believe him? Didn't he believe him? How come those two questions meant the same thing? Arkle didn't know whether he trusted Baxter any more, but he knew he didn't trust Kay, because she was the reason he didn't know whether he trusted Baxter any more.

Whitby was still burbling: 'We got talking. She mentioned she lived here and like I said . . . I was passing through.' It sounded like he was on a looped tape, a tape Arkle broke by braking. '. . . Why are we stopping here?'

'She didn't tell you about the family business?'

'We didn't get on to that.'

Arkle was already on the pavement. Whitby had no choice

but to follow. They went through a door set into the wooden gate, Arkle holding it open like Whitby was a treasured guest instead of someone he'd found snooping round old man Blake's. 'Sand and gravel,' he said, pointing. 'Not much gets built without one or the other.'

'It all looks . . .'

'Abandoned?'

Whitby gave an embarrassed shrug. 'A bit.'

'Yeah, well. He was a good businessman, the old man, but he had this weak spot.'

'What was that?'

'He died. Whole place went straight to fuck after that.'

Whitby stared at him a couple of seconds. 'Are we near the car park? I've not got a great sense of direction.'

'You don't want to see Kay?'

'I'd better be going.'

'Long way back to Oxford, right?'

'Yes.'

'Except I thought you were going to St Ives.'

'. . . I'm on my way back.'

'That's not what you said.'

'I think it is.'

Arkle said, 'Yeah, maybe, who cares? What did you and Kay talk about?'

'This and that . . . I don't remember.'

Arkle said, 'You drive two hundred miles and you don't remember why? One of us must be a fucking idiot, and know what? You think it's me.'

'. . . You're not her brother-in-law, are you?'

'What?'

'Look, if you're her husband . . . We just talked, okay? That evening, in the bar? Talk, that's all we did. And I was passing, so I thought I'd say hello . . .'

Arkle stared at him, then started to laugh. 'You think I'm Bax?'

'. . . I just want to go find my car. That's all.'

But Arkle was on a roll: this guy thought he was *Bax*? That hadn't happened before. 'Watch,' he told him. 'You think Bax could do this?' He crossed to the metal staircase, Whitby's eyes on him every step. It was like snakes and rabbits. There was always somebody in control, somebody who was lunch. Arkle plucked the crossbow from behind the bottom step: it was already prepped and loaded. Bax was smooth, everybody said so, but no way Bax was in this league. When Arkle released the bolt it whipped past Whitby's head with inches to spare, and buried itself in the wooden upright of the nearest sand container. Whitby looked ready to puke.

'I hardly ever miss what I'm aiming at,' Arkle said.

Whitby said nothing.

''Course, I sometimes hit other things too. If they're in the way.'

'You've made your point.'

'What point's that?'

'Whatever you want. Can I go now?'

'Just when we're starting to have fun?' Arkle slotted another bolt, and began to wind it. 'You had any more thoughts about that conversation yet? The one you had with my *sis*ter-in-law?'

'I've already told you—'

'Because I'm having trouble believing you came all this way just to see how she is.'

Whitby said, 'Okay, that's it. I'm going through that door. Don't try to stop me.'

'Yeah, right. And how fast do you think you'll get there?' Arkle asked. 'This fast?'

The bolt hit the gate at Whitby head height, and if it didn't go right through, there wasn't much of it left showing.

Arkle said, 'I want you to imagine for a moment what that must have felt like for the gate.'

Whitby looked like he was going to speak, but didn't. His

fists, which had clenched, had loosened again; his mouth was open, but not in a smile. Perhaps his teeth would drop out. And this, Arkle realised – fitting another bolt – this was better than back in Oxford; those precious seconds when he'd known he was about to fire at the uniformed idiot. Because this target knew it was happening . . .

And whatever had brought Whitby here, whatever he had going with Kay, what mattered more was that nobody knew where he was now. This information worked its way through Arkle, starting at his fingers and branching out into the usual parts. The big question mark over the money would be addressed in due course, and whatever Kay and this guy had been planning, well, Arkle would get round to that. But there was fun to be had first.

Whitby said, 'Let's just stop this now, right? Before it goes any further.'

St-st-stop: your genuine fear stammer.

'You reckon? What kind of brother would I be, I didn't get upset about you hanging round some hotel with his wife? In Oxford, right? She was in Oxford?'

'So was he.'

'You saw him?'

'I— No, but he was there, she said he was there—'

'Oh, right. That's what I'm supposed to believe, like I'm some fucking idiot or something. Bax takes his wife off for a weekend, then leaves her hanging round the hotel Saturday evening. That sound remotely plausible to you?'

'I—'

'You what?'

'I never said what evening it was.'

Arkle was about to reply but wasn't sure what to say, and if there was one thing Arkle didn't like, it was being made stupid. So he decided to loose another bolt instead, glance one off Whitby's shoe – well, *glance*: it would probably sting a bit. And he could see in Whitby's eyes that Whitby knew it was coming; knew it as soon as Arkle raised the bow, and Arkle in turn knew Whitby was measuring the distance to the exit – call it five yards. He thought he could get five yards before Arkle shot his bolt? Let alone the extra seconds for fiddling with the lock, pulling the door open? There was positive thinking, then there was plain religion. But what option did Whitby have? I removed his options, Arkle thought. The pleasure he'd felt earlier crawled through him again, as something the size of a tennis ball sailed over the gate, over his head, and bounced ten yards distant, and he span just like that – like he was automatic; pivotal – and hit it on the bounce. The bolt carried it maybe ten yards, and buried it in a drift of sand.

He said, 'Fuck! Did you see *that*?' but when he turned Whitby was gone and the door was hanging open.

Arkle walked over, but the street was empty.

After a moment, he closed the door and crossed to where whatever it was had landed after he'd hit it on a reaction shot. He'd feel that one in his muscles forever – one perfect fluid moment in which target and bolt were connected; like there'd been an inevitable conjunction waiting to occur, which couldn't have happened through anyone but Arkle. This was Olympic standard. Olympic, hell. Miracle standard. They should hand out the Nobel for a shot like that.

Precisely what he'd hit, he didn't know yet.

The end of the bolt protruded from the sand an inch or two, and he pulled it clear like a sword from a stone. Brushed wet sand from the lump at the end, only now beginning to wonder who'd thrown it over the gate in the first place . . .

A fucking apple.

For no reason he could positively identify, the Lone Ranger tune started skipping through his head.

*

Without a plan, he climbed to the crow's nest. Being here by himself always tugged at something inside Arkle he didn't understand and wouldn't know what to call, except that he felt more at home here than he did at home, and guessed the others did too. Just one more thing binding them together; another reason he couldn't allow them to fall apart. The money, he remembered. He was supposed to be considering the money; what Kay knew about it; whether – more to the point – she could get her hands on it. Whether this Whitby was part of some scheme to do that. And if Whitby was actually from Oxford, or if finding him again would be trickier than that.

The light filtering through the meshed window had a greasy, second-hand texture, and the air tasted of whatever Trent had eaten lately: something fast and fried, and already cold by the time it got here.

The phone rang.

Afterwards, it would seem of great significance that when he heard the news he was in the crow's nest, where he, Bax and Trent had spent so much of their shared lives together . . . It was Trent. Trent sounded sober. That was a first.

'It's Baxter.'

Arkle said nothing.

'He's dead, Arkle.'

And still he said nothing, as if this were the simplest way of undoing whatever complicated misunderstanding had infected Trent.

'It was Kay.' There was a curious vacancy in Trent's voice, a vacancy which found an echo in Arkle's heart. 'She stabbed him, Ark. He's dead . . .'

The greased and heavy light clouded over, leaving Arkle in the dark.

5

I

IT WAS A LONG drive home, and if Zoë had known it was going to end with her being dead, she'd have pulled into a lay-by and avoided it altogether. Life was too short to approach death head-on. On that journey, you took any diversion available – marriage, travel, children, alcohol. At the very least, you stopped to admire the view.

The moors folded over themselves deep into the distance, and wherever one fell from sight, another rose. Their only limit was the horizon. All the evidence suggested they kept happening the far side of that, too.

After the harried man had escaped the yard, the pair of them had raced down the street together like an elopement in progress, Zoë's heartbeat underlining their urgency. If the apple hadn't worked, she'd have had to do something else – and even with a gate between them, his attention elsewhere, shaven-head Arkle looked bad news; like somebody who'd squeeze whatever trigger was offered, for the pleasure of the damage it would cause. So she'd have had to do something, and had no idea what, though it would probably have involved being on the same side of the gate as him . . .

Thanks to the apple, that hadn't happened.

They'd hared round two corners, Zoë and the man in white chinos and black jacket, before looking back. But nobody was following. She slowed, stopped and rested, heart hammering. When she closed her eyes, a picture from her past exploded in her head: that moment she'd been pulled clear of the canal just before her lungs burst, then plunged back in again, and held under.

She was being talked to:

'. . . Thanks.'

Zoë, without opening her eyes, said, 'Don't tell me. You just popped in there, asking for directions.'

He didn't say anything.

Now she opened them. 'Oh, God. Tell me that didn't happen.'

'I was looking for somebody,' he said at last. 'I found him instead.'

'Right.' She tested her legs: reasonably steady. What was the matter with her? All she'd done was throw an apple and run. But even with the gate between them, that man had scared her. She'd recognised something dark in him, and knew that whatever she'd thrown to distract him – a kitten, a child – he'd have shot without thinking, and congratulated himself on his reflex. Her legs were okay now. It would be an idea to put space between him and her.

On being asked a third time, she registered what the question was.

'Boehm. Zoë Boehm.'

They weren't far from the car park, and judging by the relief on his face, he was parked here too. Belatedly, she asked his name: Tim Willerby, Wallaby, something like that. Who had come looking for someone and found Arkle instead, but had walked away intact. She should have advice to offer (don't go into deserted yards with strange men) but that was ridiculous: he wasn't much younger than her, and a little shop-worn himself – hollow round the eyes; creased at the edges. Old enough to know better, in other words. She had rescued him, but only because he'd happened to be there. It wasn't a big deal. Goodbye, Tim Willerby/Wallaby, she thought, and they parted in the middle of the car park. All of a sudden, she couldn't leave this town fast enough.

It was a long drive home, and it ended with her dead.

Her first-floor flat shared a downstairs lobby, where mail, mostly junk, accumulated on a small table. This afternoon a posh cream envelope awaited her, along with a hand-delivered card, taped to a copy of the local paper. She carried both upstairs. It felt like she'd been away forever: her rooms had shrunk in her absence, and mustiness tinged the air. She flipped the light switch in passing, but nothing happened.

It was an immutable law that bulbs only went when there was no spare on the premises.

She swore, but quietly, under her breath. No big deal. Sitting, she thought about getting up again and pouring some wine, but if she started now she'd drink all evening, and this would leave her wrecked. Not that she had plans demanding sobriety . . . Best to sidestep the issue and read her card, which turned out to be cheap and sombre: embossed bouquet on white background, with *Deepest Sympathy* in raised gilt lettering at its foot. Inside, in a script she didn't recognise, was scrawled *Sorry to hear you're dead.*

For a moment Zoë felt nothing – very specifically nothing. She could feel nothing's edges, the space nothing occupied. Nothing threatened to expand and swallow her whole. Nothing, for a while, verged on everything. Then she forced herself to blink, and the shadows receded.

She looked again at the envelope, but it gave no clues; just her name in block capitals, black ink. It didn't matter. Clues only work when you're already looking where they point, and this had Bob Poland written all over it. Putting it aside, she picked up the newspaper it had been taped to. A clammy knowledge of its contents was already clawing at her, the way the man in the Poe story scratched at his coffin lid, as if this would make the slightest difference.

Her name was there in the middle section, under Death Notices. *Suddenly, unexpectedly. No flowers, by request.* Bastard. She threw the paper aside, her inner debate about wine forgotten, but the first thing she found in her kitchen was a pool of water on the floor by the fridge, and this time she swore out loud, already knowing what would happen when she tried the light switch – nothing. She tried anyway, just as somebody knocked on her door. Zoë marched out; took the stairs two at a time; threw the door open so fiercely, it was a wonder it didn't splinter. The man on the other side took a step back, frightened. He lived downstairs.

'Zoë?'

'Dave.'

'You're alive.'

'It would seem so. Has somebody been here?'

'A policeman. Jesus. He said you were dead.' Dave shook his head: he was thirty-four, and wore a beard. Death was a big thing. 'A car crash?' He made this a question. If anyone ought to know about her death, it was Zoë. 'He said there'd been a traffic accident?'

'And he had ID, right?'

'It looked real to me.'

And you're an expert, she managed not to say. 'So you let him in.' They kept each other's spare keys, which until now had seemed a good idea.

'. . . I'm really sorry, Zo.'

'Don't call me Zo,' she said. Then, seeing his face, said: 'Look, it's nothing. Really. Practical joke, that's all.'

'He wasn't a policeman?'

'He's retired. He likes a bit of a laugh.'

'He said you were dead,' Dave repeated. 'That's supposed to be funny? Your friends play real rough, Zoë.'

'So do I,' she told him.

★

She thought at first he'd managed to cancel her utilities, but she'd overestimated Bob Poland: he'd sliced her plugs, removed her fuses, reached his limit. Making out she was dead, leaving her flat a stone cold tomb – he didn't get cleverer than that. Blunt weaponry was more his speed. And she felt her anger harden to a cold knot, and knew she'd make him pay for this, first chance she got.

Meanwhile she retreated to her local pub, which had drums and trumpets fixed to the walls, and player-piano music on the ceiling, and ordered a large white wine she almost finished before reaching her table. There was nothing like being reminded about one bastard to make you forget another. Poland's intrusion had pushed Arkle to one side, but now she was sitting quietly with alcohol thank God in front of her, the morning returned into focus, and her conclusion was immediate: no way did she want to tangle with Arkle. He'd toyed with that man like a cat with a cornered sparrow. Zoë didn't know if he'd have shot him or not, but she wasn't about to replay the experiment with herself in the target role, just to find out.

Zoë drank wine, and thought about Win. Win thought the Dunstan brothers ripe for robbing, and her logic was the same as her boss's had been when he'd set the Dunstans on Sweeney – who could they tell? Where this collapsed was in expecting Arkle to pout, fume and forget it. He presented with the self-control of a heat-seeking missile, and last thing Zoë planned to do was light a fire in his vicinity.

It was too late to do anything about plugs and bulbs; too early to go to bed, but suddenly that's what she wanted to do anyway – close her eyes and put it all out of view: madmen, bastards, carnage on the roads. She had another drink first. The pub was filling as the nearby publisher closed its doors, and the ambient chatter of book people masked her inner tension. Think about good things. Think about seeing Sweeney tomorrow: making her report, taking her money, pulling down the curtain. Bob Poland was a story for another day, and Arkle was history, clear and simple. Win's dream of untold booty – whatever the Dunstans had stashed from their thieving outings – was only a pirate's dream of other people's money. Sweeney's promised bounty, on the other hand, she'd earned. Take the money, pay her debts – she need never see or think about these people again. The next best thing to a happy ending was an ending.

She finished her drink and went home, where it was dark and comfortless. And when she turned on her portable radio, she found that Poland had thought of this too: he'd removed its batteries. No light, no sound; no calming voices on Radio 4, murmuring secular certainties. 'Fuck you,' she said out loud. Did he think this would bring her to her knees; make her feel she was peering over the edge of an open grave? Zoë was too solidly of the here and now to be frightened out of it by that creep. Even an angry, vindictive stalker was only a stalker: sooner or later, you scraped him off your shoe.

By light that swam through the window, she noticed, lying on her sofa, the other letter; the one she'd forgotten about after opening Poland's. It could be good news. It was, of course, a bill. Damien bloody Faraday – *for consultation.* For being told, in other words, what she already knew: that she owed the Inland Revenue more than she could currently repay. Her fridge remained disabled, but she retrieved the half-empty bottle of wine from it anyway; finished it in one large glass, and went to bed.

Thursday morning – crack of nine – she was outside the Cancer Relief shop again. No Miss Marple yet; no sign of Sweeney. She turned her mobile off, in case Jeff rang asking for his car back, and browsed the *Independent*: train fares up, military scandal, human cloning. Somebody got murdered, too: *Totnes* caught her eye, but before she could read further there was a tapping at her window, and she looked up expecting Sweeney. But no. It was Miss Marple.

Zoë wound the window down.

'I rang the council.'

Now why wasn't that a surprise?

'And they said they've nobody surveying antisocial behaviour. Nobody at all.'

'And did you complain about that?'

'Complain?'

'Council tax the way it is, you'd think they could afford a little antisocial targeting.' Anti-antisocial, she meant. She wound the window up before this could be pointed out, and decided that waiting round the corner might be quieter – where the Dunstans had lurked, in fact. It was coming to something when you had to take parking tips from a bunch of armed robbers.

Once there she felt restless, so got out and walked the block. The streets were busy now. All the other shops were open. Zoë felt, or possibly imagined, the gimlet stare of white hair/pink wool upon her, and wondered for a moment what it would be like to be that age. Then realised she was looking no more than, say, twenty-five years into her future, and tried to shut that channel down . . . Too late. What would she be doing in twenty-five years? Without a serious upturn in economic status, she might not be working in a charity shop, but she'd be buying her outfits there. This was not a good vision. She walked on, browsing windows, but found herself looking back every two minutes, because it stood to reason that one particular pair of minutes would be the one in which Sweeney appeared.

Except none of them were. And though she waited a full hour past Sweeney's usual opening time, for most of that, she'd known in her bones he wasn't coming.

11

Arkle, blind with fury, mad with loss, roared like a blood-red sunset on one of those plains he'd dreamed about. From the darkness something answered: echoing his pain, telling him to shut up, who knew?

Trent said, 'That copper? The one with red hair?'

Arkle's noise might have meant yes, he knew the one; no, he didn't care.

'He said it would have been quick. He said Bax didn't suffer.'

Trent didn't feel drunk, which was alarming. He'd been drinking all day. If he wasn't drunk, he'd possibly turned some evolutionary corner.

'I said, didn't suffer? She stuck a fucking kitchen knife in him. That's gotta hurt.'

He was sitting at the foot of the metal staircase, washed in the light of the last unburnt-out overhead lamp, and his eyes were red and aching. Around him lay torn, wadded copies of newspapers, most of which had had something to say about Bax, about Kay; all of it liberally sprinkled with inverted commas. 'Abusive'. 'Self-defence'.

Last time he'd seen Kay, she'd had that shiner decorating her face: what they call a mouse. Even a mouse'll roar, if you poke it hard enough.

Arkle was back and forth, back and forth. He looked like he was wearing a mask again, except this mask was fashioned of anger, grief and fury; the three of them working his features, making him their puppet.

What Trent mostly felt was numb.

There'd been coppers, naturally – a whole day's worth – and while they'd started out sympathetic, this had changed yesterday evening, when something tribal had occurred. Attitudes hardened, and things became more recognisable. From the unfamiliar role of innocent bystander, Trent had been shifted to his usual position of being somebody he probably shouldn't be. In a way, this was a comfort. Baxter was still dead, but at least Trent was still Trent, whom policemen eyed with suspicion as a matter of course, if only for being Arkle's brother. And Arkle was a walking war zone.

Look at him now. Back and forth, back and forth. There'd been journos buzzing round like flies on meat. At the police station, Trent and Arkle had been ushered out of the back door to avoid them: a courtesy allowed on account of their brother being the meat, despite the new-found suspicion he might deserve to be. But journos tracked them to the yard anyway, and stood outside the gates, rattling the woodwork. This was what it must be like, the wrong side of a zoo. When their noise penetrated Arkle's grief, he'd gone out and flattened the nose of the first to reach him. There'd been a scattering, as if news were breaking elsewhere. In the midst of it, Trent noticed a woman watching from over the road: late fifties, mad grey hair and thick glasses; wearing a belted brown raincoat, from under which tufts of a tatty green cardigan poked. Bag lady, he'd thought. Astonishingly, she'd yawned. He'd turned to check on Arkle, and when he next looked, she was gone.

It had become clear reasonably quickly that interviews weren't going to happen. The journalists dispersed shortly after.

Time had passed. The light was long gone; the moon a ghost under covers. Trent had two empty vodka bottles at his feet, one two-thirds full in his hands, and every time he took a swallow, he wondered why he wasn't drunk yet. If Bax had been here, he'd have had words on the subject. 'It's not just your liver you're killing,' he'd have said. 'It's your brain. Your dick. Your heart.' And he'd have added: 'I know you're not using them, but miracles happen, right?'

'Miracles happen,' Trent said out loud.

Arkle raged at the ghostly moon.

'Miracles happen,' he said again, but they didn't. Baxter was still lying the other side of town in a fridge, while Kay was on police bail; cushioned in a four-star hotel, probably, spilling her story to a sleazebag with a chequebook. *Tell me how he blacked your eye. Tell me what a bully he was.* Yeah, right: so you killed him. You couldn't have just walked out, bitch? His vision filled with tears again. You take something sharp, you stick it in your heart. That had to hurt, didn't it?

Trent tried to stand, and it turned out that he was, after all, inhumanly drunk. But being short, he didn't have far to fall.

When he woke, he was in the crow's nest. It wasn't the first time he'd woken somewhere without the faintest memory of getting there: usually, though, he'd just aligned himself to the nearest horizontal surface while unconsciousness took its course. Tonight, it appeared he'd managed to sit in Arkle's chair – which had been known to be unwise – after wrapping himself in a blanket. All of which must have happened, because the alternative wasn't feasible.

Arkle said, 'You okay?'

He tried to speak. Decided he wasn't ready yet. Nodded.

'It's just you and me, now.'

Wherever Arkle had been – his land of pain – he'd come back. And wherever Trent had been, he'd been there a couple of hours at most. Outside was full dark. One dim bulb lit the cabin. Arkle looked like a vampire: black coat, white face. When he spoke again, his tone was so unArkle-ish he might have been pretending to be somebody else; something he was so bad at, it was like watching two other people instead. Vinnie Jones doing Michael Palin, perhaps.

'I didn't want to leave you out there. You might have caught cold.'

Two days back, he'd have watched while Trent dozed off in a river.

'You're okay in my chair for a bit. I don't mind.'

Trent closed his eyes. He was going to throw up shortly, which was almost certainly the vodka, but was possibly the notion of Arkle being tender.

'When you're feeling better, we've stuff to talk about.'

He must have drifted. He didn't spew. Light returned slowly, and sketched things' edges: the window frame; the TV set. His feet ached with a cold that crept up his legs and curled icy digits round his stomach; prepared to rip the warm life out of him. If he exhaled, he'd see it hanging in the air: breath like Jack Frost's fingers . . . He came awake terrified, convinced he'd stopped breathing, to see Arkle by the window, crossbow cradled in one arm. The dawn light had a grey, second-hand look, as if it had already been one too many mornings.

Arkle had found a piece of toast somewhere, and was holding it in a palm as if it were an important element in an impending sacrament.

After a while, Trent said, 'What day is it?'

Arkle replied, 'When he told me he was going to marry her, I tried to talk him out of it. That's not hindsight. I definitely tried to talk him out of it. I said it was one thing . . . *seeing* her.' His tone indicated he'd considered and rejected synonyms. 'But marrying her . . . I told him it would be the death of us.' He turned to Trent, his eyes black holes. 'I meant the three of us. I meant it wouldn't be the same between the three of us.' He turned back to the window. 'I was right, though, wasn't I? She's been his death.'

Eat the toast, Trent thought. Don't just stand holding it, *please*. He was in that post-binge toxic state where everything hurt: everything. Even things other people were doing.

'What was it you talked about in the bar that time?'

His voice was back to standard Arkle: what Bax had once said a pissed-off speak-your-weight machine would sound like.

Trent squeezed his eyes shut. Cold grey used-up light sneaked in anyway, so the shapes that moved inside his head threw shadows.

'What was it you talked about in the bar that time?'

'Arkle—'

'What was it you talked about in the bar that time?'

He said, 'Bax said you were on the edge. Near to blowing it.'

'Bax said that.'

'Yes. Bax said that.'

Trent started to cry softly, telling Arkle this.

'What else did he say?'

'Arkle—'

'What else did he say?'

'He said that's not something we wanted to be near. When it happened. That's what he said.'

'Okay.'

Arkle dropped the toast, then laid his hand flat against the reinforced windowpane, as if testing its resistance. It seemed solid enough. It didn't, anyway, tumble and crash to the ground below.

'It was always the three of us,' he said.

'Yes, Arkle.'

It was best to agree with Arkle when he said things like this, or like anything else. Even when they were monumental rubbish.

'It's her fault, really. I don't blame you.'

'. . . Thanks, Arkle.'

It hurt just to talk. He was crying harder now.

'I don't blame you. You agreed with him though, didn't you?'

'. . . Yes, Arkle.'

'I know.'

Arkle turned and in one seamless movement smashed the stock of his crossbow into Trent's head. Trent flew from the chair and crashed against the table in the corner. The TV fell to the floor and shattered; there was broken glass and electric parts and blood everywhere, and to Trent it felt like the world, or a small significant part of it, had just ceased spinning. Then it began again, and he threw up and blacked out, in roughly that order. When he came to he was back in Arkle's chair, every last nerve screaming its distress, and Arkle was tenderly dabbing blood from his face with a cloth last used to mop spilt lager.

'It's just the two of us now,' he said, as if nothing had happened since he'd last spoken. 'And we've got to look out for each other.'

Yes, Arkle, Trent wanted to say, but couldn't.

'We're going to wait till you feel better. And then there's things we have to do.'

Yes, Arkle.

'We're going to kill that bitch for what she did to our brother.'

He licked a finger, and rubbed at a patch on Trent's forehead where a grain of glass from the TV had embedded itself.

'But first, we're gunna find out where she and Bax hid our money.'

Trent felt consciousness slip away. Last thing he was aware of, Arkle was saying, 'And don't worry, we'll get you another one. The sound was buggered anyway.'

III

She was about to make the call when she remembered the law about phones in cars, so pulled off the road; punched the number standing next to a field full of pigs whose corrugated iron sties were shaped like tiny aircraft hangars. While she waited, Zoë wondered whether each pig returned to the same sty after a day truffling in mud, or just kipped in the first one it reached.

. . . Mental displacement activity. This wasn't a call she'd been looking forward to.

'Jeff Harris.'

'Is your answering machine in?'

'Zoë bloody Boehm.' Heavy on the sarcasm, he asked: 'How *are* you?'

'I look like shit and feel like I've been kicked in the head.'

'Good.'

'I suppose you're wondering why I've not returned your car yet.'

'Not really,' he said. 'I worked it out. You're a thief.'

'A thief would hardly ring you to apologise.'

'She might if she was clever.'

'I'm not that smart.'

'There's a lot of things you're not, Zoë, but that smart isn't one of them.'

A pig, possibly the top pig, had stopped excavating the root he'd discovered and was scrutinising Zoë instead. 'Piggy-eyed', she'd always thought an insult. This, though, was a remarkably intelligent study.

'I'm sorry, Jeff,' she said.

The pig said *Yeah, right.*

'So don't tell me.' Even over the phone, she could see him: screwing up his eyes, furrowing his brow; plucking an answer from the heavens. 'You're, ah, *on a case.* You're *tracking someone down.* You need *wheels*, right?'

'I'm sorry, Jeff.'

'But not sorry enough to buy your own fucking car.'

'No,' she agreed. 'Not that sorry, obviously.'

'Last time, Zoë. Seriously, positively, the last time.'

It was also the first time, but Zoë didn't feel in a position to point this out.

'I'll return it soon.'

'You'll return it today.'

'Sorry, Jeff, this is a really bad connection . . .'

She stood a while longer, wondering if he was as pissed off as he'd sounded, or just upping the stakes for when he needed a favour in return. And then wondered about herself instead, for having thoughts like that. Jeff was a friend. Had been, anyway. And Zoë had known the moment she borrowed the car that she'd break their agreement if she needed to. So what did that say about her?

Pocketing her phone, she turned to go.

Goodbye, Zoë, said the pig.

'That'll do, pig,' said Zoë.

She got into Jeff's car and drove on.

She was driving to Totnes again. It was late Saturday afternoon.

Several times since Thursday she'd returned to Sweeney's shop, always finding the closed sign in the door, and no lights burning; the metal shutter obscuring the window. His phone rang unanswered. His home address was unoccupied, too. Sweeney lived in a surprisingly neat little house in a cul-de-sac in Headington Quarry, but hadn't been seen there lately, according to the kind of neighbour who would notice.

'Does he have family?'

'There's a sister in Dulwich.'

Zoë had contemplated breaking in, but not for long. The alarm box on the wall might not be real, but the neighbour certainly was. This was a tall, stick-thin woman with sharp features; happy to share info with Zoë, on the assumption she'd receive some in return. 'Is he in trouble?'

'Not that I'm aware of,' said Zoë. 'Thanks for your time.'

By mid-morning she'd known she had to do something, and by noon had known what it would be.

It was a calm day. What clouds there were were high and moving slowly, and the usual weekend noises that filtered into her flat – distant traffic, sirens, drunken students – were muted; mono. She'd spent hours tussling with some rebarbative accounts, repeatedly finding no way of adding the available figures together that made her future look rosy. Had mulled on Bob Poland's future, too: that needed taking care of . . . But at least he'd not severed her landline. The part of Friday she'd not been checking on Sweeney or repairing Poland's damage, Zoë had spent fielding calls from former clients sorry to learn she was dead, and also from a flat clearance firm eager for the contract. Who, she wondered, had these people imagined was going to answer her phone? And this, too, had cast a pall: no one would have answered her phone. When Zoë went, she'd be leaving nobody behind.

Last thing she'd done before setting out had been to ring Win. 'I went to see Sweeney today,' she said.

Win said, 'Have you thought about what we discussed?'

'What you discussed. He wasn't there.' This felt like two conversations at once. Or one conversation, two agendas. 'Wasn't there yesterday either. I wonder why?'

'He probably needed a break. Did you hear the news?'

'About Baxter Dunstan?'

'Spousal abuse case. Why she did it, I mean. Not the murder.' Win paused. 'Murder's not spousal abuse. More like fair comment.'

Zoë said, 'I guess the remaining Dunstans'll be in an uproar.'

'Good time for what we talked about. They already don't know what's hit them.'

'What you talked about,' Zoë said. 'And never would be a better time. That Arkle? He's a basket case on a sunny morning. I shudder to think what he's like when he's grieving.'

(The image that came to mind was of a bellowing lion: sore, confused, angry. Somewhere under a roaring red sunset, terrifying everything for miles around.)

'Strategy,' Win said. 'Hit your enemy when he's down, everyone knows that.'

'You know how to carry a grudge, don't you?'

'You use both hands. I've made a rough estimate of how much they've made. On jobs for the boss, I mean. Your share would be something like eighty thousand.'

'My share.'

'Equal partners. That's assuming they haven't blown it all. But the amount of time they hang around that yard, I doubt they've worked through two hundred grand yet.'

'Eighty,' said Zoë, 'is not half of two hundred.'

'I'm rounding things off. They're bound to have spent a bit. Where are you?'

'Heading out. Same as Sweeney's out.'

'You keep telling me that like it's my fault.'

'Did you speak to him, Win?'

'Why would I have done that?'

'Well, let's see,' Zoë said. 'He owes me five grand, or will do once I tell him what he paid me to find out. But suppose he discovered the information some other way. He might argue he didn't owe me anything. At the very least, he might try avoiding me.'

'Sounds a little paranoid, Zoë.'

'And if I don't get his five grand, well, that might make me likelier to fall in with this scheme of yours, mightn't it?'

'If we're going to be partners, we're going to have to trust each other.'

'You work for a crook, and you want help robbing his strong-arm boys,' Zoë said. 'Trust might be stretching it. That time you and Arkle spoke, what did you talk about?'

'I don't remember.'

'Let me guess. He mentioned your weight, your general appearance. He questioned your taste in clothes and made fun of your voice.'

There's no silence quite like the silence of someone not speaking over the phone.

'Possibly he queried your gender.'

'You fucking bitch.'

'It's been said. And what's the upshot of that little chat, Win? You plan to knock him and his brothers over, take them for, what did you say, a couple of hundred grand?'

There was another silence: a shorter one. Then Win said, 'Where's this going?'

'You ever get a look at Sweeney, Win? He's kind of short, kind of bald. He has these fuzzy patches he can't reach to shave, and on his best day, you'd not notice him twice. What makes you think he can't carry a grudge any better than you?'

'You think I've wound him up and pointed him, don't you?'

'I think you told him about the Dunstans as a way of leaning on me. And I think you forgot to take his reactions into account.' Zoë paused. 'Just because you're kind of funny-looking doesn't mean you have no pride.'

Win said, 'You probably imagine you're perceptive. But so what if the dwarf's upset? It doesn't affect our plans.'

'Your plans. The dwarf's my client. If he's got it into his head to even the score, Arkle will eat him for breakfast. That'll be your fault, Win.'

'We're partners. Remember?'

'Only in your head. Anything happens to Sweeney, I'll hold you responsible.'

She'd hung up before she got dragged into debate. And immediately afterwards, left the flat too; the image of Sweeney confronting the remaining Dunstans was not a happy one.

So she was driving to Totnes again. It was late Saturday afternoon.

The day's calm dissolved after she'd spoken to Jeff, as if his disgruntlement had spread. The roads grew cluttered and sluggish, clogged by inexplicable tailbacks which felt to Zoë like a mechanic's curse. It was evening before she drove into town, and the street lamps were winking on. Echoing in her brain were details of another story, about a local woman who had stabbed her husband to death in their flat. Variations on the theme had occupied her radio the whole way down.

Spousal abuse, Win had said, and that was certainly the

chorus. The facts were sketchy – Baxter Dunstan had died on Wednesday, the same day Zoë had last been here; Katrina Dunstan, née Blake, had been arrested that same day, after calling the police from the kitchen in which he lay dead – but the speculation mortaring the gaps left little room for doubt. Round-table discussions of domestic violence explored the outer limits of self-defence, and cases were exhumed in which convictions had been overturned, sentences reduced, and acquittals handed down to women who'd burned their husbands in their beds. Amid the token voices of dissent, the general feeling was that men who raised their fists to women wouldn't be missed. Zoë could get behind that. And if his brother was anything to go by, Baxter had probably thought target practice a form of foreplay.

That was the discussion thread: the headline was, Katrina Blake had been released pending full investigation. The fact that she'd not been charged indicated what a hot-button topic this was, Zoë thought. There followed one of those throat-clearing moments you get when one part of the media admits that other parts exist, allowing her to gather that a newspaper – she was guessing a tabloid – had whisked Ms Blake off to its hidey-hole. Give it a couple of months – trial safely over; acquittal safely bagged – and she'd be splurging her recently bruised emotions over pages five to fourteen, with pics. Though as far as any of this concerned Zoë, what mattered was the effect it would be having on Arkle and the other extant Dunstan.

She parked in the usual car park, walked into town – she was having visions of Sweeney nailed to a board in the Dunstans' yard; a grief-maddened Arkle taking potshots at him. She rehearsed it again: why would Sweeney come here, hunting his stolen loot? Other than that he knew this was where it was? . . . And here, counter-argument collapsed. Zoë knew what desperation tasted like. Sweeney was staring at livelihood's end. And everything she'd said to Win came back, and rang true:

never underestimate the pride of a man who was a bit too short; a bit too overlooked.

By the time she reached the yard it was dark, and a pub down the road was spilling light on to the pavement. Knocking on the big gates didn't seem a great idea. On the other hand, she wasn't sure how to proceed otherwise. After making sure there was no one around, she dropped to her knees and peered through a gap. Everything in the yard was shades of grey – mounds of gravel, heaps of sand; all spent and wasted in the half-light. The tin cabin perched lifeless in the sky. Knowing herself an idiot she banged on the door, now she was certain the place was deserted. The only response was a faster creaking from the Dunstan & Sons sign overhead. A scrabbling, perhaps, from one of the grey mounds. Probably a rat.

The upside was, there was no sign of Sweeney, either. The vision of him nailed to a board with metal bolts slapping around him faded, to be replaced by a different vision of him tied up in a cellar, she didn't know where. Ridiculous. And how much of Zoë's concern, anyway, was based on the fact that he owed her five grand? A question she'd successfully avoided so far, and planned to continue doing so: her next move was obvious. She went to the pub.

Which was themed to give the impression it had once been a library. From a distance, the rows of books looked impressive – uniform, leather-tooled – but on inspection proved to be book club editions: MacLeans, Wheatleys, *Reader's Digest*'s condenseds. Zoë ordered a glass of wine, remembering the drive home in time to make it a small one. The clock above the mirror read 7:15. After he'd delivered her drink, she said to the barman: 'You don't have a phone book, do you?'

'Yes, but I've no idea where. Sorry.'

'Doesn't matter.'

He was young, seemed pleasant enough: T-shirt and stubble,

the just-been-surfing look. He said, 'Anything else I can help you with?'

Zoë wondered if he was coming on to her. She quite genuinely lacked the equipment to be sure.

'You know the Dunstans? From the yard along the road?'

'You press?'

'Would that make a difference?'

He shrugged. 'Takes all sorts. Nicest guy I ever knew had a press card.'

'Blimey. Anyway, no, I'm not press. I just need to speak with them.'

'They drink in here, or did. You know Bax is dead?'

'I read.'

'He was the normal one. The other pair . . . I don't like to see them coming in. On the other hand, I wouldn't want to bar them.'

'I've seen Arkle in action.'

'You'll know what I mean then. It's not like he loses his temper. It's more like lost temper's his default option.'

'Seems to have been Baxter's problem too.'

The young man shrugged.

'Or you think wife-beating's just a foible?'

'Fuck, no. Just didn't seem the type, that's all. Kay comes in sometimes. Came in. I never thought she looked . . . You know.'

He seemed uncomfortable. And no: Zoë didn't know. Not exactly.

She said, 'Did she watch him closely? Or would she talk to other regulars? Did she talk to you?'

'Sometimes.'

'When he was around?'

He thought about it. She liked him for doing that. He considered it, rather than just batting away whatever she was getting at.

At last he said, 'I see what you mean. Yeah, maybe. I can't be sure, not now. But maybe you're right, she only talked to me when he was out of the room.'

It was Zoë's turn to shrug. 'Doesn't prove anything, really. I was just . . .'

'No, it's a good point. You're saying, I didn't think he seemed the type, but that's just because I thought he was an all right bloke. But if I'd watched properly, I'd have noticed she was scared of him.'

Okay: he was definitely coming on to her.

She said, 'Anyway. Do you have any idea where I'd find Arkle now?'

'Home address? Sorry. He's not the all-back-to-mine type.' He scratched his stubble. 'Not that anyone would go.'

'Thanks anyway.'

'You're not the first to ask today.'

'Who else has been in?'

'Like I said. Press.' He paused to check nobody needed a drink, then said, 'Funnily enough, I know where she lives. Kay. Where she used to live, I mean.' He seemed to think this needed a reason. 'Her dad used to be an undertaker. He buried my gran.' He gave Zoë an address at the top of the High Street. Her grasp of the town's geography was enough to give her the basic picture.

'Can I buy you a drink?'

He said, 'Why don't I buy you one?'

'I have to go. Sorry.'

And for almost a minute, she really was.

Passing an open café, she saw through its window a payphone and directory, so went in and jotted down the addresses of the four Dunstans listed. Outside, she sat on a bench and collated the addresses against her map, then worked out the quickest route round all four. At each, she would check for signs of

Sweeney. What these might be she didn't know, so it would be simpler just to get on with it.

Maybe she'd snatch him from the jaws of Arkle. Maybe as she did so, he'd notice he owed her five thousand pounds.

The first address washed out. She'd barely arrived when a car pulled up and disgorged about fifteen pre-teen squabbling boys, herded by a fraught mother and a man who looked like he wanted to get straight back in the car. They disappeared into the house, and all the lights went on. Zoë scratched it from her list, and left.

On the corner, checking her map, she found she wasn't far from the street the barman had mentioned: where Katrina, or Kay, Dunstan had lived. If she ignored this now, she'd have to come back later when nothing else panned out. This had happened too often for her to dismiss. So she followed the street round to where it ended at a railed-off dead drop, twenty yards or so below which a big road skirted the town centre. Traffic squirted along it heading west, and she watched tail lights forming ever-receding patterns for a moment, before turning to check house numbers.

The house she was looking for stood next to the drop, and even in artificial light had an air of neglect; its paintwork scuffed and worn; its wooden porch a ramshackle add-on. It was in darkness, but the front room curtains hung open, and a glow within suggested light at the rear. For no reason she could pin down, a shiver tickled Zoë's spine. Then a reason materialised.

Parked on the kerb opposite was a van she recognised – *a shaven-headed man with a smile tight as a shark's.*

Her mind flipped back, and she was outside the gravel yard again, watching Arkle torment Tim Willerby/Wallaby – would he really have put a bolt through him? Zoë couldn't know. But Arkle's smile suggested he'd do pretty much whatever he wanted, which was reason enough to give him a wide margin. Enough, in fact, to turn and walk away, but even as this sensible approach suggested itself, Zoë was trying the wooden door at the side of the house; pushing it open to find a passage leading to the back. The way was partly blocked by a hedge which hadn't been shaved in a while, but she squeezed past with minor scratches, and reached the far end to find a hearse staring at her . . .

This was not the happiest surprise to encounter in the moonlight. Kay Dunstan's father, though, had been an undertaker. The barman had told her that. The car was a tool of the trade, not a horror movie prop. She wasn't going to find Sweeney stretched out on its rear shelf.

Zoë let her heart climb down to normal before registering everything else: the stone frog next to the overgrown pond; the dilapidated shelter under which sat a freezer, a wardrobe, some other odds and ends. Hardly ideal homes and gardens, but she was more interested in the light spilling on to the crazy paving from a recessed window. Falling to a crouch, she peeped round. Inside the house, an old man sat on a chair in the middle of a room. Of his companions, one had a bandage wrapping his head, and the other was Arkle.

It took most of Zoë's nerve not to scoot away. But she was invisible: dark night, light on; the most they'd see through the window was their own reflection. So she stayed where she was, pointlessly eavesdropping – she heard nothing bar traffic. Arkle was pacing, talking; bandage-head, who must be Trent Dunstan, was slumped against the far wall. As for the man in the chair, he'd be Kay Dunstan's father, and was somewhere else altogether – his attention fixed on a spot on the wall, as if a secret window blossomed there, the view from which was all-absorbing.

Perhaps the key element in the scene was that Arkle didn't have his crossbow with him.

And at that moment Arkle turned and looked into the night, and stared directly at her. Zoë immediately forgot what she knew and ducked round the corner, her heart racketing against her ribs. *What was it with this guy?* She'd seen big; she'd handled mean. But she didn't think she'd ever looked at anybody before and seen straight through to the darkness within. He was all silhouette; the kind of shadow children fear lurks under beds and in dark nooks. That would grab them if their bare foot hit the floor.

A noise behind her froze the blood in her veins. Then she clenched her fists; forced herself to her feet. Nobody appeared. She counted three, and risked a look round the corner. Arkle had his hand raised, but as she watched, he let it drop. Old man Blake didn't appear to have moved a muscle, or possibly even breathed, in the intervening period. Nobody was looking through the window. *Feeling better?* her inner Zoë asked. Her pulse slowed. 'Much,' she muttered. *Why are we still here, remind me?* But that was one she couldn't answer. There was no sign of Sweeney, and whatever was happening in the house was none of her business.

If Arkle's here, her inner Zoë remarked, *then he's not at his own place.*

Which meant, she translated for her own benefit, that looking for Sweeney at the Dunstans' would be a lot safer than hanging round here. So would returning to Dunstan & Sons, and shinning over the gate: the fact that Sweeney wasn't visible didn't mean he wasn't in there somewhere. Maybe in that tin cabin, handcuffed to a radiator. *Or underneath a mound of sand.* Beyond the reach of help: she hoped not. *Or beyond the reach of his chequebook*: yeah, thanks. Shut up.

One way or the other, time to go.

IV

'Did you hear that?' Arkle asked. He was looking out of the window.

What Trent could mostly hear was the noises in his head.

Arkle turned to Blake. 'What about you? Anything reach your eagle ears?'

Bit of humour here: the only thing that had reached Blake's ear the past half-hour was his own finger. And that was uncharacteristically energetic.

Before today, last time Arkle had seen old man Blake had been months ago – not to speak to; just to watch from over the road as Blake meandered out of a shop and stopped dead, as if he'd lost track of what to do next – *for fuck's sake*, Arkle had thought, *you're retired: what's to forget? Get up, put your trousers on: you're already halfway through your day*. That was when he'd had his thought about growing older: that it was just another way of fucking up. Blake had puzzled his way into the café next door after a while. Possibly not where he'd intended to go, but a good place to regroup.

And now he was a room ornament, staring at a wall, and nothing Arkle said was bringing him back.

'That murdering bitch of a daughter of yours,' for instance. 'She killed my brother.'

Blake had raised a polite eyebrow, as if Arkle had mentioned a common acquaintance who was in satisfactory health, sent good wishes, and hadn't killed anyone.

By now, hours later, raising an eyebrow would have ranked as a special effect.

Arkle looked at Trent. 'Any ideas?'

But ideas didn't figure on Trent's current agenda. That was what two and then some bottles of vodka did, though admittedly the blow Arkle had fetched him with the crossbow must have smarted.

Forgive and forget, though. Arkle had forgiven Trent for needing to be hit, and had largely forgotten about it.

Since then he'd nursed Trent tenderly – bandages, ointment, toast – and explained what they had to do next. Grief had been moved to the back burner. It was just the two of them now, and it was important they had a workable plan. Which would have been much easier if Baxter had been around to talk it through, but that was upside-down thinking. If Baxter was around, this wouldn't be happening.

To Trent, Arkle had said: 'Our brother's dead. What we have to focus on is what happened to the money.'

Trent mumbled something that might have been 'Banker'.

'That's right. He was our banker.' Jesus. They weren't kidding when they said it killed brain cells. 'And we don't know what he did with the money. Remember?' He made Trent eat more toast. 'But Kay does.'

Trent groaned. That would be the hangover kicking in. One of the best things Arkle had ever done was not drink any more. He'd had a tendency to lose control after a drink or two.

'I've an idea which way to go on this.'

His train of thought was broken by Trent being sick. Once he'd cleaned him up a bit – Trent looked like a lopsided panda; it was funny, really – he continued:

'Her old man. If she blabbed to anyone, it'll be him.'

Trent was sick again.

When you were down to your last brother, it was awesome how fucking tolerant you had to be.

After a few hours in old man Blake's company, though, one thing was clear – any information that had found its way into his head lately wasn't getting loose without a struggle.

'Does he ever actually leave the house, you think?' Arkle had pretty much given up addressing Blake directly: he was talking to Trent, or talking to the air. Current state of play, there wasn't a lot of difference.

But this time round, Trent answered. 'Paper,' he said.

Which was a start. Today, Trent's vocabulary had consisted of 'fugle', 'drosh' and 'wodka', and this was after he'd finished throwing up. 'Paper' was at least English, even if Arkle didn't have the first clue what he was on about.

'Paper,' he repeated. You did this with budgies and parrots: they said something and you said it back, to make them do it again. Pretty soon they wouldn't shut up saying it, and you could pretend they were talking to you. That was the theory. Arkle, frankly, didn't have the patience. 'What the fuck you on about?'

Trent pointed.

The paper. Today's paper was on the floor by Blake's chair, which meant he did actually leave the house, or at least left his chair. All of which indicated that the ambient temperature was drying Trent's brain out, but otherwise didn't help.

He had another go. 'Your daughter. Kay. Remember her, old man?' Not on the evidence. Something occurred to Arkle: something he should've thought of already. 'Katie.' Old man Blake called her Katie, not Kay. There was a flicker of recognition. 'Katie Blake. Are we getting somewhere?'

But whatever light switch had flipped in Blake's head flipped back again, leaving them all in the dark.

Arkle tried once more. 'When she came round, what did she talk about? . . . Hello? Anybody there?' He reached a hand out, intending to knock Blake's head – not hard: just getting his attention. But he let his fist drop halfway.

. . . It had seemed simple. He'd come up here for words with old man Blake: find out what Kay had told him; discover what hints she'd dropped. She was a woman, everyone was agreed on that. Women dropped hints. This was practically a natural law. So Arkle had been *sure* Blake would know what had happened to the money; Arkle was *dead certain* Kay would have told him. It occurred to him now to wonder about the source of this certainty, and wondering that was like running full tilt into a wall. Why was he sure? He just *was*, that was all. When Arkle had an idea, the important thing about it was this:

it was *his idea*. If it didn't work out, he was going to have to come up with another one, and it wasn't like the fuckers grew on trees.

At his feet now lay the newspaper Trent had drawn his attention to. Arkle wasn't a big reader – had been known to move his lips while watching TV – but he recognised the *News Chronicle* from the typeface even before he unfolded it and read *Inside! Today!* in the colour bar across the top.

A whole new idea occurred to him, making a noise like the door into the side passage . . .

'Wait here,' he said unnecessarily, heading for the front. Nobody else in that room was going anywhere.

Time to go . . .

For Zoë, the next few minutes – which were also her last this side of the coffin – passed with the slowness reserved for accidents, though nothing that happened to her during them was accidental. She did not hesitate after her last glimpse of Arkle through the window – fist raised as if he were about to clout the man in the chair; then dropped, as if he'd changed his mind – but turned to leave; she'd go and make sure Sweeney wasn't at the Dunstans' actual address: alive or dead; captive or lurking. It would not take much to dissuade him from thoughts of vengeance, if such possessed him. A clear look at consequences would re-establish common sense. With an amateur like Sweeney, putting the fear of God into him wouldn't be a problem either. She reached the overgrown hedge and swung round the corner, expecting to push her way through to the door, the street, the outside world. Instead she met a bright light, which she did not have time to interpret immediately, and which was in fact nowhere visible to anybody else – it happened inside Zoë when the blow struck her forehead, and a universe of stars showered down on her: bright blue happy stars that lasted, each of them, a lifetime.

But lifetimes pass, and so did the stars. They winked out, one by one.

Next it was dark, and she lay on her back, unable to move for the pain in her head. Somebody had hit her: that much she knew. She'd been hit before, though couldn't remember having been struck unconscious – it couldn't be good for the brain; there would be repercussions. And it was so so dark. She tried to move her feet, and barely could, and her immediate thought was that here was the first repercussion – some part of her neural system had fused, and none of the messages her brain sent to her feet were getting through. She'd lie here forever, unable to wriggle or stretch, because her wriggle and stretch commands didn't work any more. And panic gripped her, racked her like a wave, and she kicked and pushed at the same time, and found resistance all around.

Probably she shouted. Certainly, at some point, noise was everywhere; echoing minutely in an enclosed space, and her throat was raw and painful . . . She couldn't move because there were walls all around her; close walls with no give. She could punch and twist forever and make no dent in their permanence. She was in a box, a box not much bigger than herself. It might have been made to contain her. She might have been shaped for this end . . . An image of a hearse flashed through her mind before she went blank again; lost herself in a frenzy of screaming and punching; hurting her soon to be useless hands on walls that didn't flinch. This was more than fear. It was the last moments of the scariest film she'd ever seen, and it was real. This was Zoë's coffin.

And inside it, she knew with perfect certainty, she was going to die.

THREE

THE PARTY WALL

6

I

THE HOUSE WAS AN end-of-terrace on a road no wider than a lane, negotiating which required diplomacy as much as motor skills – Katrina had already witnessed a breakdown in relations when two cars met head-on, neither prepared to reverse three yards. Opposite was a garden square, surrounded by tall black railings set in stone. Once, you'd have needed a key to get in. Now, all you needed was the usual city armour: an indifference to discarded needles, used condoms, broken glass. When the gentrifying wave washed this far, it would be retoned as a stately pleasure garden, but for now it remained a winos' dormitory: peace and tidy greenery deep in its past, far in its future.

Her third-floor room was at the back, and looked down on an actual lane, much favoured as a shortcut by those heading to or from a local club – Heaven, or Paradise, or possibly The Sweet Hereafter: something, anyway, that promised more than it could deliver. No cars used this – three concrete bollards blocked one end – but revellers' noise woke her on her first night, and she got out of bed and stood by the window, while scattered groups of people wandered past, heedless of the sleeping houses around.

Jonno said, 'Probably best not to stand by the window, know what I mean?'

'Is my room wired for vision?'

He flushed. Twenty-two, he flushed easily. If Katrina had been of a mind, she could have made his daylight hours hell.

'There's a loose board,' he said. 'Just by your window? It creaks.'

In addition to being twenty-two, Jonno had a receding hairline he disguised with a buzz cut. Girls were growing taller, and men were growing bald. To compensate, he nurtured a goatee. Without it, Katrina would have pegged him at fourteen.

'Who do you think might see me?'

'Better safe than sorry, know what I mean?'

'I think so,' she said. 'It's not terribly complicated.'

He looked at her blankly, no idea what she meant.

Jonno was a staff writer on the *News Chronicle*, or so he'd told her. Jonno, in truth, was a gopher on the *News Chronicle*: a newish daily yet to claim a grip on a readership, but whose proprietor had always wanted a newspaper to play with, and was throwing money at it like it was a snowball fight. The experienced journos he'd hired were snatching the cash, beefing up their expenses, and keeping in touch with the hirers on the broadsheets. Tyros like Jonno were fetching sandwiches and telling their mates they were press.

The actual writer on Katrina's story was a thirty-year veteran called Helen Coe: a big-boned ex-smoker whose light was fading fast – while the more cliché-prone in her trade succumbed to drink or quit to write The Book, Helen was gradually giving up the struggle to remain awake twelve hours at a stretch.

'You know how many council meetings I covered, way back when?'

A lot, Katrina guessed.

'Felt like all of them. Stayed awake, too. But these things catch up.' She was fifties, with mad grey hair and thick glasses; she wore a tatty green cardigan, and a belted brown raincoat for outdoors. 'After that, I covered Westminster, then a crime beat. Half my career happened way past bedtime. No wonder I'm knackered.'

'You never considered another line of work?' Katrina asked.

'And miss the glamour?' Helen spoke without apparent irony, but in the light from an unwashed window, the room had the charm of a prison officers' social club. 'You know why most politics happens at night? So MPs have an excuse for a London flat. Gives them the opportunity to shag their research assistants.' She paused. Jonno blinked four times in quick succession. This was code, Katrina decided, for *No way is my career going to be like this. Not even in a joke.* 'If they all went home to their wives at night, you think the transport system would be quite so far up hell's back passage?'

She seemed to expect a reply.

'Some MPs are women, I've noticed,' said Katrina.

'That's very sweet, dear.' Helen shifted on her stool. There was one usable chair in the room: a straight-backed armchair whose padding was a distant memory. Katrina had this. Jonno stood sentry by the door, a post from which dispatch was as regular and inevitable as Helen Coe's need for refreshment. 'Halfway chance of a decent pension, and I'd be into the sunset.' She yawned, without bothering to hide it. 'Then Jonno'd have to write your story. And Jonno has a *degree*.'

Katrina looked at Jonno. 'I'm sure you'll make a very good journalist.'

'And I'm sure he'll make a very nice cup of tea,' said Helen. 'Soon as you like, dear.'

Jonno left.

Once Katrina had called the police, events had occurred both very swiftly and alarmingly slowly. She was taken to a succession of rooms in a large police station, where cop-show reality swallowed her up – fingerprints and photographs; questions and more questions. She surrendered her clothes, and was given a medical examination by a male doctor in the presence of a female officer. The left side of her face was paid careful attention. 'Tell me how this happened?' She told him, then told him again. Her new clothes were baggy grey coveralls, and felt like a replacement identity; in this role, she'd carry out useful but uncomplicated tasks, such as cleaning floors or unblocking drains. The attending female officer remained impervious throughout, and Katrina attempted a similar detachment. *What happened to my face is part of somebody else's statement.* And what happened to her dress sense was somebody else's wardrobe. A switch had flipped inside her, allowing a pragmatic, purely functional Katrina to take over; who responded to a prod, but otherwise might have been laminated. Meanwhile, phone calls were made and a lawyer appeared. Possibly in a puff of smoke: she didn't notice. The plan was to get through this while noticing as little as possible, though all the time in the cold hard centre of her being, she wrapped layer after layer of unfeeling around the knowledge of what she'd done.

When she needed the toilet, she was accompanied. Washing her hands, she stared into the mirror – the face staring back was a party mask.

'Slight fracture,' the doctor had muttered, taking notes. As if he were talking to himself, and Katrina merely an onlooker at her own examination.

Now, looking into the mirror, she murmured, 'What is your favourite colour?' Purple or blue; black or crimson?

'What?'

'Purple,' Katrina said. Then: 'Nothing. Doesn't matter.'

She was taken back to the room she belonged to, and the questions began again.

All that had come to an abrupt end, she told Helen Coe.

'Oh yes. You know how things go in waves, dear? Reality TV, boy bands, Tory leaders? You're riding the zeitgeist. The appeal courts have been backed up for months releasing battered women who've crossed the line.' She reached into her bag for a cigarette, before remembering she didn't smoke. This happened a dozen times a day. 'Before they charge you with something that's going to be trampled underfoot by the law lords – always supposing you're convicted, dear – the CPS are going to be looking very carefully at the alternatives.'

'Which is likely to be?'

'Wilful misuse of a kitchen implement, if the *Chronicle*'s got anything to do with it. Mind you, you're not out of the woods yet. You know what it means, dear, having a newspaper on your side?'

'It says nice things?'

'If you're lucky. But it also means the others are going to be kicking seven kinds of shit out of you.' Helen almost leaned back, then recalled she was on a stool. 'You noticed the small print? If you're convicted, we won't be paying for your story.'

'Yes.'

'Another good reason for being innocent.'

Sometime during the second day of police, Katrina had been shown a tabloid, and found it used the word 'murderess'; the inverted commas a standard defence against libel action. That *-ess* troubled Katrina. Actress, stewardess, waitress – all had shed their suffixes; succumbed to the gender neutral. So why did 'murderess' still have that cachet? Because it was sexy, the idea that women were dangerous. It gave men the notion that taming remained incomplete.

She had the feeling that sharing this with Helen Coe wasn't a good idea.

So here she was, anyway, in what the *Chronicle*'s crocodiles probably termed a safe house: a barely furnished three-storey in an area that would be on its way up just as soon as it touched bottom. She felt like she'd wandered into an urban fairy tale. There was just enough of everything for all of them, provided

Jonno didn't mind going without – there were mugs and plates for three, but they were short a knife and fork. Plus, of course, he had nowhere to sit. Not that Helen would have let him sit much.

On the first evening, when it became apparent that Helen wasn't staying – no offence, dear, but they don't pay me enough – Katrina had wondered if this was going to be stage two of the nightmare: stuck in a rambling flophouse with a kid who hadn't been alone with a woman yet. That was before she discovered how easily he blushed.

Once Helen had gone he told her, dead serious, 'If you hear anybody at the door in the night, stay put. I'll deal with it.'

She asked who it was likely to be, this late-night caller.

'Probably no one.' He shrugged. 'There's drinkers and druggies about, know what I mean? It's the square over the road, they congregate there.'

It occurred to her that he was expecting rival journalists to turn up and spirit her off. 'Jonno? If I hear anything in the night, I'll stay where I am.'

Because if he was her protection, she'd be better off hiding under a duvet.

Later, after she'd been woken by the revellers, she lay staring at the ceiling, remembering some parts of the past few days; forgetting others. Her face throbbed. But if not for that, she wouldn't be here at all. She'd have been charged with murder. It was one thing describing how you'd been struck, hit, *beaten*, but without the bruises, it could just be a story. Baxter, dead on their kitchen floor, might have been a sweet innocent; his brothers, grieving lambs. She shuddered. If there came a knock on the door in the dark, rival journalists wouldn't be on her mind. She'd be thinking Arkle; she'd be thinking Trent. Blood revenge would draw them here. And of course, there was also the money . . .

They were not supposed to know she knew about the

money, but they'd know. Arkle, anyway, would. From the first time she'd laid eyes on him, he'd had a way of staring straight through her, as if already wishing she weren't there. He'd seen her as a threat, which was almost funny, because it was impossible to be in Arkle's presence without knowing where the real threat lay. That phrase about a riddle wrapped in a mystery wrapped in an enigma might have been coined for him, except for riddle, mystery and enigma read aggravation, hostility and blunt instrument.

For as long as Katrina had known him, Arkle's appetites had been diminishing. He drank no alcohol; never ate a decent meal. But he was eaten up by hunger all the same. It just lay in less obvious directions.

Two days after the Oxford weekend she had read about the robbery there, and had known, even without the significant detail, that the trip had been reconnaissance. This had not come as a surprise. Some things Bax had told her, others he tried not to, and it was an aspect of his masculinity that he'd imagined that the things he didn't tell her, she didn't get to know about. As if she were shrouded in ignorance, and her only light shone through holes he punched . . . Among other things, he'd told her where the money was. Which he hadn't told Arkle or Trent.

'Why not?'

'Arkle's a little . . . unsteady.'

He was telling her?

'Arkle's a little impulsive. He can only focus on one thing at a time.' This was delivered with an air of interested detachment, as if Baxter were narrating a documentary. In a way, he'd spent a lot of time doing that: providing the voiceover for whatever Arkle was up to. 'He prefers it this way. Trust me. Keeps his issues from being clouded.'

Though it didn't take much to cloud Arkle's issues. The significant detail in the newspaper report was that somebody walking past the target at the wrong time had wound up with a bolt in his leg.

Katrina closed her eyes, blotting out the ceiling, but not thoughts of Arkle, or Baxter. Arkle was straining at the leash. That's what that detail meant. Was probably frothing at the mouth, in fact. Firing his crossbow at a warm two-legged body would have been the highlight of his day.

Arkle: hostility, aggression, blunt instrument.

Baxter: simply dead.

All three had been adopted – strange that they'd forged such a unit. Or perhaps it was inevitable, after years of being harried from pillar to post, that they'd drop a common anchor in the first available harbour. No wonder Arkle had always looked at her as if she were a pirate – he wasn't a man for whom romance figured on the agenda. Arkle understood the nature of alliance, but hadn't quite sussed out what was in it for Bax. What turned out to be in it for Bax was a knife in the heart.

A passing car threw shadows across the ceiling, and when it stopped she knew they'd come for her. But they hadn't. It was lost, that was all; a lost car having to stop and reverse, because of the concrete bollards at the alley's end. After a while her pulse steadied. This room – bare floorboards, a narrow bed and a thin curtain; one wooden chair on which she'd draped a change of clothing – was sanctuary for now, courtesy of the *News Chronicle*, but it wouldn't remain so for long. She wasn't sure how they'd manage it, but they'd find her. Sooner or later, they'd find her.

And Arkle's appetite was just starting to wake.

II

Arkle and Trent. Arkle and Trent. Arkle, Baxter and Trent . . .

Baxter had been the smart one, able to work through the logistics of a given situation to the satisfaction of the important parties. And Trent generally managed to do what he was told. He could, for instance, carry heavy stuff a lot further than you'd imagine, given what a fucking dwarf he was. As for Arkle . . . Arkle, to get to the point, was a creative genius.

They were heading into London; Arkle driving, because of Trent's head. Trent had regained maybe sixty per cent vision, but only in the eye he could see out of, so there was room for improvement. Arkle was optimistic he'd be more or less sighted before long. Meanwhile, on Arkle's knee lay the *News Chronicle* he'd taken from old man Blake's, folded open to the story flagged above the headline: *Inside! Today!* – a 'special report' on 'wives who kill'. It turned out there was more than one of them. It turned out there was a fucking epidemic: the big surprise was there were any married men still upright. If Blake hadn't retired he'd be rich on the overtime, shovelling the poor bastards away. It seemed there was a legal defence available – if he left the toilet seat up, you could whack him – and women jailed as murderers these ten years gone were hitting the streets like there was no tomorrow. Kay Dunstan's name didn't figure, but more to come was promised . . .

Arkle, creative genius, could put two and two together. The TV had said a newspaper had bought Kay's story: that would be the *Chronicle*. The 'special report' was the first in a promised series: keep reading, and he'd end up with the inside dope on Baxter's killing, complete with smiling photograph. *Look at me now*, she'd be saying, and she'd be saying it directly to Arkle. *Look at me now. Your brother's dead, and I'm getting paid for the details*. Not to mention the rest of the money, of course: the money Bax had been in charge of, and which the bitch had stolen on top of everything else.

'You will ask me nicely if you can give it back,' he said, and it was only when Trent grunted in reply that he knew he'd spoken out loud.

'How's your head?' he asked. This was something he was making an effort at: showing kindness and consideration to Trent. Trent said something in reply, but he didn't listen. 'Yeah, yeah. Anyway, I had another idea. You want to hear it?'

'Are we nearly there yet?'

Trent really was milking that wound. How the fuck should Arkle know? Was he in charge of geography? They'd know when they reached London because of all the London stuff: Marble Arch, Buckingham Palace, the London Eye. Madame Tussaud's. Still, he let it pass. 'What I was thinking, we find one of these internet cafés, cruise the Web. Bax reckoned there's nothing you can't find out with a computer.'

After a while Trent said, 'Maybe.'

Count to ten, Arkle advised himself. He reached two, then said, 'For all the help you are, I should dump you by the side of the road. You want to be dumped by the side of the road?'

'. . . No.'

'And don't think I'm fucking slowing down, neither.'

'Sorry, Arkle.'

'Yeah, *sorry Arkle.* You think it's easy, having to make all the decisions? You think I'm having fun?' He drove two miles in silence. 'And another thing. You look like a mad panda in that fucking bandage. Take it off.'

'Arkle—'

'Take it off.'

Trent unwound the bandage. Parts of it stuck to his head, and he removed those bits very carefully indeed.

When it was a sticky mess between Trent's feet, Arkle said, 'There. You look a lot better.'

He looked like a burns victim, in fact, but changing your mind was weakness.

Arkle said, 'We got the name of this paper, right, and we got the name of this journo.' He glanced down at the paper to remember what it was. 'Helen Coe. She's the one writing this story. We need to talk to Helen Coe.'

He kept driving, and eventually they reached London – Marble Arch, Buckingham Palace, the London Eye. Madame Tussaud's.

So they found an internet café. Arkle didn't know where they were, exactly, but that was the point of the internet: it didn't matter where you were. He paid for half an hour, because how long could it take, then again thirty minutes later, because who knew it would take this long? Kids surfed the Web constantly, and Arkle was older than any kid he'd met. But maybe they knew something he didn't, because when he typed *Where is Helen Coe?* into a search engine all he got was a list of random websites. He'd be better off wandering the streets, shouting her name. And Trent was a help – was he fuck.

Trent – slouched next to him – hadn't touched a drop in days, but smelled like alcohol. It was a big responsibility being the oldest. Arkle had done all the driving, all the thinking, and the best Trent could manage was this shagged-out zombie act. His head was kind of splotchy, too. From a distance it looked like a birthmark, but Arkle had to deal with it up close, and frankly it was making him feel ill.

He found himself looking at a screen telling him that the page he wanted couldn't be found, and swore loudly. Then noticed he was being scrutinised by a black kid who looked about eleven or six or something. 'You got a problem?'

'You ever used a computer before?'

It was lucky Arkle was a creative genius, because anyone else would have smacked the kid. Maybe four foot high: it wouldn't have needed a big smack. Baggy T-shirt; pair of jeans he might grow into if he lived another six years. Which depended on him not bothering Arkle any more.

'You're doing it wrong,' the kid said.

This was constructive?

'You're supposed to use commas,' the kid said.

Now he fucking tells him. Arkle typed *Where, is, Helen, Coe?*, and got the same mad list he'd got before.

'Not them kind of commas,' the kid said.

Arkle looked at him. 'You work here?' he asked.

The kid stared. 'I'm nine,' he said.

Arkle had been bigger than that when he was nine, definite. 'And?'

Turned out there was an electoral register site. Arkle fed the kid Baxter's credit card number, and the kid did the rest.

Ten minutes later, forty quid and a credit card lighter, Arkle and Trent were back in the van. Trent looked more alert now. Maybe the nap had done him good.

Arkle said, 'You gunna whinge the rest of your life, or give me a hand here?'

'I'm feeling better,' Trent said.

He still sounded like he was chewing mothballs, but it was supportive not to mention this.

''Cause we got a list of Helen Coes twenty names long. It'll take a while to work round them.' He pulled out, and someone behind him tooted angrily. This happened: people saw a white van, they hit the horn. Plain bad manners. 'And every hour wasted . . .' He paused at a junction and lost his thread. 'Is an hour wasted,' he finished.

Trent asked, 'We got an A to Z?' and it was the first time in a while Arkle had heard him say 'we'.

'Somewhere.'

'And we got Baxter's phone,' said Trent. 'We can work something out.'

III

It was part of the deal: the whole of the deal, in fact. As long as she was here, she had to answer questions. All the *Chronicle* wanted was her story. What Katrina wanted was somewhere to hide.

A chair, a stool and a man by the door . . . She felt like Goldilocks, in a dwelling short one bear.

And here was Mummy Bear, her chief interrogator:

'How long were you married?'

'A year. A bit more than.'

'Had you known him long?'

'Since we were teenagers.'

'How did you meet?'

Once upon a time there were three boys, and their names were . . .

'Katrina?'

Katrina, eyes fixed on the window – through which she could see only the raggy tops of exhausted trees in the square opposite – said, 'There was a place the kids used to hang out. Not a club. Just a public space, the top of the High Street.'

'He was a skateboarder, was he?'

Katrina said, 'Well, he followed it.'

What he did was follow *them*. It wasn't hard to work out who had money. Baxter, Arkle and Trent had it down to an art: they could shake a 'boarder down in a lot less time than it took to learn a double back flip. And were good at ensuring nobody complained afterwards.

Complaint meant official intervention. First time that happened, the boy in question broke both legs the following week, and told anyone who asked, and a few who didn't, he'd fallen off his skateboard.

Kay had heard about the brothers before she laid eyes on them.

'I'd have given them the money twice over,' somebody said. 'Just to make him stop looking at me.'

Him was Arkle, of course.

'The brown one, though. Funny thing is, he's kind of nice.'

Which should have been news, but wasn't, somehow – the brown one was a thug who robbed other kids and damaged them if they squealed. This should have shown on the surface; he should have had stupefied eyes and a fixed lip curl; a face waiting for a tattoo to happen. Instead he had white teeth, open features, and a smile that suggested, if it was up to him, you'd be friends, and happy to share your wealth. All this, Kay put together from second-hand details, as if she were colouring by numbers without having been told what colours the numbers meant. So why wasn't this news? Because it was there in countless films and numberless books. The good-looking bad boy. The one who stole your heart along with everything else he could get his hands on.

Of course, now she thought about it, none of those stories ended happily.

'And did you think you could change him?'

'Change him?'

'That's the usual pattern, dear. Women choose men hoping they'll change. Men choose women hoping they won't.'

Helen had taken to pacing the room, smoking imaginary cigarettes – tucking her biro between her lips; breathing out clouds of invisible ink.

'Well,' Katrina said. 'I didn't suppose he'd be pinching skateboarders' lunch money all his life. But I expect he'd have reached a similar conclusion on his own.'

'You thought he'd graduate to mugging grown-ups?'

'I thought he'd grow out of it. It wasn't like he'd had the best start in life. Shuffled from one foster home to the next. When Roy Dunstan adopted him, it was more for the sake of the firm than anything else.'

'Seems odd he chose a mixed-race kid, then. If he was after surrogate sons.'

'That was his wife's idea. I never knew her. Baxter said she was a good lady.'

'That doesn't seem to have affected them much, does it? What did she think of their thieving?'

'She'd died by then,' Katrina said. 'Like I say, Bax didn't have the easiest of childhoods. None of them did.'

And maybe that was a connection Helen would want to know about; maybe she should talk about dead mothers. She could say a bond developed because both were motherless. Baxter, in fact, had lost mothers several times over: first the real one, an anonymous teenager he never hungered to know more about; then various foster mums, among them some real demons. And lastly Mary Dunstan, who had been kind to him and his new brothers, but who had died within two years of the adoptions. Her heart, a rock for others, had proved unreliable in the end.

But she didn't say any of that, because it would have been a lie. Or rather, would have been such a small part of the truth, but sounding so big and meaningful, that it would have allowed Helen to think she'd found the key to her whole story.

And what was the rest of the truth? That she had been attracted to Baxter because he was beautiful – the word itself: he wasn't good-looking, but beautiful, and it didn't matter how many muggings he participated in, how many threats and menaces he casually dispensed, he'd had looks that could stop a teenager's heart. Her own was no more reliable, in its way, than Mary Dunstan's.

The deal was, she'd give the *Chronicle* their story. But stories were, by their nature, untrue.

Once upon a time . . .

'Tell me about his brothers.'

Katrina said, 'What do they have to do with anything?'

'At the risk of sounding unsympathetic, dear, can I remind you of one detail?'

(Helen Coe might look like Denholm Elliot in drag, but she had a core of pure steel running through her.)

'We own you. The *News Chronicle* owns you. Which, for current purposes, means I own you. And if you do not give me a full and detailed answer to every question I ask, I will rip you up and flush you down the nearest drain. Are we agreed on that?'

'I can walk out of here any time I like.'

'And what happens when you're arrested again? Because the police aren't finished with you yet. And next time, you won't have a friendly newspaper batting for you. You ever seen footage of lions on a gazelle, dear?'

Katrina didn't answer.

'Start a feeding frenzy among the press, you'd change places with the gazelle. Believe me. I've seen people chewed up so bad, what was spat out afterwards didn't look organic, let alone human. And these were folk who'd merely put their genitals where they shouldn't, dear. They didn't murder anyone.'

'Neither. Did. I.'

'Really, dear? That's interesting.' Helen pulled back the lace curtain, and looked down on the street below. Then let it drop.

'Why don't you tell me all about it? Start with his brothers.'

'Trent,' she said, 'would have been the runt of the litter. Whatever litter he came from.'

Trent, she didn't say, spent his teenage years waiting for the next hammer to fall. At the time of life when how you looked determined your worth, he was designed to be a cast-off: sniggered at in the school corridor, laughed out loud at in the gym. Except he hadn't bothered a lot with school, and nobody was going to so much as chuckle with Arkle nearby, which was always.

'Arkle, though – he's the oldest – Arkle kind of imagines himself the alpha male in any gathering.'

Arkle, she didn't say, would have been left on a hillside in some societies; those that would sooner make the odd small sacrifice than nurture their own destruction.

'Imagines?'

'I've always thought your true alpha male had rather more going on up top.'

Jonno, from his doorway watchtower, allowed himself a quiet smile.

'He's not a clever man, then,' Helen said.

'He's cunning. And he may not be a man of ideas, but the ideas he does have, he grips pretty tight. He's not somebody you want to get in the way of.'

'Yes. I saw him scatter a crowd the other day. A bull couldn't have done it more effectively.' Katrina waited, but Helen didn't elaborate. 'Go on.'

'He's probably a sociopath. Seriously. I don't think he quite believes in other people, and he certainly doesn't care what happens to them.'

The look on Jonno's face was now that of a man contemplating somebody he knows he's superior to, who luckily isn't there.

'And this is the family you married into.'

'I wasn't marrying Arkle.'

'But they sound a unit. Did you really think they'd stop being one afterwards?'

Katrina said, 'Why are you so interested in them? They've nothing to do with what happened to . . . us.' Happened to Baxter, she meant.

Helen Coe said, 'I saw your brothers-in-law the other day. They're . . . intriguing.'

'Nice word.'

Jonno said, 'This Arkle sounds like the kind of bloke penicillin was supposed to eradicate, know what I mean?'

'When your opinion is called for,' Helen said without

looking round, 'I'll be *sure* to let you know.' To Katrina she said: 'Arkle was in a state. I don't suppose you're in his top ten right now.'

'I never was.'

'Another reason for hoping you're not charged with Baxter's murder.'

Katrina laughed: a full-out laugh which surprised all of them. It didn't last long.

In the silence which followed, she said: 'Do you seriously think Arkle's going to give a damn what the police or the courts decide? As far as he's concerned, it's a closed issue. His brother's dead. I'm to blame. End of story.'

The creaking noise the others heard while digesting this was a floorboard relaxing.

Helen said, 'Yes. Well. You're safe now.'

'That's good to know.'

'Nobody knows you're here.'

The doorbell rang.

IV

When Trent squinted he could just about achieve normal vision, and he was grateful for this; partly in a non-specific way that things hadn't turned out worse, but partly too to Arkle, who could have hit him harder if he'd wanted. Trent knew this because Arkle had mentioned it once or twice.

'It's pretty tough,' Arkle had said, 'but that doesn't mean you can't do it serious damage.'

Trent rubbed his head in agreement. Serious damage. Something might have come loose inside; be floating unanchored, even now.

'As it is, it'll probably need adjusting. You might have thrown the aim off. Just the slightest kink'll do that.'

'Sorry,' Trent mumbled.

'Yeah, well. You're my brother. Doesn't matter how often you fuck up. We're tied by blood.'

Some of which had dried by now, leaving an almost black stain on Arkle's crossbow's stock.

It had been a long day. They had a list of addresses, a map and a phone, and with patience might have found Helen Coe without moving an inch. But things were never easy. Directory enquiries squirted out most of the phone numbers, but three remained unaccounted for; of the numbers available, another three didn't answer, and two hung up on Arkle. 'Does this silly bitch expect me to come knocking on her door?' he wondered, when a voice declined to tell him whether she wrote for the *Chronicle*. No: what the silly bitch expected was, he'd fucked off once she'd cut the connection. Trent decided not to tell him this. 'Let's do the unknowns geographically,' he said. 'Geographically' was his longest word in days, and it came out funny. Nearest first is what he'd meant.

Geographically, though, left a lot of ground to cover.

So here they were, parked half-on/half-off a stretch of pavement lined with a row of black, Trent-and-a-bit high railings, on the other side of which city-type undergrowth scrabbled for life. Across the road were some tall, shabby but expensive houses; old enough to have kings' names attached – Edwardian, Georgian, whatever – instead of Wimpey or Barratt, like the estate they'd checked out earlier further west; an area hemmed in by high-rises whose balcony railings were painted bright primary colours. It had been like looking at a stack of children's playpens, piled higher than a beanstalk.

. . . Trying to move around London had been like driving through quicksand. Everything was a bastard, and their map didn't understand that you couldn't get anywhere without being diverted, or pitched into no-go zones. Arkle's patience lasted as long as a Christmas cracker, and Trent's thirst was growing. All he'd had to drink was a bottle of water.

He could foresee days of this – backwards and forwards, backwards and forwards, wearing deep grooves in their out-of-date map. Don't try telling Arkle how to do things, though. Arkle was the brains, now Baxter was history.

. . . And with that thought had come the image of Baxter, lying dead on the kitchen floor. Kay had taken a knife and stuck it in his heart, like something from a rock and roll song. To stop him hitting her, the newspapers said, or that's what they said *she* said. Well, she would, wouldn't she? Bottom line was, Baxter remained dead. And now Arkle wanted Kay dead too, and Trent didn't think that was such a poor idea. As far back as he cared to remember, Baxter had been his big brother, and while Arkle had protected Trent from the rest of the world, Baxter had protected him from Arkle. And now he was gone. No, Trent had no problem with Arkle's objective; he just thought it would be handy if they could do it without getting caught. Not using a van with Dunstan & Sons on its side panels might be a step in the right direction.

But now, anyway, they were parked half-on/half-off a stretch of pavement, and the next potential Helen Coe lived right across the road.

'I did the last one,' Arkle told him.

Trent could hardly talk. Well, he could talk, but it was a long shot anyone but Arkle would have the faintest idea what his noises meant.

'We share them between us, it'll take half the time.'

It needed Baxter to pick the holes in that one, but Bax was way too dead to be any use now.

He got out of the van, though. Arguing with Arkle generally didn't make it past his brain's suggestion box. Big soft raindrops were starting to fall as he crossed the road; were hitting the tarmac with fat plopping noises, as if a swarm of frogs had been tipped from an overhead cradle. As he approached the house, he caught his reflection in a window, and wondered for a moment what that freak was up to – the lopsided, squat accident whose face looked like someone had tried to force it through a sieve . . . Some of this, but not enough, was the crazy-mirror distortion of flawed glass.

Trent climbed three steps to the front door, and rang the bell.

V

The doorbell rang, and it was a policeman. The police knew Katrina was here, of course – she hadn't been charged yet, but it was a speeding certainty she would be: only the nature of the charge remained to be determined. 'A matter of forensics,' this particular policeman told her. 'Of seeing how the evidence holds up.'

Helen Coe snorted. 'A matter of politics, more like. Charge her with murder, there'll be public outrage. You're aware that *that* has been in every paper in the land?'

That was Katrina's face, or the red-and-ochre bruise decorating it: an angry smudge that changed its shape depending on the light – now forensics, now politics.

'If I could have five minutes with Mrs Dunstan?'

Ms Blake, Katrina didn't say.

Helen Coe left, muttering. Jonno went with her.

The policeman, who had red hair but whose name always seemed to leave Katrina's mind as soon as enter it, had come a long way to talk to her, and wasn't happy about it. 'It used to be the law ran the country. Not the media.'

Katrina knew who she was with the police. Knew who they expected her to be. So she didn't reply to this.

'But that's what happens when a newspaper boss is mates with a chief constable.' Once he'd got that off his chest, he felt better. 'How's your face?'

'Improving. Thank you.'

He glanced about. 'They treating you all right?'

'I'm fine.'

'There's a few things I need to go over. About the morning your husband died.'

'Again?'

He said, without apology, 'That's how it works.'

She was remembering a children's game, Murder in the Dark, in one of whose variations the designated detective asks everyone the same questions over and over. Whoever gives inconsistent answers was the murderer.

'I understand.'

He bent and picked a folded newspaper from the floor, then collected what had been lying underneath it. 'It seems the guardian of the free press forgot something.' He showed her Helen Coe's palm-sized dictaphone. 'Wouldn't want her to waste her batteries.'

He turned it off.

Coe was spitting feathers by the time the policeman left: who did he think he was? (He thought he was the police.) Whose story was this anyway? (It was Katrina's.) And wasn't it way past lunchtime?

Jonno already had his jacket on; was already out of the door.

'How cooperative were you?' Helen asked.

'You weren't listening?'

'You heard the man. He wanted to speak to you alone.'

And to be fair, when the policeman had checked, neither Helen nor Jonno were at the keyhole.

Katrina said, 'I answered his questions.'

'The *Chronicle*'s paying for an exclusive on this.'

Katrina stared at her.

'Yeah, all right. Can't blame me for getting irritated.' Helen Coe ran fingers through her hair, in case it was settling down. 'It seems we've spent a lot of time talking, and nothing much gets said.'

'Maybe you're asking the wrong questions,' Katrina told her.

'Maybe you're not answering them properly.'

Katrina didn't have an answer for that, true. She said nothing.

Helen Coe asked, 'Why did you marry him?'

'Why does anybody get married?'

'Try not to look on this as a conversation, Katrina. Try to think of it as an opportunity to get your side across.'

'He won't be putting his side now, will he?'

'There's people'll do that for him.'

A thought occurred to her. 'Are you on my side, Helen?'

After a moment, Helen said, 'This is my job.'

'What about the *Chronicle*? Is the *Chronicle* on my side?'

'Of course. Now, always and forever.'

'Your apprentice has gone for pizza. You can tell me the truth.'

'You're not a stupid woman, dear, so don't pretend to be. We're a newspaper. Whose side we're on depends on how many copies we're selling.'

'So long as we both know where we stand.'

'Good. So. When did he start hitting you?'

A question like any other, from a list to be completed.

'Katrina?'

'Not till after we married.'

'That right?'

'You think I'd have married him if I'd known he would hit me?'

'I don't know. When was the first time?'

Katrina glazed over. The past was to be looked at darkly. You did not easily start turning stones when you knew that under one of them, something ugly hid.

She said, 'It was quite soon after. Soon after we were married. I forgot to do something, something really stupid. I forgot to pay the paper bill. Which meant one of us had to go out again, though we'd both been out already . . .'

The windowpane rattled at a gust of wind. Fat raindrops pattered on the glass.

'I'd have gone myself,' she said. 'I didn't think it was that big a deal.'

After a moment, Helen asked, 'Where did he hit you?'

Katrina touched her cheek. Purple or blue; black or crimson. *What is your favourite colour?*

'Jesus,' said Helen Coe. She stood, and noticed she'd been sitting on her dictaphone. Perhaps it had been an accident she'd left it there, thought Katrina. Either way, she switched it on now. To celebrate the event, the pair fell silent.

Tick tick tick. Tock tock tock. In a matter of weeks, the trees across the road would have scattered their leaves on the pavements; making an untidy slippery mess; choking and gagging the storm drains. Puddles would flood the kerbs, while the grass behind the railings grew brown, and tried to dig its way back inside the earth. All as a way of underlining that time went on, regardless of what you did with it. But Katrina would be long departed before this came to pass. She hoped.

'Did you tell anyone?'

'Then? No.'

'How about later?'

'Only much later. And it was nobody important.'

'Who?'

'I don't remember. And I didn't really tell him, anyway. It was just . . . We were talking. I think he might have guessed.'

Helen said, 'This really isn't going to work unless you start being a little clearer.'

'It was in a hotel bar in Oxford. His name was Tim. Bax was . . . out on business. We got talking. I had a bruise, not as bad as this, but . . . He couldn't not notice.'

'And you told him your husband did it?'

'No. But I think he guessed.'

He might have guessed. He had seemed sympathetic; the

kind of man who might have seen a little further than his own ends required . . . On the other hand, he had turned out to be very drunk. Not noisy, stupid, scene-making drunk, but bottom-of-a-deep-dark-hole drunk, and unlikely to clamber out on his own. Perhaps, once his clouds had cleared, he'd remember their conversation. But she wouldn't bet on it.

'What about friends?'

'What about them?'

'Didn't you tell anybody else?'

'Everybody I know knows Baxter. Knew him.' Tenses were dangerous: now and then they came out wrong. 'I told some people I'd walked into doors.' Which was what everybody said when they'd picked up extracurricular bruising. It was part of the social code, a notch above *We must get together really soon.*

'Did his brothers know?'

Katrina said, 'Arkle's just barely aware the world keeps turning when he's asleep. Trent . . . Trent knew. I think he knew.'

Trent had seen her once, with a bruise in place. She was reasonably certain, anyway, that he had seen her, while sober enough to know what he was seeing.

Helen was pacing the room again. Downstairs, the door opened and closed: that would be Jonno, back with the pizzas. The thought of eating – especially of eating pizza – filled Katrina with disgust. Lately, nothing but takeaway food. Her digestive system must be starting to resemble an overstuffed binliner.

To the window; back again. It was Katrina who was unspilling secrets; Helen Coe who was agitated and unhappy.

'Why did you stay?' she asked suddenly.

'I suppose you'd have left.'

'After I'd nailed his balls to the ironing board.'

Katrina laughed: a short sharp shock that startled both of them.

'I'm not joking, dear. You stay with them, you give them licence to do it again.'

'Is this a new phenomenon to you?'

'What, he beats me because he loves me? Of course not.'

'Because you seem to have trouble comprehending it.'

'Maybe that's because you're an intelligent woman. Too intelligent to fall for that bullshit.'

'You think it's an IQ issue?'

'Maybe, maybe not. But I'd put a man's lights out before I let him hit me twice.'

Katrina said, 'Your point being?'

And up the stairs and into the room came Jonno. 'Food's on the table,' he said. Neither woman replied. 'Yeah, well,' he added, and went back the way he came.

Once his footsteps had disappeared downstairs, the only sound in the room was the humming of the bored dictaphone.

'I suppose,' Helen said after a while, 'he didn't exactly get away with it, did he?'

Another squall of wind, and the outside world turned to water.

7

I

THE RAIN, ALREADY HARD, redoubled its efforts, and for five minutes bounced off pavements, windows, rooftops, like the trailer for an environmental damage movie. From the shelter of a shop awning Helen Coe waited until it eased, thinking of this as London weather as opposed to any other kind, which made her wonder if she'd been here too long. It was still steadily raining, though less torrentially, when she moved on.

Her flat was three bus stops from the *Chronicle* house and boasted a canal view, though you'd have needed a periscope. At the corner shop she picked up milk, bread, teabags and washing-up liquid, wishing she'd sent Jonno out for them earlier. It wasn't that she didn't like Jonno; more that she regarded it a duty to make his apprenticeship unpleasant. To do otherwise would be to waste her experience. These thoughts carried her the last hundred yards; where, flimsy white plastic bag in one hand, she pawed free her keys with the other, and let herself into the building. She lived on the first floor, and had small excuse for using the lift. A small excuse, though, was all she needed. Somebody she didn't recognise stepped out as she stepped in, and for the time it took the machinery to deliver her to her landing, she endured the masculine smell he'd left behind: aftershave and hair gel, on its way to being swamped by pubs and smoke.

In her kitchen, she unpacked her purchases; transferred the milk to the fridge, left the rest on the table. The kitchen wasn't large, and unput-away groceries made it seem smaller very quickly. Helen coped with this by not minding. She poured a medium-enormous gin and tonic, then moved into her sitting room, draped her raincoat over a chair and sank into the sofa. The day's newspapers lay stacked beside her. Ignoring them, she turned the radio on, and caught the end of a report about an increase in the congestion charge, followed by a brief uninformative item about the discovery of a woman's body somewhere in the West Country. Interesting set of priorities, she reflected, turning it off again. The same stories were always happening: only their endings altered. Unknown women were murdered, and their bodies dumped in the West Country. Others fought back . . . Helen liked the idea that Katrina Blake be recognised for what she was: a victim who'd switched roles. She even liked the way Katrina seemed determined not to cooperate, as if she felt soiled by what had happened to her. Baxter Dunstan might have deserved what he'd got, but once you took pleasure in that, you were no better than the bastards of al-Qaeda or Abu Ghraib.

She took a large swallow of her G&T, then got up and rifled her raincoat pockets. From one, she took out her dictaphone, and ejected a tape. On this, she'd recorded the afternoon session with Katrina. *I'd put a man's lights out before I let him hit me twice*, she had said, and wondered now if that were true. Scaring a man: Helen could manage that – look at Jonno. But there was a crucial difference operating here; the difference between men who hit women and men who didn't. Statistics dictated that Helen had met more than a few of the former, but all had pretended to be the latter in her presence. And what would she have done if any had dropped the pretence? By its nature, it wasn't an offence that took place in public. It had the dropped shutters of a relationship shielding it; it happened behind the carefully constructed doors of intimacy. *Is this a new phenomenon to you? Because you seem to have trouble comprehending it.* No; she'd known it happened. But knowing something and experiencing it were galaxies apart, and in hoping she'd react in a certain way, she was echoing the thoughts of a generation of men who'd never know what stripes they'd have shown, had they been called upon to march to war.

Ultimately, though, you dealt with what happened to you. Anything that didn't, you filed under pending, and forgot about.

This first cassette, she put on the table next to her glass. Then she foraged in another pocket, and found a second.

She inserted it into the recorder, pressed rewind, finished her drink, and poured another. Then dimmed the light, and crossed to the window. Rain pattered the glass, while traffic splashed about on the road below. Because, like everywhere else, the parking here was criminal, an illegal amount of it was taking place on the pavement opposite. Helen didn't run a car. When she needed to be somewhere, she used a minicab. When she was in a hurry, she rang ahead and explained she'd be late.

Yawning, letting the curtain drop, she went back to her seat.

Another slug of G&T, and she took her glasses off; let her surroundings dim to a cozy fuzz. The room felt warm and private; detached from the world of men. Odd thoughts to be having when she was about to violate the privacy of others, but that was pretty much her job description. She pressed play. After a moment, the recorder broadcast the noise of somebody bending to pick a folded newspaper from the floor, and collecting what had been lying beneath it. *It seems the guardian of the free press forgot something.* What the voice was referring to was the recorder now broadcasting its words. This felt a little postmodern. *Wouldn't want her to waste her batteries.*

She wondered if he'd really been so naïve as to believe the room wasn't wired for sound; then found other things to think about as the tape unpacked its meaning.

*

Dusk had fallen, and the lights in the houses across the canal made everything look warm, comfortable and well fed. In the van, however, all was a grumbly mess. Trent would have killed for a drink, and Arkle was in that high-pitched state he reached when he went too long without sleep. This involved talking too much and tapping his fingers on available surfaces.

Earlier, Trent had done as Arkle wanted; had crossed Whatever Street – the road with the park on one side, behind big black railings – and had rung Helen Coe's bell, then waited, like, eighteen months for someone to answer it. Helen Coe, who arrived on sticks, had turned out to be old, really old: a granny – very nearly a mummy – and definitely not the Coe they were after. But a knee-jerk response to old ladiness kept him hovering on her doorstep anyway, mouth flapping as he unwrapped seven plausible reasons for bothering her, none of them remotely intelligible once they'd been scrambled by his damaged mouth, then processed by her malfunctioning ears. In the end, when she'd looked ready to pass from bewildered to downright terrified, he'd turned and walked back to the van; had got in and been driven away.

Arkle said, 'Course, that would only really work if we had two vehicles.'

By the clock on the dash, it was an actual eleven minutes before Trent worked out what he was on about.

But now here they were; the third of the unknown quantities. There were lights on but the building was divided into flats, so that wasn't a clue as such; more an unnecessary confusion. Rain drummed on the van's roof. A man walked past, with slow enough steps that he might have been a policeman, or possibly a drug dealer. Or both: you heard stories. But he walked on by.

Arkle stopped tapping, and examined his knuckles instead. 'If you had to eat one of your own fingers, which would you choose?'

Trent tried to think of something to say – anything. But all that happened was that rain kept falling; while over the road, the same lights stayed on in the same windows.

Being in the van when it rained was like sitting in a tin can being shot at.

Arkle said, 'Where are we, anyway?'

Trent showed him on the map.

Arkle said, 'Where are we, anyway?'

'Back there,' Trent said, pointing, 'is the Angel Islington.'

'That one of the blue ones?'

Now a woman walked past with a small, black, snuffly dog. Arkle mimed aiming his crossbow at it; fired an invisible bolt through the windscreen. He was remembering the apple, and how he'd hit it on the bounce: a reaction shot God would have been proud of. He'd raised the subject with Trent a few times (sixteen). He raised it again now.

Trent said, 'Wish I'd been there,' feeling like he had been.

Arkle said, 'What's that?'

Another dog walker, thought Trent. Another office worker arriving home; another cleaner heading out to scrub offices. But he looked anyway, because Arkle expected a response when he voiced a thought, and Arkle didn't mean someone else was coming down the road; he meant someone was standing by a window.

Second floor. She was framed by background light, and had mad grey hair and thick glasses; wore a tatty green cardigan which bunched into tufts around the shoulders. Even as Trent watched he saw her yawn, and remembered not believing it the first time.

'That's her,' he said.

Arkle looked at him, waiting for the follow-up.

But all Trent said was 'It's her' again, and the pair sat watching Helen Coe drop the curtain, while rain hammered the roof as if what it really wanted to do was pound their heads.

*

I remember *a cold morning. I remember a hailstorm last April. It was late in the year, but there aren't any rules, are there? He'd just washed the car when this hailstorm left little powdery marks all over it. He hit me that day. He said it was for something I'd done, but it was because he'd had to wash the car twice.*

This voice, this tape, this recording Helen had made – it barely sounded like dialogue. It was simply a given; a situation trying to make itself understood. It included the odd question, the odd prompt, but the policeman might as well not have been there. This was Katrina, talking to herself. Or talking to an empty room, rather, which just happened to contain a policeman.

He never used to care where he hit me. When you read about men . . . When you hear about men who hit women, hit their wives, they're careful to do it so no one'll know. You see women in supermarkets with smiles and nice haircuts, who can't reach the top shelf because their ribs are taped up. But he'd slap me in the face. I had black eyes. He loosed a tooth once. I'd tell people I walked into doors. Some of them even believed me. And you know what? Even the ones who didn't, they never asked. Never said anything. You see, if it happens to you, it's bad. But if it keeps happening, it's your fault.

This woman, downstairs. The journalist. She wouldn't let it happen to her. You only have to look at her to know that. Or at least . . . You only have to look to know she believes that. And belief is not something you can argue with. What people perceive about themselves, they assume is hard-won knowledge. Who knows them better than they do? It's hard to accept that things don't always work like that, that you're not always the person you think you are. Something happens, and it takes part of you away. And then you're frightened in case it happens again. And when it does, you're more frightened, because you're not sure how much of you is left.

All this stuff, I allowed it to happen, so what does that make me? A coward? And why didn't I tell somebody, instead of lying about these stupid injuries I kept sprouting, covering them up with paint and powder? I think about it now – non-stop – and I wonder if what I really wanted was for somebody to find out without me having to tell them. For somebody to know there was no door I kept walking into. Maybe what I was hoping for was a knight on a silver steed. Not to carry me away. But to slay the dragon.

He didn't come, of course. And because there was no door, I couldn't walk through it. So I stayed and it kept on happening. Because I let it happen, yes. Because I was ashamed enough to let it keep happening. As if it were my fault. But then, that's what we're told, isn't it? We're told that women in that position think it's their own fault. So when we're in that position, we think it's our own fault.

Helen stood and turned the machine off. The room felt smaller, its walls bearing in. She went and poured another drink. For a couple of days, she'd been talking to Katrina – asking the usual questions; the ones where you hoped a story would eventually appear, even if you had to change the words to help it come. But these words flowed without Helen's intervention, and now she understood that Katrina would have been better off talking to anyone but her. Even this policeman whose name nobody could remember. Because every time Katrina looked at Helen, what she saw was somebody who'd insisted *I'd have nailed his balls to the ironing board . . . I'd put a man's lights out before I let him hit me twice.*

She emptied her glass standing by the sink; in a kitchen in which no man had ever hit her. What did she know, really? When had she decided she was the judge? She didn't notice pouring another drink, or drifting back into the other room, but that's what she did; and sank into the sofa again, and turned the recorder on.

You're going to ask about the police now, aren't you? About why I didn't go to the police. Do you mind if I make a very particular observation here? Don't make me fucking laugh. There. Let's move on.

I think one of the reasons I didn't walk was, I was scared. Not just of him, I mean. I was scared of the world, of what might happen to me out in the world. I'd married a man I thought loved me, and he was hitting me black and blue. What other wrong choices would I make? The next man to say he loved me might have a toolkit under his bed.

There was someone in a hotel, though. I talked to him. I thought he knew what I was trying to tell him, but I suppose he had his own troubles. If I'd been drowning, he'd have reached out. But he didn't know I was drowning, so what did I expect?

Silence fell. It took Helen a while to remember that it was a recorded silence; was merely being repeated now. The silence she was listening to had already been broken.

And they could find this man, she thought, if they tried hard enough . . . *It was in a hotel bar in Oxford. His name was Tim.* Hotels offer paper trails; even Jonno could follow one. And a stranger Katrina had talked to about her bruises: that might play in court. The impartial witness – it was always good to have one on your side. Unless he turned out a complete bozo, of course, and believed she'd walked into a door. And the odds on a random man not being a complete bozo weren't so strong you'd bet your future on them.

Besides, if he was going to be a witness for Katrina, he couldn't be part of any story Helen would write. Not before a trial, anyway.

Even as she had these thoughts, she was wondering how far she was straying from the line she'd once been told it was the journalist's duty to walk.

But Katrina was talking again.

Arkle's last words, leaving the van, were, 'This won't take a minute. Don't go anywhere,' which was a joke, because where would Trent go? If he wandered off he'd get arrested or possibly taken to a zoo – it hadn't been a good move, taking the bandage off. But there was no talking to some people. This usually pissed Arkle off, but Trent was his brother, so he made allowances.

It was taking more than a minute, though, and he was getting wet.

This was despite the cap, which he was wearing because Coe had seen him once already; she'd been watching when he'd scattered the journalists outside the yard. But what had she seen? A bald guy . . . As well as the cap he was wearing a pair of shades: in the rain, at night. Still, this was London. What counted as a disguise everywhere else, round here they wore to go shopping.

As for the plan, it had been pure simplicity: he'd come across the road, talk to Helen Coe, find out where Kay was squirrelled. If the front door hadn't been locked, he'd be back in the van by now. Instead, he'd had to improvise. This had involved an expenditure of £6.95.

And then a shape appeared in the lobby of the building: all macked up, umbrella hanging from its arm like a giant bat. Arkle, who'd been lurking at the foot of the steps, bounded up them just as the man pushed through the door; just as he stood there holding it open – his automatic politeness allowing Arkle into the building, even as his city instinct kicked in, causing him to say: 'Who you for?' Or words to that effect.

Arkle showed him the £6.95 box. 'Pizza.'

'Who for?'

'Davies. Flat 7.'

The man nodded, turned on his way. Pizza: like some kind of magic key. Abracadabra, and hold the anchovies.

But he was glad he hadn't had to say Coe's name. Coe's name might become an unpopular association, depending on the next twenty minutes. Coe was in flat 5, according to the tenants' board by the lift; two names above the Davies Arkle had picked at random. Of course, if that had been Davies leaving, things might have become tetchy . . . But here was Arkle, in the lobby, facing the lift. Arkle didn't believe in lifts, so took the stairs instead. Under his arm, the pizza cooled, and he wondered if its oils were seeping through the box and staining his coat . . . The image in his head was from a film he'd seen once, in which blood soaked through a ceiling. He couldn't remember what had caused this exactly, but it could have been one of a number of things. Some of them came to mind as he climbed.

II

There was a board that if she stood on, Jonno would hear it, and wonder what she was doing – Jonno was in the room directly below; the one they did the talking in, furnished by a chair, a stool, a space by the door. Jonno slept in a sleeping bag, which was always gone by the time Katrina rose in the morning. What hour he got his head down, she didn't know, because each evening, as soon as Helen Coe had yawned her last and left for home, Katrina made her excuses – the appropriate journalistic term – and came upstairs; frightened that if she spent much time in Jonno's company, she might discover she liked him, or something equally dreadful. Might talk to him. The possibilities weren't precisely endless, but were worth avoiding.

Tonight, she sat on the edge of her bed and brushed her hair.

She supposed, if anyone were to catch her doing this, they'd take it as an admission – of guilt, or just of numbness. You didn't kill a man, particularly your husband, and then brush your hair a few days later. It indicated that you gave your grooming a higher priority than you'd given his life. That was the line she walked now. Her future rested on the opinions of others; something it was important to bear in mind, even when alone.

There was a mirror on the wobbly table next to her bed, but she didn't use it – she already knew what her face looked like. Only in the evening did she take the painkillers she'd been prescribed. The same onlookers might interpret that as a penance, though again, they'd have been only partly right. Not taking painkillers was a way of maintaining focus. Maintaining focus was a necessary part of survival.

She finished, and laid the brush down. It was quiet now, but the late-night revellers would be around soon: teeming in gangs to the nightclub; smooching back in pairs, if they were lucky. Heaven, Paradise or The Sweet Hereafter – something like that; a name with pleasant associations, which traditionally you had to be dead to enjoy.

A car alarm sounded, then choked off. Katrina undid the latch and opened the sash window. A breeze met her, tasting faintly of petrol and newly laid tarmac. The drop to the ground three storeys below was deep but seemed climbable, with frequent window sills and jutting brickwork for hand- and footholds. Not that she intended to make use of them. It looked doable, but being wrong would be a swift messy business.

And Katrina knew about death, of course. Death had been her father's business partner. In any other line, your father's business partner could be relied on for a favour; in this instance, Katrina preferred him at arm's length, though he'd visited lately – had been in her kitchen, the morning Baxter died.

Did you think you could change him? Helen Coe had asked.

Katrina had forborne from pointing out the obvious: she'd changed him, all right. He was different now.

That's the usual pattern, I've heard. Women choose men hoping they'll change. Men choose women hoping they won't.

Though Baxter, as it happened, had been changing anyway.

She pulled the window mostly closed; drew the curtain. Immediately, rain pattered the glass. Perhaps she should take her clothes off, get under the covers, turn out the light. It wasn't late, but she felt exhausted anyway; drained by the constant vigilance her situation demanded. But if she lay down in the darkness, thoughts of Baxter would invade . . . If she asked, Jonno would go and find her a bottle of something, which might help. But even aside from other considerations – the degree to which this would impair her focus, for instance – drinking with Jonno on the premises was not a great idea. She sat on the bed and closed her eyes. Bax arrived immediately.

They were in the kitchen of their flat, and he was telling her about the change of plan; about Arkle, who'd always been close to the edge (did she really need Baxter to tell her this?). Though he didn't tell her Arkle had shot a man with his crossbow, and she didn't tell him she already knew.

'I've spoken to Trent about it. The other day, in the pub.'

'What did he say?'

'He thought I was suggesting we squeeze Arkle out.'

As if he would. This made-up family, however out of order to outsiders, was bound together with bonds of steel.

She opened her eyes. There was somebody coming up the stairs: it could only be Jonno – it had to be Jonno. Someone knocked on her door: 'Katrina?' It was Jonno.

'What is it?'

'I just wondered . . .'

The way his voice trailed off was a way of telling her communication would be easier if she opened the door. But no way was Katrina opening the door.

'. . . I was just wondering, you okay?'

'I'm fine, Jonno.'

'Only . . .'

She waited.

'Only there's been a lot of noise out front. Cars coming and going.'

'I'm fine, Jonno.'

'. . . Okay.'

For a while, the only sound was that of Jonno not going anywhere.

'. . . Katrina?'

'What is it, Jonno?'

'Would you like a drink?'

There quite probably was a God, she decided, but he was taking the piss.

'No thank you, Jonno,' she said.

For a while longer Jonno hovered on the landing, carefully balanced on the one board that didn't squeak. And then she heard a sigh, which might have been the boy expelling breath, or the woodwork relaxing. The next thing was, he was making his way down the stairs. By this time Katrina was standing by her bed, her right hand making a tight perfect fist around nothing. In her left she held the little bedside mirror.

Black and purple, crimson and blue. Politics, forensics.

Your husband did this to you, is that right?

Yes.

On the morning he died.

There had been something in the policeman's voice; not doubt, precisely; more what you might call open-mindedness. As if he were not immune to the possibility that other scenarios existed.

On the morning he died. That's right.

Perhaps you'd better tell me about it.

. . . It was a cold sunny morning, a proper autumn morning. Wednesday. I was downstairs first. He . . . he was having a lie in. That usually meant I had a couple of hours to myself. Especially those mornings when we'd made love the night before.

And here, listening, Helen heard Katrina pause, as if the detail struck home as she spoke it aloud . . . The tape whirred; one silence captured and broadcast into another. Helen could almost feel the story cohering in Katrina's mind: that this man had been her husband; that there'd been happy times. That they'd shared a bed, shared the act of love. And this same man who'd abused her, whom she'd killed on the morning she was about to describe, had been inside her with her consent just hours before . . . Despite everything, there had been two lives involved here, and now there was only one.

I'd showered and dressed. There were things I had to do that morning, I can't remember what. You'd think the details would be tattooed on my memory. But whatever they were they involved leaving the house, and I suppose I must have been smartly dressed, because he came downstairs before I'd left, and the first thing he asked was, why was I all dolled up?

That was his expression. All dolled up.

There are moments when what's coming next is all too clear. When a fridge powers off, the ear catches its hum just before it coughs into silence, or so the brain pretends. Something of the sort, Helen picked up in Katrina's voice now. There'd been a moment of realisation, a second or so after the ordinary morning switched off, that events had just jumped track; that what was coming was brutal, but had to be lived through. It started when Baxter spoke. Katrina had yet to say his name.

We were in the kitchen. I'd washed up, and everything was where it should be . . . Cutlery in its drawer, mugs on their tree. Glasses in the cupboard. We have one of those wooden blocks, do they call them butcher's blocks? Whatever they call them, we've got one of those. Blocks for sliding the kitchen knives into. They're all slightly different thicknesses, so each has its own slot. I always used to think this silly thing when putting them away, that it was like the sword in the stone, only backwards. That if I could put each one into the right slot first go, I'd be . . . a princess. Queen of England. They were all in their slots. I didn't get them all right first go, though.

He was waiting for an answer, so I told him I wasn't dolled up, I was going out, that was all. I'm not sure why I said this. It was one of those . . . Sometimes you try to pretend everything's okay, in the hope that everybody else will join in. That's how marriages survive, even the ones where nobody's hitting anybody. By both partners pretending everything's normal, that nothing terrible's happening.

But he was shaking his head before I'd finished, as if I'd already failed the test. As if I hadn't even managed to write my name at the top of the paper – Kay. That's what he called me. Never Katrina. Kay.

. . . I've just thought of one of the things I had to do that morning. I had to renew the TV licence.

Maybe I mentioned that to him. I don't remember.

. . . Your job's quite tough, isn't it?

Helen found herself nodding in agreement; kept nodding until, like an alarm clock interrupting a dream, a male voice broke in. What it said, she didn't register. *Yes* or *no*, or something less committal: just a punctuation mark in Katrina's monologue . . . This was between Katrina and the policeman. Helen hadn't been there, and she barely felt here now. When the policeman had said whatever he said, Katrina continued:

I expect there've been times you've known violence couldn't be avoided, that it was your duty to confront it. And that the best you could hope was, it would be over quickly, with no permanent damage done . . . But you're a man. Probably you have different ideas about your role in a violent situation. All I'm saying is, I knew what was coming. Not its specifics, but the general outline . . . Things were familiar. Already familiar, and they hadn't started yet.

It would be good to be able to say that a difference came over him. That there were two of him, that he was taken over by some – inner demon, some Hyde. But he wasn't. He was just himself. The same man I'd married, without wanting him to change.

And he didn't say another word. You'd think he'd need to rev himself up, wouldn't you? To change gear, to give some acknowledgement this wasn't ordinary, wasn't what everybody did, you didn't just wake up, get dressed and smack your partner round. But that's what he did. No pretence about regrettable necessity or painful duty or . . . It was just what he did next. In between combing his hair and putting the kettle on.

Helen stood abruptly, and pressed pause. For a moment there was silence, and then the usual noises intervened: the slap of rain against her window; the buzz of electricity making her flat work. Somebody walked past her door in what sounded like work boots, but were probably de rigueur clubwear. She had intended to listen to the tape right through, and then bed: ten hours' sleep. Now she wasn't sure. Not sure she could stand the rest of it; not sure she'd sleep afterwards, either. Luckily, there was always the third option: the drink you poured while you made your mind up. Helen was out of ice now, and almost out of tonic, but she didn't let these things stop her. Before she knew it, she was back in her chair with a fresh glass; before she'd noticed what she was doing, she was reaching for the pause button . . .

Somebody knocked on her door.

'I didn't order pizza.'

'You sure?'

'Do I look like I can't remember whether I ordered pizza?'

Hell, she looked like she couldn't remember last time she changed her shoes: with her mad hair, and a cardigan probably saw service in the Crimea. She was blinking fiercely, and Arkle remembered she'd been wearing glasses when she'd drawn her curtains earlier. She wasn't wearing them now.

He said, 'Helen Coe. Flat 7, right?'

'Flat 5.'

Fuck. 'Five. What I meant.'

'No thanks. Goodnight.' She made to shut the door.

He said, 'You're the journalist, right?' and his words must have scraped through the gap just before the lock snapped into place.

A second passed. Two. The pizza box had grown clammy, the way a shirt does on a muggy day.

The door opened again. Same mad hair; same cardigan.

Standing in her line of sight, though, Arkle felt like a target – like there might be twin red dots appearing on his forehead. 'You're not pizza delivery.'

He said, 'They have those yellow jackets? So they don't get knocked off their bikes? I'm not wearing one. I bought this round the corner.'

'Do I know you?'

He grinned. He was pretty sure he could take his cap off, plus his shades, dance naked in her hallway, and she wouldn't recognise him. Though she might suspect something was up. 'We've not met, no.'

'Which paper do you work for?'

He said the first one came into his head.

'Tam Dalgliesh still running your news desk?'

'That's right.'

'Well tell him to keep his fucking hands off my story.' And the door was closing again, only this time he got his foot inside it first.

'I'll tell him. Only it's a little late for that.'

'Get your foot out of my door.'

'Okay. But you want to hear this.'

'Hear what?'

His brain was working overtime now; it was like hitting the apple with the bolt – the trick was to keep moving. Not to stop and wonder whether you'd miss, because if you did, you'd miss.

. . . Had he faded, just then? No – he was still in the flow.

'They know where she is.'

'Where who is?' But she was backing down, he could see; mentally adjusting to the idea that wherever she had Kay, it wasn't the safe place she'd thought it was.

In his mind, Arkle could see tonight unfolding. He'd go back and sit in the van with Trent; wait for Little Miss Mad here to go beetling off to Kay's hidey-hole . . . He wished Baxter was here. He'd be shaking his head in amazement, saying *And everyone thinks I'm the smart one?* And Arkle would say, *Who's the oldest?* . . . Yes, Baxter ought to be around when they found Kay. That would have a sweet justice to it, though Arkle was prepared to admit it wasn't entirely logical.

'. . . Are you listening?'

Shit.

'Get your foot out of my door. Then we'll talk. But as long as you're trespassing, I've nothing to say, though I might be doing some shouting soon.' She nodded towards the neighbouring flat. 'The couple over there? They work doors down the West End. How many knots do you think they could tie you into?'

Arkle made to run a hand over his shiny head; realised he was still wearing the cap. 'It would be interesting to find out,' he said. 'But it wouldn't really solve anything.' He moved his foot. The door stayed open. He said, 'If you want to make sure she stays hidden, you're going to have to cut a deal.'

'The only deal I need's already made. She talks to me. Nobody else.'

'Maybe a couple photographs?'

'No way. We've got an exclusive. Words and artwork, they're ours alone.'

That was okay. Arkle had set his bait; now it was a waiting game. They could talk newspapers some more, but they'd done words and mentioned pictures, so unless they moved on to the TV guide, he was out of ideas. He'd worried her, though. She was imagining stuff going on, wherever Kay was; imagining a gang of journos laying siege – an exclusive leaking away in a battery of flash photography and noisy questions. Give her five minutes, she'd be on her way. All he had to do was follow.

He said, 'Well, you can't blame me for trying,' and turned to go.

'That's it?'

'Can't con a pro, can I?' There you go: flatter the cow. 'You want the pizza, anyway? It's got those little fish on.'

'No thanks.'

'Go on, spoil yourself. Or take it for Kay, I don't care.'

'Katrina,' she said. And something in her out of focus eyes shifted, and Arkle knew he'd fucked up . . .

'Oh, Christ,' she said, but he was too fast; had a foot and a shoulder in the gap before she could slam the door. And she was about to shout, but he was too quick for her there, too.

Kicking the door shut behind him, he pushed her into her flat.

III

The bell rang again. For a safe house – a phrase from a seventies spy novel: all Moscow Rules and frightening shadows – it was pretty busy. On the edge of her bed, she listened to Jonno troop downstairs, and barely took a breath while he answered the door. He said something she couldn't make out. So the bell goes at, what? – she checked her watch: after ten. So the bell goes after ten, and he's supposed to be safeguarding her, and what's the boy do? He opens the door, instead of calling reinforcements . . . She'd been led to believe the *Chronicle* was a busy newspaper. There must be another grown-up on the staff. Katrina wasn't sure she liked Helen – she was too much the cynic for comfort – but she trusted her. Helen wouldn't open the door without being damn sure who was on the other side. Katrina looked to the window once more. Which was open, too: just a crack. If worst came to worst, which recent experience suggested was not unlikely, that was her escape route. Three floors down, but plenty of brickwork, plenty of window sills. Somehow, this did not reassure her. Getting up, she walked out to the banister; tried to hear what was happening several flights below . . .

The smell of pizza came wafting up.

So Jonno had sent out for pizza again. This was what happened when you left the kids in charge: they took the easy option. She went back into her room. Downstairs, voices stopped abruptly, and the front door closed. Outside, no doubt, a guy in a luminous jacket would be mounting his scooter. Katrina felt a hunger pang, and wished Jonno had asked if she wanted anything, then remembered she'd been short with him about the drink. There you go. She could starve to death: he'd care. Door shut, she sat on the bed once more. Her face was throbbing again. No: her face was throbbing *still*. It was important to keep your story straight. Small mistakes occurred, and people picked everything to pieces. Her face hurting wasn't a story: her face hurting was a pain. Katrina lay back and closed her eyes. More fireworks went off; another souvenir of her fractured cheekbone . . . In the darkness she'd created, Baxter's face lit up like a Hallowe'en pumpkin. And the creaking she heard was somebody coming up the stairs.

Do you want to know something funny? Don't worry, it's not very funny . . . But do you want to hear it anyway? How my face got hurt? He did it with the door. There. I told you it wasn't very funny. But after all those excuses, all those made-up stories about doors, there's a kind of . . . I'm trying to avoid the word 'irony'. There's a kind of circularity. As if I deserved it, after bad-mouthing doors for so long. What did doors ever do to me? Up till then, nothing. Not really.

I'd turned my back on him, you see. I knew what was coming, what he'd do next. In between combing his hair and putting the kettle on. And I wanted out. I wanted to walk away before it happened, instead of having to make up stories afterwards. I thought if I could just leave – get outside, into what passed for a normal world – he'd have time to calm down, and get behind the foul mood he'd woken up in. Because when he wasn't in that mood, he could be the sunniest person I've known. And that part of him was always there, somehow. The way the sun's always shining, it's just that clouds get in the way.

He reached out to stop me. But instead of grabbing my arm or my sleeve he caught the door, and jerked it back into my face as hard as he could . . .

On the landing, a floorboard creaked. The whole house was a deathtrap; you could sit quiet as a mouse, and work out where everyone was by ear alone – next to the kitchen sink; in the centre of the bathroom. You'd know not only when they moved, but when they were thinking about it; when they remained in the same place too long. With patience, you'd know how heavy they were; how slow, how fast . . . And recognise, too, which boards were deceivers, and groaned in response to invisible pressures rather than intruders – weather, damp, boredom. There were a few of these, here and there. When they made a noise, you ignored it. It was just one of those things happened in old houses, to old wood.

But the board outside her bedroom door wasn't one of them.

Katrina froze. All other noise faded into the background, like a trick scene in a horror film. One moment she'd been distracted by squabbling in the lane below; the next, the only thing audible for miles around was the body hovering on her bedroom landing. She opened her mouth, intending to say 'Jonno?' but no sound came out. This was self-preservation, not fear. That's what she told herself. No sense in letting whoever was out there know her voice was wobbling. It was ridiculous, anyway, to suppose there was anyone there who shouldn't be. It was Jonno, gearing up the nerve to knock. It was Helen Coe, back for more, and pausing to catch her breath.

But on the other hand, the possibility existed that something had gone horribly wrong, for reasons she couldn't know.

She looked to the window. It was true that, in a sober moment, she'd reckoned it possible to climb down to the yard.

On the other hand, that had been based on the assumption it was never going to happen. Reality had a way of chipping at the edges, so what you'd imagined to be smooth could draw blood. Besides, what would it be like, being found by Arkle clinging halfway down a building? With him above you, crossbow in hand? The image that swam into mind was thin-lipped, sharp-toothed. Some things were better faced in the light.

Unfreezing, she got to her feet. Crossed the room without making a sound, and flung open the door.

I didn't see stars. You're supposed to see stars, aren't you? Well, I didn't. There's no end to the disappointments in life. What I saw, for what felt like a second or two, was nothing at all, was a big black nowhere. I could have stepped into it quite easily. If I had, everything would have been different . . . I'd have woken up later, and he'd have been . . . Well, I don't know what he would have been. It would be nice to think he'd be sorry. But I think the most he'd have been was still alive.

For whatever it was – a second, two – I stood in the kitchen waiting for everything to make sense again. I couldn't see him. I could sense his presence, though, close but not touching. It was a sunny morning, did I mention that? The kitchen must have been full of sunlight. But not right that moment.

I tried to take a step, almost fell, and must have staggered to the draining board, because next thing, I was leaning against it . . . I think I threw up into the sink. You'd probably know more about that than me. That would be forensics, yes? . . . Anyway. There was a pain that started on the surface and worked its way to the centre of my head, and however much you know about violence, sergeant, or whatever your rank is, I hope you've never felt anything like it. Because it felt life-ruining. It felt like a new permanence.

He came to me. And I wasn't sure . . . I don't know what he intended to do, sergeant. Take that as a confession, if you like. I have no idea what he intended. Usually, once he'd hit me, he made himself scarce. When he came back, we'd pretend an accident had occurred in his absence. Not that we gave names to it. We simply failed to acknowledge the truth. But once in a while his better self, or whatever you'd call it, would seize him before he'd left, and then he'd take me in his arms, and make promises . . . That didn't happen often. But like I say, I don't know his intent. All I know is, I was very very hurt, very very frightened. He'd never hit me so hard before. He'd never slammed a door in my face. He'd crossed a line, and I wasn't sure he knew his way back.

Perhaps you could say I'd been pushed across the same line.

Unfreezing, she got to her feet, crossed the room without a sound, and flung open the door. Jonno was there, on his knees on the landing; looking, for a foolish moment, exactly what he was: a kid, embarrassed to be caught doing what he was doing.

Which was sliding a pizza from a box on to a plate. The plate sat on a tray. The tray also held a glass of red wine.

No doubt, if he'd had access to a single rose, he'd have laid it across the base of the glass.

'I thought you might be hungry,' he said after a moment.

'That's sweet,' she said. 'Did you bake it yourself?'

'No, I— ' And here it was: the flush. But he had the composure to come up with something. 'I took it out the box, though. That's the tricky bit, know what I mean?'

'Thank you, Jonno.'

'I figured you'd rather eat up here.'

'Thank you, Jonno.'

He got to his feet, and handed her the tray. She took it, restraining herself from making a little curtsy as she did so.

'I hope you enjoy it.'

'You're doing a great job, Jonno.'

'I'll be downstairs if you need me.'

Helen likes you, Jonno. It's her job to give you a hard time.

This was what Katrina didn't say as she carried her supper into her room.

Downstairs, the bell rang again.

It was as if it found its own way into my hand. You think I'm trying to avoid responsibility, don't you? And you're right because . . . because this really was not my fault. Not right then. Not with lightning flashing in my head, and my whole body scared it would happen again any moment . . .

I don't remember reaching for it, that's what I really mean. There was nothing deliberate about the way it fetched up in my hand. It was just the first thing there when I needed to hold on to something.

He put his hand on my shoulder and squeezed. I still have the bruise.

There was noise in my head, white noise. The kind that blankets everything, like a migraine, so you can't see or hear and don't know what's happening.

I had the impression he was talking, but the words weren't making it through. It was like being in a fog, hearing cannon in the distance . . . There were big sounds going on, but everything was muffled by the weather inside.

He shook me, and jolted my back teeth . . . I remember the way they clacked together, sending a shock through every bone. I couldn't see him, but I felt him move, and all I could imagine was, he was about to punch or slap me, continue punishing me for whatever it was I'd done. Which was simply be there . . . I was there and I was his. Anything I did that he didn't approve of was automatically an infraction, do you see? He was allowed to punish. It wasn't his privilege, it was his right. It was almost his duty.

I put my hand out, and he walked straight into me. It was as if he couldn't see I was holding a knife.

. . . Do you remember what I said about the sword in the stone? That if I could slide each knife into its slot first go, I'd be a princess? Well, this one found its slot straight away. All those bones it could have glanced off, but . . .

I didn't feel like a princess, though. Instead, I felt

Arkle turned the tape off.

They were in the van again; rain bouncing off the roof. Arkle pressed eject, and the tape slipped into his hand the way it had back in Helen Coe's flat, when he'd removed it from her machine; fingers tingling, as they still did now. Adrenalin buzz. She had given him, by then, the address he needed. She had had little choice. It was unsurprising how easy it was to make people do things; it exactly fitted Arkle's view of how the world worked. People bent and broke without difficulty, and on the whole were pleased to do things that made the breaking stop.

This woman, downstairs. The journalist. She wouldn't let it happen to her, you only have to look at her to know that . . . To know she believes that.

Whatever. She'd stopped believing it now.

Trent said, 'That one. On the corner.'

He double-parked opposite the house: end of the row, with a lane bending round the back. It was three storeys high, with lights burning on each floor.

'Just the two of them, right?' asked Trent. His face was pulled into a Hallowe'en grin, but he probably couldn't help it.

'Kay and a boy. He makes the tea.'

'And Coe won't have called the cops or anything?'

Arkle said, 'Trust me. She won't have called the cops.'

Not without psychic intervention, she wouldn't.

Staring through the windshield, Trent said, 'You didn't kill her, did you?'

Arkle said, 'All I meant was, I left her trussed up. On her sofa.'

'. . . Okay.'

'And I pulled her landline out and took her mobile. See?'

He showed Trent Helen Coe's mobile.

'. . . Okay.'

But Arkle, thought Trent, hadn't actually said he didn't kill her. Taking the mobile was something he'd have done anyway. Arkle didn't altogether approve of mobiles, and definitely objected to other people having them.

And then Trent had an even worse thought, which was: what *if* he hadn't killed her? No way in the world was she not going to know it was Arkle. She'd seen him once already. Leaving her alive was like signing a neon confession.

But there was the money to think about. Revenge for Baxter, too. But also the money.

'. . . Fuckin' lot of money,' he mumbled, as his train of thought audibly derailed.

'Yeah,' said Arkle. 'Revenge for Baxter, too.'

He described his plan, which was not complicated, then got out and crossed to the house where Kay was hiding, and rang its doorbell.

Jonno called up the stairs: 'Are you still there?'

'Yes.' She'd come out on to her landing. Jonno hadn't ordered another pizza. It wouldn't be the police again: not this time of night . . .

Kids. One of the local drunks or druggies, looking for a handout. Or somebody lost, wanting directions. Collecters for Christian Aid or Shelter; trick-or-treaters; carol singers . . . Anyone, basically. Anyone except who she already knew it was.

'Maybe you should stay quiet while I answer it.'

'Why don't you call the police, Jonno?'

He said, 'Because it's only somebody ringing the bell. What are they gunna do, send the flying squad?'

'It's not who you think, Jonno. They're not interested in stealing your story.'

'You think I'm just a kid, don't you?'

'I don't think anything right now, Jonno, except that you should call the police.' She could hear her voice rising as panic bit into her. 'You were there when we were talking about his brothers? That's who it is, Jonno. His brothers.'

Jonno fell silent; a silence broken immediately by the doorbell ringing again.

'They couldn't possibly know where you are.'

'No. Not possibly. That's who it is, though.'

'You're nervous, that's all. And it's late, and—'

'Jonno. That is fucking Arkle Dunstan at the door, and if you let him in, he'll kill me.'

'Then I won't let him in,' said Jonno reasonably. 'And I'll call the police. But I can't do that without knowing it's him, can I? It would be . . .'

It would be embarrassing.

'Jonno . . .' Her voice dropped to a whisper. 'Please. Don't answer the door.'

And knew immediately that that had been the last thing to say; that what a kid like Jonno was dying to hear was what you didn't want him to do, so he could do it, and prove you wrong.

'It'll be okay,' he said, and the next she heard his feet were on the stairs, dancing down two flights.

She'd have retreated into her room then, but her hands stayed glued to the banister. Strange things happened – life, for instance, had arranged it that she end up in a barely furnished house, waiting for the hammer to fall – and it might be that here was another of them, and the bell-ringer was indeed a trick-or-treater/bleeding heart/lost wanderer: anyone. Anyone but Arkle. But she stayed glued to the banister anyway, while the truth emerged a few floors below. Jonno hit the hallway with a whump, as if he'd leaped the last stairs in his eagerness to put her heart to rest. She heard him open the door and say something, though she couldn't make out what – it was too big a drop; there was too much space between them. Then came a noise which didn't sound like anything in particular, though it involved bone. And then came another whump as Jonno hit the hallway again, this time with his body.

Her hands pulled free of the banister as the front door clicked back into place. For a moment there was silence, then she heard footsteps making their way across the hall, and up the stairs. She thought she was imagining the rough breathing accompanying the ascent, then understood it was real, and her own. That and the beat of her heart: he had all the time in the world. It wasn't like hiding would make a difference. He could track her blindfold, drawn by the volume of her panic.

With nowhere to go, she retreated into her room. The most she could do was jam the door closed then scream out of the window: judging by the area's nocturnal activities, the police might hear of this sometime in the next fortnight. But before she could get this far, the window was opening; was being pushed up from the outside, and through the gap a woman with pale skin and dark wet curly hair was climbing; a woman with a round red mark on her forehead, as if she'd been struck there recently. She hauled herself over the sill and stood up straight.

'Where is he?' she asked.

Katrina pointed.

'Put some shoes on,' the woman said, then went out on to the landing.

8

I

You do this quickly, else you won't do it at all. Fear hides in corners, and once it leaps you're caught forever. So Zoë bounced out of the room, put one hand to the banister, and launched herself down to the next landing in a single movement. Arkle, two steps below, looked up in surprise, astonishment – something, anyway, which was replaced almost immediately by pain as she kicked him in the throat. There followed a second's gravity-grasping charade before he tumbled down the stairs. Zoë shouted, 'Bring the chair,' then rushed up to fetch it herself.

Katrina, shoes on, burst from her room holding the wooden chair by its neck.

Grabbing it, Zoë jumped back down the stairs. On the landing below, Arkle Dunstan was getting up, both hands to his throat. Zoë hit him so hard with the chair its legs broke, then threw what was left at his head. 'Now,' she shouted. Katrina came clattering down behind her, to the hallway where Jonno lay in a confused heap. The front door was open. Zoë pushed Katrina through it; slammed it behind them. Down for the count Arkle might be, but she wanted barriers in place regardless.

'This way.'

She hauled Katrina, who'd been about to head left, off to the right instead, and even as she did, spotted the white van idling over the road with the remaining Dunstan brother at its wheel. He saw them too. Visible questions – who how what where – crossed his face, then he snapped to life, and the van's motor roared. 'Round the back!' Zoë shouted, but Katrina was way ahead of her; had turned the corner before the van kangarooed forward, narrowly missing the car parked opposite. Zoë lit up as its headlights found her, and then she too was round the corner, two yards behind Katrina. Down the lane, she tried to shout: the words came out an incoherent roar. But Katrina understood and swung left again, down the back lane the nightclub revellers favoured. She pulled further away on the straight, while Zoë's smokey years dragged her back: her feet like lead; her lungs stone-filled buckets. There was a car waiting at the far end. She picked up speed as the van cornered too, its lights peeling her from the darkness like a moth. And something caught her foot . . . For a moment she was airborne. And next she knew she was sprawled headlong, and the van was almost upon her.

This is not how you're going to die.

It was a moment for ignoring everything, except the absolute need to be moving. The van at her back; her scraped hands and knees . . . All that mattered was to be moving, so with those same scraped hands, scraped knees, she launched herself. Up ahead, Katrina had stopped: a matter of yards, a hundred miles away. Headlights swallowed Zoë. The van behind her was a light-breathing juggernaut. She could feel it at her spine as she bent double into her sprint, aching for the finish . . . Swore ever after that she felt its kiss one split moment before clearing the concrete bollards that guarded the end of the lane.

There was a tearing sound as the van crunched to a halt: spat glass and furious rubber; a noise like a dustbin hitting a wall. Something bounced away to Zoë's left. Ahead, the car waited, doors open. She scrambled in behind Katrina. 'Go.' As it pulled off she looked back at the van, which was reversing from the concrete soldier. One of its headlights was out, and its front had been radically reshaped. Smoke drifted across the scene like a last-minute special effect.

From the driver's seat, Tim Whitby said, 'Are you all right?'

Zoë opened her mouth to reply, and closed it again when she realised he was speaking to Katrina.

They were on the M40 before Katrina Blake started asking questions.

'What just happened?' was her first.

Tim, who'd been waiting, said, 'That guy who came after you? He's Ar—'

'I know,' Katrina said. 'I was married to his brother.'

'Oh. Yes. Sorry.'

Zoë said, 'I don't think he had friendly intentions.'

'You climbed up the outside of the house.'

'It seemed the easiest way of getting past him.'

'We saw you through the window,' Tim put in. 'I'd have climbed up, but Zoë—'

'You were in the hotel in Oxford.'

'Tim,' said Tim. 'Whitby,' he added.

'You, I don't know.'

'Boehm,' said Zoë. 'Zoë,' she added.

'How did you find me?'

Tim said, 'Zoë did.'

Katrina looked at Zoë.

'A friend of Zoë's,' Tim amended. 'She must be, what? Twelve?'

'Fourteen,' said Zoë, checking the view behind them. Through a rain-lit blur of lights in motion, she could identify nothing that was positively following. 'I think you're missing a few important details.'

But Tim had latched on to this as the key issue: how they'd found Katrina, with everywhere to choose from. 'Vicky's a hacker. A computer whiz?' Katrina's expression indicated that she was familiar with basic vocabulary. 'Sorry. She traced their van. We tracked it because . . . Well, because we didn't know what they were driving otherwise.'

Katrina said, 'Leaving aside for the moment why you were trying to find me in the first place, are you seriously telling me some fourteen-year-old plucked one white van out of the ether?'

Zoë, still studying the road, said, 'It seemed likely that whichever newspaper had hidden you would have picked a city to do it in. They make for better hiding places. London was an obvious choice.'

'It's the biggest.'

'With the most surveillance. My friend hacked the congestion charge system. She found the Dunstans' van late this morning, entering the zone. We've been following them for the past three hours.' She shrugged. 'Sometimes the odds pay off.'

'And Arkle? How did he find me?'

Spray thrashed the windscreen as they passed a sixteen-wheeler.

After a while, Zoë said, 'If it was me, I'd have gone through the paper. The *Chronicle*. Journalist, accountant, something like that.'

'Helen,' Katrina said.

Zoë didn't reply. When Arkle had come out of that last place, before leading them to the safe house, he'd carried himself like a man who'd just enjoyed violent exercise.

'Arkle will have hurt her,' Katrina said after a while.

'We'll find out in the morning,' Zoë said.

Her bones ached; her palms were raw and stinging. When Katrina subsided into silence Zoë closed her eyes, and was instantly back in her coffin: that cold hungry space which had swallowed her whole. She didn't know how long she'd lain inside; only knew that when Tim opened its lid to release her, her throat had felt like torn sandpaper, and she'd expected to be spitting blood. Instead, she had found herself in a decommissioned freezer which sat between an old workbench and a wardrobe with its doors removed; all three beneath a carport-cum-shelter with a corrugated plastic roof. A two-foot-high stone frog with a crack in its head crouched to one side. And beyond it lurked the hearse; its grille gaping wide as a skull's mortal grin. *Could have been me*, it was saying. That, or *How* you *doin'?*

She couldn't believe she was back in the world: on shaky legs, on solid earth. When she'd looked at Tim, who sensibly stood back in case she savaged him, he'd seemed limned in light, like a man in a doorway. It had taken a moment to recognise the faded chinos, the black jacket; the man she'd saved from Arkle Dunstan with an apple . . . And now she opened her eyes again, and was in a car speeding from London: Tim Whitby's car. Her time in a counterfeit coffin was behind her, and whatever didn't kill her made her stronger.

Whatever did kill her would fuck her up no end, of course.

Lights splashed all around, blurred or polished by the kaleidoscopic rain. Way off the motorway, a lonely pair of beams explored the wilderness, scratching a route through the dark. On a distant hillside, a garage floated on a tide of nothing, its overhead spotlights pooling on an invisible forecourt. These would be places the dead gathered; empty places, hungry for life. Places which left lights blazing, in the hope of company.

Zoë did not believe in ghosts, on the reasonable ground that they don't exist, but she was acquainted with the dead, and knew that the space between them and the living was a heartbeat thick. The dead were in the next room, as the comforting lie had it. If so, death was the party wall. And the older you got, the more time you spent leaning against it, wondering if you heard murmuring from the other side; and knowing that it would collapse one day, perhaps when you least expected. Or worse, when you most did. Two nights ago, she'd put a hand through that wall, only to pull it back – frozen, aching, but still attached. Possibly, there had been moments when her life had come closer to ending; episodes she could never know about – the virus shunned by the healthy cells; the multi-car pile-up that didn't happen. All the accidents that wait round the corners we choose not to take. But she'd never before felt so trenchantly that this was it; the dim and distant become the here and now. When the lid lifted, she thought for a moment her heart had burst. It was something she would never speak of to anybody.

White eyes bore into her own across the central divide; grew the size of comets, then hurled past, leaving a red blur in their wake. If she relaxed, the car's motion might rock her to sleep, but she doubted it. She didn't like being a passenger; felt it incumbent upon her to remain alert, in case of emergencies. Though Tim was doing a reasonable job . . . It had been for Tim's sake that she had looked for Katrina. He had freed her, so she owed him. She recognised, too, a certain quality in his determination to track Katrina down: something – duty or guilt – that wouldn't subside until satisfied. Zoë had known similar hungers. Trying to convince him they couldn't be quelled would have been futile. Besides, Tim Whitby had the air of a man coming awake after haunted sleep, and Zoë didn't have the right to get in his way.

The reason she'd climbed the wall to Katrina's room, though, had more to do with her life-sized fears the other night . . .

Tim said, 'You still awake?'

'Yes.'

'Nearly there.'

She knew. But knew, too, that his reason for speaking was just to hear a voice reply, so said, 'Thanks, Tim.'

. . . The reason she'd climbed that wall had been that Arkle

Dunstan had almost scared her to death. It must have been Arkle Dunstan. Zoë had a small round bruise on her forehead where he'd hit her with, she guessed, the heel of a torch, before dumping her in the freezer and taking off. She could have died. Worse, she could have died knowing it was happening: locked inside her fear as securely as she was boxed in a no-longer functioning device. It was the fear that reverberated. The chances of her winding up in a freezer twice were reasonably remote; the memory of the fear, she'd carry forever. And Zoë hated that notion; belonged to the school that would have forced her back on the horse, though she'd never belonged to a school where there'd been horses. She'd climbed the wall to show she wasn't scared, and it didn't have to be true to make the point. She'd been scared, but had done it anyway. She might live with fear, but she damn well wasn't tidying up after it.

When Tim had released her, he'd been full of garbled stories: that Arkle Dunstan had burst out of the front door, and looked up and down the street as if expecting someone. That he'd gone back in and re-emerged moments later with a bandaged man who must have been Trent: they'd got in their van and driven away. That somebody else had passed by, but Tim wasn't too coherent on the subject, because what he wasn't saying was what seeing Arkle had felt like – the man who'd terrorised him with the crossbow: a nightmare given flesh. Tim must have shrunk behind his windscreen; hoped he was invisible, the way a child hopes, if he keeps his foot clear of the floor, that the monster won't grab him. When you were a child, that often worked. In the grown-up world it wasn't a sure thing. Zoë was thankful Tim had held out long enough to be there when she needed him.

He had heard her thumping the sides of the freezer . . . At first, he'd thought it had been coming from the hearse. This with a laugh that lasted longer than it needed to. As he'd opened the lid to release her, he'd wondered if he was making a grave mistake.

And then had turned and seen, through the window into the back room, old man Blake watching them, a totally unreadable expression on his face.

Zoë blinked. They were coming off the motorway, a few miles from Oxford. She wondered whether the old man had actually been watching, or just staring out blankly, fazed by the disturbance . . . Tim had helped her to his car and brought her home. As for her own car, Jeff's car: that was still in the car park in Totnes, unless it had been stripped and redistributed since. Something else she was trying not to think about.

The rain had eased. The road narrowed. Big empty buildings appeared, lit only in the stairwells. Road signs promised twenty-four-hour shopping at the next junction, or perhaps the one after. When Zoë glanced at Katrina, she seemed to be sleeping, though it was hard to be sure. The shadows that played across her as they drove into the city simulated movement, or perhaps disguised it. It depended on how you looked at things.

II

'Why did you come looking for me?'

Zoë said, 'Tim came looking. I helped, that's all.'

'Are you lovers?'

'No.'

Katrina said, 'You were lucky, you know. With Arkle, I mean.'

'I know.'

'You took him by surprise.'

'Perhaps I should have given him a warning.'

'All I meant was, it won't be so easy next time.'

'There'll be a next time?'

'He won't stop looking for me just because you knocked him over.'

'But maybe I won't be there next time he finds you.'

'No. But maybe Tim will.'

Zoë said, 'Tim's got some stuff he's getting over, I don't know the details. But he seems pretty decent. I'm sure he'll do his best not to let you down.'

'That's good.'

'On the other hand, Arkle Dunstan'll make mincemeat of him.'

'Yes.' Katrina put down her glass, and looked around. Took in the minimal furnishings; the shady lighting. They were in Zoë's sitting room. Both were drinking water. Katrina had turned down the offer of food. 'You live here alone.'

It wasn't a question, so Zoë didn't answer.

'Have you ever been married?'

'Once.'

'What happened?'

'It came to an end,' Zoë said.

'Mine too.' Katrina raised a hand to her face. 'He did this to me.'

'So I heard.'

'Have you ever let a man hit you?'

'Let one? No.'

'But it's happened?'

'I've been roughed up,' said Zoë. 'But only by strangers.'

'Do you despise me?'

'No.'

'But you wouldn't have let somebody do this to you.'

Zoë said, 'Things have happened to me that I wish hadn't. I'm not in the business of judging other people's mistakes.'

'But you judge your own harshly.'

'I try not to make the same one twice.'

'Is that why you said "once" when I asked if you'd been married?'

'I don't usually think six answers ahead of myself,' said Zoë. Then added, 'I'm glad I knew Joe. That part wasn't a mistake.'

'What did he do?'

'He was a private detective.'

After a while, Katrina said, 'You are too, aren't you?'

'That's right.'

'But it wasn't really me you were looking for.'

'No,' said Zoë. 'I was looking for the money.'

The sitting room's bay window overlooked the quiet street below. A sofa faced this window, and a standard lamp stood at one end of the sofa; there was an armchair, too, backed into a corner. Other than that, the room's story mostly spoke of absences – no TV, no bookcase; no art on the walls, though outlines showed where pictures had once hung. A visitor might remark on their removal; might wonder if Zoë's minimalist mode signalled depression. But depression would have meant leaving everything the way it was. Zoë had simply grown to dislike her pictures, and hadn't yet found any she liked more. Besides, art was a luxury she couldn't currently afford.

A short way down the road was a street light, partly obscured by a tree. After dark, orange light threw branch shadows on Zoë's walls, and when the wind blew, they thrashed like a make-believe wood. Taken in all, it didn't seem Zoë's room lacked for much: it was furnished with weather, and anxious movement.

None of which was Zoë's. She sat in the armchair in the corner. Katrina perched on the sofa, at the opposite end to the lamp, legs tucked beneath her. Her face, mottled by bruises, was also splashed by weaving shadows.

'Don't you ever draw your curtains?' she asked.

'Do you want me to?'

'. . . I'm okay.'

Tim had left an hour before. He had become mumbly and awkward while Katrina thanked him; had barely remembered to say goodnight to Zoë. Zoë was neither surprised nor distressed by this, but noted it for what it was: a response rooted in Tim's needs rather than genuine connection. Tim and Katrina had met, by his own account, just once; he had been quite drunk. His reasons for having been in the hotel in the first place remained obscure, though Zoë had her suspicions.

It was late now – after two – and the closing-time refrain of drunks and sleepless traffic had subsided. Sometimes, the sound of a night train would carry this far; channelled through streets and round houses until it seemed to be coming from an entirely wrong direction, as if trains were running up the Woodstock Road. Given the local transport strategy, that wasn't impossible. For the moment, though, there were no trains; only the thrumming of rain on glass, and gentle breathing.

'So . . . You went looking for the jewellery money.'

'The man they took it from wanted it back.'

'But you haven't found it.'

'I found the Dunstans. That was my job.'

'Are you always this controlled?'

. . . Zoë remembered pounding on the freezer lid, before it turned out to be a freezer. When it had still been a coffin. She said: 'What will you do now?'

'I'm not sure.'

'You thought the paper would keep you safe, didn't you?'

'From Arkle? Yes.'

'Well, there are other hiding places.'

Katrina took a sip from her glass. 'What would you do? If you were me?'

'I'm not you.'

'That's what "if" means.'

Zoë chewed her lip. This wasn't what she wanted right now. On the other hand, action involved responsibility. She wouldn't pretend that saving somebody's life meant you had to keep on doing so, but she couldn't turn Katrina out into the rain, either. 'You haven't been charged with anything, have you?'

'Not yet.'

'Meaning, it's going to happen.'

'Helen . . . Helen thought it would be a minor charge. Given the circumstances.'

In dappled orange light, Zoë saw the late autumn shades of Katrina's cheek.

She said, 'You might not have to worry. The Dunstan brothers could be under arrest by now.'

'For evading the congestion charge?'

'For assaulting your friend. Helen.'

'They hurt her to find me, didn't they?'

'I think they must have done. I'm sorry.'

Katrina said, 'What if they killed her?'

'Killed her?'

'Yes. If she's dead, who's left to tell stories? Jonno?'

Jonno was the kid who'd been lying in the hallway.

'Because once Jonno opened the door, that was it. A goldfish would make a better witness. At least their memories last a couple of seconds.' She paused. 'As far as the police are concerned, I just legged it.'

Zoë said, 'You've given this some thought.'

'It's a pressing issue.'

Maybe that was a train now, off in the distance. Trains at night were a melancholy sound. They rendered every country song Zoë'd ever heard redundant.

Katrina said, 'I know Arkle. He's an accident waiting to happen to whoever's nearest.' She looked up sharply, but it was only the wind, the rain; the same imaginary train Zoë had heard. She relaxed. 'He'll happen to me. First chance he gets.'

'So what do you want to do? Run?'

'Is that what you'd do?'

Full circle. This was the question Zoë hadn't answered yet. She chose her words carefully: 'I'd make sure he couldn't hurt me.'

'Not the same thing, is it?'

'Running's a serious business. It's not like the police'll think, Well, she was probably innocent . . .'

Katrina said, 'My husband's dead. My father's losing his mind. What's left of my family are who I'm scared of. I don't care how serious it is. The alternative's not a barrel of laughs either.'

'My specialty's finding people, not helping them disappear.'

'But I bet you've got contacts.'

Zoë didn't reply. She was thinking about Joe's filing cabinets, in which he'd kept a record of everyone he'd ever met: bookies, off-duty cops, civil servants with marital problems, and the boys and girls causing them. He'd known ex- and future cons, without ever feeling the need to judge, and maybe because of this, his cabinets had grown fuller and fuller . . . He'd never been much cop as a detective, but if he'd opened a dating agency, he'd have been quids in.

He'd known a boy who hot-wired cars and a man who could finesse locks, and he'd paid for lessons from both, without staggering success.

He'd known a woman who kidnapped cats, then waited for flyers to appear on local lamp posts, offering rewards.

And he'd known a man who recycled passports, suitably adjusted, at scary prices. For the right customer, he'd throw in credit ratings, driving licences, NI numbers; probably old bus tickets and pocket lint too. Zoë had never met him. But Joe had his name, number and address; and had probably been his best friend once, for half an hour.

So yes: she had contacts.

She said, 'Supposing I did. Where would you go?'

'Out of the country.'

'That takes paperwork.'

'Will you help me?'

There was a bad feeling nagging at Zoë; one hard to push aside. Over the past few days, she'd been dumped in a freezer and nearly flattened by a van, while harmless Tim Whitby had been bullied by a crossbow-wielding maniac. Something had happened to Helen Coe, and a kid named Jonno had been left in a heap. Not to mention Baxter Dunstan, who wouldn't be feeling pain again. All of it revolving round this woman in front of her. Maybe it would be an idea not to get involved further.

She wasn't sure how to say any of this, but a short answer occurred. She would say no. That covered the bases. Zoë was good at saying no, and it was an answer that rarely got her into trouble. She finished her water, and looked up.

Katrina said, 'The money from the robbery? All the robberies?'

Zoë nodded.

Katrina said, 'I know where it is.'

'. . . Right,' said Zoë.

III

Tim, alone in his sitting room, paced back and forth, back and forth, waiting for the background noise to start again.

Background noise meant anything – cars grinding to a halt nearby, or grinding to a start; kids laughing their way to a party, or crying their way back. Anything to distract him from the unreal photoplay of the last few days.

Background noise meant things happening elsewhere, instead of cluttering up his head . . .

But it was late, and unlikely that real-world distractions would turn up soon. His car had been the last to disturb his street's silence; his door the last to close. Anything in the wider distance was smothered by rain, which no longer counted as noise. Once inside, the first thing Tim had done had been pour himself a drink. It would also have been the second, if drinking the first hadn't intervened. Then he removed his shoes and coat, put the light on. It would be wise not to start drinking now. Two didn't count. His eyes were strained and dry from night driving; he was wired and tense, and a strange bubble in his chest kept threatening to burst . . . Tim dimly recalled this feeling from long ago, his first year of courting Emma; a bad week during which she had told him she wasn't sure they should see each other any more. For days, he had harboured an alien life form; one he was desperate not to give birth to, for that would be to admit its reality. In the end, it had withered and died during one tear-stained phone call. And this . . . This was similar. Not the same, but similar. And so, for the first time since her death, he thought about Emma in relation to the way he was feeling, rather than the other way around.

But that didn't register. What did was a simple fact: that he had decided to do something – to find a woman he'd met in a hotel, and help her out of the difficulty she was in – and had achieved it. It wasn't just that he felt a sense of accomplishment. It was that he felt anything at all, other than empty, hung-over or angry; the constant soundtrack of his recent months.

Over his head, the light flickered. Upstairs, a board creaked. In a movie, these would be signs that all was not right; that what had been accomplished was a false ending. Arkle Dunstan was still out there, which was no way to finish a story. But life followed untidier arcs, and left narrative strands ungathered. Lights flickered in response to local conditions. The electric pulse beat weaker at night. And boards creaked; houses rustled; everything was acted on by everything else . . .

Tim, for instance. Tim sipped his drink. Tim, like everybody, lived life buffeted by pointless information; a ceaseless update on events he had no chance of influencing, along with intimate details about people in whom he had no interest. 'News' happened elsewhere, only occasionally scratching reality . . . Once, Tim's picture had appeared in a trade newspaper. He couldn't, at this moment, recall why. And Emma's death had been reported, though he'd been too untogether to register the details. But it would have been a minor paragraph only, inhabiting that border between the human and the statistical – the shading of a woman into a number; the nth fatality on the roads this year. Otherwise, Tim had never troubled the public eye. It had been strange, then, to open his paper and find a story in which he felt implicated, even if tangentially. Katrina's photograph had floated from the page. The facts had taken a while to focus, but 'death', 'stab' and 'fatal' had figured. This was the woman who'd tried to tell him her husband was beating her up. He had done nothing for her, and this had happened . . . In his mind, it was hard not to hear the word 'therefore' sliding into place in that sentence. He had done nothing for her, and therefore this had happened.

Pacing was not conducive to drinking, he discovered. Pacing while drinking created spillage. He set the glass down; would have set himself down, but was too nervy, too agitated, too alive. So kept pacing: striding forwards, thinking backwards; recreating the lucky dip of reasons he'd had for returning to Totnes, looking for Katrina – guilt, surprise, uselessness, alcohol, worry, excitement. All these, plus the sense of having got something wrong; of having missed a cue or turned away at a crucial moment, as if life were a spectator sport, and a moment's inattention meant you'd missed the drop kick, the dropped catch. None of which differed from everybody's feeling about their everyday life, every day. But not everyone got to read about the consequences in the paper.

Out loud he said, 'This time, I got it right.' His voice felt thick in his mouth.

It was funny to think he'd worried about skiving off work. Not the crippled-by-indecision worry of the previous week – he was going, and that was that – but worry, nevertheless; an apprehension that he was storing up problems he'd have to deal with later. And then it had occurred to him, with the suddenness of a light going on, that they knew, of course – of course they knew. His colleagues, his staff: all of them knew his wife had died; that eight months was not a long time; that grief was not only embedded in Tim's life, but was still rubbing away at the surface, altering texture, appearance, colour: everything. And all were human, and remained involved in the emotional network her death had loosed him from. So he could say 'I won't be coming in for a few days', and their only response would be a sympathetic murmur . . . This was how things worked, among the kind and reasonable. It was how life answered death. And besides, it didn't truly involve dishonesty. If Emma hadn't died, none of this would be happening. None of it would be happening to Tim Whitby, anyway.

So he had returned to Totnes, shovelling from his mind as he drove the image of a shaven-headed maniac with a crossbow in a gravel yard . . . Tim had little doubt Arkle Dunstan would have shot him, if not for Zoë Boehm. Not to kill him. (Probably not to kill him.) But to see him squeal and run . . . What Tim had found more frightening than the crossbow was the pleasure in Arkle's eyes when he'd picked the crossbow up, as if this were the only connection he cared to make: one that rendered whoever was nearest a target. Tim guessed a lot of cats had gone missing round Arkle Dunstan's childhood home. So Tim's plan, inasmuch as he had one, boiled down to this: stay out of Arkle's way. And as he'd formulated it, he'd felt a long unfamiliar tug at his heart, or some other useful organ; that fish hook jerk that pulls you back from sleep. Not fear, but excitement. There had been a reason he hadn't died in that hotel room, and even if it came with crossbows and blunt, bald-headed threat, it beat the stasis of these past months. Because it also involved apples that bounced out of nowhere; and a hurt woman in a hotel bar, who had looked to him as if he might help. If nothing else, he'd found out this much: he was worth shooting, and he was worth saving from being shot. However you added the two, it came to more than worthless.

Another noise from overhead interrupted him: a sound both

familiar and unwelcome – a rattling, scratching disturbance; it took Tim a moment to pin it down. The roof. There was a loose slate on the roof, and when the wind hit a certain angle it worried it, trying to prise it out with no other tool than its own blustery nothingness. Perhaps the slate would survive the night; perhaps not. Either way – Tim made a mental note – he'd get around to fixing it soon. Perhaps next weekend.

. . . When he'd arrived in Totnes, after dark, he had parked near Katrina's father's house. He couldn't think where else she'd fetch up – news reports indicated she'd been released, but Tim didn't think her likely to return to the marital home, which was, anyway, in need of a new form of address. Circumstances had rendered 'marital home' Orwellian in its incongruity. It was now the murder flat, the death location; a starter home for widows. He'd been parked a while before what should have been his first observation struck him – that the Dunstans' van sat a short way down the road . . .

Staying put wasn't an act of courage. Fact was, Tim was afraid that starting his car would attract attention . . . It occurred to him that, last Wednesday, Arkle hadn't even been pissed off. Firing his crossbow at strangers was Arkle in neutral. Since then, his brother had been killed. This wasn't someone whose attention Tim hungered to attract.

Thoughts like this only took you so far, and in the end left you where you started: behind the wheel of a parked car, watching a house whose front windows were dark, but shone with the hint of lights round the back. Tim unpeeled his fingers from the steering wheel. Somebody sneaked down the passage by the side of the house: *Katrina.* She was out of sight before he'd decided it hadn't been. Too solid. In his mind, Katrina had assumed an ethereal quality not entirely consistent with the details his memory had processed: Matisse-print dress; healthy hair; autumnal bruise carefully powdered over . . . Jesus, enough. It hadn't been Katrina because she looked too big; she moved differently. It was another while before things had started happening.

First, Arkle appeared in the street, looked up, looked down, then returned inside, to re-emerge moments later with somebody shorter, his face bandaged like the invisible man's. They got in their van and drove off. Tim's fingers had stuck to the wheel again, and sweat had broken out over his upper body . . . But Arkle hadn't seen him; Arkle's tail lights were turning the corner, and would be down the hill any moment. Tim wondered what had happened to the woman. Soon, when he could trust his legs, he was going to find out . . . When he looked up, another man was heading past. Whether he'd come out of the house, Tim didn't know, and he'd vanished into shadow before Tim got a good look.

He yawned suddenly. Hugely, in fact. Stopped pacing long enough to finish his wine and wonder about pouring another, but that would make three, and he'd decided not to drink tonight . . . He'd sit instead, while remembering what happened next: how he'd gone into the back yard, to hear muffled thumping from, he'd thought at first, the hearse . . . Tim didn't believe in ghosts, but it was instructive how ineffectual lack of belief was in the face of spooky thumping.

Except it had come from the freezer, not the hearse, and when he opened its lid, he found the woman who'd rescued him from Arkle with an apple. He hadn't recognised her sneaking in: memory, in fact, was shaky all over. 'I thought you were a redhead,' he told her later.

'Yeah, I get that a lot,' Zoë said.

. . . And then Tim must have slept, because light was creeping through the curtains, and the rain's soft hiss had been replaced by proper noises; the hum of life. The toytown rattle of a milk float. His bladder ached and his mouth felt rusty. Misplaced priority had him switch the kettle on before rushing to the bathroom; after which he checked upstairs for – what, exactly?

Intruders? A dim recollection of nocturnal rustling nudged him. Now it was safe, he was making sure. How smart was that? But he did it anyway, and of course both rooms were empty . . . There was a loose slate overhead, that was all. Feeling ridiculous, he returned downstairs. How could Arkle Dunstan have traced him anyway? They'd not been followed last night. Zoë had been sure of that.

He spooned coffee into a mug, opened the fridge, and found no milk. Toast, he thought. This was the way the mind worked: leapfrogging the immediate problem. Lack of milk was the immediate problem, but he'd already heard the float; there'd be a pint on the doorstep. How could Arkle Dunstan have traced him anyway? Out of nowhere, a smell arrived: a damp mouldiness of the sort that lurks on beaches. Wet sand . . . Tim shook his head to clear the image, but it persisted. Wet sand piled up in pens whose wood had rotted, spilling their contents over the concrete ground.

Passing through on your way where?

Oh, uh . . . St Ives.

From?

Oxford.

. . . What's your name?

And this, too, he had answered. How could Arkle Dunstan have traced him? Because Tim had given him all the information necessary . . .

He reached out on automatic for his coffee cup, to find it held dry granules: duh. He added water from the kettle, then reached for the milk. Duh. There was milk on the doorstep, though . . . So Arkle Dunstan could have traced him, and it was important to let Katrina – let Zoë – know this, but what was more important was, it hadn't happened yet. First thing first, which was fetching the milk. As he passed through the hall, he heard the slate rattling on the roof again: next weekend he'd fix that. It was a bright morning. The front path was five foot long, and spiders' webs decorated the hedge that bordered it. From Tim's angle of vision sunlight caught the overnight rain that clung to their threads, turning the hedge to lace and lattice-work; a dream of somebody else's wedding. A milk bottle seemed to hover in front of him. He blinked. A milk bottle hovered in front of him. Wrapped round it was a hand, attached to an arm, attached to Arkle Dunstan.

'Looking for something?' Arkle said.

IV

It was late when they got to bed. Even so, Zoë didn't sleep right away. She'd put Katrina in the spare bedroom; had to shepherd her around stacked boxes, unhung pictures, Joe's filing cabinets; had nearly apologised for the mess. Now she lay staring at the ceiling, sums of money dancing round her head. Katrina knew how to put her hands on the Dunstans' treasure; the cash Win's boss had converted their stolen jewellery into. Zoë had flirted with this possibility once already, and it hadn't seemed realistic. But this edged closer to the plausible, and she couldn't deny the money would be useful . . . A lifesaver. The only downside was, it was stolen money. Well, not the only downside. Others were that the Dunstans wanted it too, and that Arkle had a crossbow.

'You mean, they don't know where it is?'

'Baxter was in charge of the money,' Katrina had told her.

Because that was how they'd done things: each of the brothers had their role to play.

'No wonder they came looking for you,' Zoë said.

'Don't imagine they've given up yet.'

Round and round her head it went, like tigers round a tree. At length she must have been sucked into sleep, because she was wandering a corridor which kept turning corners without arriving anywhere. Overhead lights flickered nervously, while drawers were opened and closed, almost – but not quite – noiselessly. Electrics fizzed and plumbing burped. Somebody stepped into her room and Zoë woke with a start. Katrina stood by her bed, a cup of coffee in her hand. 'I didn't mean to wake you.'

Creeping into her room wasn't the best way to achieve this. Zoë sat up and took the proffered cup. 'What time is it?'

'Just gone eight.'

Which meant she'd had about four hours' sleep. 'Thanks.'

'Sorry. I couldn't sleep. I was worried.'

'About whatsername,' Zoë said. Katrina's brow furrowed. 'Helen Coe,' Zoë remembered.

'Yes. There must be someone we can call.'

'Must be. Not from here, though.' To stop another brow-furrowing, she added, 'I don't want my number on anybody's callback. Not while people are looking for you.'

'Oh.' Katrina sat on the end of Zoë's bed. Zoë moved her feet to make room. 'I'm not too good at this.'

'I'm not an expert myself,' said Zoë. The coffee was too hot. Probably be non-supportive to mention this. 'Look, go and lie down. I'll get dressed and find out what I can.' Which would not be much, and nothing good. Pretending to rub her eyes awake, she squeezed them shut instead; mentally replaying moments on a rainy road in the city last night – she'd known what Arkle Dunstan was looking for; felt certain there'd be no good news of Helen Coe. But what could she have done to stop the bad things happening? Fragments assembled in her mind, and curled into excuses. *I climbed a wall. I rescued Katrina.* Which was all very well, and might be a comfort to Helen Coe. If she was in any shape to receive it.

'I can do it.'

'That's okay.' Her response to having somebody in her flat was to want to leave it. She meant nothing personal by this, she would say if ever asked.

She banished Katrina, showered and dressed. Afterwards, she spent some time with Joe's filing cabinets, then went online and collected phone numbers. In between, she made more coffee. Things weren't always better with coffee, but they were reliably worse without it. Then she warned, or perhaps just asked, Katrina to stay inside, and left for the nearest phone booth, a few streets away.

Not far, but she wasn't there before her mobile rang. She leaned on a railing to answer it. Mobile phones had led to an alleged increase in brain cancers and tumours of the head, and a verifiable increase in people not looking where they're bloody going. Zoë made a practice of coming to a halt before engaging in conversation with an absent other.

'Zoë Boehm.'

'Wonders never cease. Your phone's switched on.'

It was true she'd had it turned off lately, because she'd been avoiding Jeff, who might still wonder where his car was. But this morning she'd reactivated it, in case Tim called. As Katrina said, the Dunstans wouldn't stop looking. Anything might happen yet.

But it wasn't Tim, it was Win – the pale baby-soft driver with lips like roses and buzz-cut hair; all of it perched on the body of a pro wrestler. Even bounced off a signal tower, her voice came over like a speech bubble. 'I thought we had a deal.'

'I know you did,' Zoë said.

'My boss has been trying to call the Dunstans.' There was a sameness to the conversation already. This was how it was going to be: Win would carry on saying whatever she had to say, and nothing Zoë added would make the slightest difference. 'Can't get an answer. Like they've fallen off the planet.'

'Perhaps they've gone on holiday.'

'It's as if they're deliberately avoiding him. The way you've been avoiding me.'

'Win. Win?'

'I'm listening.'

'There's always a first time. Win, whatever you thought we agreed the other evening in the café, we didn't. Can you follow that?'

Win paused. 'You know what I think?'

Zoë shook her head. Behind the railing was a children's playground, and though there were no children about, there was playful movement all the same: swings swung gently in the wind, and the roundabout creaked as it inched backwards and forwards over the same two degrees. There was a slide too, and a small smudged plastic horse or something, mounted on a thick spring; the only toy in evidence of which there'd been no direct equivalent in Zoë's childhood playgrounds. The horse, if that's what it was, was blue, and—

'Zoë?'

'. . . What do you think, Win?'

'I think now would be a good time to check out their place. The Dunstans. While they're elsewhere.'

'Not answering your phone doesn't mean you're somewhere else. I've had mine switched off, and I haven't been anywhere.'

'But yours is a mobile,' Win reminded her. 'You can be anywhere whether you're answering or not.'

Dream logic was nothing Zoë wanted to dispute. 'Win, I'm expecting a call. We'll continue this some other time.'

'You're not going after the money yourself, are you?' Something in that cartoon bubble carried the weight of the body it came from. *This would not be a good idea* was its undertow. 'You wouldn't do that, would you?'

'It's stolen money, Win.'

'That's often the best kind.'

'You've been driving cars for the wrong man too long. People die over that kind of cash.'

'People die anyway,' said Win. 'Money's as good a reason as any.'

'I'm about to go into a tunnel,' Zoë said, and broke the connection. She turned her phone off, put it in her pocket; walked on to the post office.

But when she reached it she kept walking; went as far as the bookshop before turning down a short road ending at a wall. Making this call from her mobile didn't matter. Harold Sweeney already had her number; besides, his were stored in her Nokia, not in her head. She rang the shop first, and got the same nothing as last time . . . The image it conjured was the same, too: a rotary phone rattling on a dusty counter, while junk mail piled up behind a locked door, and brittle sunlight chiselled through flaws in the metal shutters. There was a certain bleak romanticism here, but it didn't encourage Harold to answer. After a while Zoë gave up, and tried his home number instead.

She wasn't expecting a response. Why was she calling then? Because you tried all the doors; when you were looking for something, you kept opening doors until you found it. That it was always in the last place you looked was one of those irritating universals you had to put up with . . . These past days, when Zoë hadn't been reflecting on the death she'd lived through, or looking for Katrina Blake, she'd been wondering where Harold Sweeney was, and whether he'd indeed gone hunting Arkle Dunstan. A picture which kept morphing into one of Elmer Fudd: little brown suit and cap, shotgun at the ready . . . Either way, he remained her client until he'd paid her bill, and while Zoë's occupation probably ranked near politician in any public grading, she liked to think she'd retained certain standards. Knowing where her client was seemed a bare minimum. At the very least, she'd know where to send that bill.

All this in her head: no wonder she started when the phone was answered: 'Yes?'

'. . . Harold?'

(Hard not to call him Harold, given that's how she thought of him.)

'Is this . . . ?'

'It's Zoë Boehm.'

'Ah.'

Deep breath. 'Where've you been, Mr Sweeney?'

The building she was facing, back up the road – a multistorey block in the hospital grounds – was currently undergoing renovation, and scaffolding masked its façade. Across this was stretched, like some Christo-inspired event, a huge sheet of canvas, which whapped and smacked in the wind. It was the sound of a body at rest, aching to be in motion. Zoë had plenty of time to notice it while waiting for Harold Sweeney to reply.

'You're annoyed. You've a right to be.'

'Thanks.'

'You're pissed off.'

'If I need a thesaurus, Mr Sweeney, I'll ask. Where've you been?'

'I went away.'

'I'd got that far.'

'I was on the south coast. Near Brighton.'

'Did you have a nice time?'

'Ms Boehm—'

'Because for all I knew, you'd gone off on some hare-brained scheme. I thought you'd gone after—' She'd been about to say the Dunstans. 'I thought you'd gone after those thieves on your own.'

And then there was another pause, during which the canvas sail audibly grieved for open seas.

'Ms Boehm?'

'I'm still here.'

'Why would I have done that?'

It was a good question. One she didn't answer.

'I thought this was what I'd paid you to do.'

'You've paid me nothing yet. And I thought you'd be around to hear what progress I've made.'

'So. What progress have you made?'

Zoë tried not to sigh. She was obviously no wabbit, or Fudd wouldn't be tying her in knots.

'Ms Boehm?'

'Not too much,' she said.

'You haven't found them?'

'No,' she said. 'I haven't found them.'

Another pause. She leaned against the wall. A group of students crossed her line of vision, heading townwards. The moment during which she could have given Harold Sweeney the names of the men who'd robbed him, and arranged to collect her five thousand pounds, slipped out of sight about the same time the students did.

'I'm glad.'

It wasn't the response she'd expected.

'Ms Boehm?'

'I heard. I'm wondering why.'

'Because I did the wrong thing, sending you after them. It was dangerous and it was wrong. They shot a man, you'll remember.'

'I hadn't forgotten.'

'With a crossbow. Even if you'd found them, Ms Boehm – and I know now it was an impossible task – but if you had, then what? You might have been hurt too.'

That would have been another nice moment to tell him: the one in which he'd just said what she'd done was impossible. But she held her tongue.

'I was greedy. What they stole, I shouldn't have had in the first place. I told myself I didn't know for sure the . . . items were already stolen property. But I knew.'

'We all cut corners,' Zoë said, just to be saying something.

'We don't all drive a bulldozer, to be sure of making the

short cut,' Harold Sweeney said. 'Something else occurred to me, down at the seaside. You go to the seaside much, Ms Boehm?'

'Once in a while.'

'It's a good thinking place. The other thing that occurred to me was, maybe it was my own fault. You get involved with a bad crowd, you can't complain when things get nasty. You follow me?'

'Loud and clear.'

'The man I used to sell the items to, the under-the-counter items, his name's Oswald Price.'

'You didn't have to tell me that, Mr Sweeney.'

'No, but in your line of work, maybe it'll be useful sometime. I'm glad you came up short, Ms Boehm. I bet you don't hear that often.'

'Not really, no.'

There was another pause. The open connection swelled like an ocean, and the canvas sail flapped again. This should have been conducive to thought, given the seaside theory, but all Zoë was thinking was, maybe you did get to hear the ends of some parts of the story . . . It seemed she didn't have a client any more. And she tried to tell herself that his change of heart made it okay to lie to him; that anyway, she'd been lying for his own protection. That all this was getting a bit nasty for the likes of Harold Sweeney. But the fact remained: back in Zoë's flat was the only woman who knew where the stolen money was, and there was no chance poor Harold was seeing any of it . . . She'd given him, effectively, his five grand back. Didn't that give her the right to play her own game from here on in?

She wasn't sure. But thankfully he didn't know any of this, and broke the silence of his own accord.

'I was frightened,' he said simply. 'I was frightened they'd come back. The bald one? The one with the crossbow?'

'Yes,' Zoë said. Then added, 'You mentioned him.'

'He didn't have to shoot that man. He shot him because he wanted to.'

Zoë said, 'He's no reason to come back. He got what he was after.'

'Yes. So long as we don't stir things up.'

She said, 'Okay, Mr Sweeney. I think you're doing the right thing. I won't be sending a bill.'

'You don't need to do that.' Not do that, he meant. 'I'll pay you for your time.'

'I hadn't spent much time on it. Good luck, Mr Sweeney.' She disconnected before he could say more.

Then she walked back to the post office, where the coin box waited. Behind her, the wrapped building flapped and rustled, but it wasn't going anywhere.

Another place, another phone call.

'I was looking for Dennis.'

'Is that right? And what made you think you'd find him here?'

'A friend gave me the number.'

'A friend of yours or a friend of his?'

'Both. He was my husband.'

'Did he have a name?'

'Joe. Joe Silvermann.'

There was a pause. She heard a rasp, or maybe imagined one: a match being struck. A dull intake of smoke. 'I heard he died.'

'Yes.'

'I was sorry about that. You'd be Zoë, then.'

'That's right. And you'd be Dennis.'

'Possibly. Any friend of Joe's . . . owes me money.'

'He always spoke highly of you, Dennis.'

'Really?'

'No. I found your number in his files. First time I'd come across your name.'

'He kept a file on me? Jesus!'

'Don't feel paranoid. He had files on his primary school teachers. You were one among many.'

After a beat or two, he said, 'So, Zoë. Zoë Boehm, that right?'

'You've a good memory for names.'

'Being good at names is my main thing,' he said. 'As you'll know, if you've read my file.'

'That's exactly what we're going to talk about,' she said.

She didn't have a phonecard. She could have called from home – Bob Poland, after all, hadn't sliced her landline – but she didn't want to be an entry on a callback record. She fed coins into a slot instead.

'Chronicle.'

'I'm trying to reach Helen Coe.'

'Putting you through.'

But she wasn't put through to Helen Coe; was transferred, instead, to a male voice affecting boredom, but whose undertone had an elastic twang. 'She'll get back to you. What was it in connection with?'

'Isn't she well? I spoke to her yesterday.'

'At home or at the office?'

Zoë hung up; flipped through numbers she'd found in Joe's files – journos one and all, though guessing which among them had retired, descended into alcoholism, or quite rightly been put behind bars was anyone's guess. She scratched lucky third go: 'Coe? She went to work for the *Chronicle*.'

'Do you have her home number?'

'I think it's listed in my mobile. One second.'

Which multiplied to eighty. Zoe spent them finding a pen in her inside denim pocket, then smoking it . . . If she'd noted Coe's address last night, she wouldn't need to do this. Cars passed. A young couple scrutinised the blackboard roped to the railings of a restaurant over the road . . . The voice returned, and gave her Helen Coe's number.

*

Children had invaded the playground when she passed it heading home, and were watched from the periphery by groups of women and one or two men. By now, Zoë was suffering the exhaustion that comes from seeking information from strangers. She needed coffee. She needed peace and quiet. And she was returning to a flat with somebody else in it, which she wasn't accustomed to, and which was making her tense. One of the men caught her eye as she passed, and communicated envy: she was walking away, and he couldn't. The playground squawking sounded louder the further she got, which was either an aural illusion caused by nearby buildings or a horrible truth caused by children.

When she got home, Katrina was on the sofa: pale, calm, dressed. In daylight, her damaged face looked appalling. Her plum-coloured wound cast shadows. Automatically, Zoë raised a hand to her own bruise; the circular mark on her forehead she'd collected before being bundled into the freezer. It would pass, and she'd forget about it. What had happened to Katrina, though, wasn't something that would fade – the face would recover, the swelling subside, but the memory was going nowhere; would pop up with every startling noise, every sudden flash of light . . . A man had done this. She had killed the man before he could do it again. Most juries, Zoë imagined, would look at the photos of her injury, then think about themselves, their wives, their sisters, their girlfriends. Few would be thinking about the other photos: the ones showing Baxter Dunstan with a knife in his chest.

'Did you talk to her?' Katrina asked.

'I talked to her sister,' Zoë said.

'And?'

Zoë shut the door behind her. 'She's not dead.'

'Thank God.'

'She's in a coma.'

'. . . Is it bad?'

'I'm not sure how they grade them. I think you find out afterwards. She'll come out of it or she won't.'

'What about Jonno?'

'Okay, I think. Doesn't seem to be hospitalised, anyway.'

'And the Dunstans?'

Zoë sat. 'Remember what you said last night?'

'Most of it.'

'You could be right. Helen Coe's not talking. Jonno won't know what hit him. As far as the cops are concerned, the missing link is you.'

'They can't think *I* hurt them.'

'They'll certainly be interested in hearing your point of view.'

'But—'

'And it's not like you've not hurt anybody else.'

The phone rang. Zoë, not taking her eyes off Katrina, picked it up.

'Zoë?'

It was Tim Whitby, out of breath, as if he'd been the one who'd had to run to catch the phone.

'What is it, Tim?'

'I'm sorry, Zoë . . .'

There came the sound, unmistakable in the circumstances, though unidentifiable in any other context, of somebody taking the receiver from him.

Arkle Dunstan said: 'You're the one hit me with the chair, right?'

'It seemed like a good idea at the time.'

'You threw the apple, too.'

'There wasn't a chair handy.'

Watching, Katrina had got the message; had hardened into something like waxwork. Arkle Dunstan was on the line – his voice was in the room. She sat motionless, as if hoping it wouldn't notice her presence; as if it were crawling the walls like a spider on surveillance, waiting for a twitch on its web.

'What do you want, Dunstan?' Zoë asked. She'd already worked through the various ways he might have found her, and it had dawned on her that he hadn't: he'd found Tim. This couldn't be undone. What mattered was what happened next, which was going to involve Katrina, who was going to have to pull herself together. At the moment, she looked like she'd shatter if spoken to. Zoë thought: *Hell, woman, you killed the last man raised a hand to you. Get a grip . . .*

'She's with you, isn't she?'

'Who would that be?'

'And I've got your friend Tim.'

'Tell me, Arkle, do you think this is a gangster movie? Am I supposed to say, okay, let's swap? You think that's what I'll say? You're out of your fucking mind.'

'Listen—'

'No, you listen. You're halfway through a home invasion less than a mile from where you shot someone with a crossbow. How long do you think it's going to take to arrange an armed response? Ten minutes from now, you'll be looking back on this as your last free conversation.'

'No, you daft cow. I meant *listen*.'

Zoë heard him lay the receiver down. And then heard what happened next.

FOUR

THE ULTIMATE STALKER

9

I

'THIS MIGHT HURT.'

It did, of course, but what most shocked Tim, reconstructing the moment afterwards – no. What most shocked him, afterwards and at the time, was pain. But the second most shocking thing was, the way the brothers acted in total unspoken accord, as if there'd been a hidden meaning in Arkle's words, decoded only by Trent. Who, without hesitation, pulled Tim to his feet and pushed him against the wall of the living room . . .

. . . A while, this had been going on. There'd been conversation, mostly consisting of Arkle asking questions to which Tim didn't know the answer. A lot of them involved money. Tim was starting to put pieces together: it was like a mystery jigsaw puzzle he'd done once, which involved reading an incomplete murder story, whose villain the accompanying jigsaw revealed. A jigsaw minus a picture was tricky, but at least you approached it without preconceptions. You filled in the edges, and then you were on your own. Bits that looked like a hand could turn out to be a pigeon, or a juggler's hat. He'd finished it in the end. Here and now he was starting to get a vague outline, but a lot of the pigeons might still be jugglers' hats. Katrina knew where the money was hidden – money the Dunstans had stolen. It seemed Katrina hadn't been involved in the robberies, but Tim knew enough about the shallows of the human mind to recognise that this might be wishful thinking.

And then Arkle Dunstan, tiring of asking questions Tim didn't follow, had said, 'Who's the woman?'

He was looking at the photo of Emma on the mantelpiece. It wasn't the best picture Tim had of her, but it had been there for years, so it was still there now.

'My wife,' Tim said.

Arkle had glanced at the ceiling, as if she might be upstairs. 'Where's she, then?'

'She doesn't live here any more.'

'Not been lucky lately, have you?'

You could find truth anywhere, Tim supposed.

'Where's Kay?'

. . . Photographs apart, in the weeks following her death, Tim forgot Emma's face. It became impossible to conjure it from the black cupboard of his memory, and when he tortured himself trying to imagine her about her normal everyday tasks, the visions that arrived were of a walking corpse washing dishes, or dealing with the kettle. It was as if his most recent sightings of her, wired to various important pieces of medical machinery, had supplanted all trace of his living wife. And while the best way of quantifying the pain this caused him was to compare it to something heavy and sledgehammer blunt, another part of it was sharp as a stiletto, and went straight to what remained of his heart. Because, of course, the impossibility of retrieving her face was exactly his first memory of Emma, and brought back all the joyful pain of their early days, and his inability, in her absence, to picture the woman who had captured him. It was as if she'd been another jigsaw puzzle – an undoable one – though he'd been the one falling to pieces. And then he found she loved him too, and after that, he carried a constant perfect image of her in his mind . . . She had been younger than him, and now always would be. Would have been in any case. But more so now than ever.

And sitting on the sofa – Arkle prowling round him – trying to remember exactly what Katrina looked like instead, all Tim could summon up was dark hair falling over a pale face; the shifting pattern on a dress that sunlight played with. But when he stopped trying, Emma returned to him: wearing the same dress, crossing the same sun-patched stretch of hotel bar . . . For a moment, this took his breath away in familiar sledgehammer/stiletto fashion. And then the pain passed, as if it had been the ordinary cardiac warning after one drink too many, and he attempted again to summon up Katrina, because she, after all, remained living and vital, while Emma was gone forever. But he couldn't. Last night had been only their second encounter, but already she was lodged in – in what? In his heart, he should say, though it felt more like his bowel or lower intestine; somewhere not just organic but digestively functioning – wherever it was, anyway, there she clung, or there he clung to her . . . Tim wasn't so naïve as to think there was more to this than a grief-swung heart changing its beat. It had everything to do with loss, and nothing with connection. But it was happening, and it was happening to him. What else did he have to measure against?

Arkle said, 'Where is she?' again, and Tim said, 'I don't know.'

'It was you last night, wasn't it? Driving the car?'

'I don't know which car you're talking about.'

Even to his own ears, that sounded stupid. Which car didn't matter.

'We tracked her down.' Arkle sounded proud of this. 'The whole world, she could have been hiding. We found her.'

'I don't know who you mean.'

'Kay,' Arkle said patiently. Kind of patiently, anyway. It was possible he'd explode any second. 'Katrina.'

'We met once. In a hotel—'

'I know. You told me, remember?'

'You threatened me with your crossbow.'

Arkle said, 'I hit an apple. On the bounce. You should've seen it.'

'I was otherwise occupied.'

'It was a fucking Olympic shot.'

'I don't know where Katrina is.'

Trent said, 'Who's Zoë Boehm?'

Now they both looked at him.

Trent was standing by the phone, though Tim hadn't noticed him get up; he was looking at the scrap of paper on which Tim had scrawled Zoë's name and number. The first such note he'd made in a long while. Trent had pronounced Boehm *Bome*, which a lot of people did. Without Zoë to check him, Tim would have spelt it *Beam*.

'Nobody,' he said; way too late to be even quarter-way convincing.

'She's the one hit me with the chair, right?' Arkle said, in a tone of voice that suggested he was remembering what Zoë did for a living.

Actually, when Zoë had mentioned she'd hit Arkle with a chair, her tone had been much the same.

Tim said, 'You can't make me do anything I don't want to,' but even at this relatively early stage of his personal development, he knew that wasn't so.

Arkle said, 'Actually, I think you'll find I can make you do pretty much whatever I feel like.'

The important thing was to keep your cool. Arkle had acquitted himself brilliantly so far: despite recent aggravations, he'd yet to lose control, except with Trent a couple of times, and also with Helen Coe. Which memory was still working its way through him, with special reference to his knuckles and the palms of his hands. But maybe he was being harsh on himself.

You couldn't call that losing control. Circumstances had demanded he become physical. What kind of man failed to rise to the occasion?

Anyway: he wasn't going to hurt Tim Whitby until necessary. Control meant timing, if it meant anything.

He asked Trent, 'Any other numbers?'

Trent shook his head.

Arkle said to Whitby, 'Okay. I'm going to assume this is the woman who's been helping you and Kay steal my money.' Our money, he thought. 'Our money. Which pisses me off, but I'm prepared to let it pass. Call her up.'

'She's not involved—'

'She is now.'

Trent dumped the phone in Whitby's lap, and Whitby looked at it as if it were a strange machine he'd not been taught to use. Christ. It wasn't as if Arkle couldn't push the numbers himself. Whitby doing it gave Arkle the edge, that was all; an admission he was on the right track.

'Something you might want to think about,' he said.

Whitby looked up.

Arkle backhanded him, not too hard; it probably looked worse than it felt – probably hurt Arkle more than it hurt Tim Whitby. Well, not literally, but it jarred his knuckles. 'That didn't hurt much,' he said. Whitby, tears in his eyes, looked like he disagreed. 'Trust me, that was nothing. Make the fucking call.'

A couple of minutes later, when his hands had stopped shaking, that's what Tim Whitby did.

'Listen—'

A calm buzz on the other end of the line was all Tim could hear. Zoë taking charge of the situation.

'No, you daft cow. I meant *listen.*'

And then Arkle was saying, 'This might hurt,' which it did,

of course, but what shocked Tim almost as much was the way the brothers acted in total unspoken accord: Trent pulling Tim to his feet and pushing him against the wall of the living room; kicking his feet apart the way cops did in movies, though it wasn't *Tim* who was the bad guy . . . Then Arkle dropped the receiver and stepped across to him, and then Tim wasn't thinking anything, because lightning had struck. The world fizzed into black noise and static. Breath sucked out of him, immediately replaced by blind cold pain, focused on his stomach. Later he would think of penalty shots he'd seen in internationals; of tries converted, and know that Arkle hadn't kicked him much less softly than that. It was a wonder his balls were still attached.

Meanwhile, black noise and static:

'. . . already know you've got her . . .'

'. . . keep this up all day . . .'

'. . . how much of him do you think there'll be left, by the time the cops get here?'

He wondered if Emma were looking down on the mess he was making. Nothing remotely like this had happened when she'd been around. Or if it had, it had happened elsewhere, to other people, so didn't count . . . That's what he thought he was thinking anyway. It might have been something he added later. At the time, things were mostly pain: brightly coloured pain in fantastic blotchy shapes that swallowed each other then spat each other out, like an animated Rorschach test. What did they all remind him of? They all reminded him of pain.

'. . . hundred grand, two hundred. What's it to you, bitch? It's ours . . .'

Something was being hung up. Probably the phone. Now something was being picked up. Probably Tim. Hands hooked under his arms and threw him back on the sofa, where he curled into as small a Tim as possible, in case this hurt less. It didn't. He squeezed his eyes so tightly shut the darkness shone. The ache in his stomach was a balloon, into which air was steadily pumped.

There was more conversation. Tim, head buried in cushions, heard: *worra worra worra worra worra.*

Time must have passed. Light span and buckled. Bells rang.

The next English phrase that made any sense was, 'Okay. Let's go.'

II

On a road heading away from the city centre, past the university press and the arts cinema, a walled drive ran off to the left just before shops and restaurants yielded to houses and flats; a drive lined by trees big and old enough to cast heavy cover, even now, in their largely leafless state. It had been June last time Zoë was here, and the trees had shed deep green light on the rough ground. The cemetery gates kept daylight hours, according to a board hung in the big stone porch, and were imposing, serious gates; might have been planted to guard some moneyed, exclusive community, though money and exclusivity were not entry requirements here, or not the primary one. On that June day Zoë had wandered through the open gates to find a path, also tree-lined, which wound into a circular area made up of brick-built flower beds, a bench and a litter bin, so visitors could rest among plantlife without making a mess. A breeze, as it happened, had done this anyway, and papers and wrappers were scattered about; some coming to rest against gravestones, as if taking rubbings. The graves were nominally arranged in rows, but the years had tilted the majority from the perpendicular; now, like English teeth, they leaned this way and that, though rooted in straight lines. The cemetery had a bedded-down air; told a tale of grief surrendering to neglect, and was hemmed on several sides by the ironworks, whose green-tinged windows overlooked the mostly forgotten. Zoë found few recent dates, and no recent offerings. Somehow, this was irrelevant. It is not why we die but when that matters. And such places paid testimony to the fact that even the forgotten have their memorials; and that though we'll all end up history, history always stakes a claim on the present. Or something like that. A hard-edged comfort, but at least it was honest.

Today, she'd chosen the cemetery because almost nobody went there.

On the phone, Arkle had said: 'I can keep this up all day. 'Course, he's likely to get tired of it sooner than me.'

What Zoë had just heard had been blunt and violent; had ended in a high-pitched yelp, as if a puppy had been chastised.

'You bastard—'

'Yeah yeah. How much of him do you think there'll be left, by the time the cops get here?'

She could feel Katrina's eyes burning into her; a lasered accusation of impending betrayal.

'What do you want?'

'She's with you, isn't she?'

'What do you want?'

'Her. And I want my money. Our money. She knows where it is.'

Zoë said, 'How much are we talking, exactly?'

'A hundred grand, two hundred. What's it to you, bitch? It's ours . . .'

He didn't know. All those robberies; all those pay-offs. But Baxter had handled the money, and Arkle had no exact idea how much was involved.

'Don't hurt him any more,' she said.

'I wish I could promise. But the longer I don't have my money, the crosser I get.'

He was enjoying this. He was top dog again, taking potshots with his crossbow.

Zoë raised a hand, palm flat, to keep Katrina quiet. 'So what do we do?'

'Where is she?'

'Not far.'

'We swap. Kay for your friend. While he's still worth trading.'

'Don't hurt him any more,' she said again.

'Clock's running . . .'

And then they'd been alone again, just Zoë and Katrina. Arkle's voice, which had crawled round her walls like a spider, had been sucked back down the line, leaving the same vacuum that happens when a TV set switches off.

Katrina said: 'He'll kill me.'

'All you have to do is tell them where the money is.'

'You think?'

'We're past the stage where they can do anything to you and hope to get away with it. They'll settle for the money at this point. After that, they'll run. And let's face it, it's not like they'll get far.'

'You're forgetting, Baxter was the brains. What's worse, Arkle thinks he's got brains too. He does whatever he does, and tells himself afterwards it was a plan. So he's never had a plan that's failed yet.'

'He should run for office.'

'I'm glad you're finding this funny.'

'He just hurt Tim. Tim's the reason Arkle hasn't got you already. So no, I'm not finding it funny. Where'd you hide the money?'

'Somewhere nobody can get it.'

'If you don't trust me, who can you trust? I saved your life, remember? Tim and me both.'

'Maybe that was part of your plan.'

Zoë laughed. 'Right. Think about it, Katrina. You approached Tim in that hotel, not the other way round. How'd we work that?'

Katrina seemed to be holding her breath, and the bruise covering half her face flushed redder, like a sunset on the turn. 'I'm sorry,' she said at last. 'It's in a storage facility. Just outside Totnes. One of those security depots, full of cargo containers.'

Zoë said, 'And that's safe?'

'Safer than a bank. People rob banks. Those storage places, they're where you stash Grandma's furniture once she goes into a home.'

'Arkle doesn't seem clear exactly how much we're talking about.'

'Only Baxter knew that,' said Katrina.

'How about where it came from?' Zoë asked.

Katrina looked away. 'He started by telling me it was cash that came out of the business. Cash they weren't declaring.'

'Can't have sounded too convincing once they'd closed the business down.'

'I tell myself I wasn't sure, couldn't know for certain. I knew it was dodgy money, but . . . I told myself I didn't *know*.'

And that, Zoë thought now, passing the lane to the graveyard, had the ring of truth. Confessing she'd lied to herself, Katrina had sounded honest . . . Not that Zoë would have believed her otherwise.

On the next corner, she turned left. A couple of hundred yards along the road, she found what she was looking for, which made her smile for the second time in fifteen minutes; this one a tight smile, without humour in it. Then she turned and went back the way she'd come, and headed into the cemetery.

'I should have worn the suit,' Arkle said to no one in particular.

No one in particular answered.

His tropical suit; the one designed for a cheap country with big landscapes. One he could wear marching home by torchlight, kill strung from a pole. The one he'd not worn because he'd not been hunting yet.

They were in Tim Whitby's car: Arkle driving; Trent and Whitby in the back. The van was history. They'd left it in a lane ten minutes from the house they'd nearly taken Kay from; smashed, but drivable; keys in the ignition. Local kids were probably using it for handbrake practice now. Ten minutes after *that*, they'd boosted an illegally parked car they'd later dumped on the outskirts of Oxford. Tim Whitby's house, they'd found using the phone book: no internet nonsense this time. He reached a junction, and behind him Trent poked Whitby, making him yelp and release information.

'Straight on,' Trent said.

He drove straight on. A cemetery, the woman had said, when she called back; a cemetery was where they'd do the swap – Whitby for Kay. St Saltpetre's? Something like that. Not a major landmark, which was cool. Last time they'd gathered, furniture had been damaged. However this went, an audience probably wasn't a great idea.

Whitby, answering questions, had made these huffy little gasps, though Arkle didn't reckon he'd kicked him that hard.

The sun was out, bouncing unexpected dazzles off shiny surfaces. The breeze was warm, lacked bite. Arkle was wearing his long dark overcoat: unnecessary, but it wouldn't draw attention in an empty graveyard. And in the car he was anonymous; gliding sleekly through post-rush-hour streets. At a roundabout, guided by Whitby (prodded by Trent), Arkle swung almost full circle to avoid the town centre, and found himself driving past a row of primary-coloured restaurants. This was the city of dreaming spires. So far, spires were outnumbered by buses and off-licences.

. . . Last time they'd met, this Zoë had broken a chair over his head. Which had hurt, but that wasn't the point. The point was, she'd *broken a chair over his head*, and that was just taking advantage.

Focus, though. He reached another junction; took another

instruction. Focus. Revenge was important, but you had to pick your targets . . . Soon, in the next ten minutes or so, he'd have his hands on Kay, and she'd lead him to the money.

One way or the other, Arkle would get his hunt. He might not be bringing her home strung from a pole, but that had never been the main purpose of the exercise.

In the cemetery, on the bench by the flower beds, Zoë sat. The wind whispered in the trees, but she couldn't catch what it was saying; the branches tore all meaning to shreds before the words reached ground level. She stood and looked about once more, in case the whispering was a cover for other, earthbound noises, but saw nobody. To all appearances, she was alone in the graveyard. Though of course, no one is ever really alone in a graveyard.

From the road came the sound of the occasional car. From the flats a few hundred yards distant life hummed, in its non-specific way.

At home, before she'd called Arkle Dunstan back to arrange a rendezvous, she'd asked Katrina: 'Where's the key?' The key to the money; the key to the storage facility. 'At your father's?'

'What makes you think that?'

Zoë said, 'If it were at your flat, you'd already have it. And you don't, do you?'

'No,' Katrina said. 'I don't.'

And she'd told Zoë where it was, producing Zoë's first smile in a while.

She leaned back, conscious of being watched, and looked at the tree overhead as the wind rippled it, turning its leaves their other colour. One span free as she watched, and pirouetted madly earthward, then lifted suddenly to twirl off like a butterfly – death's last and neatest trick: making something seem most alive in the moments immediately following its extinction. An irony worth bearing in mind, as adrenalin pumped through her system . . . That nerve tickling Zoë now was her nicotine centre. Starved for so long, it was taking the opportunity to fuss. She tamped it down, willed it back into submission, and saw Arkle Dunstan heading down the path towards her.

He was followed by Tim, who was followed by the one who'd driven the van into the bollard last night – Trent Dunstan, she supposed – whose face was a match for Katrina's, if only in respect of the damage it bore. Stand them at opposite ends of a casualty ward, and they'd bookend all the injuries between. But that was a slow-growing thought, taking root to blossom later. What mattered at the time was Arkle: his long black coat which seemed unnecessary for the weather, and which might hide just about anything. The way the sun shone off his shaved head; flashed off his eyes too, and even his teeth, as his lips parted in a thin smile. Which wasn't a smile but a snarl.

'You're the woman,' he said.

'That would be me, yes.'

'Where's Kay?'

She looked past him, which took an effort. 'Are you okay, Tim?'

Tim said something, cleared his throat, tried again. 'More or less.'

'Have they hurt you?'

'They—'

'Fuck, am I invisible or what?'

'There's people buried here,' she told him. 'Watch your tongue, would you?'

Arkle Dunstan watched hers instead; his gaze fixed on her mouth as he undid two buttons on his overcoat. Then he laughed. 'There's a bump the size of an egg on the back of my head. Good job it was a chair you used, not a table.'

'Trust me,' Zoë said. 'If I'd had a crane, I'd have hit you with that instead.'

'Where's Kay?'

'Not here.'

'Right.' He looked round, as if expecting her to pop out from behind a gravestone. 'This is some fucking joke, right?'

She would really, really have liked to be smoking right now. 'It turns out she didn't like the idea of being swapped, Arkle. She thinks you might hurt her.'

'Me?' he asked. 'The bitch killed my brother and stole my money. Does she think I can't take a joke?'

'Well, your big brother slapped her around—'

'My little brother.'

'Oh.'

'I'm the oldest.'

'Either way, he slapped her round. I suppose she's worried it runs in the family.' She couldn't help looking at Trent when she said this. For some reason – where did notions like this come from? – for some reason his bruise looked more mechanical than Katrina's, as if crude technology had been involved in its creation.

Arkle undid another button. 'So now I know where she isn't,' he said. 'Where is she?'

'She's staying out of your way,' Zoë said. 'I'm all you get.'

This was what they'd decided, or what Zoë had decided. Or maybe it was what Katrina had decided, while allowing Zoë to think she had. Here in the graveyard, Arkle Dunstan two feet away, it didn't feel like a situation Zoë might have willed on herself.

'He wants to kill me,' Katrina had said.

'He wants the money more.'

'You don't know him like I do.'

'I don't know him at all. But he'll go for the money. Anyone would.'

She'd been sure of that. She'd thought of all the people she'd like to wreak havoc upon – starting and finishing with Bob Poland – and knew she'd take the money too, if only to crawl out of this hole she'd found herself in. A phantom figure, her tax debt, swam through her mind: £4,731.26. Phantom because it didn't exist: she didn't have it. Going by what Katrina had said, you could lose that much from the Dunstans' stash just rounding down to the next whole number. The problem was, it was dirty money.

On the other hand, there was an awful lot of it.

'I suppose,' Zoë said, 'it really belongs to whoever owned the jewellery that was fenced to the guys the Dunstans stole it from.'

'Or their insurance companies . . .'

'Well, we've got ten minutes,' Zoë said. 'We should be able to come up with something.'

So here she was, saying: 'She's staying out of your way. I'm all you get.'

'That's nice. But what if I don't want you?' Arkle undid the last button, and his overcoat dropped open heavily. He thrust his hands into its pockets.

'Oh, you'll want what I've got.'

'What's that?'

Zoë looked at Tim. 'You sure you're okay?'

He shrugged, swallowed. 'I've felt better.'

'Let him go,' she said to Arkle. 'And I'll tell you.'

He didn't laugh. Instead, he said, 'Ho ho.'

Trent looked round. 'She's called the cops, Arkle.'

'Uh-uh.' Arkle's eyes remained on Zoë. 'She's not a cop-caller. She's a chair-breaker.'

Zoë didn't like him looking; didn't like his unbuttoned coat. Didn't like the here and now. But no other reality presented itself, so she made do with what was.

She said, 'I know where the money is.'

'Our money,' Arkle said.

'If you like.'

'The money Kay stole.'

'Well, the money you stole, if you want to get technical. She knows where it is, that's all. So do I.'

For a moment his gaze drifted, and he stared at a nearby copse – a copse, in a cemetery? Bunch of bushes, anyway. Behind her, but that's what he was looking at: she'd made sure she knew what was there before she'd sat down.

He looked back. 'Where is it?'

'Let him go. Then I'll tell you.'

'Tell us. Then we'll let him go.'

'Ho ho,' she said.

He glanced towards the copse again. 'You picked here because it was quiet?'

'I picked here because I know it and you don't.'

'Where's Kay?'

'You're not going to find her, Arkle. I don't even know where she is myself.'

'Oh, I'll find her.'

'I don't think so. Not if you want the money.' God, she needed a cigarette. 'I didn't call the cops, Arkle, you're right about that. But I wrote them a letter. You want the money, you've got twenty-four hours to collect it. And if you want to stay free, you'd better be on a plane the same day, because I also told them it was you put Helen Coe in hospital.'

Arkle said, 'What if I don't believe you?'

'Then stick around. The post here's not great, but it gets there.' Three times out of five, she didn't add.

Trent said, 'I don't think she's bluffing, Arkle.'

His wound didn't so much muffle his voice as scratch it, as if something sharp was lodged in his mouth; snagging his words as they left his lips.

Arkle tilted his head to one side. 'What's your angle?'

'Let him go.'

'She got to you, didn't she? Same way she got to Bax.'

'Clock's ticking, Arkle.'

'You keep using my name like you know me.'

Zoë felt as if she did. Felt as if her first glimpse of him, on a busy street in Totnes, had been lifetimes ago; that ever since, he'd been at her shoulder like a perverted guardian angel. For a long time, she'd thought he'd tried to kill her – had sealed her in a fridge and walked away. And knowing he hadn't didn't alter her opinion: that he was out on an edge; the edge you only noticed when somebody else fell off it. That his head probably glowed in the dark. That of all the people whose attention she didn't need, he was way up there. And yet here they were, talking.

She said, 'Does Big Red Box mean anything to you?'

Arkle said, 'Is that English? Start making sense.'

'It's a storage place,' Trent said. 'Off the Newton Abbot road.'

'So you're the Yellow Pages now?'

Zoë said, 'I'm telling you where the money is, that's all.'

A better way of halting conversation, she'd yet to find. *That couple of hundred grand you were wondering about? Here's where it is.*

After a bit, Arkle said, 'She told you that? It doesn't make sense.'

'No?'

'It's too public. Anyone can go in.'

Trent said, 'Well—'

'Shut up.'

Zoë said, 'You need to be an authorised user. You need a key.'

'. . . So where's the key?'

'This is where you let Tim go.'

Tim said, 'I'm not leaving you here with this pair.'

'Tim? You shut up too, okay?'

'I hate being interrupted, don't you?' Arkle asked.

'Time's wasting,' Zoë said. 'Let Tim go. Then we discuss where the key is.'

Trent said, 'Arkle—'

'Shut up. I'm thinking.'

You could almost watch it happening, too. Almost see the cogs turning behind pale blue eyes, which seemed to look out on a different landscape to everybody else's. The world according to Arkle. Whose coat hung lopsided, as if there were something heavy in a pocket.

For the minute it took him to reach a decision, everything came to a stop in the graveyard: no wind, no noise, no overhead birds. Then Arkle snapped back to life and said, 'Right.' He looked at Tim Whitby. 'Fuck off, then.'

Trent said, 'Arkle—'

'Shut up.'

Tim opened his mouth, but Zoë shook her head. 'I'll see you later.'

'I could—'

'Don't. Don't do anything. Just go. Now.'

It was always possible that if you very quickly told a man four times to do something, he'd get the message.

He didn't like it, that was obvious, and Zoë, in her turn, liked him for that. But mostly what she wanted from him was to leave without fuss, and she was relieved to see that's what he was doing. He cast a look of pure venom at Arkle – never underestimate the anger of a gentle man – but Arkle wasn't looking. His eyes were fixed on Zoë; his stare so unrelenting, he might have been taking her pulse.

Tim said, 'Take care, Zoë.'

'I will.'

He headed off along the winding path, towards the outside world.

Arkle said, 'If this is all a big lie, it's gunna piss me off something rotten.'

'Katrina wants you out of her life,' Zoë told him. 'Money's a small price to pay.'

'Long after the money's spent, my brother will still be dead.'

Tim had gone. Zoë was alone with Arkle and Trent. The fact that things had gone to plan so far wasn't a great comfort.

'We don't even know how much we're talking about,' she said. 'Baxter covered all that, didn't he?' She looked around. Nothing was moving. 'I'm working on the assumption it's about two hundred grand.'

'Where's the key?'

'I tell you, then you leave, right?'

Trent said, 'Arkle—'

'Shut up. You think I'm stupid? You're coming with us. Bax reckoned he had the brains, but I'm still the oldest.'

'It's falling apart, you know that. You've left a trail a mile wide—'

'So stop wasting time. Where's this key?'

She said, 'Back where you started. In Totnes.'

'I'd worked that out. Where else would Bax keep it? Where exactly?'

'Uh-uh. Not till we get there.'

He sneered. 'You don't trust me, do you?'

'You think?'

Trent said, 'Arkle—'

'Yeah, I see him.'

The time he'd spun on his heel and put a bolt through the apple – Zoë hadn't been watching, exactly. She'd been aware of it happening, but had been on the other side of a wooden gate, her attention focused on making sure Tim Whitby got through it. This time, she had a ringside seat. Something had moved behind her; somebody had edged into view, and Arkle had seen them do it. With his left hand, he opened his overcoat;

with his right, he drew out the crossbow Velcroed to its lining – she heard a velvet rip as it tore free. It was loaded and primed already; she had a notion you had to wind them like a watch – did she think that at the time, or afterwards? Doesn't matter. What happened was as he'd boasted: an Olympic reaction. One moment he was talking; the next, the bow was in his hand, its bolt flashing past her like a natural event, and even before she'd fully registered this, a scream had burst through the already skewed normality of the morning, and she knew his bolt had found its mark.

'He one of yours?' Arkle asked, unperturbed.

'Not exactly,' Zoë said. 'But I know who it is.'

Without waiting to see what he thought about it, she turned and headed for the copse he'd been eyeing earlier, behind which a man lay full stretch on the ground, clutching his thigh and running out of breath. A scream was whistling away into the big blue nowhere. He was gearing up for his second when Zoë reached him.

She said, 'Golly, Bob. Somebody's shot you in the leg with a crossbow. That must hurt.'

'Call a . . . fuckenambulance!'

'Sure, Bob. Right away. I don't even know why I'm wasting time discussing it.'

'. . . Bitch.'

'Definitely. But not a stupid bitch, Bob. Shall I tell you what your big mistake was? It was cutting every electrical connection I've got except my landline. That's what you call a clue, Bob. If you'd ever been a policeman, you'd know about those. Oh, hang on. You were a policeman, till I killed your job. If you'd ever been a good one, I meant.'

'. . . Fuck you.'

'Yeah, right. Or maybe I could just dump you in a fridge.'

This was another of those occasions when she really ought to have been lighting a cigarette. It was practically a moral obligation. But she had to make do with looking down on him, hands on hips. There was a saying, if you stood on the banks of the river long enough, the bodies of your enemies would float past. Standing over them while they writhed in pain had its moments too.

The comment about the fridge penetrated, and he managed a response. 'You should have fucken died in it.'

But she didn't need his confirmation. Once she'd realised he'd tapped her phone, she'd known it had been Poland tipped her into the freezer. He'd been the man Tim had seen outside Katrina's father's house; had been the man in the pub, too, pretending to be press – *You're not the first to ask today*, the barman had said, before sending Zoë in the direction of Blake's house. All this on the day Win had called her. *You plan to knock him and his brothers over*, Zoë had said; *take them for, what, a couple of hundred grand?* That's what had drawn Bob on. Fake death notices were one thing; the scent of big money another. And the opportunity to bop Zoë on the head and drop her in a box was evidently unmissable, which was why she wasn't too upset he'd been shot – though if she had to put hand on heart, she'd probably admit to being glad she wasn't smoking.

But all she said to Bob was, 'I didn't.'

Arkle was behind her. 'Who,' he said, 'is this prick, anyway?'

Poland had given up screaming, but hadn't stopped writhing yet, and still clutched his thigh, from which Arkle's bolt protruded. There was surprisingly little blood. Zoë guessed it had missed the bone, but she'd be the first to admit she wasn't a doctor. Either way, bones mended. He'd get over it.

'Somebody else who's interested in your money.'

'You invited him?'

'No, he crashed,' said Zoë.

Arkle, maybe absent-mindedly, maybe not, took another bolt from his pocket, and fitted it into the slot of his bow. For a moment, Zoë saw this slipping out of hand – any second now, she'd be watching Arkle fire a chunk of metal through Bob Poland's head. And while there'd been times she'd imagined similar punishments visited on the creep, the key word was 'imagined'. Reality was too harsh an arena. She'd seen dead bodies before, and knew they weighed like an albatross round the neck.

With her left hand, she gently pushed the crossbow upwards. 'Don't.'

'I don't like being told what to do.'

'Murder him in cold blood,' she said, 'and everything finishes here. You'll have to shoot me too.'

At the back of Zoë's mind lurked the possibility that he'd judge this an appropriate course of action.

Bob Poland said, 'You're all fucken meat, you know that? Dead fucken meat.'

I've changed my mind. Kill him. No: she stopped herself in time. Instead she said, 'Be quiet.' And to Arkle, 'It's time to move. You might want to take his car keys. You'll certainly want his phone.'

'. . . Why his keys?'

'Because Tim'll have reclaimed his car. He's the type to carry a spare set.'

Trent said, 'We'd better go, Arkle.'

Zoë was getting better at interpreting him, though he still sounded like he was speaking through a mouthful of doughnut.

Arkle bent and said something to Poland, who without hesitation reached inside his jacket for mobile phone and car keys.

Trent said, 'Arkle—'

'Don't you ever shut up?' So suddenly none of them were expecting it, Arkle pulled the bolt from Poland's leg. Poland whooped – the noise of a bird shot down – and blacked out.

Arkle wiped the bolt on Poland's jacket. 'These things cost money.'

After a moment, Trent said, 'I was going to say, where's his car parked?'

'. . . Fuck.'

'It's round the corner,' Zoë said. Finding it had made her smile, though there'd never been much humour in it.

Arkle looked at her. 'All this turns out to be a scam—'

His eyes were pale blue bottomless holes.

'It isn't,' she replied. Hoping her voice was steady; imagining it wasn't.

They left the cemetery.

III

Through the stone arch, up the lane, out on the street – if Tim Whitby had fashioned a self-image at that point, it would have been a mole thrusting its snout into the air after too long underground. He found himself hauling in great mouthfuls of air, savouring its petrol aftertaste as if it were a fine wine, or at least a cigarette . . . One of which he could murder right now, though first he had to fetch help for—

'Tim.'

He turned, heart pounding: it was Arkle. But it wasn't.

Katrina said, 'Come on. We have to hurry.'

'Yes. They've got Zoë—'

'It's okay. I'll explain in the car.'

How could it be okay? But what he actually said was, 'Which car?'

'Yours. It's round here, isn't it?'

'Yes, but—'

'And you've got keys? Zoë said you were the type to carry a spare set. If Arkle's got the others, I mean.'

Tim said, 'I don't see why she thinks I'm—'

'Do you or not?'

'Well, yes, but—'

'So come on.'

And because she took his arm, he went.

If she'd thought he might leave her on the kerb, Zoë would have told Arkle where the key was then and there. Would have called the police the moment they were gone – there were times to cut your losses, take your licks; put a brave face on your favourite cliché. But Arkle just opened the door and waved her in. She was driving, apparently. The car was a Beamer, a real boat. Poland had once boasted that he changed wheels every October, but this one had a few years on the clock.

She wondered what their chances were of reaching Totnes before the car was reported stolen, and what Arkle's reaction would be to flashing lights in the rear-view, and an invitation to pull over. Or to open his coat so the nice policeman could see what was under there . . .

But it was pointless dwelling on what might happen. Best to get on with it; to deal with whatever came up.

Arkle said, 'I was aiming for that.'

'. . . What?'

'His leg. I was aiming for his leg.'

Arkle was behind her, next to Trent. Zoë felt like a chauffeur. Every so often something nudged the small of her back through the seat, and however much she knew it was his knee, her stubborn mental picture remained that of a crossbow: primed and ready to tear her insides out.

'Well,' she said. 'That's what you hit.'

'I could have aimed for his . . . navel. Aimed for his navel, I'd still have hit it.'

'Navels are pretty small,' Zoë agreed.

'You taking the piss?'

'I'm trying not to,' she said. 'I saw you hit that apple, remember?'

'Olympic shot,' he said. 'The Lone Ranger couldn't have pulled that off.'

'. . . No.'

There was silence for a few moments, and then Arkle whistled the first few bars of the William Tell Overture.

At times, joining the dots of somebody else's thought processes was a joy and a delight. At others, what worried you was the gaps in between.

Zoë kept her mouth shut. Concentrated on the road, whose white lines flashed like dots: now here, now gone. The picture they formed drawing her closer to Totnes.

'Big Red Box?'

'It's a storage place.'

'And we're going there why?'

. . . Though, truth to tell, Tim didn't care. Why had mattered when he was being assaulted in his own sitting room; when Arkle Dunstan was kicking him in the crotch. Why was best reserved for the bad things in life: *Why is this happening to me? Why did Emma have to die?* There were many such questions, but answering them improved nothing: Emma still died; Tim's stomach still hurt. Why was he in a car with Katrina? Didn't matter. She told him anyway.

'The Dunstans? My husband, his brothers? They're crooks, Tim. Robbers.'

'And this Big Red Box place . . .'

'Is where Baxter hid the proceeds. The others don't know about it.'

Well, it was good to get that established.

He said, 'So it's a stash of stolen jewellery?'

The notion of a pirates' lair, loaded with rubies, wasn't any more ridiculous than some other recent events.

'Not exactly. They fenced the jewellery. It's cash.'

This stretch of road was bordered with fields grazed by

cows; big dull placid creatures who didn't care about the whys either.

Tim said, 'So once the police have it, the Dunstans'll be off your case, right?'

'In an ideal world.'

'I mean, if the money's out of their reach . . .'

'We've got to get it first.'

'Well, yes . . .'

'No, I mean we've got to get it *first*. Arkle doesn't know where it is. But Zoë will tell him. He'll hurt her otherwise.'

Tim glanced at her. She was staring straight ahead, the damage to her face hidden from him, and he could imagine her unblemished. He'd yet to see her so. That first night, in the hotel, there'd been the bruise she'd tried to cover with make-up; which was what had started all this, for Tim. He had planned that night as an ending, but it had turned out the opposite. Life was what happened while you were making other plans. The same was probably true of death, but in Tim's case, Katrina's bruise had shelved that for the moment.

'Well,' he said at last. 'We'd better make tracks then,' and put his foot on the accelerator. The cows, already some distance behind them, fell further and further away. Tim had forgotten their existence already.

Arkle said, 'You ask me, old people, we'd be doing them a favour if we rounded them all up and had them quietly shot or something.'

Trent had fallen asleep. Zoë didn't answer.

Arkle said, 'You ask me, old people, we'd be doing them a favour if we rounded them all up and had them quietly shot or something.'

She said, 'That's your considered opinion, is it?'

He didn't much care what your reply was. But you had to reply, so he could say what was on his mind.

'Take Kay's old man. Not long back he was like normal people. Then he gets old, and it's like flicking a switch. These days, staring at a wall's about all he can manage. He probably fucks that up too, if you pay attention.'

They were on the outskirts of Totnes, heading for Katrina's father's house. The roads had mostly been clear, though twice Zoë's heart had skipped when police cars appeared. The first had been speed-trapping in a lay-by, and hadn't budged. But the second had flashed past at upwards of ninety miles per, and from the moment its siren screamed into her consciousness, Zoë had been certain they were its prey. She'd driven faster as it swept up the outside lane, and only once it had torn off into the distance did she ease up, its howl still doppling in her ears. Throughout, neither Arkle nor Trent said a word. For Arkle, she thought, stuff didn't exist if he didn't want it to. 'Stuff' here included other people, who he didn't mind hurting because he barely believed in them.

Now Arkle said: 'I ever get that old, I hope somebody shoves me off a cliff.'

'Oh, there'll be a queue.'

But she said it quietly, so he didn't hear. She was navigating the roundabout now: they'd be at Katrina's father's house in minutes.

Tim, not much earlier, had navigated the same roundabout, responding obediently to Katrina's every instruction. Not that he'd needed it. He'd been here so often lately, he felt part of the neighbourhood.

'We've made good time,' he said.

'The roads were clear. So will they.'

'But we set off first.'

After a while, Katrina said, 'She'll try to delay them. The more time she can waste, the better.'

'Arkle's on a short fuse.' Tim's judgement was sound on this. 'Zoë needs to be careful.'

'I didn't say it was the best plan in the world. We had ten minutes to hatch it.'

'I don't want to do anything that'll get Zoë hurt.'

'None of us do,' Katrina said. 'But the plan was to stop Arkle getting his hands on the money. Getting his hands on me, come to that.'

'I won't let him hurt you,' Tim said.

'That's very sweet. How would you stop him?'

Tim didn't reply.

She said, 'Straight ahead here.'

'But your father's house—'

'We're not going there. Trust me.'

So he did.

Nothing had changed since last time: same loose guttering; same ramshackle porch looking like the first good wind would batter it to sticks. That wind might be cutting across the moors now, by the scudding of the low-lying clouds. But she didn't have long to register this, because the moment she'd parked, Arkle was breathing heavily in her ear: 'If this doesn't go the way you promised, I'll hunt you down.'

'You won't need to,' she said. 'I'm already here.'

'Don't worry. You'll run.'

He got out of the car and waited for her, exactly like someone polite would do.

Trent emerged too, and stood blinking for a moment in the open air. His hands were deep in his pockets, and his posture spoke of expected blows; but indicated, too – to Zoë, anyway – that when the blows stopped, he'd still be standing . . . He noticed her watching, and showed his teeth in what might have been a smile in some cultures. She looked away. The clouds were still bashing overhead, and Arkle was waiting for her to get a move on.

Ignoring the front door, they headed straight for the side

passage, with its clutching accompaniment of out-of-control hedge. It smelled of damp, and something else too quick for Zoë to register – not unpleasant; a wild herb, or possibly a flower previously associated with friendly occasions. It would be interesting, her inner Zoë remarked, to keep track of whether future associations remained as positive. If she had a future in which to associate, of course. She scribbled a mental note to her inner Zoë: *Shut up*. Arkle had made her lead the way, and the first thing she saw at the other end was the hearse, though the first thing to make her shiver was the freezer . . . Which sat under the same makeshift carport-cum-shelter it ever had: next to the workbench with its rusting tools; the wardrobe with its doors removed; the two-foot-high stone frog, with the crack in its head like the slot in a money box. She wouldn't have been surprised, right then, if the freezer had lifted its lid in a welcoming sneer: *Hiya, Zoë. Back to stay?* The imagination was a useful tool, but there were times she'd have happily sunk hers in concrete boots.

Arkle said, 'If all goes according to plan, that key's in my hand in about twelve seconds, right?'

'If all goes according to plan,' Zoë agreed.

Arkle put his hands on her shoulders and moved her aside. Even as he did so, Trent closed in behind her; his short wide body solid as a fire hydrant. Brushing him off wasn't on the cards. Hitting him with a shovel might help, but even then he'd probably cling to her legs until Arkle reached her.

Which wouldn't take long, because Arkle moved fast. She'd barely blinked before he was at the hearse; long coat flapping like a vampire's cloak. And she could feel a hollow sensation swelling inside her, because she knew what was coming. How could she not? This was, in the realest of senses, the story of her life. As Arkle stretched through the driver's door for the ignition, which was where she'd told him the key was, she remembered what Katrina had said: *I'm going to need time, Zoë.* I'll give you as much as I can, she'd replied . . . There was movement to her left, and she turned her head to see Katrina's father at the window, staring blankly, wondering what they were up to. Then Arkle pulled his arm out of the dead folks' car, and turned to show her his empty hand.

'Looks like the plan just fucked up,' he said.

10

1

With Big Red Box in his rear-view mirror, and Katrina beside him in the passenger seat – she'd only been in the depot fifteen minutes; the key was all you needed to pass security – the tightness in Tim's chest loosened at last, though it threatened to bulk up again with every thought of the two holdalls now in the back of the car. Canvas bags with thick zippers, they bulged in odd, irregular ways. He wasn't clear on how much money they held, but it was more than he'd seen in one place before. Not that he'd actually seen it yet, because it hadn't come out of the bags.

'Where are we going?' he said. It was important he knew this, because he was driving.

'Straight ahead for now.'

Straight ahead would take them on to Dartmoor eventually.

'What about Zoë?'

'She's meeting us later.'

'If she gets away from the Dunstans.'

Katrina turned, and he felt her gaze burn his cheek. 'Do you trust me?'

'I— Yes. Yes, of course I do.'

'Zoë will be okay. She'll tell them I tricked her. They'll believe that. They'll believe that all too easily.'

'But won't Arkle—'

'Trent won't let him go overboard. I know these people,

Tim. Trent's not as useless as he looks, almost. He's Arkle's anchor.'

'Where's she taken them?'

'To my father's. That's where she's told them the key is.'

'That your father's hidden it?'

'No, that I hid it at my father's.' All this time she was looking at him, though he couldn't look back. 'In the hearse. In its ignition, in fact.' Now she looked away at last, and, like him, fixed her gaze on the road ahead.

'But it's not, is it? Because you've got it.'

'It wouldn't fit an ignition anyway.' She held it up, and he registered something credit-card sized with holes punched into it, and a familiar magnetic strip down one edge.

'. . . Okay.' But how come Katrina had it, he wanted to know. When everybody seemed to think it was somewhere else . . .

She said, 'Tim. Tim?'

'I'm still here.' Pitching for a jaunty tone, but falling between nervous and stupid.

'There were two keys, Tim. Baxter had one. I had the other.'

'. . . And that one's Baxter's?'

'I took it from his wallet.' As he lay dead on the kitchen floor, was the gloss she didn't need to make. 'It seemed the sensible thing to do.'

'. . . So yours—'

'Mine's at my father's,' she said. 'Hidden.'

'And they don't know there's two keys,' Tim said. 'So once they've got it, they'll think the money's theirs.'

'By which time we'll be gone.'

'But Zoë—'

'Zoë will tell them where it is. Long before Arkle hurts her.'

'I bloody hope so.'

'But she'll keep them guessing first,' Katrina said.

'That's where she said it was,' Zoë told Arkle.

'Right.'

'In the ignition. It's what she said.'

'Right.'

'She tricked me.'

Right . . .

Arkle, it struck her, looked at home leaning against a hearse, even a clapped-out no-go hearse like this. Maybe he'd had the wrong adoptive father; should have been reared by one whose daily dealings with death might have lent him respect for natural forces, and helped him appreciate the consequences of violence wrought upon once living bodies. This might have fostered gentleness, or at least tempered brutality. Instead, he'd grown up with sand and gravel and concrete, in a yard where hard things ground against other hard things until some of them became dust. Same general outcome, but a less forgiving process. And either way, he looked at home leaning against the hearse . . .

'Do you think I'm fucking stupid, or what?'

Trent said, 'Arkle—'

'Shut up.' He brushed a hand over where the hood ornament should have been. 'Do you think I'm fucking stupid, or what?'

'Why would I think that?' Zoë asked.

He stood straight, reminding her how tall he was, and the movement emphasised the hang of his overcoat; underlined the crossbow Velcroed in place. 'I hate it when I don't get a straight answer,' he said, and then he was on her.

She tried to sidestep but he grabbed her anyway; threw her against the freezer, pinning her head by a hank of hair. His body thick against hers, his face inches away, he said, 'When did you decide I was joking? About wanting that fucking key?'

'I know you're not—'

He slammed her head against the freezer lid. 'Then *why* this *shit* about *where it fucking is*?'

Lights swam apart, then swam together again . . . She could

feel his body hard against her own: tense and taut; a collection of cables knotted together. *It'll take tools to dismantle this one*, was the thought she thrust away, struck by the need to answer him before he bashed her head again. 'I told you—'

Arkle did it again. 'You told me *shit*. I don't want to hear *words*, I want to see *keys* . . . Oh, fuck. Who have we got here, then?'

He let go, and before she could grope her groggy way upright, a queue of suspects had trooped through her head – someone watching over her? Not Katrina, surely. And please not Tim. But Win wasn't out of the question; or even Jeff, tracking down his borrowed car . . . Or the man from her past who owned her old leather jacket, which she was going to go looking for one day.

But it wasn't any of them.

'Up here,' Katrina said.

How she could tell beat Tim. This particular lane was indistinguishable from any they'd crossed since leaving the main road an hour ago: little more than a passage between hedges, with a ditch either side to keep things interesting.

It was growing dark, and he couldn't tell whether the sky was giving up or his eyes giving out. The morning's blue had surrendered to troubled purple, lit by pink smudges to the west. It was probably his imagination that the car felt heavier. He was struck by a ludicrous image, of the bags behind him honking like stolen geese in a fairy tale, and shook his head.

She said, 'What?'

'Nothing . . . Are we nearly there? Wherever we're going?'

'I'm sorry, Tim. You must think I'm a madwoman.'

Again he felt her gazing at him.

'I think you've been through a bad time,' he told her. 'It's over now.'

The car crested the hill, and Tim switched the headlights on as they went into a descent. He knew the moors began not far away. The boundaries between here and there felt blurred, as if he might tip into wilderness without warning, and he was glad of his seatbelt, and wondered when the day would be over.

'Second on the left.'

At first he looked for another turning, then realised she meant the cottages lining the dip ahead – shepherds' cottages, he thought, but what did he know? They might be local sewage workers', or computer programmers'. Old, anyway, and small, and built of stone, and unlit. The second on the left was also the last on the left, and Tim didn't wait to be told it was okay to park on the gravelled area beyond. Killing the engine, he turned to Katrina, who flinched, or he thought she did. And at once Tim felt guilty; implicated in that vast engine of male aggression that had damaged her face, and left it the same brooding purple as the sky overhead.

'This is it,' she said.

It took him a second to shift from his viewpoint to hers. 'The cottage?'

'Baxter rented it. A six-month let. In case they needed a hideaway, he said.'

'But his brothers didn't know?'

'The emergency never came up. So no, he never told them.'

He could watch her now, for the first time since getting into the car, and he thought: yes, she's beautiful. Even with that bruise plastering her face, like the birthmarks you sometimes see on people on the street – though never on people you know – she was beautiful. Admitting it, Tim felt a missing part of his heart slot back into place. 'And we can get in okay?' he said. It surprised and comforted him that his brain was keeping pace with the conversation.

'There's a key by the back door.'

'Isn't that a bit . . .'

She said, 'Somebody wants to break in, it'd be easy enough. It's not like there's anything to steal.'

Tim unsnapped his seatbelt, which whipped back into its socket. He felt absurdly conscious of the mole under his jawline, of the fact that he'd not showered today, and supposed this was writ large on his face, though Katrina evidently read something else there, because her next words were sharp: 'Yes, he told me about it. Okay?'

'I didn't mean . . .'

'We were married. Have you been married, Tim?'

'Yes. She died.'

'Oh . . . I'm sorry.'

He said, 'Me too. I didn't mean to throw it at you.'

'No. No, you didn't – I'm so sorry. I just meant, when you're married . . . There aren't secrets. Not for long.' A car rolled down the road, and kept rolling. She said, 'I knew about the robberies, too. It doesn't mean I liked it.' She touched her cheek. 'Bad things happen,' she said. 'You'll understand that.'

'Yes,' he said. 'I understand that.'

She reached and squeezed his hand. 'Come on,' she said. 'Let's find the key.'

Zoë's head was ringing, or possibly only her ears. Trying to draw a distinction was in itself not a good sign . . . She was upright, resting against the hearse's bonnet; Arkle in front of her, Trent to her left. And newly on the scene was Katrina's father, surprisingly tall; almost imposing with his iron-grey hair and shaggy beard, if not for his misbuttoned cardigan, and the fact that he wore slippers, and had them on the wrong feet.

'Katie?'

'Go back inside, old man.'

'Are you all right, Katie?'

Arkle turned to Zoë, raising eyebrows as if they shared an in-law problem. 'This is Kay's dad. He's kind of senile.'

There was nothing senile about the look Blake flashed Arkle. 'You're Baxter's brother. What are you doing?'

Trent said, 'You'd better go inside, Mr Blake.'

But Blake turned to Zoë instead. 'Katie? You're not Katie.'

This with an air of disappointment, as if she'd let him down.

'No,' she said. 'But I'm a friend.'

'Oh . . . Would you like a cup of tea?' The word 'friend' pushing a button, perhaps; or just the universal fallback asserting itself. When mayhem erupts in your back yard, offer it tea. Normal service will be resumed.

'Old man,' Arkle said, 'we're sort of busy.'

'You're on my property,' Blake said. 'I want you to leave. This lady can stay. I shall make her a cup of tea.'

'Nobody's going anywhere,' Arkle said, 'until I've got what we came for.'

'Then I shall call the police,' Blake said. And he turned and strode towards the house.

Arkle watched for a moment, then looked back at Zoë, a sly grin opening his face. He twitched at his overcoat, reminding her what hung beneath. As if she'd forgotten. Then he turned his back again, and she could tell by the way his shoulder dropped that he was reaching for the bow.

Zoë shouted, 'Wait!' and everybody stopped.

The key to the back door was in the second place they looked – behind a loose brick – which might have delayed a burglar half a minute, supposing he hadn't used the time to pick the lock instead. But once inside, it wasn't clear what he would have stolen, unless he was in the business of outfitting holiday cottages. The kitchen was a drab affair – bare essentials arranged in the usual manner on peeling tiles – and the sitting room the same: an ancient dusty sofa, a ditto portable TV; last year's calendar on a wall that needed painting. The lampshade, thick with dust, gave a yellow, elderly quality to the light. Tim knew without looking that in the wooden chest by the sofa there'd be a pile of last year's magazines – *OK*, *Hello*; the odd *Railway Enthusiast's World* – and somewhere on a window sill would sit a row of forgotten bestsellers: MacLeans, Wheatleys, *Reader's Digest*'s condenseds. For a moment, he was reminded so explicitly of childhood holidays that he felt actual pain. Then he turned to Katrina and said, 'So this is where Baxter planned to retire with the stolen millions.'

She laughed. Then said, 'It's not millions. This was just in case they needed somewhere to hide in a hurry.'

'Playing board games until the heat died down.' He was getting into the swing of this. 'There'll be jigsaws too, no doubt.'

'And food in the freezer, and alcohol somewhere. Baxter was big on contingency planning.'

'How will Zoë find us? I mean, even I'm not sure how we got here. And I was driving.'

'She's got my number. We'll work something out.'

Tim was carrying the two bags of money, which wasn't a sentence he'd featured in before. New experiences cluttered his life. Putting them in a corner, he drew the curtains; then, in afterthought, moved them under the table instead. Katrina watched with an amused expression. This, too, was new; he'd not seen Katrina amused. Except, perhaps, in the hotel, but he hadn't been paying full attention then.

'You must be starving,' she said.

He supposed he must. He hadn't thought about it. 'We need to decide what to do,' he said. 'I mean, shouldn't we call the police?'

'Not until we've heard from Zoë,' Katrina said.

'But—'

'I know Arkle. If he's threatened, he'll hurt people. Whoever's nearest. Right now, that's Zoë. Maybe my father.'

Tim had spent the past few days in women's hands: obeying their directions, seeking their advice. After months of only his own counsel, and most of that despairing, this was a relief. And he was very hungry . . . 'We'll give her an hour,' he said. 'But no longer. I'm worried about her, Katrina.'

'Me too. But she's a tough lady. And this was her idea, Tim. Buying time so we could get clear.'

In this faded, papery light she looked younger, for some reason. Maybe because she was starting to feel safe . . . The idea pleased him. Of course it did.

'Okay,' he said. 'An hour, then. So. Where's this food?'

'A cup of tea sounds a good idea, Mr Blake,' Zoë said.

'This man was rude to me.'

'He wasn't terribly nice to me,' Zoë agreed. 'He's annoyed because he's looking for something, and he thinks I know where it is. Maybe tea will calm him down.'

Arkle said: 'If you seriously fucking think—'

'Or you could do both of us,' Zoë told him, trusting 'do' was outside the old man's vocabulary. 'Then spend the rest of your natural life tearing this place apart.'

'You know where it is.'

'I guarantee this much,' Zoë said. 'Harm him, and you'll never know the answer to that.'

Trent said, 'Arkle—'

'Shut up.' Arkle, coat back in place, jammed his hands in its pockets. His mouth worked furiously: he was possibly chewing his tongue. 'You think you're protecting him, right? But keep pissing me off, and I'll use him for target practice.'

'I'll bear it in mind,' she said. Old man Blake was hovering uncertainly a few yards away. Zoë took his arm. 'Come on,' she said. 'Show me how your kettle works.'

Together Tim and Katrina raided the kitchen, and found a collection of ready meals in the freezer – mostly Indian and Italian, from a low-fat 'be good to yourself' range. Both would have preferred a high-carb fuck yourself up selection they'd remember eating half an hour later, but warmed the oven anyway, loaded it with foil containers, and waited for the smell of lasagne to overpower the damp.

There was alcohol in the fridge: three bottles of Stolichnaya.

'That'll be for Trent,' Katrina said. Then added, redundantly, 'Trent's a drinker.'

'Is there anything to mix it with?' Tim asked. He needed a drink, but wasn't sure he needed neat vodka.

'No,' said Katrina. Then added, more pointedly, 'Trent's a drinker.'

And Baxter a weight-watcher, given his choice of meals. But Tim held his tongue. There was presumably an etiquette governing questions addressed to a woman concerning the husband she'd killed, but it was likely to be complicated, and didn't need exploring right now. He explored the freezer again instead, and found ice cubes. These would dilute the vodka; or at any rate, make it colder. Tim's initial disinclination to get stuck into hard spirits was diminishing, and unlikely to survive the conclusion that there was nothing else available.

He chiselled ice from its tray into glasses, listening to Katrina moving about in the sitting room. And as he did so, he noticed – how long had this been going on? – that something had changed. At first, he thought it was his hearing; that his reception had broadened somehow, and sounds of a previously unavailable pitch were coming through. But that wasn't it. It was internal. It was as if he'd laid a weight down, or had it surgically excised. Something he'd carried for months, and had variously labelled grief, terror, self-loathing, *whatever*, was gone; had melted the way this ice would, and had done so while his attention was elsewhere. He paused, the bottle hovering over a glass. He was trying to measure the difference. It was ease of movement, he decided. Not just that he could hold the bottle without it trembling, but that he could do so without undue consciousness of the event; without some part of him holding back from doing it, out of fear that every action hardwired him deeper into an Emma-less reality; a fear balanced by the equal and opposite anxiety that every action refrained from had precisely the same effect.

The over-examined life, which had proved not worth living.

Enough. He willed himself into movement; poured vodka over ice; felt his tastebuds grip at the cracking sound this made. Then carried the drinks next door, where Katrina was gazing at the pile of money she'd created by emptying the bags on the floor.

'I wanted to see how much there was,' she said.

'Ah.'

She looked from Tim to the money, then back to Tim. 'It seems there's loads,' she said.

Zoë had never liked tea, and if there were a single reason she might start believing herself the plaything of a malevolent deity, it was the frequency with which she ended up nursing cups of the stuff she was expected to drink. Well, that or the number of times she'd pissed off armed and dangerous men.

Arkle said, 'This is nice. Isn't this nice? I think it's nice.'

His tone of voice, his savage eyes, suggested he'd sooner be pulling teeth.

'Katie's been away,' Blake replied. 'But I expect she'll drop in soon.'

A conversation between these two, thought Zoë, could run for hours without touching the sides. It would be like watching two rubber balls bouncing round a locked room. They might collide eventually, but it was down to chance.

Trent, watchful, leaned against the wall. He was hard, squat and morose, and in a previous life might have been one of those concrete bollards he'd driven his van into the night before.

Let's not forget: Trent had tried to run her over.

. . . How long it was taking to dawn on her: she was in serious trouble here.

Arkle said, 'The key.'

Zoë took a breath. 'I've told you. Katrina – Kay. Kay tricked me. She told me it was in the hearse, in its ignition. That's all I know.'

'Why don't I believe you?'

'You think I'm happy about this?'

'We had a deal.'

Sounding actually affronted, as if Zoë had wantonly cheated him out of harassing and torturing Tim.

Blake said, 'She's never happier than when she's sorting through my books. Are you, Katie?'

'I'm not your daughter, Mr Blake,' Zoë said.

His eyes clouded, then cleared. 'No. No, of course not.' He looked at Arkle again. 'You're his brother.'

'I was,' said Arkle.

'She used to turn up here with bruises.' He looked back to Zoë. 'Vicious. Somebody should have stopped him.'

'Somebody did,' said Zoë, before she could help herself.

Arkle bent low. 'His brain's fucked. What's your excuse?'

Trent said, 'Time's moving on.'

'Shut up.' Back to Zoë: 'Where's the key?'

'I don't know.'

He nodded at Katrina's father. 'You want me to pull bits off him? Till you get your memory back?'

'It's not a question of memory.' Her words coming out tighter, the more he wound her inner spring. 'I've no idea where her hiding place was.'

'Katie has a hiding place,' Katrina's father said.

They looked at him.

'She says she's going upstairs. But I hear her slip outside. Watched her once. By the window.'

He pointed, to clarify 'window'.

'Like dropping a coin in a slot. Except it wasn't a coin.' He turned to Zoë, as if expecting a clue. 'Don't know what it was.'

The old man had acquired momentum now; determined to prove that the brain, if rusty in places, remained the tool of choice for piercing secrets. That sharp as his Katie was, he still knew a thing or two.

Like creatures in a pantomime Arkle and Trent were on the move; gathering round him, guiding him to the window. 'Okay,' Arkle said. 'Show us.' Zoë got to her feet too – to protect him?

So at the window, he pointed again. And all four looked out on the cluttered mess of his back yard: a hearse on bricks, an old workbench, a decommissioned freezer, a wardrobe with its doors removed; and to one side – next to what might have been a pond, if its overgrowth were napalmed – a two-foot-high stone frog, with a crack in its head running ear to ear, as if it were an oversized money box.

II

Katrina counted. Tim watched. At some point, he went to refresh his drink – odd term, 'refresh': his drink was beyond repair. Poured a new one is what Tim did. When he returned, she was still at it; sorting through bundles of money of differing thickness, each wrapped by a rubber band. After a while, the bands fascinated Tim more than the money. They came in various colours, various widths – he wondered whether Baxter had collected them in advance, or just dug them out of drawers and cupboards. Tim couldn't remember ever buying rubber bands himself, but he'd usually been able to put his hands on one when he needed to.

'One hundred and eighty-three,' Katrina said.

Not rubber bands: pounds. Thousands of pounds.

'That's a lot,' Tim agreed. His tongue felt thick and unusual. Neat vodka obviously required practice.

Katrina stacked it all back into a single bag; flinging the bundled bricks in any which way, as if the money weren't important to her; the counting a necessary administrative task, no more. She had rolled her sleeves up, and tied her hair back with one of the rubber bands. The effect was brisk and efficient, as if she might be about to start vacuuming, or whip a duster round.

She noticed him watching, and smiled. 'Are you okay?'

'Yes.'

'Arkle hurt you, didn't he?'

'He did. But I'm all right now.'

Katrina zipped the bag up and stood. 'How's the food doing?'

'Five minutes?'

'I could do with another drink.'

'You haven't touched your first.'

'Watch me.' She retrieved her glass from the table and drained it in a draught, not taking her eyes off Tim. Then rattled the remains of the ice. 'See?'

He held his hand out, and as she handed him her glass, their fingers touched.

'I don't even know what you do,' she said.

He was about to answer, then shook his head. 'That's real life,' he said. 'Let's not worry about it now.'

'And this is make-believe?'

He thought: thugs, crossbows, bags stuffed full of money . . . Yes, this was make-believe. None of it connected with real life: the get up/go to work variety. His finger tingled where hers had touched it. That wasn't true either: he was conscious of their fingers having touched, that was all; a consciousness which manifested itself in imagined tingling. 'Time out, maybe,' he said. 'A reality break.'

'My ice is melting,' she said.

For a moment he wasn't sure what she meant, then understood. Her ice was melting.

'I can fix that,' he said, and went to fetch more.

The house felt calmer without Arkle in it. Most houses would; he seemed to trail a cloud like that kid in the Charlie Brown strip, except instead of dust and dirt, Arkle's exhaust blew violence and threat. He might as easily have put that bolt into Bob Poland's head as through his leg. And Zoë's complicity in that imagined act frightened her, now it was too late to retract: it was as if a door had closed just before she'd stepped through it. The view on the other side had been familiar – she had once killed a man herself – but it wasn't anywhere she wanted to visit again.

Her face must have clouded, because Trent said, 'What's the matter?'

'I was thinking.'

He nodded, as if that would do it every time.

They were in old man Blake's sitting room, because there seemed no point in putting him anywhere else. He was sitting now, largely focused on something happening on the other side of the wall his chair faced, but every so often he'd look at Zoë, who was leaning against the same wall, balanced on a stool. On the mantelpiece sat an oddly shaped metal figure she guessed was the hearse's missing hood ornament. Trent, meanwhile, stood with his back to the door, reminding Zoë of one of those dogs which, once it's clamped its teeth round part of you, you have to saw its head off to get free.

Arkle had left them twice; the first time to fish the key from the crack in the stone frog's head. From the window, Zoë had watched him pull on a length of thread looped round the creature's ear. What emerged on the other end resembled a credit card that had been run through a hole punch: a swipe key, of course; nothing you'd fit into an ignition. Wrapping his long, surprisingly clean fingers round it, Arkle had stared directly at her; for a while it was as if their lines of vision had knotted, and neither could break away. *You knew*, his gaze said. And beneath that, something not entirely susceptible to language; an inchoate mess of suggestion, bloody with the split infinitives of all he yet intended: *to seriously hurt, to definitely maim*. She did not look away, on the principle that once you'd shown fear, you were lost. In the end it was Arkle who had broken the connection, as if the intensity were too much to maintain.

She'd thought he was going to hit her once he was back in the house. Her body felt both hard and soft at the same time; either way, she was a target. Yield or not yield, the result wouldn't differ . . . He didn't, though; barely looked her way, in fact, as if the gaze they'd exchanged through the window had set the seal on a promise he could redeem at leisure.

Instead, he said to Trent: 'Where's that place again?'

'Big Red Box?'

There was a slight pause.

Trent continued, in a hurry, 'You go out towards the roundabout . . .'

He lost her in a blether of instruction.

When Trent finished, Arkle said, 'Tie her up. I'm going for the money.'

'By yourself?'

'You stay with them. Tie her up. Something's going on, and I don't know what.'

Then, in case Trent hadn't followed, he went and found some garden twine, and tied her up himself.

So here she was, wrists bound behind her, propped against the wall the old man faced; the only available good news the fact that Arkle had left the building, and even this tempered by Trent's repeated use of 'it's not far' when explaining where the storage facility was . . . Arkle, from what Win had said, had lived here as long as Trent, so should have had a similar grasp on local geography. But it was likely that trivia didn't cling to Arkle's consciousness that tightly; trivia in his case being anything that didn't immediately affect his well-being.

For now he was gone, though. Him and his weapon both.

She said, 'I need to use the bathroom.'

'Piss yourself.'

'You sure? We might be here a while.'

Trent touched his damaged nose. 'My sense of smell's fucked. I couldn't give a toss.'

If she'd been kidding, this would have rankled; the fact that it was soon going to be a live issue made it worse. But she put that out of mind, as far as she was able. 'You think Arkle's coming back?'

'Why wouldn't he?'

She laughed. God knew what it sounded like outside her head; to her own ears, a rattlesnake had just entered the room. 'We're talking about a couple of hundred grand, right? What's that divided by one?'

'He's coming back.'

'If you say so.'

'I just did.'

Playground stuff . . .

She said, 'Besides.'

'Besides what?'

'. . . What if the money's not there?'

They had eaten and were on the sofa now, and if Tim closed his eyes and threw his mind back to when he and Emma were starting out – to when a whole minefield of nuance and between the lines silences had to be negotiated before he braved an arm round her shoulder – he could drum up a soundtrack to match the moment. REM released *Automatic for the People* the same month he first kissed her, and everywhere you went, everybody hurt. He could hear it now: a quiet song, best played loud.

When the chorus loomed, he was surprised Katrina couldn't hear it too.

'. . . Are you asleep?'

'Sorry. It's the vodka.'

'You've done a lot of driving. It's okay if you sleep.'

'Has it been an hour?'

'I'll call her now.'

She did, and the pair sat listening to the curiously chirpy response: *The number you requested is not available* . . . Not a lot of clues in a verbal cul-de-sac like that. Zoë might be anything – upright, sideways, downright dead – and all they knew was, she wasn't *available.* Whether this was temporary or permanent, the future would tell; meanwhile, Katrina switched her mobile off.

Then they sat quietly, while 'Everybody Hurts' looped through Tim's head, and the melting ice in his glass fizzed in time.

. . . Katrina said, 'How do you see the rest of your life?'

'How do I what?'

'You think this will change things? What's happened these past few days?'

He said, 'I live an ordinary life. I mean . . . When Emma died, it nearly killed me. Went on nearly killing me. But it didn't, in the end. I'm still here. My life's pretty boring, you want the truth. Electrical goods aren't as exciting as they sound.'

That was a joke, but Katrina didn't laugh.

'But it's not a bad life. Until Emma died, it was enough. And would be again, if missing her stopped. And what they say, the things people tell you, they talk about two years or whatever, a specific passage of time, that you get better, that it stops hurting. And maybe that's true. It's not, I don't mean, she wasn't replaceable . . . Isn't. Isn't replaceable. But the gap she left in my life, if that was filled, everything else would work too. It would be enough again.'

'Yes.'

'It would need to be something special. Somebody special. Emma . . . I loved Emma so much. I've never stopped. I thought I had . . . You hate people when they're dead. At first. But really you're hating yourself, for not being there when it mattered. You think you're the reason why they died. But you're not. And you always love the ones you love. That's what love means. It means nothing if you stop.'

'You're a nice man, Tim.'

'No, I'm just me. Everybody's just themselves, it doesn't matter how nice they want people to think they are. I'm not making sense. All I mean is . . . All it is, things are what they are, that's all. Emma's dead. I'm still here. Life goes on. Will go on, I mean. You're nice too, Katrina. I'm not just saying that because I'm drunk.'

She kissed him: a light feathery kiss that barely brushed his cheek. But it would have hurt her to kiss him any other way; her cheekbone hadn't knit together yet. Her face was still the colour of pain. But her lips touched him, and for a moment he forgot the song in his head, because not everybody hurt after all.

'I think I need another drink,' she said.

Tim was pretty sure he didn't, but went and poured two all the same. When he returned, she'd drawn her knees beneath her, and taken the band from her hair. He remembered the first time he'd seen her, with a bruise just a ghost of this present damage, and knew there'd come a time when this hurt too would fade, and he'd have to study her face for signs of its having existed. That was what the future looked like in that moment; a long drawn-out passage of time in which Tim studied Katrina's face. He was still holding both their glasses, so handed her one, and sat down.

The bag under the table stared up at them.

Katrina said, 'Do you really think they need the money?'

'. . . Who?'

'The insurance companies?'

'Probably not *need*, no.'

'It seems . . . idiotic to give it to them. So much good could be done with it.'

'What sort of good?'

'Any sort. You could start a whole new life with that much money.'

He laughed. 'I thought you were going to say you could feed the starving, or fund a cure for something.'

'It's a lot. But it's not enough for that.'

'It's not really enough for a new life, either.' He mushed some syllables there, but he was making sense. 'It's a pile, sure. But hardly enough to buy a house with, not most places. Even supposing they let you pay cash.'

'So the insurance companies won't miss it.'

'It's not a question of them missing it, it's about whose it is. It's stolen, is what it comes down to . . . I'm not trying to be all high and moral. But the money's not a secret. Once Zoë's safe, we call the police, and they arrest the Dunstans. The money will be mentioned, Katrina. And it's not like the police'll call it finders keepers.'

'It seems a shame, that's all.'

'Worse things happen.' Than not having a huge lump of untraceable cash dumped on you, he meant. 'Look, when the police come . . .'

'They'll arrest me too.'

'Will they?'

'Of course. They're still deciding what to charge me with for Baxter's death. And now the journalist who was looking after me's in a coma, and God only knows what other mayhem Arkle's caused . . . I'm involved in all that. They're going to want to know how deep.' She looked at him. 'They didn't know Baxter was a crook,' she said. 'But once they get hold of Arkle, it'll come out.'

'But you weren't involved.'

'Can I prove that?'

'You don't have to. They have to prove you did. Were, I mean. Involved.'

She said, 'Tim, I'm not worried about being found guilty of something I didn't do. I'm worried about how many years of my life'll be eaten up before people forget I was suspected.'

Years of her life, thought Tim. She must have been about the same age as Emma – who had died at thirty-four – but he wasn't the world's best guesser, and this wasn't the moment to ask. He wanted her to kiss him again, but that might be out of line too. Years of her life: leaving plenty of years . . . It occurred to him – a thought that came with its own lack-of-sobriety tag – that he could offer himself as a kind of long-life guarantee. Because if she, say, married him, what were the chances of her dying young? Of that happening to him twice? Even allowing for the fact that it wouldn't be him it was happening to, or not primarily.

Another car passed the cottage. Its headlights briefly probed for breaks in the curtains, then threw bright pools through them, which splashed on the walls and drained away into the corners.

She said, 'There are places you can go, people you can turn to. Who can help you with identities and such. It only costs money.'

'What are you talking about?'

'Instead of turning the money in. I could just disappear.' She looked at him. 'Then I wouldn't have to worry about being proved innocent.'

Tim said, 'I've got a better idea.'

'You saying she tricked you?'

'You think I'd have come with you if I'd known the key wasn't here?'

'But the key was here.'

'Not where she told me.'

'So you say.'

'If Arkle comes back without the money, what do you think he'll do?'

'. . . He won't be pleased.'

'I know he won't be pleased. I'm wondering what he'll do.'

After a moment, Trent repeated, 'But the key was here. So how could the money be gone?'

'How many keys could there be?'

Trent looked away. 'You'll have to tell him where Kay went.'

'I don't know where Kay went.'

'But you were with her. You took her from that house. You saying you just let her go, when she was the only one knew where the key was?'

Zoë said, 'That's sort of what "tricked" means, in the circumstances.'

She thought she could hear a clock ticking, but it was some obstruction in the old man's breathing.

Trent said, 'I can control him.'

'You think?'

'He knows where to draw a line. That's how come . . .'

How come he's still walking round free, Trent didn't finish.

Zoë said, 'Looking back on our brief acquaintance, I suspect whatever controls Arkle has pretty much rusted away. Did he do that to your face?'

Trent didn't answer. Didn't have to.

'So what do you think he'll do to me? Or the old man here?'

'It's Kay he wants.'

'Right. And there's a woman in a coma because she was in his way. It's not about what he wants, Trent. It's that he doesn't care how he gets it.'

'It's our money.'

'Forget the fucking money. Were you there when he beat up Helen Coe?'

Trent said, 'I don't know what happened. I was in the van.'

'Good for you. You planning on waiting outside when he loses his temper today? Because anything that happens here, you're guilty too, you know that? Whatever he does, you're doing it too. That's the law, Trent. They call it collective responsibility.'

'I won't let him . . .'

'Let him what? I've watched him take potshots at Tim with a crossbow. I could smell the blood on his teeth. You really think you can stop him?'

'. . . Did you really send a letter to the police?'

'Yes,' she lied. 'Another thing. The guy he shot in Oxford this morning? He's a copper.'

'He didn't look like a fucking copper.'

'He's not supposed to, Trent. He's undercover. The whole point of being undercover is you don't look like a fucking copper.'

'So what was he doing?'

'Being shot by your brother. That's the part he'll remember, anyway. And what happens when policemen get shot, Trent? You think the rest of them throw up their hands in disgust and knock off early?'

'. . . What's your point?'

'You're already a mess. They'll say you were shop-soiled when they arrested you. If you're lucky, they'll give you a bag to carry your teeth in.'

'You're just trying to get me to let you go.'

'I'm trying to get you to help yourself. Arkle comes with an expiry date. That doesn't mean you have to spend your life in prison.'

'He's my brother.'

'And how much fun has that been?'

Trent said, 'You think you know a lot, don't you? But you don't know nothing. Baxter's dead. Arkle's all I've got. You think I'm going to take sides against him?'

The deadness of his tone told Zoë she'd hit a wall.

The things she'd said, the lies and the truths, were volleying around the room now; colliding into each other, spinning off in all directions. She could have sworn old man Blake hadn't twitched in half an hour. If it weren't for the odd fractured breath, she'd have thought him dead. And the fact that he wasn't might merely be intermission, because one of the things she hadn't been lying about was how much damage she thought Arkle might do when he came home without the money . . . There didn't seem much hope in his turning up sheepish and rueful. Torch and run was more likely. He must know he had little time left. He was leaving the same trail of clues in his wake as a hurricane.

She said, 'I'm all out of things to tell you. He's your brother. Nothing I say can change that.'

'Right.'

'So I'll ask a favour instead. No tricks. I really need to go to the bathroom. Could you let me have that much dignity?'

He said, 'No way am I taking that rope off.'

'You don't have to take the rope off. You can leave the damn door open if you want. But let me have that much control for when he gets back, can't you? Please? You think I want to wet myself when he takes his crossbow out?'

'. . . You're trying to trick me.'

'I watched him put a bolt through somebody this morning, Trent. For being there. He thinks I've tricked him out of a couple of hundred grand, you reckon he'll write that off to bad judgement? Please. All I'm asking is a little human decency, before the bad stuff starts.'

Blake said, 'Katie?'

They both looked, but it was a momentary lapse, no more.

Blake was already back on the other side of nowhere, though there was a pulse throbbing at his temple which hadn't been there before.

Zoë said, 'Please. You don't have to untie me.'

Trent said, 'If this is a trick, my brother's the least of your worries.'

Tim stopped talking, and raised his glass to his lips. It was empty. He didn't remember finishing it, but his mouth felt powerfully dry; a dead giveaway. He wondered if his words had come out right. There had been an awful lot of them, and they had started by trying to explain why disappearing wasn't a great idea, and ended by saying she should come with him to Oxford instead. Not in that way, he had probably added. He wasn't trying to suggest. Which wasn't to say he didn't think. And so on. By the time he had backtracked out of several verbal dead ends, only to walk slap bang into a number of conversational lamp posts, he couldn't have found his way back to the subject with a map and a torch.

In the quiet that followed he could hear new weather coming; the noises clouds make when they roll over themselves in the late grey sky.

At last Katrina, 'I was right, though. You are nice.'

'Katrina—'

'You're worried I'm digging a hole I'll never get out of.'

'Yes.'

'Take the money and run. But if I do that, I'll never stop running.'

Yes, that's what Tim had been saying. If her version sounded more coherent, that was because she'd had time to digest it, whereas he'd been improvising. 'I don't want you to run,' he said. He put his glass down. 'Nothing that's happened was your fault. He hurt you, he—' Running out of words again, he touched her face instead. She didn't flinch. When he put his fingers to her cheek, it felt hot, as if her whole body were still working on the pain problem: converting Baxter's damage to dischargeable energy. What was washing past him was the by-product of anger, brutality, outrage. All she had to do was stand up in a courtroom and it would come blazing out of her: that was what Tim thought. That a jury wouldn't just acquit her; they'd dig Baxter up and kill him again. And he heard himself finish, 'He deserved it,' which left nothing more to say.

After a while he took his fingers from Katrina's cheek, to find their tips still glowing with her heat. Our hearts should always be in others' keeping, he thought. Having sole custody of his own had nearly broken him. Was that pathetic? Maybe so, maybe so. Something once firmly attached inside him slipped away with the admission, the way a label glued on a jar floats free after soaking.

He looked into her eyes. They were dark and deep, and it was possible he could spend the rest of his human span gauging their secrets. But first, there were things that cried out to be done. 'We need to call Zoë again,' he said.

'Yes.'

'And if we don't get her this time, we've got to call the police.'

'. . . Yes.'

Zoë went ahead of Trent, her wrists behind her back. The stairs were narrow, steep, and curved slightly in a way that didn't seem deliberate. Perhaps the house was folding up in accord with its owner's slow withdrawal . . . If she fell now, she'd send Trent crashing to the floor below with her. The way her luck was running, she'd be the one who broke her limbs. Reaching the top, she felt his push.

'That way.'

On the landing was a bookcase on which sat a dusty vase holding a plastic spray of flowers. Cobwebs stretched between petals, and scattered round the vase's base was a drift of husks: spider's leftovers. The bookcase contents looked like they were on their way to or from a charity store: a mishmash of MacLeans, Wheatleys and *Reader's Digest*'s condenseds, among which nestled a pamphlet outlining the uses of a pressure cooker. *She's never happier than when she's sorting through my books. Are you, Katie?* But Trent was hustling her away already; pushing her against a door which swung open to reveal very much a bachelor toilet.

'Make it quick,' he said.

'I can't manage like this,' she told him.

'I told you. I'm not untying you.'

'You think I'll run? There's not even a window in there, for God's sake.'

'I'm not untying you.'

'I still need your help.'

He looked at her.

'You'll have to undo my jeans. You think I'm Houdini?'

'I'm not your fucking nurse.'

'Trent, please. What's the point of bringing me up here otherwise?'

From downstairs came a rattle of some kind: faint and indeterminate.

He said, 'If he's going walkabout, I'll throw you down the fucking stairs.'

'That's a fair and reasonable response. Are you going to help or not?'

He didn't want to. She could see that. But could see, too, that she'd backed him into a corner, one he was too accustomed to to leave easily. Being round Arkle had done that for him. Sooner or later, he'd end up doing whatever he was told, because otherwise he'd suffer.

She hunched her shoulders; allowed a whine to stain her voice. 'Trent? This has got to happen soon.'

'. . . What is it you want?'

'Just undo my jeans, that's all. I can manage the rest, but I can't undo my jeans with my hands behind my back.'

He shook his head, but it was surrender, not refusal. Muttering something she couldn't catch, he edged forward, hands fumbling in front of him.

'You try anything—'

She closed her eyes.

And then he was in front of her, hands still fumbling; attacking the clasp of her jeans like a man in boxing gloves peeling an orange. This close, his stench was a physical object: stale tobacco and alcohol burying something grimier and forgotten. When she opened her eyes, she was looking down on the top of his head, where hair had matted into a nest; any moment, she'd see something stir in there, and scream . . . She spoke instead:

'Have you done this before?'

'Fuck off.'

'Don't be alarmed if I . . .'

'What?'

'Oh, nothing.'

As he pulled the clasp apart she moaned slightly, and he looked up in alarm.

Zoë brought her forehead into his face as she kneed him in the crotch.

. . . The crotch is the soft target: every good girl knows that. But in Trent's case his damaged face was softer still, and his howl as he staggered back pierced the ceiling. She dropped her shoulder and charged, hitting him chest high, thumping him into the bookcase – the vase smashed against the wall, and books went everywhere: flopping down the stairs like poor imitations of birds. Zoë tripped, lost her balance, landed on her knees. Trent had pitched forwards, and was scrabbling to get up. She bunny-hopped on to his back before he could, feeling the air leave him as she landed . . . Five seconds in, it was going her way. But there was a law of slim returns operating, and the longer this continued, the greater his chances of shrugging her off . . . Raising herself, she dropped on him as hard as she could; and was again rewarded with a breathless grunt. But he was gathering now, and pretty soon, he'd throw her off . . .

She scrabbled to her feet, swallowed hard, and kicked him in the head.

. . . There were those who wouldn't have been shocked to watch Zoë kick a fallen man in the head. Others might have expressed surprise that she refrained from it so often. But it didn't feel good, it wasn't who she wanted to be, and a large black lump reached her throat as she kicked him again, because however bad it felt, it was necessary Trent stay down long enough that she get her hands free. He grunted again and was still. She made to kick him a third time, but stopped. She looked at her feet, the black zipped boots she wore, and thought for a moment she saw blood on them, but that was a trick of her eyes. And she didn't have time for this: Trent was out of action, but Arkle would be back any moment. She needed to find a knife or scissors – get out of the knots she'd been tied in. Then start bringing all this to a close.

. . . Among the scattered books was a pamphlet outlining the uses of a pressure cooker. When it had hit the ground, it had shed a load it carried; a sheaf of newspaper clippings hidden among its pages, held together by a paper clip. They'd landed facing away from her, and she squinted, trying to read the uppermost headline . . .

That's what she was doing when the front door opened, and Arkle returned.

'Still no luck?'

'Her phone's off.'

'It's late, Katrina. We need to call the police. We should have done ages ago.'

'But—'

'No. She's in trouble. Or she'd have been in touch.'

'. . . Okay.'

'Do you want me to do it?'

'. . . Yes. That'd be best.'

She handed him her mobile. As she did, her fingers touched his, and he smiled . . . This was strange, was practically supernatural, but it would keep happening, of that he was sure. No matter what else was going on, there would be moments of connection with this woman, and once enough of them had been laid down, they'd have a foundation on which to build.

'What's the matter?' she asked.

'Nothing. Just . . . Where are we?'

'What do you mean?'

'The police. It's the first thing they want to know, where you're calling from. What's this place called?'

'I don't know . . . There's a leaflet somewhere.' Katrina went into the kitchen, and found one on the window sill: a photocopied sheet with instructions for use of the premises – hot water, binmen, recycling. She called out, 'Poachers' Cottage.'

'Does it have an address?'

She read it out.

'Okay.' He looked down to figure out her mobile, and she came back into the room, arms folded across her chest.

'Tim?'

'What is it?'

'Once you call the police, everything changes . . .'

'I know.'

'They'll arrest me.'

'I'm sorry. But we've got to do this. You know that, don't you?'

'Yes.'

'So is it okay? I have to do it anyway. But is it okay?'

'Yes, Tim. It's just . . .' She half laughed, or perhaps half sobbed;

something, anyway, that tore Tim three ways at once. But how many times could he tell her? The only future she had was if they buried her past, and however dismal a prospect that was, they'd survive. It wasn't as if she was heading for prison. She had done nothing wrong. She had defended herself. And he tried to explain all this once more with his eyes, because words wouldn't come; he was awkward and inarticulate again: a boy on one end of a sofa, with a girl on the other and the world in between.

But women, the world reminded him, always know which move to make.

Katrina's eyes were wet when she said, 'Could we stay this side of it a moment longer, Tim? Just hold me for a while before you call?'

Could he? He could. He put her mobile on the sofa, and took her in his arms.

Holding her – she felt slight, vulnerable – was coming home. To feel someone else's bones beneath their skin, to feel them move between your limbs . . . To have all this taken away from you, and then brought back: it was coming home. He closed his eyes, she shifted in his arms, and his heart opened like a parachute. There was a reason for this. When he looked down, his eyes met the blunt handle of the knife protruding from his chest where she'd left it. So this is why we die, Tim thought. Oh. Katrina stepped away as he fell, and watched until she was sure he was dead. When she'd killed Baxter, she'd made the mistake of pulling the knife free, and had ended up washed in his blood. That didn't happen this time, but there was no shortage of the stuff, all the same.

Once Tim was done, she stepped over him to tug at the curtains where they didn't fit. There was little chance of anybody peeping through – they hadn't chosen the cottage for its busy location – but you took no chances. She couldn't think of any way Zoë might find her – for some reason, it was the very specific Zoë rather than the generalised police she was worried about – but there were always exits left uncovered, and no point relaxing yet. She'd drag Tim out of sight of windows, curtained or not, then carry the money upstairs, where it too would be safe from view.

There is always a moment when the heart stops in perfect time with the brain – when all falls blank and quiet, and the body's on its own. When Arkle came back, Zoë's body was abandoned for that split second at the top of the stairs; stuck and solitary, no clue what to do. And then whatever it was within her that habitually overrode fear kicked in – her sense of self, or her pig-headedness, or perhaps her fundamental belief that it was wrong that the thugs, creeps and stalkers of the world should hold sway. So she rolled out of his line of vision even as he registered events, and was flat on the floor when his first bolt hammered into the wall behind her at stomach height.

And then there was quiet . . . Only the gentle rain of plaster dust flaking down.

Until she heard him move.

It might have taken seconds . . . Arkle could have been up the stairs in seconds, leaving the tiniest splinter of infinity before he put his next bolt wherever he wanted. But he wasn't; he was crossing the hallway, to where lay a chance of an angle on some part of her head.

Zoë tried to flatten herself further . . . Aiming for the instant diet: lose a stone in seconds.

Trent grunted, and a shudder passed through him.

Arkle said, 'It's like I'm the only one I can trust round here. Do you get that a lot? Nobody doing what you tell them?'

In case he took silence as provocation, she replied, 'You can't really blame him. I lied.'

It was surprising how steady her voice was. As if somebody else had charge of it.

'You told him you weren't going to trick him?'

'Something like that.'

'That's the oldest one there is,' he said, with genuine wonder in his voice.

Zoë didn't dare raise her head, didn't know what he was doing . . . A picture flashed through her, of him sighting down the stock of his bow . . . Of one injudicious glance, and his next dart sailing through her open eye . . .

. . . Inches from which lay a bundle of newspaper clippings, their upside-down headlines swimming in and out of the recognisable alphabet: G T H E o V Σ . . .

And now something had found its way into Zoë's side – something sharp and painful enough to pierce her as surely as anything Arkle sent flying up the stairs.

He said, 'The money wasn't there.'

'. . . I guessed.'

'You knew.'

'No, Arkle. She tricked me too.'

'I always knew she was a bad one.'

The thought of Arkle passing moral judgement would have been funny, if she wasn't lying at the top of the stairs, wrists bound behind her back.

It was a shard of vase. The object biting into her side. With a little wriggling, she could get it into her hands . . .

Arkle said, 'Did she have a key all the time then?'

'There must have been two. One for her, one for Baxter.'

'And she took his from Bax's body.'

'I guess . . .' Zoë had hooked her feet around the toilet door frame, and was easing the rest of her body that way. The shard of vase scraped with her, snagged on her top.

'That makes you an idiot, doesn't it?'

'You might say so.'

She couldn't tell what he was up to: priming his bow or just folding himself in righteous anger . . . Which was something

Zoë was starting to develop herself. This had been the plan: Katrina got here first, grabbed the key, then took half the money from Big Red Box, leaving enough to satisfy the law. Then she'd send the cops . . . Once the key turned out to be still in the frog, Zoë'd known Katrina had fooled her, which meant she'd fooled Tim too, from the moment they'd met . . . For a second, the possibilities of treachery revealed themselves as a long long corridor, at the far end of which lay a body. What all this meant for Tim, she didn't want to think about.

Daring to roll on to her side – becoming a larger target – she groped behind her and located the fragment of vase; took as tight a grip as she could manage between finger and thumb, and began sawing at the twine binding her wrists.

Arkle said, 'Funny, really. She fooled Baxter. You fooled Trent. It's like it's only me nobody's fooling, but I'm still standing here without the fucking money.'

'A real heartbreaker.'

'You didn't kill Trent, did you?'

'No, my hands were tied. All I did was knock him unconscious.'

'They still tied?'

'You want to come and find out?'

There was a thud two inches above her head, as a second bolt buried itself in the wall.

He said, 'I've got four of these. Reason I'm still playing is, I only need one.'

Zoë's numb fingers fumbled the shard.

'So you've no clue where she's gone?'

Again: nearly funny. She was lying here while he took potshots, and she was supposed to share information . . . 'She might be anywhere, Arkle. She's a rich woman.' Her scrabbling hand found the fragment again.

Trent groaned once more and stirred. Head down, Zoë couldn't see, but could sense him trying to pull himself up . . .

Arkle said, 'Trent? You okay?'

Okay or not, he wasn't answering yet.

Then Arkle said, 'The way I see it, my money and the woman who killed my brother are getting further fucking away every second. And you're not helping.'

Sawing again, Zoë felt her numbed fingers pick up a rhythm . . . How long did it take to sever a length of garden twine with a broken vase? . . . Or rather, if *X* was the time so required, and *Y* how long it took a man with a crossbow to climb a flight of stairs, what was *Z* going to do about it? Not that algebra had ever been her strong point.

She said, 'You seem very sure we're on different sides here. She fooled me too.' Trying not to let her efforts break her speech into separate gasps.

'And kept you from getting your hands on my money.'

Well, yes. He had a point.

. . . Zoë felt something give behind her, a sudden loosening, only it wasn't twine; it was her fingers . . . Slick with blood, they'd dropped the tool again. And her heart slipped with it, because time was getting away here; Arkle was playing, but she doubted his attention span ever cleared cruising speed. And Trent was shifting too, like the bit at the end of the scary film where the villain lurches upright, and the violence begins again.

In a garden once, Zoë had found a dead duck behind a bush: it looked intact – eye, feather, beak – but when she shifted it with glove and shovel, it proved light as a blown egg. The organs that had anchored it to the land of the living had been subtracted. This evisceration was what death's hungry agents did; and the same harvest death claimed from the body, fear of death stole from its energies: sapping its vitality, pruning its enthusiasms . . . Fear was performing those actions now. Everything was draining out of her along with the blood trickling from her fingertips, where the shard of vase had bit.

From below, Arkle said, 'There's a stain on the wall above your head. Can you see it? About the size of a penny.'

She said, 'So what?' her voice not much more than a whisper.

'So this.'

And another thump, like a nail being driven straight into her mind – down into its dark places, where things she couldn't put a name to crawled. It was a noise that, if you'd been on the other side of it, would have been the last you heard.

Arkle said, in a bright conversational tone, 'I've only got one left, but we both know I can put it wherever I want. And after last night . . . Putting another hole in another woman isn't going to make much difference.'

Not to him.

She said, 'I don't know where Katrina is.'

'Then you're no use to me, are you?'

'What do you want?'

'I want you to stand up.'

'You're going to shoot me.'

'If I want to do that, I'll do it anyway.'

'Not from there.'

'I can see the top of your head through the banister. You want proof?'

She didn't.

'So . . .'

Zoë got to her feet.

She almost stumbled, standing; it wasn't easy, any of this – being in fights; suffering frights. A woman her age shouldn't be having this kind of fun. She staggered on reaching her feet; banged backwards into the wall, hooking her hands rather neatly round the bolt buried in it, though that was no use to her . . . Too smooth to fray the twine that held her wrists. Her vision swam, then cleared. Trent was trying to get up; pushing against the floor on arms that trembled as they took his weight. She still had a pain in her forehead from butting him. It was true:

acts of violence damaged both parties. Though with a little practice, it would have hurt Zoë a lot less.

The newspaper clippings that had slipped from the crashed bookcase lay at her feet. The topmost headline read *Abused Wife's Murder Conviction Quashed.*

Arkle said, 'Catch,' and tossed something up the stairs at her.

The apple bounced off her knee, and rolled through the open toilet door.

She watched it wobble to a halt, and said, 'You've got to be fucking kidding.'

'It was you gave me the idea.'

'I've told you, I've no idea where she's gone. Where the money is. That storage place? She might even have been lying about—'

'I'll find her.'

'So find her. But don't play stupid games.'

Games whose losers wouldn't get a second chance.

Fear of death had gripped her again, and was rapidly starting to squeeze. And something clutched her leg too; she almost screamed – but it was Trent, grabbing at whatever was nearest.

She pushed with her knee and he fell back, but reached his feet with the help of the banister. He was shaking his head now; either trying to rattle confusion loose, or just denying any of this was happening. When he focused, he was looking directly at Zoë. 'Have too,' he said.

'. . . What?'

'Done that before.'

'Get the apple, Trent,' Arkle told him from the foot of the stairs.

It was one of those His Master's Voice moments: with no fucking idea what Arkle was on about, Trent looked for the apple anyway. And Zoë . . . Zoë didn't move. The knots at her wrist hadn't budged an inch, and Arkle, down below, was smiling at her; bow in his hands, primed and ready to fire.

The landing wasn't too deep . . . He couldn't hit her below the knees, but other than that, she was open country.

And something slowed inside her; her internal clock, she thought – this, too, was what fear did: it made the bones heavy, so they ached to stop; to come to a halt against a flat surface, and put up with whatever was about to go down.

Trent put a hand on her shoulder to steady himself, then placed the apple on her head as carefully as if it were a joke they were both taking part in . . . As if it were as important to her as to him that it didn't slip and fall.

Arkle said, 'This is going to be so cool.'

. . . And Zoë didn't have words . . .

Trent moved aside. Arkle raised the bow.

Old man Blake appeared behind him, and struck the back of his head with the hood ornament from the hearse.

Arkle crumpled from the knees up in a manner that might have been comical if – well, no, Zoë later amended; in a manner entirely comical, in fact. The look on his face was one there isn't a word for. When his body hit the floor, it was as if all the air his presence had sucked out of the surroundings came rushing back at once.

The old man said, 'Katie? Are you all right?'

Trent stepped in front of her; looked down at the pair below.

Zoë took a deep breath, and felt the vampire fear lift its teeth from her neck. Bracing herself against the wall, she kicked Trent hard in the small of the back, and sent him flying down the stairs.

Then she said, 'Yes, I'm fine. Thanks.'

Her mobile was in Arkle's pocket; she retrieved it, switched it on, but before she could call the police, it rang.

'Zoë Boehm . . .'

'Zoë bloody Boehm,' a voice said.

'Oh, hi, Jeff. Funny you should call. I was just on my way to pick your car up.'

She hoped like hell it was still there.

III

When you piled all the money your immediate future held into a single bag, for ease of carriage, it was hard not to pack all it had cost into a second; or not exactly a bag; more like a black box – your internal recorder; the one you might wish broke down occasionally, and transcribe white noise in place of grey deeds. But no, those deeds were all there; from clipping newspaper reports about acquittals of abused wives, to practising with make-up in shades of burnt sunset, the better to paint a convincing bruise. And choosing the right witnesses, so if it came to court, you'd not be alone.

Sometimes you picked strangers in hotel bars, because who was more impartial than a stranger?

Katrina had always laid contingency plans. It was something she'd learned from her father.

Now she placed her coffee cup on the saucer in front of her, the lipstick ring on its rim as bright and obvious as a country song. No matter how careful you were in its application, make-up always gave you away; leaving temporary scars on cheap china, or drawing attention to the fact that your foundations needed work. By and large, Katrina had no worries about her foundations. She wore make-up today for the exact reason she had pretended to wear it on that evening she'd met Tim: to conceal her bruising. Which then had been fake, of course; cosmetically applied, and intended to be noticed. But there was nothing made up about her damaged cheekbone now. This bruise was real, and needed toning down – it was a detail that would figure largely in descriptions . . . In truth, cosmetics weren't doing much in the way of concealment. She'd have worn a headscarf and sunglasses, but would have looked like a film star shamming anonymity.

On the street, everything looked the way it had done twenty minutes ago: different passers-by, but doing the same city shuffle. The shops lining the pavement opposite were low-end electrical stores, second-hand CD shops, and outfits with whitewashed windows offering a bewildering array of services, from takeaway delivery to unlocking mobile phones; this last so much in demand round here, you had to wonder how forgetful the locals were. Up the road was a market where once – in this patch of London shading into the east – you might have bought bread, fish, vegetables, but which now mostly boasted the greetings cards and kitchen knick-knacks trade. Electrical goods in battered dusty boxes were stacked in shop doorways. Somewhere, a stall sold burgers in buns. Katrina imagined the smell of hot fat wafting visibly past the window, like cartoon aromas in *Tom & Jerry*. She picked up her coffee again, but it was still too hot to drink.

. . . *I walked into a door.* That was the common lie she'd relied on in fabricating her backstory, and she'd always known it would hit her in the face eventually, like a dramatic truth. A truth which would then seep backwards, granting her lies retrospective validity: *this is real* – so everything else must have been real too. Her black box ticked away as her coffee cooled, bringing back those moments during which Baxter cooled like coffee on the kitchen floor, and she slammed a cupboard door in her own face. One moment of white hot pain, she'd expected, and had not been entirely wrong about this. But what she hadn't been prepared for was the dull ache afterwards, that never went away. Or how livid her face would look – she'd imagined a rich mishmash of purples and blues that would flower long enough to look good on the photos, then fade picturesquely to a Chanel smudge. And instead here she sat, still looking like someone had hit her with a shovel.

Over the road, between one of those whitewashed windows and a fast food place – whose logo might be taken, in a hurry, for KFC – was an alleyway leading to a back yard. Nobody had entered or left it while Katrina had been here, and nobody passing had shown interest. Of the cars illegally parked nearby, none had occupants. If anyone was watching, they were too good for her. It was more likely that nobody was watching. But still she sat.

The café floor was white lino squares, checked with seemingly random reds. But nothing was random. The placement of each red tile dictated the pattern around it, the options decreasing with every choice made . . . If Baxter hadn't worried that Arkle was losing it; hadn't decided to protect him by calling it a day – even though they had nowhere near their target amount – things would have continued as normal. Katrina would have carried on being Baxter's wife, and carried on convincing him that life could be better without Arkle and Trent – that two could live twice as cheaply as four; or exactly as cheaply, perhaps, but for twice as long. Once they'd arrived at the right magical number (a million had a ring to it) they should cut their losses, the losses being Arkle and Trent. What she hadn't reckoned on was how deeply Baxter's bonds to his so-called brothers went . . . So when the maths didn't work, the bottom line appeared instead. One could live much more expensively than two, because there was no division involved.

Some bonds had to be cut cleanly, the way losses should be.

This time, when she picked up her cup, it was too cold. That familiar Goldilocks feeling. She drank it anyway, and continued staring through the window; something tickling her ear she couldn't put a name to . . . A mosquito in the room. A bluebottle at the window. A police siren . . .

Katrina put the cup down as quietly as she could. This happened every day in the city; hell, every half-hour. There was always an emergency somewhere; that was practically a definition of London. Handbag snatchers, muggers, pensioners stuck up trees. There was no reason a passing noise should have anything to do with her . . .

And it didn't. The wailing hit a peak then took the slow slide into distance, cutting off abruptly as it reached a destination, or cornered a building large enough to swallow it. Katrina still had a finger locked around the handle of her cup. As she eased it free, she knew how stupid she'd been: if anyone had the slightest notion she was here, they wouldn't be sending cars screaming after her; they'd be waiting in corners. Which was why she was watching the street; alert for the studied indifference of the far too casual passer-by. Alert, specifically, for Zoë Boehm. But seeing no one who didn't belong.

Enough. She'd be here all day if she didn't take a grip, and too much care was as dangerous as too little – sooner or later, the man on the counter would wonder what the lady with the bruise was waiting for. Hoisting her bag, she made her way to the door, noticing how warm the café had been when the chill outside hit her.

It wasn't a great distance, the alleyway over the road. At its end was the back yard she'd expected; a grim sunless area where a drain gurgled in a corner, and a black door was covered by a metal grille, like something out of Prohibition. A buzzer beside it looked too shiny for the brickwork. She pressed it anyway. After a moment it awoke in a crackle of static, and a voice said, 'What?'

'Dennis?'

'What?'

She said, 'I'm Zoë Boehm. Looking for Dennis,' and released the button.

That night she'd spent at Zoë's, in the spare room, she'd gone through the filing cabinet; Zoë's dead husband's records. The cabinets were unlocked, and Zoë had put her there – Katrina didn't need asking twice. Information was hard currency, and provided you hid it in your head, you could carry it over any border there was.

My specialty's finding people, Zoë had told her. *Not helping them disappear.*

But I bet you've got contacts.

And Zoë hadn't denied she had contacts, or that Joe had had contacts, and this was where they'd be: alphabetically sorted into drawers. He'd shelved Dennis under Identity. Katrina bet Joe had sorted his socks by the day of the week.

When Zoë had left to make her phone calls, Katrina had phoned Dennis from the flat: *You'd be Zoë, then*, he'd said.

That's right. And you'd be Dennis.

(What was one more name among many? Kay, Katie, Katrina. Find the Lady – you overturned a name to see what it uncovered . . .)

And here he was in the flesh: a big man in black jeans and white T-shirt, which might have been XXXL, but didn't cover his stomach. He was mostly bald with a fraying grey beard, and his eyes' paranoid glint matched the grille over his door.

She said, 'We spoke on the phone.'

'I know.'

So what was he waiting for, she wondered.

After a while, he said, 'The way Joe spoke, I thought you'd be taller.'

'He didn't mention you were morbidly obese, either.'

'It's glandular.'

'Is that right?'

'Yeah, I got glands keep demanding more food.'

'I heard that happens.' She was slipping into Zoë's speech patterns, as if an imitation of a woman he'd never met would convince him that's who she was . . . A scratching noise made her turn, but it was only a cat, its paws clicking on a drain cover. The look it granted her was part contempt, part indifference; all cat.

When she looked back, Dennis had unhooked the grille and was pushing it open. She had to step back sharpish.

'Get a lot of unwanted visitors?' she asked.

His raised eyebrow suggested he'd never encountered any other kind.

Dennis's hallway was surprisingly bright, surprisingly clean, as if its main aim was to dispel the image he radiated of a bear disturbed in hibernation. Once he'd closed and locked the door, he led her into a white-walled, windowless room which must have been his office, the clues being a lot of electronic equipment and the absence of comfortable furniture. The only decoration was a framed print of a naked blue woman, conjured from a few swirls of paint. Matisse, Katrina thought. A memory swam away from her, as if it belonged to somebody else.

He said, 'You bring photos?' He held a hand out: a meaty paw. 'From before that happened?'

'Yes.'

He grunted. Her injury might have been a pain if it showed up on the photos, his manner implied; but otherwise, she could merrily bleed to death. Once she was off the premises.

Taking the photos, he sat at his desk; sliced them into individual shots, then took a bundle of papers from a drawer – her new identity, she supposed. For something to say, she said, 'You can add the photos afterwards, can you?'

Dennis didn't feel the need to confirm that. 'You might want to sort my money out,' was all he said.

He bent to his tasks; adding her portrait to those parts of her paper identity that required it, while she bent to her bag; took out the envelope she'd prepared. Three thousand pounds was a lot, but you had to pay for the best . . . Odd that she trusted dead Joe, whom she'd never met, to come up with that. Perhaps because he'd married Zoë. She didn't give the envelope to Dennis, but stood holding it, staring at the print on the wall . . . Which reminded her of Tim, who lay dead in the cottage, bundled into a cupboard under the stairs. This had not been an easy manoeuvre. The dead were uncooperative – his very weight had been a reproach. But what had he expected? Tim had had the air of a man who thought he'd entered a love story, though you'd have imagined life had taught him better than that. He'd loved his wife, after all, and look how that ended.

From an early age, Katrina had known death was coming. The knowledge had lit her father's every working day . . . She had not wanted to kill Tim, but hadn't wanted to give up the money, either. Tim had been an impartial witness, that was all; a man on his own in a hotel bar, who could be counted on to notice her bruise, not quite hidden by make-up. Except he turned out drunk, which wasn't ideal . . . With only limited time while Baxter was casing the jeweller's, she'd made do with what she had, and look what happened – Tim had turned out a knight in shining armour, when all she'd needed was a stable-boy. You couldn't rely on appearances, and that was the truth.

Other witnesses she'd chosen to her cosmetic damage included a local shopkeeper (always keen to study her legs, but less so to look her in her bruised eye), a taxi driver, a librarian, Trent – a risk worth taking; she could handle Trent – and her father. She'd become expert at applying the artificial bruise, then stripping it away. As soon as Baxter's back was turned, she became his abused spouse. And never said a word about it, in case it leaked back; she'd always just walked into a door. A code not hard to break, if a little effort was put in.

Dennis was speaking. She blinked: 'What?'

'You want to know your new name?'

A moment of rebirth . . . She supposed she did want to know. It was information that might come in handy. 'Tell me.'

'Emma,' he said. 'Emma Standish.'

Emma, she thought. Well, Tim would have appreciated that, wouldn't he?

Kay, Katie, Katrina, Emma . . .

She looked for a response, but he wasn't waiting for one; he'd returned to his task of gluing pictures to pieces of card before running them through a laminator.

Emma Standish went back to studying the Matisse, Baxter on her mind now more than Tim. If he'd listened to her – if he'd appreciated that it was her he was married to, not his not-even-blood-brothers – she could have shelved her make-up with no harm done. Same applied to Tim. All he'd had to do was understand that settling into his cosy electrical goods supplier life wasn't as appealing as he thought it ought to be. However well researched her abusive husband story – however solid her chances of acquittal – there was little point persevering with it once she had the money in her hands. Difficult to explain to somebody who thought happy ever after involved holding hands into the sunset. Why did men think women the softer sex, when the evidence pointed otherwise?

Dennis was done now: standing waiting. She gave him the envelope and stood while he unsealed it and counted its contents; one big gorilla thumb peeling through the notes like a banker's. Watching her money in his hands, Katrina wondered how many days' freedom it represented, and whether there were alternative ways of settling up with Dennis . . . Whether he'd open easily, given the right tool. Baxter had folded like a deck of cards; Tim had expired like a sigh. Bulky Dennis would be a different proposition; and besides – besides, Katrina wasn't a killer. She was a woman with contingency plans, that was all.

He handed her the bundle he'd put together – passport, driving licence, birth certificate; a slew of credit and loyalty cards. Maybe not such a bad deal after all.

'There's open accounts on the plastics,' he said. 'You owe a couple hundred. Here's your address.' He handed her a scrap of paper. 'That'll work for a month.'

'Do you get many repeat customers?' she asked.

He caught her drift. 'This is quality paperwork. How smart you are's up to you.'

'And Emma Standish is virgin, is she?'

'How long do you think I'd last, I was into recycling?'

'Just checking.'

'Like I said, you have to be smart. Real smart is checking before you hand over the money.' What he'd done with the cash, she wasn't sure. It wasn't visible any more, though. 'If we're done, I can let you out.'

'You're a charmer, Dennis. Joe forgot to mention that bit.'

'He gave a different impression of you, too.'

Toting the bag, she followed him through the hall. He closed the grille and shut the door behind her without another word.

The cat was still in the yard, though what it thought it was doing there was anybody's guess. It stopped examining its underbelly long enough to watch Katrina head back to the street, then returned to its slow auto-caress. When the drain gurgled again, it paid no mind.

The street looked every bit the same to Emma Standish as it had to Katrina Blake. Being a different person wasn't the big deal the makeover magazines made out; on the other hand, she'd shed more pounds in fewer minutes than any of those ever promised. But now she had to keep a grip on her next move, which was leaving London.

A quick departure needed a taxi. This meant heading for the main road; leaving the backstreet with its market stalls, its café windows, its youths in hoodies. Threading among them, her canvas bag marking her a tourist, wasn't calming; Katrina had to remind herself she'd walked these streets already without being robbed . . . But the fact that something hadn't happened once didn't mean it would keep on not happening. Picking up her pace, she reached the corner, and walked into someone coming the other way . . .

. . . A woman, though Katrina took her for a man at first

– mostly for her size. Few women bulked up like this: broad shoulders, branchlike arms, thick legs; all encased in black leather, as if some vaguely unhealthy role playing was scheduled for the near future. But her skin was pale and baby soft; her lips full roses; her eyes brown and damp. Her buzz-cut hair so blonde it was colourless.

'Emma?' she said.

And her voice high-pitched: a cartoon awaiting a paint job.

Then what she'd said struck home . . .

Katrina's grip tightened on the canvas bag. But it was the kind of grip you take in a dream, where it doesn't matter how firm your grasp, the dream's grasp is firmer, and nothing short of waking loosens it. Katrina tried, but didn't wake. The cartoon woman spoke again: 'I've been waiting.'

'You've got the wrong person,' Katrina managed. 'My name's not Emma.'

'Then that's a fucking expensive bunch of waste paper you're carrying.'

Katrina turned, but the woman took her by the elbow.

'It's like the song says, isn't it? Who you gonna call?'

And it was: it was just like an old song. One of those where the winner takes it all.

The woman was relieving her of her burden, and Katrina's fingers offered no resistance . . . *Who you gonna call?* This woman could swat her into the gutter, but didn't have to. That was the point. She knew everything – even knew Emma, a stranger to Katrina until minutes ago. She had to be Dennis's accomplice . . . Katrina opened her mouth, looking for words to put everything right, but those words didn't exist. A threat suggested itself, but Queen Kong was way ahead of her.

'Word from a mutual friend. Mentioning Dennis isn't a good idea. Where you're heading, there's people it's best not to have as enemies. Understand?'

Where you're heading . . . She thought she understood.

'So now we say goodbye.'

And like that she was gone, and Katrina was alone on a corner; her hands as empty as her future.

She turned again, because there was nowhere to look but back. And there, standing by his alleyway, Dennis was watching; big arms folded across his bigger chest, the look in his eyes unreadable at this distance. And next to him a woman with dark curly hair, talking into a mobile phone . . . Katrina couldn't read her eyes either, but had little doubt what they held. They'd be black fire. They'd be red fury. She blinked, and Dennis was gone, returned to his world of made-up people; his duty done to the wife of his dead friend. Not just to take Katrina's money; but to allow her to think it was over, and she'd won. Which was Zoë's revenge, of course . . . But Zoë was gone too now, and there was only the crowd milling around the stalls, and the usual market noises, and now, somewhere behind the buildings – round the disjointed corners – something tickling her ear she couldn't put a name to . . . A mosquito in the room. A bluebottle at the window. A police siren.

Katrina waited alone on the corner, because there was nothing else she could do.

IV

Last time she'd been in a hospital, death had occupied her mind . . . Zoë had been interviewing a man shot in the leg with a crossbow, and it occurred to her that she'd barely given him a moment's thought since. Derek the Deer Hunter: probably he'd be back in his life by now, boring his local pub stupid with tales of his derring done-to. He'd think he'd cheated death, when in fact death had chosen to ignore him; the big clue to this being, he was still alive. Nobody cheated death. Death was the ultimate stalker: confident and inevitable, where the rest were inadequate perverts. You could run, and you could also hide, but all that meant was, you'd die tired and hidden.

Like Tim Whitby, though it was Katrina who'd hidden Tim. His body had been found now; she'd told the police where it was. Zoë had no desire to see the place, but in her mind's eye it was clear enough: a stark grey cottage on the edge of the moors, on which a sky the colour of stone pressed down. She hadn't known Tim well, but had understood he was nursing grief, and had been a good man who deserved better. But in the long run, we all get the same. She hoped the sky hadn't pressed too hard on Tim's final moments. And that he'd been allowed to die with some illusions intact, even those revolving around Katrina.

The room she needed was on the fifth floor. Zoë took the stairs, a knee-jerk reaction to being in a hospital, and grudgingly had to admit they were easier than they'd have been six months ago. Which wasn't much recompense for not smoking, but you took what you could get. When she reached her level she pushed through swing doors to a corridor identical to the one five flights below. At the far end a man sat on a chair, and she headed towards him.

Thinking, as she did, about the money. Zoë thought she'd made peace with the money, but it still stirred occasionally; reminding her that it was gone, and that whatever she did next would have to involve acquiring some from somewhere . . . But that was a question everybody faced every day. Zoë had debts – and Zoë hated having debts – but worse things existed, among which would have been touching the money Katrina had killed Tim for. Most money came with strings attached, but there was a difference between knowing that and agreeing to be a puppet. And so she thought instead of the empty look on Katrina's face as Win had taken her money away – a hundred grand memory, that. Along with the one of Arkle opening his eyes just after the cops arrived, looking like a boy whose toys had been taken away. Trent, interestingly, had looked only relieved . . . And by then old man Blake had resumed vigil in his empty room; studying the wall for the secrets it hid. Maybe surfacing every so often to gaze through the window at the hearse that had once been part of his living, and was now a clue to his future.

And everybody else's.

Zoë reached the man on the chair, and told him who she was. He asked for ID, checked a list and nodded. She went past him into the room, which was surprisingly quiet – she'd half expected a technological chorus to greet her; the beeps and chirrups of sci-fi machines, fending off the medieval silence which was all death had to offer. But the room was largely bare – the light was low; there was a single chair; the narrow window had a blind drawn over it. There was a bed, though, and on this bed lay Helen Coe; a much smaller figure than descriptions had suggested. But then, those who had described her had known her upright: a broad and baggy woman; a furious smoker, until the twenty-first century had hooked her. Cardigans, spectacles and shabby old raincoats . . . Now she lay wired to a drip, and the rise and fall of her sheet was so shallow, it was barely more than the memory of breath.

. . . Helen Coe had long been tired, Zoë had been told; would have liked to spend days relaxing between naps. The old story: a life too crammed with event to allow time for reflection. Well, Helen's events had come to a halt, and rest was her foreseeable future. Zoë wondered if dreams were involved, and hoped, for Helen's sake, they weren't. Dreams were overrated.

The last dream Zoë remembered was one in which she wandered a corridor which kept turning corners, while lights flickered overhead, and drawers opened and closed almost noiselessly. But that part hadn't been a dream. She'd been hearing Katrina in the spare room, searching Joe's filing cabinets for whatever she needed. It hadn't taken Zoë long to work out what Katrina had been after; not once she'd known that Katrina had skipped with the money.

My specialty's finding people, not helping them disappear.

But I bet you've got contacts . . .

Had she ever trusted Katrina? She wasn't sure. She been blindsided by the money, certainly; Katrina had dazzled her more than Win . . . The stiletto rather than the blunt instrument. Though in the end, Win's blunt instrument had proved effective enough. And Dennis – not taking kindly to being tricked – had smoothed the path.

Before sitting, Zoë put her fingers to the blind and tweezered two slats apart. Below, the street lights were lit; endless chains stretching far as she could see, casting a pale orange glow on the underside of distant clouds. A fine rain cast a halo round every bulb, and dark figures walked beneath them: paired and singled; purposeful and vague; the coming of night dragging them out to search for the promises darkness held. Of all the metaphors for death, nightfall was the most comforting, because it was the most populated. When she'd lain in her coffin, Zoë had been alone, and it was a surprise to her – who'd always thought herself a solitary – that that was the hardest thing of all. That what she'd miss was the people; the crazy stupid beings who caused all the bother.

She sat on the one available chair, looked straight at Helen Coe's blank unstirring features, and began telling it the whole way through: from Harold Sweeney's call to Win taking the money from Katrina, before fading into London's crowded hours.

It mattered to Zoë, though she wasn't sure why, that this woman lodged in death's doorway should hear the end of the story.